Praise for Jim Nesbitt's
THE RIGHT WR
An Ed Earl Burch Novel

"In *The Right Wrong Number*, Jim Nesbitt writes like an angel about devilish deals, bloody murder and nasty sex. His beat is Dallas — not the glitzy spires of J.R. Ewing, but the back alley bars and brothels of Jack Ruby and Candy Barr. His PI, Ed Earl Burch, is steeped in Coke-chased bourbon; cured in the smoke of Zippo-lit Luckies; and longing for hard-bitten girls who got away. Nesbitt channels the lyricism of James Crumley, the twisted kick of Jim Thompson and the cold, dark heart of Mickey Spillane."

   – Jayne Loader, author of *Between Pictures* and *Wild America*, director of *The Atomic Café*

"Jim Nesbitt serves up another raunchy slice of Texas-style revenge and redemption in his latest hard-boiled thriller, *The Right Wrong Number*, featuring his scarred and guilt-ridden Dallas PI, Ed Earl Burch. In Burch, Nesbitt has created a colorful, authentic and deeply-flawed character who is nobody's idea of a hero but also turns out to be nobody's fool."

   – Robert Ward, author of *Cattle Annie and Little Britches*, *Red Baker* and *The Best, Bad Dream;* writer producer on *Hill Street Blues* and *Miami Vice*

Read what fellow authors say about Jim Nesbitt's first award-winning noir thriller,
THE LAST SECOND CHANCE
An Ed Earl Burch Novel

"If Chandler's noir was a neon sign in the LA sunset, Nesbitt's noir is the Shiner Bock sign buzzing outside the last honky-tonk you'll hit before the long drive to the next one. On the way you'll pass towns with names like Crumley and Portis. Roll down the window; it's a hot night. It's a fast ride."

    – James Lileks, author of *The Casablanca Tango*, columnist for the *National Review* and *Star Tribune* of Minneapolis, creator of *LILEKS.com*

"Make no mistake. *The Last Second Chance* may be a classic noir tale full of bullets and babes and booze. But at heart, it is a western. And our ex-cop hero, Ed Earl Burch, is a modern day cowboy, minus the spurs. . . . smart, tough, profane and reckless. . ."

    – Mike Ludden, author of *Alfredo's Luck*

"In 'The Last Second Chance,' Jim Nesbitt gives readers a splendid first opportunity to meet Ed Earl Burch, as flawed a Luckies-smoking, whiskey-drinking, serial-married hero as ever walked the scarred earth of Dirty Texas. . . . In Burch, Nesbitt has created a more angst-ridden and bad-ass version of Michael Connelly's Harry Bosch and a Tex-Mex landscape much meaner than the streets of

L.A. Add hate-worthy lowlifes and a diminutive dame, Carla Sue Cantrell, who cracks wiser than the guys, and you've got a book with gumption."

    – Bob Morris, Edgar finalist, author of *Baja Florida* and *A Deadly Silver Sea*

"If you like to read, if you appreciate words and the people who run them brilliantly through their paces, give Jim Nesbitt's *The Last Second Chance* a read. And his next one, and the one after that. You'll be enthralled, like I was."

    – Cheryl Pellerin, author of *Trips: How Hallucinogens Work in Your Brain*

"Cowboy noir for the cartel era ... *The Last Second Chance* is a gripping read with a cathartic ending, and it takes you places you've likely never been."

    – Jeannette Cooperman, author of *A Circumstance of Blood*

To Mitch — buckle up for a lethal ride.

THE RIGHT WRONG NUMBER

An Ed Earl Burch Novel

Jim Nesbitt

Spotted Mule Press

This is a work of fiction. All the characters, organizations and events portrayed in this novel are either products of the author's imagination or are used fictitiously.

THE RIGHT WRONG NUMBER
An Ed Earl Burch Novel

Cover photograph by Andrew Palochko.
Used with exclusive permission.
Author photo by Bill Swindell
Cover design by SelfPubBookCovers.com/Island
Interior formatting by Polgarus Studio

For Pam and The Panther

ONE

It wasn't San Francisco or London, but the fog was thick and flowing — like tufts sucked from a bale of cotton, carrying the muddy tint of a used linen filter. It made him think of trench coats, lamp posts and the low warning moan of a ship's horn sounding somewhere out on the water. Rolling across the flat fields, it made dark gray ghosts of the trees that huddled along the far fencelines and left cold beads of moisture on his skin and memories of old black-and-white movies in his mind.

But there were no ships in the harbor, no waterside buckets of blood, no Rick or Ilsa. Just lightless farmhouses, barns, open-sided equipment sheds and squat corrugated feed bins for cattle, all cloaked by the fast-moving fog, glimpsed only if the wind parted the curtain of stained white wetness as you rolled by.

And it wasn't the Left Coast or Britain. It was Texas and the scrubby coastal country north of Houston, beyond the Intercontinental and its roaring planes. Take a left off the farm-to-market road with the four-digit number. Find the third dirt road on the left, take it for three miles. Splash through the potholes and set your teeth against tires juddering across the washboard track. Hit the T of another dirt road. Look for a faint gravel trail at your 10 o'clock. Rattle over the cattle guard. Close the gate behind you.

Easy to remember. Hard to do with visibility down to zero. Even with the window rolled down and the Beemer's fog lamps flipped on. Nice car. Leather seats the color of butterscotch taffy. Mahogany inserts flanking the instruments and fronting the glove box. Killer sound system and a cellular phone. Shame to bang this baby along back roads, splashing mud and gravel against its polished flanks of forest green.

Not his car. Not his problem. Fog and time were. He was already a half hour behind schedule when his contact finally drove up with the car, the briefcase of bills and directions to the meet. Fog was adding more minutes to his travel time. He had to double back when he missed one turnoff and that made him slow and leery of missing another.

Not good. Not good. Patient people weren't on the other end. They never were. But they would wait because he had the money, they had the product and both sides wanted this deal closed tonight. And if they were pissed and wanted to wrangle, he could deal with that; a matte-chrome Smith & Wesson Model 6906 with thirteen rounds of 9 mm hollow point nestled in a shoulder rig underneath his black leather jacket.

Always the chance of a wrangle on a run like this. Rip-offs were a run-of-the-mill business risk, even between long-time associates. But on this deal the probability of gunplay was low. He was just nervous about running late. It wasn't professional. He thought about using the cellular phone but shook the idea out of his head. Not something a pro would do.

And not something his people would appreciate. They were security-conscious and worked the high-dollar end of the street. No cowboys. Pros only. Running a well-oiled machine. Not that he knew them well. He was strictly a cutout man, a well-paid delivery boy who made it his business to stay ignorant about those who hired him and their business partners.

He wasn't totally in the dark about his paymasters; no prudent pro ever was. But he kept his curiosity in check and his focus on the amount of money he was paid and the demands of the night's job.

It was a relaxing way to make a living. A phone rings. A voice on the line gives him the name of a bar or cafe. A man meets him with an envelope and instructions. And he goes where he is told — to deliver money, to pick up a truck or car loaded with product, to put a bullet through the skull of someone he doesn't know.

Command and control. Just like the Army and those over-the-border ops in Cambodia. Project Vesuvius. Studies and Observations Group. Words both grandiose and bland to cover what he and his comrades did. Slip over the fence, gather the intel, slit a few throats along the way. Set up the Big Death — from the air and on the ground. Operation Menu. Operation Patio. Operation Freedom Deal. Cambodian Incursion. More bland words for killing the enemy in his safest sanctuaries. Parrot's Beak. The Fishhook. The Dog's Face.

A sputtering string of electronic beeps startled him. The car phone. He glanced down and saw a red pin light flash to the time of the beeps. He pulled the receiver out of its cradle.

"Talk to me."

"Where the hell are you?"

"You don't want me to say."

"You're late and that's making some people nervous."

"Your man was late and this phone call is making me nervous. It's not very smart."

"We decide what's smart. We pay you to get things done and be on time. How long till you get there?"

"Ten."

"Get there."

He snapped the receiver back in place and shook his head. Not good. Not good. Lots of snoopers scanning these cellular circuits. A pro would know this and wouldn't risk a call unless the other side was making a ruckus. Made him wonder if the players in this game were as big league as he thought they were.

Those thoughts rode with him as he wheeled the Beemer down the dirt road, looking for the T intersection. There it was. He looked for the gravel trail, slowly turning the car to the left and letting the fog lamps cut a slow sweep across the far side of the road. There. At his ten o'clock. Just like he was told. He stayed alert, but his nagging nervousness and doubts started to fade.

The trail led from the gate and crossed the field at a sharp angle. He crept along, easing the car through ruts and washouts. He saw the shrouded form of a tin shed and weaved the car so the lights would pan across its open door. The yellow beams caught the wet metal of an old tractor and two men in dark slacks and windbreakers — one tall, bald and lean, the other short, squat and slick-haired.

He stopped the car, fog lamps still on. He pulled his pistol, letting his gun hand drop to his side and rear as he stepped out, keeping his body behind the car door.

"Wanna cut the lights, guy?"

A purring voice from the short guy, coming from a full, sleek face that made him think of a seal.

"Not really. Let's keep everything illuminated. Makes me feel safe."

"You're among friends, guy. Nobody wants monkeyshines here. We just do the handoff and the call and we can all get the hell out of this fog. You're late and we're cold."

"No arguments from me, my man. But let's do this by the numbers."

"Numbers it is, guy."

He stepped away from the car.

"Money's in the front seat. Have your buddy do the honors."

A nod from the talker. His companion walked to the passenger side of the Beemer and leaned in. He heard the latches of the briefcase pop open.

"Looks good to me."

"Make the call. That okay with you, guy?"

"By all means. Make that call. Tell Mabel to put a pot of coffee on."

A laugh from the talker. He could see the other guy reach for the cellular phone. Somewhere across town, a phone would ring. Assurances the money was in hand. Somewhere else another phone would ring. Product would change hands. Then the Beemer's cellular would ring again and the night's business would be done.

He was alert but relaxed, ready to wait, the screw-ups behind him and the deal running smooth and professional now. He had a clear view of the talker and his companion. He had his gun in hand. He was thinking about a cup of coffee when the baseball bat cracked across the back of his skull.

"Cut those damn lights. Secure the money."

A nod from the companion. The talker moved toward the third man, the man with the baseball bat, a hulk with the arms and shoulders of a lineman and the on-the-balls-of-the-feet stance of a third baseman. They stood over the slumped body.

"Give me a hand with this sumbitch. He's heavy. Get that gun, Jack."

"Got it. Who'd this guy piss off?"

"Nobody you need to know about, guy. Or me. He's just a poor soul somebody wants whacked."

"Awful lot of trouble just to whack a guy. What the fuck are we stagin' this thing for, Louis? Why not just pop him and get it over with?"

"Not your worry, guy. Just muscle him into the driver's seat and let me dress him up pretty. Bill, did you wipe your prints?"

"Does it matter?"

A glare from Louis. The companion shrugged, pulled a bandana from his back pocket and leaned into the Beemer. When done, he hoisted the briefcase and walked back toward the shed.

Louis kept his eyes locked on the bald man as he walked away, his head swiveling like a table-top fan, his eyes popped with anger. He broke the stare and fussed with the body, pulling the head back, reaching into the mouth, then his pocket, then back into the mouth. Jack watched and shook his head.

"Bill!"

"Yo!"

"Get me that bundle, guy. The jacket and the trench coat. And bring that bag with the stuff in it."

"Yo."

Bill hustled to the car. Louis patted him on the shoulder, thanking him in that purring voice, his face soft and placid again. He turned back to the body, peeling off the leather jacket and unfastening the shoulder rig. He fished through the pockets, pulling wallet, keys and a checkbook, leaving loose change. He replaced these items with wallet, keys and a checkbook he pulled from a crumpled brown paper bag. He pulled a ring from the right hand and a fake Rolex from the left wrist, digging a wedding band, a class ring and a real Rolex — an Oyster Perpetual Datejust — from the bag.

The jacket and trench coat came next — a nicely tailored Burberry, pity the waste. Louis started to sweat as he pulled and smoothed the clothes onto the body. He unbuttoned the shirt down to the navel, then reached into the bag and pulled out a squeeze bottle, the kind with the thin nozzle that could poke through the bars of a footballer's facemask. He squeezed water onto the body's chest then reached under the dash to pop the hood of the Beemer.

"Jack — hook up those cables, guy."

"Jesus."

"I know it's unpleasant, but just do it for me, guy."

Louis fired up the Beemer's engine then waited for Jack to hand him the twin clamps. Clamps to the body's chest. The smell of burning flesh and electrified ozone.

Again. Again the smell.

And again. Clamps to Jack. Engine off.

"Bill. The acid, guy."

A glass bottle of sulfuric acid. A small glass tray. Fingers and thumb from one hand in. Then the other hand. He handed the tray to Bill.

"Careful with that, guy. Dump it."

"Yo."

Louis turned back to the body. He pursed his lips as he lined up the shoulders, the head and the arms to stage the proper angles of a kill shot.

The head was the difficult part. Without a helping hand to hold it in place, it rolled about and wouldn't stay upright. Louis pulled the hips forward then shoved the shoulders deep into the folds of the leather seat, pressing them into place. The head was now resting lightly against the butterscotch leather padding of the headrest.

That's how it would line up. He stood up and pulled a snub-nosed Colt Agent in .38 Special from the paper bag with a gloved hand. He eyed the angle for another second then nodded Jack away.

Louis eased the pistol barrel into a sagging mouth, eyeing the angle one more time. He pulled the trigger, blinking at the pistol's flash and sharp report. He dropped the gun to the floor.

The bullet had blown off the back of the man's skull, obliterating the pulpy mark of the baseball bat and spraying a dark stain of brains, blood and bone shards across the light-colored leather seats. The impact canted the body across the console and gearshift, head and shoulder jammed between the seats.

"Jesus, Louis."

"What?"

"Christamighty, it's one thing to whack a guy up close like that, another to do all that shit with the battery cables and the acid. But to have to fish out his dentures first? They'd have to pay me double to do that."

"They are, guy. They are."

"Whadja have to do it for?"

"They were making his gums sore. He needed a new pair."

"Like he'll need 'em where he's going."

"You never know. Blow the car, Jack. We gotta get us back on home, guy. Get us on the outside of some gumbo down to Tujague's."

"I'm for that. A shame though. This is a nice car."

"That it is, guy. Blow her just the same. Make it burn pretty."

"Lotta noise. Lotta flash. Cops'll be here like flies on a dead fish."

"Do it quick then, guy. So we can be long gone."

TWO

The candlelight flickered across her sweat-slickened skin, highlighting the flush that spread above her heavy breasts and darkened the sharp lines of her face. She pursed her lips and blew a strong puff of breath up toward the plastered strands of unruly black hair that stuck to her forehead, arcing her eyes upward to see if the curls would come unglued.

They wouldn't. With a frown of annoyance, she swiped a hand across her eyebrows then flicked her head like a horse fighting bit and rein, sending thick curls flying forward and back — a quick curtain for her face, freeing wet strands from her cheeks, shoulders and neck, then a wild cascade down the middle of her deeply tanned back.

She reached for the bottle of dry Spanish white, plucking it from debris scattered across the top of a small side table — a string of gold-foil condom packets, a Zippo lighter, a pack of Lucky Strikes, a pack of Virginia Slim Menthol Lights, cartons of Chinese food, a Seiko wristwatch with a band of brushed stainless steel, packets of soy sauce, plum sauce and hot mustard.

Two fat candles, red and burning, oozed hot wax across the white plastic lid of a pretzel bucket.

Wine spilled into a ridged juice glass with a green tint, part of a set an old girlfriend bought for him in a Fort Worth thrift store. Some spilled on the floor because she had to stretch across him to

9

reach the bottle and pour; the wine pooled around two spent condoms and a plate of cold pancakes and moo shoo pork.

Chinese burritos, he called them. Sex food, she said. To go along with the sex candles and the sex sofa — the convertible of sex, she said. Funny girl. And very carnal.

Red lipstick marked the rim of her glass. She downed a big slug of wine and shook her head back and forth again.

His left hand cupped the right cheek of her ass, a curve of white between solid bands of brown. He trailed his fingers through the curls of her sex and parted the lips, stroking slowly, watching as she clenched her eyes tight and hissed with pleasure when he hit the right spot.

She pitched her head back and smiled, eyes still closed, then spun away from him suddenly, pushing his hand and arm away.

"Uhn-uhn."

"Yes-huh."

He edged toward her, banging his hip across the bar that arched against the underside of his sofa bed's thin, sagging mattress. More fingers. Another hiss. Another push.

"Uhn-uhn, I said. Don't get me hot again. I have to go home."

"What for?"

"My dog is out."

"He does fine in that back yard of yours. Hell, Secretariat would do fine back there."

"He's afraid of the dark. He starts barking. The neighbors call and bitch at me. Really, I have to go home."

He forced his chin between her thighs, flicking his tongue out to taste her.

"We'll see what you say in a few minutes."

A shallow breath of protest punctuated by a hiss. Hands that gripped his hands — long, red nails gouging his palms. Hands that grabbed his wrists. Fingers that tapped a fluttering, spastic beat on his forearms.

Deep, ragged breaths. Hips moving. Stomach muscles flexing in and out below the hard wings of her rib cage. A sharp cry. A strong push against his head and shoulder. Legs scissored shut. Eyes clenched. Brow furrowed. Teeth over lower lip. Hands lightly slapping the sheets.

He was on his belly. She sat up, pulling him toward her for a kiss — all teeth and tongue. He felt his neck bones crack. She rolled him onto his back, pushing his shoulders down into the mattress. The springs screeched.

She rolled a condom onto his cock and straddled him.

"You made a little animal out of me."

Didn't have to go far, he thought, timing his thrusts to match her downward plunge. Her shadow bucked across the wall. The slap of flesh marked the pace. He heard her name in a long, low growl that crawled from the back of his throat. He lost himself in that hard, fast run up the mountain.

There was no name in her cries.

"I'm getting where I'm fond of you, Burch."

He was still lost, circuits blown, eyeteeth missing, spiraling down from that fine, white place that pulsed and sparked with a fierce energy burning everything down. Good and bad. For a second. She was resting on her side, a rolled pancake of cold moo shoo pork in her hand. She took a bite, a thin stream of juice spilling onto her chin, caught with two fingers.

She licked the fingers clean then saw him watching. Eyes locking onto his, she sucked one finger, then the other, then both. She popped them out of her mouth and traced a wet line down the middle of his forehead.

"Yes — fond, I think. That's the word. Fond."

He grabbed a handful of her curls and pulled her face close to his.

"You'll wake me up and tell me when it's a full-fledged like, won't you?"

She pulled away and smiled at him, curls plastered to her forehead. The time for a quick reply passed. She took another bite of Chinese burrito. She shifted gears.

"You're a nice guy . . ."

"Not hardly."

"No, I mean it. A niiice guy."

Her fingers traced a line from the middle of his chest to his cock.

"I've been divorced too many times to be nice."

"No, you're niiice."

"You don't know me very well, then."

She nodded her horse head nod, hair flying back and forth, teeth white and smiling against brown skin.

"Yesssss. I do. Ree-ally, reeeeally niiiiice."

Her fingers circled his hardening cock. He pulled her closer. She turned her face, expecting a kiss. He twisted her hair in his fingers until her eyes snapped open.

"You know somethin', Slick? Guys like me hate it when gals like you say we're ree-ah-lee, ree-ah-lee nah-eye-ce. It usually means you're taking us for granted or sizing us up for a sucker suit."

Her eyes cut him a look of annoyance. She shook herself free and hopped up, walking across him to the foot of the sofa bed and her pile of clothes. He watched her dress, her back turned to him as she slid panties over slim hips, snapping the elastic band straight, then hooking her bra together.

Jeans, pullover, sandals and purse. Cigarette pack from the table. One to her lip. The flare of a match. A jet of smoke toward the ceiling. Hair falling across his face. A quick kiss. No tongue. Just the taste of tobacco.

"I gotta go."

"Call me when you get home?"

"For what, a bedtime story?"

"So I know you're safe."

"Don't be ridiculous."

"You won't let me walk you to your car."

"Because it's silly."

"Not in this town."

"Please. Not another lecture about the real Dallas, the real city."

She cupped a hand to her ear and launched into a mock radio voice.

"It's the dark side of a city that only a cop can know. Or a private dick. A place where young damsels can only be protected by bear-like men full of lethal weaponry and Southern hospitality. Or is it Southern macho pride?"

"Try common sense. You'll know real quick when you need some macho."

"Look, I've been living here for fifteen years. Nothing has ever happened . . ."

Her voice trailed off. He was standing, holding her close, looking down at the top of her curls. He cupped her chin.

"It only takes once. Call."

"C'mon. This is Dallas."

He kissed her.

"Yeah, this is the D, a town where even the preachers have been known to ice their wives. So call, tough guy."

"So okay. You'll call me tomorrow? Let me know if you have to go out of town?"

Her voice went up a little-girl's octave on the questions. Cute was also part of her repertoire.

"You bet."

He lit a Lucky and closed the dented Zippo with a sharp and practiced snap. Saloon reflexes. His bartender would be proud. His thumb rubbed the single word one of his ex-wives had etched on the side — Nationwide. As in the old ZZ Top song, not the insurance company. As in their love being nationwide and too badass to die. As in a bold notion that missed the mark on their love and her own life.

She was dead, killed by a black hit man with a bad toupee and a choirboy's voice outside the entrance of the world's sixth-largest bat cave. She was dead because of something he got sucked into. He killed the bastard with a .45 slug to the brainpan. A Flying Ashtray to the forehead, dead center. The Third Eye, big and bloody. He straightened the man's toupee and left him lying in bat guano. It didn't even things out. But he was only bothered by bad memories every third or fourth week of his life.

He blew a stream of smoke toward the ceiling and watched as it rippled over the heat waves rising from the candles. He popped the bridge out of his mouth and dropped it in a half-empty glass of wine, his tongue tracing the hole where four teeth were pistol-whipped out of their sockets by a border narco scumbag, now dead. Blown to one of hell's lower chambers by slugs from the .45 of an ice-cold Tennessee blonde with a taste for muscle cars, crystal meth and the high-wire double-cross.

Saved his sorry ass from getting his heart carved out of his chest by the scumbag while trussed up like a hog on the butcher's block. Settled an old score — the scumbag had killed his partner, Wynn Moore, the man who taught him how to be a big-city homicide detective, adding layers of savvy and toughness that backed a shield he could never wear again.

But it didn't make up for his ex getting killed. He still carried that weight. Always would.

Burch leaned back and jetted more smoke across the candles, his back pressed against the curve of the sofa's rear cushion, its rough nap scratching his bare shoulders and outstretched arm.

His legs splayed out across the damp sheets. Surgery scars ran up the sides of both knees like a pair of poorly aligned zippers, dull and white against his sunburned legs and the black, wiry hair that covered them.

Football knees — permanent parting gifts from his playing days in high school and the Army, back when he was a clean-shaven offensive tackle with a full head of hair and twenty-five fewer pounds around his gut. They ached when the weather changed, when he climbed into his truck or up a flight of stairs, when he went jogging. They popped, growled and sent him sharp, warning jabs whenever he did anything particularly strenuous — like try to keep bedroom pace with a woman fifteen years younger.

On the other hand, the pain made him last longer in the saddle. And it never stopped his cock from standing up and asking for another ride.

"You fuck like a nineteen-year-old."

"Too fast and too soon?"

"Don't be stupid. You know what I mean. We just get finished and you're knocking on my door again."

"Part of my clever plan. I never show John Henry my driver's license and he never asks to borrow my truck."

"Where the hell do you come up with these lines? A better question — why the hell am I dating a guy who talks like this? You drive a pickup. You drink that foul bourbon. You listen to country music. And Jesus, you've got two first names. The guys I usually date are named Carlos or Giancarlo or Fernando. Sweeping names. Latin names. Names of candles and romance."

"Names of sissy Chicano guys with pomaded hair."

She slapped at him.

"No, stupid. Names of grandeur. You need a name like that. Something that conveys your size and style."

"How 'bout El Gordo?"

She slapped him again.

"You just want to give me a new name to make it easier to

remember who I am when all those other guys call."

"How could I ever forget you, baby doll? You don't put grease in your hair."

"Damned little hair left to put grease in."

She was unreliable, emotionally unavailable and probably unfaithful. In ways little and big, she made him feel like one in a string. It only annoyed him on mornings when he was feeling his age, when he stood before the mirror and checked out his bald pate and the new gray hairs in his beard, when the ruins of failed marriages and broken relationships loomed over his shoulder. Which made it most mornings before he had his coffee.

On the other hand, she was relentless in the rack and her exotic patter made him feel like he was living in the middle of a Raymond Chandler novel. A conversation with her had him thumbing Luckies onto his lip and talking out of the side of his mouth like a cheap gunsel.

He hated to think he just kept her around for the sex and the dialogue, but that seemed to be about it. He knew he was too burned out for love. He also knew his annoyance about the other guys wasn't so much jealousy as it was the nagging knowledge that he used to have a code about such things but no longer did.

Walkin' the line used to be important to him. He left one wife who couldn't. Or wouldn't. Now it didn't seem to matter. He was hanging around a younger woman who left his mattress for another man's as often as not. And he was bothered by it not seeming to matter anymore.

He was obsessing again. He took another sweet drag of Lucky, reaching for the ashtray perched on the sofa's armrest and grinding out the butt. A muffled ring. He rolled across the mattress, grunting as he leaned over the side and searched for the phone, buried underneath his clothes and a scattering of newspapers and magazines.

"What took you so long — a quickie at boyfriend's or did you walk the dog?"

"Excuse me?"

He froze. It wasn't her voice. It was a woman's voice but not her voice. He felt his face flush.

"I'm sorry. I thought it was someone else. Can I help you?"

"This is the AT&T operator. I've got a collect call for an Ed Earl Burch. Am I reaching the Burch residence?"

"I don't know if this is fancy enough a place to call a residence, but a fella named Burch lives here. Who's calling?"

"I have a collect call for an Ed Earl Burch from a Mrs. James Crowell. Will you accept the charges?"

"I don't know a Mrs. Crowell."

A voice broke in.

"It's Crowe, operator. Not Crowell. Crowe. Eddie? Eddie, is that you? Of course it is — I'd know that growl anywhere. I'm glad I caught you at home. Take the call, Big Boy, will you please?"

His flush of embarrassment was now a chill. She was the only one he ever let call him Eddie. She also called him Big Boy, usually when they were in the rack and the sheets were stained with sweat and sex. She was on his line again and wanted something from him. And that could only mean another dose of something bad for him.

The operator broke in.

"Will you accept the charges, Mr. Burch?"

"Yeah, yeah. I will. Thank you, operator."

A click. Silence.

"Thanks Eddie. I'm in a phone booth. I know it's late but I needed to call you."

"What is it this time, Savannah?"

"Oh, my. Such a cynical edge on that question. What makes you think I want anything from you? Maybe I want to do something for you, like toss some business your way. Or maybe this is just an overdue phone call between two old friends."

Old friends, he thought. Trouble and pain.

THREE

She was married now. Living in Houston. The wife of an attorney and investment advisor who specialized in setting up those cozy oil and gas partnerships that guaranteed a paper loss and a fine tax write-off for attorneys, doctors and other businessmen in the market for some shelter from the IRS. Five years gone from his life and his city.

The night he met her in Louie's, his favorite Dallas saloon, she was single, working for an insurance underwriter and muttering drunkenly about credit card debt, scuba diving and a feckless guy named Klaus.

She was standing next to Burch him at the bar, tall and unsteady, with wild, rusty-blonde curls falling across a broad, Slavic face, chewing on an olive from a vodka martini. She was a big girl, almost six feet tall. Not big-boned, not fat, but not classically proportioned enough to be called statuesque. Rangy and just a few pounds and years beyond coltish. It was as if God had started out making a power forward and decided to throw in some killer curves to keep a man cross-eyed and guessing.

"That goddam Klaus. You go on down to Cozumel. I mean, you drop ever' damn thing just to go on down to Cozumel. I mean, can you do that? Nobody can do that just ever' week in the year, right? Damn right. It's what I said to him. `Klaus, I just can't go down there to dive the reefs right now. Too much shit going on at work. Too many damn bills. MasterCarded right up to my damn tits in debt.' `What is debt when there is love, *Leibchen?*' Passes for charm in Munich. Not with me. Then this goddam storm trooper bullshit about me being his woman and doing what he says or he will leave me on the side of the road and find a little *schatzie* who wants to go to Mexico with him."

She giggled and gave a short Nazi salute — not the full stiff arm, just the casual upward flip of the hand Hitler used in all those candid newsreel shots.

"*Sieg Heil*, y'all. By Gott-in-Himmel, yav-ohwl. Silly squarehead. How can a girl just take a powder from work just to follow a guy down to Mexico on a weekday for some divin' even if he fucks like a tiger? What good is all that? And what good is he out of bed? The man would diddle a snake even with you watchin.'"

She was speaking to her empty glass, one of those oversized, overturned cones on a stem that Louie used to serve up Silver Bullets. Louie poured a drinker's drink and his martinis were the biggest guns in the house, a signature of sorts. A tipped glass and an olive marked the sign above his door and the T-shirts he sold behind the bar.

With the slow precision of the thoroughly plowed, she placed the glass on the bar and picked up a pack of Salem Lights, tapping out a cigarette, smoothly placing it on her lip and moving her hand to drop the pack back on the bar, missing by three inches and not hearing the plastic thump when all those Grade A smokes hit the floor.

Boston Sean, the bartender with the face of an altar boy, the body of a jockey and the soul of a bookie, stepped up quickly to light her cigarette and swipe the shaker away. She held his wrist lightly, inhaled and locked her eyes on Sean's.

"Thanks. And what's the name of the man who makes such great martinis only to take them away when a girl really needs one?"

Sean gave his name, moving his mouth around the toothpick that hung from his lip so the sliver never moved. She changed her grip to a handshake.

"Sean. Savannah. You're going to pour me the rest of my drink, right Sean?"

"Not if I can avoid it."

He said that with a slight Southie accent and a smile. She smiled back, control and poise fighting the alcohol, erasing all the slur and street talk from her voice.

"You can't and you shouldn't worry. You're going to pour, watch me drink it down and then you're going to call me a cab."

"What if you fall down? I'd hate you to mess up that nice suit."

"Sean, I don't plan on falling down. And if I do, I'll get this big guy over here to pick me up. He seems interested enough to eavesdrop, I'm sure I can get him interested enough to help me put my foot back on the rail if worse comes to worst."

That broke the bubble that surrounds perfect strangers drinking shoulder to shoulder in a bar. He took his time, sipping Maker's Mark from his shot glass, chasing it with ice water from a juice glass, tapping ash that wasn't there from the Lucky that burned near the knuckles of his left hand. He turned and looked her up and down. Slowly.

"It looks like an interesting foot. I'd try to keep it on the bar rail."

"Ah, he speaks, Sean. Thought he might be one of those true-life statues you see. You know the ones, Sean? The businessman eating lunch off his briefcase, the bum sleeping on the park bench with the newspaper over his face, the fat man scratching his belly in the lawn chair?"

"I'm the Disney version — the regular bellied up to the bar. An automaton. Look."

He took a sip of Maker's.

"I drink."

He took a drag.

"I smoke."

He smiled, turned away from her, winked at Sean and took a parting shot over his left shoulder.

"I even listen to drunk women rattle on about scuba diving and German boyfriends. *Sieg Heil*, y'all."

He flipped his hand up Hitler style then finished the Maker's shot. She cracked him across the back of the head with a half-filled bottle of Old Style, the pissy beer of Louie's beloved Chicago, catching him where his hairline ended and his bald pate began, opening the type of shallow head cut that only looks like a major artery has been popped open.

The blow caused him to pitch forward, his forearm and forehead plowing across the bar, sending his glasses, his ashtray, his Luckies, his Zippo and his ice water flying over the bottles in the well and onto the duckboards near Sean's feet. As his head cleared and his ears stopped ringing, he could hear the cackles from a table full of regulars — Mike the Mick, Lizard Brad and Mister Injured Reserve, most likely.

"That's for mocking me, you smartass sonuvabitch! Do it again and I'll crack you again."

She was red-faced fury, curls flying, the blood and anger coarsening the surface of her cheeks and forehead like rough-cured concrete. The bar was dead silent with the sudden quiet that hits when the church choir sings the final amen to a long, soaring hymn about God's saving grace.

Sean handed him his glasses. He nodded and put them on.

"Another Maker's, Sean."

"You're bleedin', man."

"I know. Another Maker's, bossman. And a drink for yourself, the lady and those assholes behind me."

"She's flagged and 86ed."

"Give her one for the road, Sean."

"I can't do that. She smacked a regular — Louie's rules, man."

"And the regular wants to buy her a drink. Do it before I bleed all over your damn bar, Sean."

"I'll pour what's left of this one, but that's it, Burch."

He could feel the cut begin to heat up, tighten and swell. He could feel the wet track of blood through his hair and on his neck. He could hear the guffaws from the boys.

"Better polish up them pickup lines, boy. She ain't buyin' that one."

"She's a southpaw, Burch. You ain't worth a shit against southpaws."

"Sign her up, Double E. She's like all your exes — drunk and difficult."

"Hey, Burch — you don't have to marry that one to know she'll clean your clock."

He said nothing. He could feel the heat of her stare. He looked straight ahead. He waited for Sean to pour his shot, rattle the shaker of martini remnants and pull down a bottle of Jameson for himself. Out of the corner of his eye, he saw Young Suzy the Virgin Waitress, brown bangs over black, button eyes, rack up a tray of beers for the boys.

The wild woman was standing to his left, wobbly and breathing hard. He didn't look her way. He could hear her breathe, but only saw her when she weaved into the edge of his vision. She set the Old Style bottle on the bar with slow precision and hoisted the spun glass cone that held her final Silver Bullet of the night.

"Wait just a second, please."

"What?"

"I bought you that drink. I'm bleeding because of you. The least you can do is wait when I ask you to."

He picked up his Maker's and turned toward the boys.

"Ladies, gentlemen. Grab your beers and join me in a traditional toast."

Chairs scraped the floor as the boys stood up.

"Repeat after me. IT JUST DOESN'T MATTER!"

"IT JUST DOESN'T MATTER!"

"Again. IT JUST DOESN'T MATTER!"

"IT JUST DOESN'T MATTER!"

He threw back the Maker's, tilted his face toward the ceiling and began to howl. The guys and gals barked back, yipping and yowling to the laughter of the crowd.

Barks started breaking out across the bar, from SMU youngsters in baseball caps, baggy shorts and page boys, from a table of drunk lawyers in dark suits, French cuffs and bad tie-and-suspender combos that looked like amoebas with the bends, from Fast Sketch Harry and the East Dallas Lifetime Waiters Association, from Delores the Dwarf Accountant and the Slut Sister Real Estate Choir. From everybody except a tall, round-shouldered man with a beer gut, a pink golf shirt, squinty gray eyes, lank black hair that hung to his shoulders and a badly pitted face.

He slapped Burch in the chest with the back of a hard-knuckled hand.

"You think you're funny, doncha?"

Burch started eyeing the bar for a loose bottle. The man slapped him in the chest again.

"Doncha?"

"Mister, when a woman smacks you in the head with a beer bottle for no damn reason, you got to make a joke out of it. What do you want me to do, smack her back?"

"Seems like she had plenty reason to crack on you."

"Care to name just one?"

"You made fun of her with that little Hitler routine."

"Come on, son. You can do better than that."

"I don't have to. All I have to do is say I don't like your damn looks and smartass barkin' and tell you I'm the sumbitch that's gonna kick your ass."

Burch saw the loose bottle he was looking for. It was too late. His glasses flew over the spouted bottles in the bar well one more time. His Zippo and his Luckies, soggy and dented from their last trip to the duckboards, stayed put.

He didn't get up.

The barking resumed. So did the laughter.

He didn't hear it.

"My husband's been murdered."

"Hmmmm — no emotion in your delivery. Do better with the cops, Irish. Might make you less of a prime suspect."

"Or he might not be."

"Might not be what — dead? Or murdered? Is this a multiple-choice test? Can I pick D — none of the above? What do you want to hire me for, Irish? To take an SAT?"

"Knock it off, Eddie. I'm in trouble and it ain't from the cops. It's serious. And it's business — big time business with some big players."

"I didn't think it was love. With you, it's sex, money or action. Maybe all three in the same package. Did you get the trifecta with this dude, Irish? Or just left with the short end when the cops came knockin'?"

He called her Irish because her last name was Devlin. And in a sentimental moment brought on by one Maker's beyond his normal whiskey curve, he trotted down to the Bodine's Fine Cigars on Commerce in the first flushed days of their affair and had that nickname engraved on the side of the best-known product from Bradford, Pa.

The new Zippo flashed in the winter sunlight. And there were the fresh-carved letters — Irish. That's what he called her, but the genes that dominated her face, frame and temper came from her mother, a Czech émigré. Her father was a saloon sport and a Radio Free Europe announcer; she inherited his smooth words and capacity for alcohol.

She slipped away the night he got decked. So did everybody else in the bar before he came to. Sean and Louie's brother, Chris, stretched him out across an empty booth in the back, his long legs and snakeskin boots splayed out into the aisle, a wet towel under his head and the bleeding cut, nose pointed toward the white neon ring of an old Mobil Oil clock with the winged red horse flying between midnight and six o'clock.

When his eyes opened, it was well past closing. His jaw was stiff and swollen. His head throbbed. The overhead lights were out. So were the neon signs in the windows. The clock was still lit. A light was on in the kitchen and in Louie's cubbyhole office. He could smell cigar smoke. The boss was in, working the books.

A small desk lamp bounced harsh glare off the wide, white pages of a ledger, casting Louie's craggy face in an up-from-the-furnaces-of-hell light, like the old Life magazine portrait of the patriarch of the Krupp family, cannon makers for the Kaiser, for Hitler and for the west half of the Germany that followed.

A Partagas double corona jutted from the bar owner's bushy, iron-gray beard, giving him the appearance of an aging *barbudo* from Castro's Rebel Army. The castors of his oak desk chair squealed as he swiveled around and shook Burch's hand.

"Mister Burch — always a pleasure. Rough night in Jericho, I hear."

"Sideswiped by a blonde and a bubba. Usual Saturday night in the D."

Burch never called his home city by its name or the nickname touristas and the Chamber of Commerce hung on it. To him, it was a merciless, mirthless town unworthy of any term of endearment, worthy of only a single initial and an anglicized version of the formal construction Hispanics used when referring to servants or a family member they had little fondness for. As in, the Maria, the Pedro, the Sebastian — the D.

"Least you quit bleedin'. Thought we might have to take you in for stitches. Marty gave you the once over and said you'd live so we let you stay zonked."

"Nurse Marty. You let that chesty thing fondle me and didn't bother to give me a wake-up call?"

"Hey Burch, if them tits of hers aren't enough to wake you up, too fuckin' bad, I say."

Louie's voice was an even mix of gravel, whiskey and smoke. When he started to laugh, it turned into a deep cough. The cigar never left his mouth.

"You still keep a private bottle back here?"

"Only ouzo."

Burch made a face.

"You know a sick man shouldn't drink licorice. What happened to that bottle of Barton you used to pour for your favorite customers?"

"Top shelf on your right, next to Ditka and the boys. Bring the bottle back and we'll have a few pops."

Burch wandered behind the bar, searching in the dim light for the photo of the Chicago Bears and their coach, grabbing the bottle of Very Old Barton bourbon and two short glasses. He walked back to Louie's cubbyhole, feeling unsteady and light-headed.

Louie poured — ouzo for himself, bourbon for his guest. They drank. Burch smacked his lips and pronounced himself healed.

"Good whiskey — all a man ever needs when he gets his bell rung."

"I'll let you in on a little secret — you're really drinking Evan Williams poured into a Very Old Barton bottle."

"Ol' Evan makes a fine whiskey. If I could find it everywhere, I'd drink it. Which is why I drink Maker's Mark. It's always around and it ain't an uppity bourbon that tourists drink to keep in touch with the masses. It ain't all that high dollar, so Greek `tenders won't try to switch it for something shitty like Cabin Still."

"Cabin Still, huh? Never heard of it."

"You're missing one of life's rawer pleasures, son. It's the Sportsman's Bourbon. Guaranteed to be less than a year old."

Louie laughed then coughed. He poured out two more shots.

"Who was my unruly date?"

"Don't know her. Neither does Sean. Little Hutch says she's been in a time or two. Not a tourist. Not a SMUster. Not a Park City Ranger drinking in coach. Random traffic. White-collar type. Business suit and briefcase, he says. And always a martini."

"The right drink for this bar."

"Not for her. She's 86ed for life."

"Don't be a hardass. You can't toss a woman who drinks that much and looks that good."

"Hey, she whacked you with a beer bottle, opened your scalp and got you clocked by a bubba. Can't have that happen in my bar, not to one of my regulars, no matter how many martinis she buys."

"Didn't know you cared."

"Hey, the broad fucks with my regulars, she's fuckin' with my bottom line. Bad for the business."

"Well tell Hutch to give her my name and number when he throws her out. She at least owes me dinner and drinks."

Louie shook his head.

"You don't learn do you?"

"Not since I left school."

She called five days later. From a pay phone. Mad because she just got tossed out of Louie's. By Hutch. Who gave her Burch's name and phone number. Sometimes life works that way. Most times you wind up wishing it didn't.

She called him an asshole when he said she owed him dinner and drinks. She hung up before he could call her a bitch. She rang back an hour later. His machine picked up that call — a terse time and place for dinner the next night. The message did not include a rude name this time.

Steaks at the Hoffbrau. Drinks at the San Francisco Rose, up on the bar where the regulars hung out, poured with a wink and a leer by Tony the Softball King, who always teased him about the young heartbreakers he squired and the doubles he always ordered after they left him a flaming wreck.

The night started cool and smooth and ended up hot — clothes flying, bodies banging together, sheets tangled. Lots of laughter. Lots of lewd talk backed by action that matched the words. He was hooked again and they both knew it. She wasn't and they both knew that too.

By the end of a week, he had told her about his three exes and she knew every emotional wound on his soul. By the end of three months, she was using that knowledge to add fresh cuts and gouges of her very own.

The garden-variety slashes came first — the all-nighters when he went out of town, then the all-nighters when he was in town. And his favorite — the date canceled at the last second because an old friend just hit town. The phone would just ring-ring-ring in his ear when he couldn't help it and made those three a.m. calls. And those old friends never had a woman's name. It was a man. Always. Rick, John, Bill, Ricardo. Never Klaus though. She *Sieg Heil*ed him out of her black book.

"Just because your first wife cheated on you doesn't mean every woman does. It doesn't mean I do. I'm with you — what more do you need me to say? That I love you? I can't say that so I won't. I can say I'm with you and don't want to see anybody else. And I don't."

She said these lines perfectly, like the smooth talk she used on Sean that first night at Louie's, nudging him her way with the calm sureness of a pickpocket until Sean yielded his bartender's eye for the terminally drunk and poured that last Silver Bullet. The set of her jaw was just right. The tone was just emotional enough but cool at the same time. And the words had their desired effect — you stepped away from your best instincts, you stayed in one spot until she was ready to blow you down and blow you off.

"Look — how long have you been poking this doxie?"

"Doxie?"

"Yeah — doxie, frail, skirt, gash. That's the '30s riff on women who are no good. Want me to go modern? Okay — bitch, cunt, whore. Want me to go Gloria Steinem? Okay — a woman exercising the wandering sexual prerogatives that men thought were only theirs. Want me to go Western? Okay — no-good, two-timin' cunt whore bitch. Got it? Because she's got you, my friend. By the *cojones*. And fist-fucking you with the other hand for good measure."

"It gets worse."

"I hate when friends tell me that. Look — let me order another round here. If I'm going to listen to misery, I need more whiskey."

Krukovitch shot his cuffs through the sleeves of a padded, mock-mohair jacket from the Gap, smoothed his thin, slick-against-the-skull blond hair and signaled Whitey for two more Maker's.

He was a short, balding man with rounded, wire-frame glasses, the intense glare of Leon Trotsky and the steely straight posture of a weightlifter and little guy always trying to be taller and bigger than God made him to be. He chain smoked Carltons from the flip-top box and poured cup after cup of thick, black coffee down his gullet — from wakeup till late evening, which usually found him at Louie's, arguing politics, writing and literature with the other would-be poets and novelists who roosted in the rear of the bar.

Except that Krukovitch, a cranky and brilliant conservative whose forefathers hailed from the steppes of the Ukraine and whose father ran a Texaco heating oil business in Fargo, was a successful novelist, newspaper columnist and syndicated essayist. He wrote yuppie thrillers. His stock character was a food columnist who always stumbled into bizarre murder mysteries with a culinary element, like the Shining Path disciple who decided to spike all the hot dogs sold at the Super Bowl with a powerful hallucinogen so he could kill the president. That one was called *Hold the Mustard*. His collection of columns and essays, many of them reruns from the local alternative weekly, the *Dallas Observer*, was called *Jangled Mutterings, Confused Complaints*.

"What could be worse, my son, than being in love with a woman who is making such a total fool out of you that everyone in your favorite bar knows about it? Are we talking a social disease here? Are we talking about one of the other guys coming after you with a lead pipe? Did you take her to Vegas and tie the knot?"

"Cut the crap."

Burch downed his shot, blew out his breath and lit a Lucky. He looked at Krukovitch and hesitated.

"What? What could be so bad? Tell me."

Burch told it fast.

"She said she wanted to buy a house. I loaned her five K for the down. There wasn't a house. There was a drug deal. It was a sting. She told the boys downtown she was fronting for me."

"And with friends like the ones you've got on the force, they were only too willing to believe, right?"

"That an ex-cop and former murder suspect might also be a drug dealer? Pavlovian salivation would be the phrase. I got the full-court press — the midnight arrest, complete with knocked-down door, cuffs and a night in Lew Sterrett. Plus four grand for the bond and eight grand for the lawyer. Not to mention the five I loaned her."

"No, I don't guess she would be giving you a refund, would she?"

"Seized as evidence. And I can't touch it because I had to deny that I gave her the money. I had to make it her word against mine, which was easy to do because I gave her cash and didn't give her a check."

"But they could still pull your bank records, right?"

"Yeah, they did that. They found a six K withdrawal that matches the time of the deal. It gave 'em a hard-on until my lawyer told them it was money for past legal work and provided them the dummy records that proved it."

"Good legal work."

"Yeah. Well worth the extra three K I had to pay for this service."

"On top of the eight for representing you in court?"

"And the four for the bond and the five K I dropped on Irish."

"Ouch."

"Ouch is right. I had to take out another loan. And business is going in the tank right now."

"But hell, this shithole is finally bouncing back from the bust. Business should be good."

"Not for a pee-eye who specialized in tracking down deadbeats for banks and S&Ls. I did right well off the bust. A counter-cyclical business, mine is."

Burch signaled Whitey. Krukovitch shot his cuffs, lit another Carlton and held up his coffee cup. Bourbon and caffeine — the poor man's speedball.

"Love has a price tag. Where is the lovely lass now?"

"Not in hell, unfortunately. Long gone. She dropped dime on me and her suppliers and split town home free."

"No charges?"

"Dropped. Smooth talk and good looks will take you a long way in this life."

"That they will, lad."

"Any advice?"

"I'll tell you what an old friend used to tell me when I'd pour my heart out about some lying, faithless, feckless bitch and start crying on his shoulder about my pitiful existence. He would push my face up out of my beer, cock his head and say `Krukovitch — I wish you well.'"

Krukovitch chuckled, pleased with his story and its perfect fit with their conversation. Burch stared at Krukovitch and didn't laugh. The smaller man looked uncomfortable. One man's perfect fit is another man's insult.

"That line is always delivered with a flat nasal accent and an ironic tone. Consider it a roughhouse term of endearment."

A joke explained is a joke that missed. Krukovitch tried to smile but it froze into a grimace. Burch broke his stare and let him off the hook.

"A comfort."

Krukovitch raised his glass in salute. Burch did the same.

"I wish you well."

"It just doesn't matter."

"No — I guess it doesn't."

FOUR

"Look — can the cute lines, Big Boy. Here's the deal — either he staged his own murder or got fried to a crackly crisp when his car blew up in a field out by the Intercontinental."

"What do the cops think?"

"You think they let me in on their pow-wows? Like you said — I'm a suspect. They did show me some personal effects. Most were badly burned but I recognized a Rolex I gave him last year — my name was on the back."

"Rolex — you ain't playin' with Zippos anymore."

"What?"

"Never mind."

"Did you say Zippo? Oh, yeah — that damned lighter you gave me. I lost it."

"Hey, it was extra weight. You were climbing the ladder."

"I was doing what I had to do."

"And doing whoever you met along the way."

"That was five years ago. Man, you bear a grudge."

"You bet — I'm Scots-Irish. We're worse than Sicilians — we don't forget, we don't forgive and we like to serve up our revenge hot and frothy. Fuck that plate of cold stuff."

"Great speech."

"I'll get off the soapbox then. Assuming I'd want to take a

fucking job from you, why hire me? Hire the best defense attorney in Houston; he'll come complete with a good brace of investigators. Hell — hire Racehorse Haynes. If he can get Cullen Davis off, he can save your piss-ant ass. Percy Forman's dead but the DeGuerin brothers are still around — if you can figure out which one spells his name which way."

"Cut it, Eddie. I'm not trying to hire you to prove I'm innocent. I want to hire you to either find that worthless puke of a husband of mine or find the guys who offed him. They, or he — or all of them — took some assets that belonged to some people who are holding me accountable."

He yawned into the mouthpiece.

"An interesting story Irish but you can't afford to hire me — your account is already heavily in arrears."

"Are you still pissed about that little business deal?"

"Pissed is what I was while it went down. Pissed is what I felt while those cops were sizing me up for those fashionable gray work clothes they give all the residents down at Huntsville. Pissed is what I felt when I had to peel off about twenty K to get myself out of your mess. Pissed is what I was as I watched my bank account drain like a kitchen sink."

"What are you now?"

"Not interested."

Burch hung up. He lit another Lucky. Two drags later, the phone rang again. The operator. He refused to accept the collect call and hung up. Two more drags and a stab of a finger to turn off the answering machine. A ringing phone. He ignored it. The rings stopped at ten, leaving a sudden silence that sent another disturbing wave of memory and doubt through his mind.

No way, son. Bad news. Let it roll on by. Wonder what she really wants? What type of sucker suit has she got me sized up for this time? Jee-zus — you never do learn, do you? Not since grade school. What are you gunning for — a PhD in trouble and pain? Nah, I just audit these classes. Christ, you're a

34

stupid sumbitch. True enough — wonder if I can beat her at her own game?

Slowly, unevenly, like a mover trying to wrestle a chest of drawers up a narrow staircase, sleep muscled his consciousness aside. It took a long time. His eyes were shut but his ears stayed alert for that ringing phone. He knew she would call again. He knew she would keep at him. He was thinking that as he finally drifted off, mouth agape, snoring, a thin line of drool running into his beard.

His eyes snapped open four hours later, his heart lurching in his chest, his mind frozen by a loud, burring sound. The phone was finally ringing. It was on the nightstand above his head, a crafty move for a common household appliance that was on the floor when he went to sleep — too crafty for his addled mind. He fumbled for his glasses and squinted at the digital alarm clock. 7:54. In the ay-yem. Early riser. Had to be her. After those nights when she did stay over, she used to leave his bed then call from her office to make sure he made an early morning meeting with a client. Had to be her.

"This is Ed Earl Burch — I'll accept the charges, operator."

"What? This isn't the operator."

That made no sense. There was a woman's voice on the line. Had to be her.

"You finally get a phone card, Savannah?"

"Mr. Burch, my name is not Savannah. I'm calling for Wilbert Nofzinger, attorney at law. You're familiar with his name, are you not?"

Burch groaned. Fat Willie, his shyster. Broker of the twenty K note that kept him from tending a clock ticking a load of hard time. Forger of phony legal bills that kept the cops off his back — for a price. Holder of another eleven K note on his business, his pickup and his bass boat. Owner of his financial hide and what little hair that hadn't been scraped from it.

"Been sittin' here thinkin' about my fav-o-rite client. Yessir —

you bet. Jus' sittin' here, stirrin' a little bourbon into my morning coffee and runnin' a little mental image of you. Wanna know what you were doin'?"

"Not if it has anything to do with animal husbandry."

A laugh that sounded like a gymnasium toilet flushing in a tile-lined room.

"Animal husbandry — that's good. Stump fuckin', right? Slippin' the salami into ol' Bessie, right? You got a dirty mind, Burch. Thas' what I like 'bout you, boy."

A gurgling sip of coffee and bourbon — the sound a dog makes sucking down his first chunk of Alpo.

"Naw, naw. You weren't stump fuckin' anything in this picture. Naw, see — what you were doin' was walking right into my office with a nice, fat envelope in your hand. You had on that fine leather blazer — the black one, the one that covers the Colt up real nice. And you were wearin' a smile. You walked right up to me and said, `Willie, I believe I've fell behind in my obligations to you. Here's what I owe and a little somethin' extra for your trouble.'"

"That's the trouble with dreams — they never come true."

"Hey! Listen up, fuckhead. You're five months down and your big note just got called. That's eighteen large — one and an eight with a K waggin' behind it. Not to mention what I'm carryin'. Am I gettin' through to you?"

Burch hung up.

The phone rang before he could pull his hand back.

"Try this for a mental image, jackass — you're in prison for shylockin' and accepting stolen property. A big buck named Cleotus is trying to cut a new path between your asshole and your tonsils. Am I gettin' through to you?"

Silence on the line, then a cough.

"Ahhhh — this is the operator. I have a collect call from a Savannah Crowe. Will you accept the charges?"

"Ah, Christ. Yes."

"Interesting way of greeting an operator, handsome."

"Kiss my ass, Savannah."

"Another interesting image. You're really rolling and it's barely eight, darling. In the old days, I had to call you twice and suggest something really nasty to get you up and out before ten."

"That's if you weren't too busy sucking off Gene or Bill or whoever the hell else you were banging after you left my bed."

"A nasty temper this morning. Have you started mixing Seconal and red wine again, darling? It makes you meaner than a boar hog."

"No — my shitty attitude comes from old memories of you, lover."

"Hmmmmm. Maybe I can sweeten you up a little bit."

"Damn unlikely. No — let me amend that. You can make my shitty attitude rise up to the level of white folks and high-dollar whores."

"Fuck you, Eddie."

"No — fuck yourself, lover. Or find one of those other guys you used to fuck when you were fucking me. Go yank on his chain. Go bring back somebody else's bad memories of having a big turd dropped on his head and ruin his damn morning. Get the fuck out of mine."

"Wait! Don't hang up."

"Do you hear a click on the line? DO YOU?"

"No."

"So why don't you just tell me what the fuck it is you want from me?"

A snarling delivery that ended in a growl. A soft voice on the other side of the line.

"I told you. I want you to find that sorry puke husband of mine. Or the guys who fried him."

"Forty K."

"What?"

"Forty K. Forty grand. Forty large. Twenty of it up front, sent to my lawyer. And I get expenses."

"Forty K. You want a lot."

"I got financial obligations. You got bad trouble that nobody else would handle."

A sigh on the line.

"Forty K?"

"That's right."

"Done."

"Done?"

"Done."

"What kind of trouble has your money bought me?"

No answer. No need for one.

FIVE

Jason Willard Crowe was a 42-year-old Houston comer in monogrammed shirts and Hickey-Freeman suits, a smiling-eyed, white-collared hustler with coal-black hair you couldn't comb with a rake. That was before he got cooked in his own $34,000 sled of leather-trimmed German steel.

Maybe he just ripped off the wrong client and got turned into a crispy critter, an unlucky player of the gray margins of the tax codes who ran into a true badass mad about a big loss. Or maybe he worked the shadier zones beyond the lights of legal commerce, a frequenter of art gallery openings with a regular table at Brennan's and a secret business life who had his own death staged to get away from angry playmates, partners or associates. And a wife who had as lethal a lust for money and action as any hood, hooker or financier.

Or maybe he just disappeared himself so he could escape the dogs of banking, securities and law enforcement that were loosed on his slick little world of smooth paper and thirty-to-one guaranteed partnership losses, regulatory revenge for the carnage of the oil bust and the real estate collapse that started rolling across Texas like a tsunami in the mid-80s, drowning the big and small. It was a relentlessly grim comeuppance for all that Lone Star hubris when oil was $30 a barrel and greedy dreamers lusted for $60, a rude stopper to all that bragging about being the nation's Third Coast.

That seemed like an eternity ago and Texas was on the rebound, tracking the national economic upswing ushered in by a bubba from Arkansas in the White House with his famously wandering eye and battle-axe wife, the Lady Macbeth of American politics.

Ol' Jace left a bag of questions — why get cooked for a little tax and securities fraud or a limited partnership soured by tax code shifts, why stage a disappearing act just to get out from under a crowd of fleeced and angry doctors, lawyers and accountants? Bankruptcy was as much a part of Texas as the Alamo, the safety it offered the busted bidnessman almost as sacred as the mission ground. Stealing was another fine bit of Texas legend and lore — from cattle rustled from the Mexicans by John Chisholm or Charles Goodnight and land stolen from Indians, ranchers and farmers by anybody rich, powerful or ballsy enough to get away with it, to the dead folks who rose up and voted LBJ to his first congressional term.

All the boy had to do was stash his loot in some offshore accounts, take a hit of jail time and come out on the other side with a nest egg for life. Or get a fast lawyer to get him off the hook. Might get a little uncomfortable being around the crowd at Brennan's or Cafe Annie's, but he'd be breathing free, gulping lungsful of that fetid Houston air. Getting caught was one of the reasons God stuck the world with lawyers and crooked judges. Might as well take advantage of the Good Lord's graces.

Unless he wasn't fast enough to build a pile before the bust and the tax code shift of `86 sucked him under. Unless he was playing a different game on the side and his playmates got pissed. Unless it was those guys he needed to escape forever, not the lawdogs. Unless he needed to slip away from Savannah before she slipped something sharp and lethal into him.

Burch took a drag from a soggy-ended Lucky and a sip of

American **oneworld**

TSA PRECHK

PASSENGER NAME
MCCARTNEY/MITCHELL

FROM:
DALLAS/FT WORTH

TO:
COLORADO SPRINGS

GROUP 6

MAIN

BOARDING PASS

DOORS CLOSE 10 MINUTES PRIOR TO DEPARTURE

FREQUENT FLYER #
M3V0356

RECORD
LOCATOR
FZSJIQ

FLIGHT	CLASS	DATE	DEPARTS
AA5960	V	26AUG	441P

GATE	BOARDING TIME	SEAT
411P	15D	

0012364719510

((•))
oneworld

BOARDING PASS

PASSENGER NAME
MCCARTNEY/MITCHELL

FROM:
DALLAS/FT WORTH

TO:
COLORADO SPRINGS

FLIGHT		SEAT
AA 5960		15D

GROUP 6

DATE	CLASS	DEPARTS
26AUG	V	441P

AAdvantage® Aviator® Red
World Elite Mastercard®*

TRAVELING THERE BEGINS HERE

with a Companion Certificate good for
1 guest at $99 (plus taxes and fees)*

Cardmembers also enjoy other great benefits like:*

· First checked bag free
· Up to $25 back on inflight Wi-Fi purchases
  ...and more!

Ask your flight attendant for an
application or apply online at
ApplyAviator.com.

* See Terms and Conditions for full details.   **BARCLAYS**

Maker's. He was sitting at the short end of the bar at Louie's, grabbing background on Crowe from a folder full of Lexus-Nexus printouts Krukovitch cadged off the *Observer's* account and smaller nuggets stored on the columnist's PowerBook. He leafed through a long profile written shortly after Crowe disappeared. Son of an oilfield roughneck. High school studhoss, quarterback and object of desire for every school in the Southwestern Conference. Picked A&M. Aggieville. Blew out a knee — Burch's zippered hinges ached in sympathy.

Sidelined from the gridiron, Crowe showed as much feel for a spreadsheet and finances as he did for the soft spots in a safety-up zone. Transferred to Rice, which still wanted him for the gridiron. Did a double major — accounting and pre-law. Went to Austin and the big university for his law shingle. Went to work for LQ, Lon Quantrell, the man who turned Glenn McCarthy's wildcatting empire into an energy conglomerate. Quantrell was a big Rice booster and probably the stake horse for Crowe's academic career. Married the boss's daughter, a classmate at Rice. Got cut in as a partner on lucrative oil and gas deals. Pictures of Crowe and wifey at all the right social galas and gallery openings.

Divorced from the boss's daughter after he crashed a society queen's Porsche 911 Targa into a guardrail on the Gulf Freeway, the splashiest and most scandalous example of his life outside the pop of the society photos. Blow found in her purse and their bloodstreams. Charges quietly dropped. But the transgression was not forgotten. Crowe violated a key rule of the upper crust, one any cracker who has crawled up to that level of life should have etched on his eyeballs — keep the dirt private and the family name unsoiled.

A dive out of the public eye. A comeback as a financial advisor for the young, the rich and the nose-candy dependent. Hints that he serviced their finances and their habits. And those of some shadier interests as well. Married Savannah. Back on the gallery and gala circuit, this time for Houston's hip and thirtysomethings. Back in the rumor mill — name bandied about after cops busted a ring of coke hounds working the same fast, rich young crowd Crowe was working. Called before a grand jury. Not indicted. Never called to testify in court.

Burch hit a key on the PowerBook, one he thought was supposed to call up the next electronic clip from Nexus. It didn't. All he got was the sound of a fart and Krukovitch's voice yelling one word: "DUMBASS!" He hit the key again. The noise and the name.

"Fuck! What the hell's wrong with this damn thing?"

"Wrong question. What the hell's wrong with you — forget which key I told you to hit?"

"I told you I didn't know how to run these damn things."

"You did fine until that last little item. You've been sitting there staring at the screen for the last ten minutes, muttering and smoking those damned Luckies. Made you forget what to do."

"The smoke?"

"The muttering. It makes you absent-minded. Here — this is the key you hit for the next story. Got it?"

"Yeah. Yeah."

They were sitting in the cool, empty gloom of Louie's, some three circuits of the minute hand away from the happy hour blitz. Little Hutch was walking the duckboards, checking bottles and glasses, filling wells with ice and coolers with beer, squaring the count in his cash tray.

A phone line ran from the back of Krukovitch's gray laptop, snaking across the bar, looping over the edge and running between the glass necks of vodka, rum and whiskey to a jack in the wall just to the left of Louie's liquor license — a private line where Louie's bookies could reach him. A postcard of thonged, greased and sunbaked Florida hardbody ass was stuck in the pressboard frame that held the license. Once it had held a Polaroid of Burch's third wedding, the one that took place in the court clerk's office in

Waxahachie, the state's simple marital vows delivered by a skinny assistant with a whiny voice as the couple stood next to a tank full of goldfish, sweating with doomed nervousness despite the blast of air conditioning.

Burch knew he would find Krukovitch here. It was Monday, column day, and Krukovitch could always be found at the short end of the bar, banging Carlton 100s, drinking cups of inky coffee that he made himself on one of Louie's double-burner rigs, spinning out another cranky 800 words on his obsession du jour — the pinheaded, dictatorial ways of Ross Perot; the revolving door of bimbos and ethical questions surrounding Slick Willy; the teeth-grinding mercantilism and intolerance of the D; the state's execution rate for Death Row inmates, which Kruk damned as too slow; welfare cheats, art mavens, Deep Ellum hipsters and smiling civic hustlers; Robert Tilton and the endless stupidities of Bubba, the state's mythical mascot, a pickup-drivin', gun-totin', beer-swillin' Neanderthal who lived somewheres out there, beyond the lights of the D, out where the creek forked and the farm-to-market road seldom crossed another of its kind.

A hip monarchist, that was Krukovitch, a conservative Burke would have loved, with no blind loyalty to the business class. Which made him a Bolshevik in the eyes of those who practiced the Dallas Way, those lock-stepped waltzers of business, civic and political interests who set the city's tempo, filled its dance card behind closed doors and tolerated no step out of time.

But the boy also had a bit of the anarchist in him. In his teens, he was an all-world computer hacker, routinely tapping into Defense Department mainframes, phone systems, bank networks and, the move Krukovitch considered the triumph of his squeaky-voiced youth, a foray into the electronic brain of Merrill Lynch that netted him $300,000 worth of Exxon and 3M stock. All on a crude Kaypro, a machine that had the blue-collar appeal of a lunch box and the power and speed of a dying light bulb. Krukovitch never got nailed for his wanderings; he reigned in the days before the Justice Department started putting teenagers in jail for dialing up the Pentagon's computers. He even wrote two books on his passion — *The Hacker's Bible* and *Whipping the Wire: Confessions of a Computer Thief.*

When Burch walked in, Krukovitch was sending his column to the *Observer's* mainframe, staring intently at the screen, waiting for the laptop to tell him the product had been delivered. When the words were safely home, Burch told him what he wanted and Krukovitch started briskly punching keys, telling him about CD-ROMS, stacking programs, virus sniffers, the new software rig that allowed him to tap into IBM-skewed databases and the near future of cellular modems that flashed 14,400 bits of information a second and would let him work at Louie's without tying up the boss's private line.

"It'll be great. I can work without this damn umbilical cord and — the best thing — I'll be able to get those stupid, mindless faxes everybody sends just like I'm working in a real office. All I need is the cash to buy it."

"I don't know what the fuck you're talking about. Just find me what I need and show me the keys to punch."

Krukovitch gave him a hurt look, tapped into the Nexus database and called up the stories Burch wanted to see. Then he sulked, turning his back, picking up a magazine and firing up another Carlton as Burch fumbled with the laptop. Silent tension was broken only by Burch's mutterings to himself. When he finally screwed up enough to throw the laptop into terminal gridlock, drawing Krukovitch's little lecture about absent-mindedness, Little Hutch laughed.

"You guys are worse than an old married couple."

"Fuck you, too, Hutch. Another Maker's and ice water back, son. And toss me an ashtray. Asshole here has this one filled to the rim. You know you're a walking ad for lung cancer, don't you, Kruk?"

"Jeezus — why don't you turn around and come back on in," Hutch said, pouring the shot and topping the glass of ice water. "Leave the pissoff at the door and enjoy that drink."

Burch gunned the shot and stared at Little Hutch, who carried twenty more pounds of muscle and twenty fewer years of age.

"I'll drink your liquor Hutch, but when I want your advice, I'll walk into the can and flush the toilet."

Hutch's eyes widened with anger then he shook his head.

"Suit yourself, dickhead. And serve yourself. Don't bother to leave a tip, either. Just drink up, pay up, do your business and get the fuck out of my bar."

Hutch moved away. Krukovitch stared at Burch.

"Christ, you're in a fine mood. This is your living room, Jack. You don't piss on the carpet here and you don't abuse the help."

"Yeah, yeah."

"Who smacked you in the balls, today — one of the exes?"

"Worse."

"What could be worse than an ex-wife?"

"The hellbitch."

"Ah, bud — I hate to tell you this, but that's a good nickname for just about everybody you go out with."

"Savannah."

"Ah, Christ. Is she what all this is about?"

"Could be."

"Bullshit — it is. You've got that look in your eye, the one you always get when you're about to go over the falls in a barrel again."

"It's part of my charm. Makes me the valued patron of this establishment that I am."

"Makes you a prize chump, bud."

"She's payin' the freight this time — twenty grand to my shyster. In advance. Twenty grand later."

"You're going to work for her?"

Burch said nothing. The phone rang. Hutch answered then slid the cordless unit down the bar to him without a word.

"Eddie?"

"Yeah."

"Make up your mind yet?"

"Told you we had a deal."

"When are you coming to Houston? Tonight?"

"No can do. Got some lose ends to tie up. Day after tomorrow probably. Your check has to clear."

"Jesus, you're a hardass."

"No, just an experienced businessman."

"Can't you get on down here and call about the check later?"

"Not hardly."

"Look, I need you down here yesterday. I got some nasty folk asking questions about Jason that I can't answer."

"Buy a dog. Or a handgun."

"Cute."

"That's what you used to say about my cock."

"My, my — we're in an expansive mood today."

"The company I keep."

"Cut the crap, Eddie. I got people puttin' heat on me, so I'm gonna go to ground till you decide to get your ass down here to start earning my money. You remember Consuela Martin — my old runnin' mate?"

"Hard to forget since that night I got to fuck both of you on her couch."

"Glad you still pack your brains in your balls, lover."

"What about Consuela?"

"She'll know where to find me."

Savannah rattled off a number. Burch reached over the bar for a napkin, then reached into Krukovitch's jacket to fish out a pen, startling the brooding columnist.

"Give it to me again."

"You know I hate it when you beg, lover."

"Gimme the damn number, honey. And stick the smartass."

"Stick it where, Big Boy? Same place you like to stick John Henry? Hot `n nasty in there, remember?"

Burch didn't answer. He drew down on his Lucky and waited. He took a sip of Maker's and waited some more. After a twenty count, Savannah rattled off Consuela's number again.

"Eddie? Are you just staying put to yank my chain? I really need you down here."

"Don't push. I got other commitments. I'll call when I'm on the way."

She hung up. Krukovitch was watching him.

"No sense being coy. She's hooked your ass again. Might as well shoot on down to Houston and start your suicide early."

"Got commitments."

"Commitments?" Krukovitch arched an eyebrow. It made him look like a devil's helper trying to sell a package tour of his master's choicest stretch of hell. "What commitments?"

"A date."

"With who?"

"The youngster."

"The Cuban?"

"The same."

"Ah, Christ. Why don't you take a razor and slit both wrists right now. At least you'd die among friends."

SIX

Two hours, five cigarettes and three cups of coffee into his wait for her call, the phone rang. Across town, a movie was rolling, twenty minutes into its first reel. One she said she wanted to see.

"I'm sorry, Burch. I just got out of the bath and my hair's still wringing wet."

"Don't worry about it. We'll grab some drinks and hit the midnight show."

Silence.

"Did you hear me? Drinks and the midnight show? Or maybe just drinks?"

"I don't know. I've been on the phone and I'm depressed."

"Who's twisting your tail this time?"

"The usual cast of characters."

"How is the old boyfriend — tell him about us yet?"

"I can't do that. I can't be cruel. His kids call me, and now his mother. I'm trying to find a way out that doesn't hurt him more than I have already."

"Simple way to do that Slick. Tell him you've moved on. Unless you haven't."

The sound of a deep breath on her end.

"I have."

"Then what's the problem? Not telling him is crueler than

telling him."

Silence.

"I don't want to talk about it. Look, I don't think I'm good company tonight. I'm depressed and the dog just ate another stopper from the bathtub and I cut my leg shaving and my period's really heavy."

"Then come on down. We'll get some Chinese burritos."

"Didn't you hear me?"

"Yeah, I heard. It doesn't matter. John Henry will wade through the Red River any ol' time. Just so long as he doesn't have to take a drink from it."

Laughter.

"You're awful."

"Naw, just animalistic. In'ersted?"

"Hmmmmm. Tomorrow. I'll buy you breakfast."

"Do better than that. Surprise me with a personal wake-up call."

"I will. And Burch? I'll never do this again."

"What?"

"Stand you up."

"Yes, you will. You specialize in keeping men waiting on you to stand them up. And men keep hanging 'round, hoping they'll be the one you don't stand up. Now the smart man goes about his life without waiting on you. He's patient and grateful for those times you do come 'round and doesn't pay attention to the times you say you will and don't."

"Some speech. Are you that man?"

"No. I'm nowhere near that patient, grateful or smart."

And he never could ignore a woman's lies, either spoken or silent. But he didn't tell her that. He didn't tell her he was about to leave town.

SEVEN

Heat bored through his forebrain as he turned off Esplanade and started walking down Dauphine. The rays of the mid-afternoon sun bounced off car windows and waxed auto metal like laser shots mixed with diamonds and glass — hard and cutting, sudden and painful to the naked eye.

For the tenth or fifteenth time on this ten-block walk into the Quarter, Louis tapped his coat pockets for shades that weren't there. Another pair of Ray-Bans lost, probably sitting on the last bar he left, next to the loose change scattered for a tip and the dregs of his bourbon and soda.

On second thought, not the last bar, not that place — he was focused and hyper-careful in that dive, watching himself waltz another man to the subtle rhythms of his will with the Third Eye the true pro uses to dispassionately monitor his moves. He ran the movie back in his mind — no Ray-Bans on the bar, just the bourbon and soda.

His shades were sitting on another stretch of stained, gouged wood, in another room that was whiskey dark and flat beer stale. He saw that somewhere near the front end of the day's reel.

His plum-colored linen coat was blackened across the back with sweat. Sweat ran through his slicked-back hair and down across his sloped forehead, stinging his eyes. It left sheen on his tanned, round face and soaked his black silk shirt, his matted chest hairs visible through the translucent fabric.

He kept the jacket on despite the sopping heat. It covered the holstered Taurus 9 mm riding on the back of his belt, a large chunk of chromed steel rubbing a raw spot into the skin between his kidneys. Riding a clip on the inside pocket of his jacket was a five-inch spike of sharpened, case-hardened carbon steel — the business end of an ice pick, tricked up so the handle looked like a pen top, a tortoise shell cap with a gold-plated band, mocking a Pelikan or a Mont Blanc. The top could be popped off the steel at the proper moment, ready to receive a replacement for the spike left buried in somebody's neck.

The Quarter smelled as it always smelled — beyond ripe and rotten, a mix of the dank, the sweet and the occasionally disgusting, a place where a wrought iron gate promised passage to a life of old lace and ancient gentility, but all too often covered up one of life's untended privies, rank beyond belief, alive against all odds, compelling and repugnant, a lover and a fiend, the essence of the feckless harlot. A city without a heart of gold; a town that ate its weak and young, and celebrated its darkest impulses with masked parades and drunken salutes to the pagan and the debauched.

A wino sprawled across the entrance of a renovated home of old French brick and glaringly white stucco, gripping the iron scroll work of a gate that closed off the Quarter's lowlife from its gentry, keeping their vomit off the garden oleanders and the polished brass urns that held the orchids or the miniature banana trees or whatever tropical life the homeowner wanted to grow in this ever-humid air. A dog nosed the bottom of a pile of plastic garbage bags, pulling mystery meat from a dark green tear.

He was walking back to where his car was parked, a block above Decatur, and he hated walking. Ruined his shoes — thin-soled Italian loafers in a buttery gray-black, made for tapping the accelerator of a plush Caddy, not pounding pavement in the Quarter.

That would be a jet black Caddy, a '75 Eldo with 12 layers of midnight covered by six layers of clear, windows smoky with the darkest tint the law would allow, leather seats the same color as his shoes. Black and gray, cut and dried, shades of a 40's movie, his favorite time and his favorite colors. Offset by a tasteful burgundy, like the pinstriping that ran underneath the Caddy's clear lacquer, or the plum jacket he wore today. A splash of color now and then. Throw the squares off stride. Keep the shitheads guessing.

Jewelry? Nothing but silver, like the heavy, square-linked bracelet that dangled from his left wrist, like the antique Elgin pocket watch with the roaring steam locomotive on the cover, like the beveled hunk on his right ring finger with the butte of solid onyx rising up from the metal.

Louis slipped the watch out of his pocket, popping the catch of the cover and squinting through the glare that rocketed off its glass face. He was cutting it close to make his next appointment, but that one would keep. The man was patient and professional. His last bit of business wouldn't. Now that poor bastard was in a hurry, rushing into that bar on Decatur, the place where his Ray-Bans weren't carelessly left next to the watery remains of a bourbon and soda, pushing him for his cut on that Houston business, pushing him for the next bit of wet work, pushing him for a drink, pushing him for a connect on some Mex brown or some blow.

"I don't wanna press ya but some guys is pressin' me. Picked some losers. Just wanna find out where y'at on the next bit of work. Got the bookies callin' me. Don't want one of your crew showin' up with broken kneecaps, do ya?"

He flashed the poor bastard his best smile, one that showed all his expensive denture wear and caused his cheeks to rise and partly cover his eyes like a pair of No Sale signs ringing up on an old-timey cash register. He donned his most soothing voice. The record started to spin. He started his slow waltz.

"I gotta make a call, guy — your cut is someplace else. Pick me up in a half hour, corner of St. Louis and Decatur, and we'll run get it. About the next deal, guy, I might have a line on that too. If I'm right, guy, I'll need your help with some equipment we'll need to stash."

"Great, Louis. Just great. Gettin' short on my end. Gettin' short in other ways too, you get my drift." He pressed the side of his nose with a long forefinger.

"I think I can help you there too, guy. Be patient. Go get your ride. Lemme make my call."

That poor bastard. All fast talk. Real friendly. None of that sullen shoulder-shrugging that almost earned a bullet to the brainpan on the Houston job. No hardass pose. Eager to please. Eager to get his money and a line on the next job. Hustling him so hard with so much single-minded purpose, with only his own agenda on his mind, leaning over like a homerun hitter thinking fastball, fastball, fastball. Never thinking of the curve or change up. Never thinking of the other man's agenda.

Which made it easier to spin the poor bastard out of the bar, then linger for another drink or two so no one would remember them sitting together. Which made it easier to get the poor bastard to drive him to an empty warehouse in Metarie, out off the Airline Highway, so he could drive that special pen spike of his just below the line of his skull, in that soft spot between the brainpan and the spinal column.

Right hand gripping the face. Left hand darting quick and sure, popping the spike past the first line of resistant gristle. A twist then a flat hand to the butt of the handle to push the steel all the way home. A pop to free the handle from the spike. A grunt from the poor bastard, the sound of a man dumping last night's dinner into the crapper. A click, then a grinding of molars as the poor bastard clenched his jaws in a death grimace, his life already over. A slow spin to the concrete floor of the warehouse.

A quick drive back to the city, hoping the poor bastard's

sputtering Impala wouldn't die on I-10. A fast wipe of the wheel and door handles. Keys in the ignition along an Esplanade curb — hello, joyriders, take this auto, please. A long walk to his Caddy for a short ride to his next appointment. So much for Bill, bald-headed coke whore, long-shot loser and second-string muscle. And an extra chunk of change for Jack — Bill's cut.

Just us. When he handed the envelope of cash to Jack, a look would pass between them, the type of look they had passed back and forth since school days in a tough neighborhood off the Irish Channel and through a joint stint at Angola. Just us. You and me. I lead, you follow. Jack was slow-witted — that helped him maintain unblinking composure when the pressure was on, when spade bull fruits tried to make Louis a punk and Jack calmly drove a shiv through the ribs of a very surprised and muscle-bound smoke named `Dozer Dick.

But Jack wasn't dumb — the windfall and the knowledge of how it came about would strengthen the bond between them. You and me. Just us. Remember that. And this was just where Louis wanted his best and steadiest muscle to always be. Tied to his side by just the right balance of fear, gratitude and the inertia of a timeworn relationship neither would break. Glad to be on his good side, wary of his sudden turns, but not so worried to consider a turn against him. Just us.

He would need Jack for this next bit of business, solid and wired in. He would need an absolutely trustworthy backstop because he was about to move against some big people, people he worked for and knew well, people who always paid him well for the teams he put together for their special and nasty projects.

They didn't accept him as they did family or closer associates, but they did show the respect due a contract player who always executed his assigned duties with speed, economy and not the slightest trace of fly ash on the silk of their two-grand Versace suits or the polished lenses of their Wayfarers. They kept him at a distance bridged by subtle nods of the head, solemn handshakes in dark restaurants and the whispery electronics of wire transfers to a Caymans account.

The thought. Just the thought of moving against these people. It gave him a chill of delight. A sliver of icy fear and joy, thin as a heroin needle, rode just above the semi-automatic that dug into his back. He smiled to himself, pleased at that private feeling only he knew was there, one that wouldn't show on his face or in his eyes or handshake at this next meeting with a patient professional in a Versace suit.

Cold air blasted from the Caddy's vents, smoking condensation that froze the sweat in his shirt as he headed the black boat uptown, bumping behind the St. Charles trolley, heading toward the manicured lawns and dripping oaks of the Garden District, the home of New Orleans' old-line silk-stocking set, the place where wealthy American newcomers settled when the French gave up control of La Louisiane, staking out territory separate from the Creoles of The Quarter.

The missing Ray-Bans were on his head now; they had been waiting patiently on the grey leather of the Caddy's front passenger seat, surprising him with their presence, causing a frown of worry to cross his brow. That wasn't in the movie of his day's movements — he still saw them sitting on a bar, next to a highball glass.

That contradiction worried him. It meant the fear was fatter than the thin, cold spike he felt along his spine as he walked along Dauphine, big enough to knock him off stride and put images in his head that didn't happen. He had to get on top of this, keep the fear as a small thing of pleasure and motivation, a reminder that he was about to make some deadly moves, but not something that screwed up his concentration and control.

Well, guy, fear is only an old friend. Something to be savored. Like good bourbon with just enough soda to tingle the nose and throat and carry the sweet burn of whiskey up into the brain.

Nothing that should cause your gears to lock up or your bowels to turn to water.

Not you, guy. You hold your mud; it stays solid. You keep your main man close; he won't turn. You do the deal — bigger than all the others. Just a taste of the fear needle, guy. Not enough to blow those chilly circuits that keep the mind icy and focused when maximum heat starts blowing its breath all around. And blow it will with these players, guy.

He smiled and glided the Caddy into the white gravel lot of Papa Saulnier's, a restaurant just off St. Charles with a name that promised a jolly Cajun as owner and chef, or maybe a sophisticated old-line Creole with a waxed moustache and a memory of when Arnaud's was truly Arnaud's.

But the promise of white tablecloth, dark bentwood chairs and a French name in gentle brown script on a background of tasteful parchment didn't extend past the dining room or the menu. The owners were two of the men in the Versace suits who gave him money, tight smiles and quick handshakes, brothers of a more southeasterly Mediterranean extraction. He was meeting one at a back table. The man would be sitting there, squared on the wooden oval of a cafe chair, leaning forward, a deep-water tan below a thick mane of white, razor-cut hair, elegantly tailored elbows on either side of a cup of coffee and an ashtray with a cigarette curling a white line of smoke toward the ceiling.

Louis gave himself a little taste of the needle as he walked up, registering a satisfied jolt because his expectations were met by the reality of the suit's table pose, tingling his spine with an illicit droplet of primal feeling, meeting the man with a firm handshake as he rose from the cafe seat, whipping off the Ray-Bans to lock eyes with the suit, holding the gaze steady and clear until the man found what he was looking for — loyalty, greed, murder, intelligence, a winning Lotto number — nodded briskly and gestured toward the empty seat on the opposite side of the table.

The Third Eye was in high gear, recording every shooting of the cuffs, every smoothing of the tie, every elaborate swirl and swoosh of a heavy-ringed hand as the suit brought the cigarette to his lips.

The Eye caught Louis nodding to a waiter with pomaded hair the color of iron filings, knowing the short-jacketed servant would bring him the same cup of coffee as the suit and a second ashtray for his cigarette; it saw him smooth his hair and make a small, smiling apology for his sweaty appearance and his slight tardiness. A nice touch, this last move — it let the suit see him sweat and firmly placed him where the suit wanted him to be, below the salt, a murderous blue-collar hod carrier coming to kiss the bossman's ring and get his next set of instructions.

The suit waved a hand through exhaled smoke.

"Think nothing of it — you been out in this damned heat, making your rounds. Like a Turkish bath out there, I know. Ruins the shit outta good clothes like you got on. Oughta just wear a fuckin' loincloth or a toga in heat like this. I was out in it earlier and had to change shirts when I come in. Chilly as shit, lemme tell you. Give a man Vegas throat like that."

A snap of the fingers. A smile on the faces of both men. The waiter stepped up.

"Ice water for Louis, Rene. He needs to cool down. 'Less you want somethin' stronger."

Louis shook his head. The suit nodded. Louis fired up a Camel Wide and shot the smoke through his nostrils, leaning back to ease a kink in his shoulders, then sitting straight and attentive, matching the suit's silence. Two men smoking at a table, waiting for the waiter's bustle to be done so they could conduct their quiet business.

The suit leaned forward again, signaling the end of the prologue, but not necessarily the end of ceremony. It was the true start of their meet, complete with full-dress flattery on a gilt-lettered scroll. The suit's words cut under exhaled smoke.

"You showed the right touch in Houston, Louis, and we appreciate it. Not your normal job, right? But handled like a pro, like always. That's why we like workin' with you. Things get done right. We try to show our appreciation in long green, but we want you to know it goes beyond the cash transaction. We appreciate talent. We appreciate what you bring to the table and want you to know that."

Louis looked down at the tabletop, feigning embarrassment, forcing a small smile to cross his lips.

"You give me too much credit. Houston was a simple thing. I trust it gave you the top cover you needed."

The suit nodded, taking a sip of coffee.

"It did, Louis. More than. Kept the cops lookin' the wrong way while a certain friend of ours tied up some loose ends for us. Let him get the hell out of the country while the cops were runnin' dental records and tryin' to sift through the ashes you left behind. We knew it wouldn't fool 'em long but it didn't need to."

"Good."

The Third Eye kicked into overdrive, lamping every tic and every gesture the suit made. This was new territory for Louis; he felt the suit draw him closer, to a place above the salt, speaking to him on more than a need-to-know basis. Somewhere short of intimate but closer than the distance the suit usually maintained. It was unexpected and Louis fought two feelings — the needle of fear increasing its gauge and the seduction of a boss feigning familiarity with a subordinate. The fear he could handle, the seduction was a different matter. Every blue-collar stiff secretly wanted to sit at the boss's table no matter how much he cursed and hated the white shirts; every dog wanted a scratch between the ears from the master who kicked it and fed it table scraps.

The suit took a sip of coffee then signaled Rene with an index finger shooting into the center of the cup. He took another drag on his cigarette. A Dunhill. Louis could see the red pack with the gilt lettering paired with a gold Ronson JetLite on the edge of the table, close to the suit's chest.

"I appreciate your confidence in me. I try to do a good job and get satisfaction from doing something well. Having you speak to me this way is an unexpected and delightful pleasure, but I sense something is wrong. Is there a way I can be of service to you again?"

The suit said nothing, taking in Louis' elaborate courtesy, turning over the surprisingly polite words, checking them out for subsurface insolence or irony.

"You been takin' charm lessons, Louis. From who — my brother or my cousins? You keep this up an' we'll have to make you an auxiliary goombah, maybe an honorary Sicilian colonel like they do up in Kentucky. Give you a scroll or somethin'."

"I didn't mean to offend, guy. I was just picking up a vibe, something that told me this wasn't just a routine meet."

The suit's gaze searched Louis' face then broke toward the coffee cup.

"It isn't. We got a problem — our friend is off the reservation and he has some things that belong to us."

"The Houston guy, right?"

"The same."

The suit was relaxed now that Louis was back below the salt, his brief excursion into bossland nothing more than a cheap manipulation straight from the minute manager's textbook, dropped like a used match when its moment was over. Other manipulations, other ploys weren't on the suit's mind — just his own, his problems and the delivery of new marching orders to an employee.

The sorry bastard. Louis checked his contempt. He didn't relax; he fed himself more of the needle to stay sharp. This was where suckers slipped up, turning themselves from hunter to prey with a careless word or gesture. Or the wrong question at the wrong time — like how much property was at stake.

The right question was what and who, not how much. He would have to know who he was looking for and what the guy had but the suit would tell him only as much as he thought Louis needed to know. Look for a strongbox key, look for a ledger, look for some account numbers, look for a warehouse, look for a cassette. That type of thing. Not the nature of what was in the strongbox or what was on the tape or how much the account held or what was sitting in a locked steamer trunk in a numbered stall in a grimy warehouse.

"Our wayward friend is named Jason Willard Crowe. Big, good lookin' sonuvabitch — black hair, blue eyes, a real glad-hander. Everybody's buddy. Used to play ball at one of them big Texas schools. The one with the letters. Blew out a knee before he could make it big. Turned out he had a mind for law, figures and the tax code. Made him real valuable to us. Put our money in oil and gas leases, limited partnerships and the like. Made us legal and made us a good return until the bust. Which put him into us for several million he couldn't pay back."

Time for a dumb question from the hod-carrier.

"How come he isn't dead yet, guy?"

The suit laughed — a short snort of disgust and smoke.

"Turned out he also had a mind for the import-export business, our style of import-export if you get my drift. Knew a lot about those plants down on the Mexican border, whatchacallit — mackquila somethin', sounds like tequila, but with another sound or two tacked on in spic talk."

Maquiladora was the word; Louis read Business Week and Fortune and knew all about the special deals American factory-owners could cut by setting up on the south side of the Rio Grande, where labor was cheaper than a clapped-out Chevy and there was no such thing as OSHA or the EPA. Louis could guess the set-up — smuggled goods traveling north in the cavities of manufactured goods from the maquiladoras, greased by *la mordita* spread among the right *federales* on both sides of the border and the taste of a factory manager for augmented income or other nastier pleasures.

"Interesting set-up. Once you get past the GMs, the Motorolas and the other big boys, it gets real fluid. People in and out. Factories open and close. Gotta know the players. This guy did and it made him real valuable to us. The plan was to cool him down in some offshore locale then let him work his magic from the Mex side of the border."

The suit shook his head and took another sip of coffee.

"The plan. Plans and then real life, right Louis?"

"I take it he picked a bad time to disappear. Am I right, guy?"

"Nah. From his standpoint, the time was perfect. From ours, the absolute worst. Two shipments — a load of coke and China pearl comin' in; a shitload of diamonds goin' out. The front money to grease everybody. And about five mil in fresh-washed cash from what I like to call our Mexican laundromats. All gone. Him too."

Louis already knew all of this from one of the cousins, a man with low family status and high ambition, the one who taught him the Italianate footwork of the subtle insult delivered in the wrapping of elaborate courtesies. He also knew the other suits were pissed at the man talking to him, angry that he let an outsider have such a hold on their operation. The suit baring the total sum of their losses to him was proof of this.

Bad enough he's got us fuckin' around down in Mexico and Texas, pissin' off who knows all in Houston and Galveston, but to trust this cheap fuck of a smilin' jack after he burns us so bad in these oil and gas deals. Jeezus, what's the man thinkin'? Fucker shoulda been whacked right then. Instead, dumbfuck's got him runnin' our business through Mexico. What the fuck, man — have all them bayous dried up? Did they turn Vermillion Bay into a parkin' lot? Fuck no, man.

All said to Louis several months ago over oysters, po' boys and cold Dixie beers at Uglesich's, a clapboard cafe in the middle of a badass block of junkyards and crack houses just off of St. Charles, close to the rattle and thump of the steel and concrete overpass of

I-10. Natural that the same cousin would tell him the latest twist in this Texas catastrophe when it happened, about two weeks ago. Natural that it would give him a sense of division among the suits, the hint of a blood squabble and an opportunity for an outsider.

"We want you to track down Mr. Crowe and end his pain. We also want you to find out what happened to our goods. The coke and pearl got diverted, we think to Houston. We'll tell you where to check. Four or five possibilities there. The jewels haven't moved otherwise we'd of heard. He's probably stashed 'em along with the money. He's had help on this — find out who, whether it's on this end, down at the border or in Houston. Could be some people we're familiar with but maybe not."

The suit slipped an envelope from the inside pocket of his jacket.

"We want this done fast and at a distance from us. We don't care how messy it gets long as it gets done. This here is a twenty percent down — the fee is a quarter mil plus a cut of what you recover. Say ten percent."

Louis puckered his mouth in a silent whistle, playing the hod-carrier overwhelmed by fat money. The Third Eye recorded the suit's pleased reaction, the slight smile around the Dunhill that rode on his lip.

"One other thing. Crowe's wife. We don't know if she's in on this or not. Looks like he split and left her holding the bag on some other deals. People are leanin' on her. And we hear she's tryin' to track him down. Could be bullshit though."

"She's still in Houston, right?"

"You got it."

"My first stop then. Familiar territory, guy."

"A bitch of a town. No class. Buncha rednecks who struck oil trying to buy culture. They got a Brennan's there, though. Same folks as run Commander's. Try it."

Louis pocketed the envelope and took a last swig of coffee. It was cold. So was the sweat that still caused his shirt to cling to his chest. He shook hands with the suit and left, stepping into the stinging rain of an afternoon thundershower. The clouds were black and purple, fresh-boiled from the Gulf, full of moisture that just added to the fetid humidity that wrapped itself around New Orleans, close and rancidly suffocating, like the breath of an old whore, a whore as ancient and alive as the city itself.

EIGHT

Years ago, when his homicide shield still had some of its shine and his coarse black hair wasn't streaked with white, whenever the phone rang after midnight, Cider Jones knew one of three people would be on the other side of the line — his partner, drunk and whining about a lost love or sober and summoning him to duty; his ex-wife, hysterical about an alimony check that bounced or angry about a matrimonial offense committed years ago and brought up during therapy he was paying for; or some desk-bound stiff whose belly bulged the buttons of his uniform, telling him to go pull his partner out of a bar or go look at another fresh kill.

If he had to drive out into the night to rescue his partner, he would work himself into a frothy rage that swept away the grogginess of sleep, his knuckles white and hard as a roll of quarters as he gripped the wheel, ready to yank Cortez out of whatever shit he had drunkenly stepped into — by the necktie, the collar or the first thing handy he could wrap his hand around — willing to slap the bejesus out of whoever was hassling the man who watched his back.

If he was headed to another killing, the drive across town took forever and the knuckles were white with something other than anger. He dreaded going there and couldn't get there fast enough, the same mix of fear and anticipation that filled him before the gridiron games that left both his knees scarred by the surgeon's scalpel, giving him a lifelong hitch in his stride.

Used to be, the victim would always be a male or a female — but that was no long a constant you could count on. Sometimes, it was a child, the toughest of all things to look at and still maintain a cop's detachment. Not often though, not back then. Now was a different story — parents and babysitters and strangers and siblings snuffed children all the time.

From there, the permutations multiplied, serpentining their way through the mind in set upon set, angle upon possible angle. But back in the days when he could always count on the identity of his after-midnight callers, these random and endless patterns of homicide seemed more orderly to him.

The methods of death were many and varied and Cider learned them all; he registered their throw-weight, their specific gravity, their particular atomic composition and the terrible light they threw upon the capabilities of the human animal when it preyed upon another. The victims would be suffocated, garroted, shot, stabbed, strangled, gassed, gagged, chain-whipped, tire-ironed, electrocuted, splattered on the concrete from ten floors up, cleaved with an axe, clobbered with a baseball bat, sawed in disposable pieces, drowned in the pool or bathtub, hung from the closet clothes rack or any of the other creative ways one human being can find to end the life of another.

Cider tallied the other distinguishing differences like an accountant making entries in a ledger — the age of the victim, his or her economic station and social status, the place of the kill and the accompanying degree of savagery or calm coldness, whether the walls were painted with blood or whether the victim looked peaceful and asleep, with only a trickle of blood from the mouth and small, neat holes in the forehead and the base of the skull to let you know this was someone who would never wake up from a professional's quick and sure caress.

There was the small, eye-catching detail that might mean everything or nothing. The hand turned up like a casual wave across a crowded lobby. The ripped fingernail with the tiny flecks of skin. The banana-yellow panties with the Chiquita logo. The thumb-shaped bruise on the throat. The half-eaten sandwich. The smear of blood from the anus or the vagina. The fat snake of milk that pooled across a kitchen floor in a lazy S past spatters of blood and a spilled bag of groceries — cantaloupes, a can of Community Coffee, a box of Rice Krispies, a twelve-pack of Charmin. An open bottle of The Macallan 12 that still stood upright in a living room looking like a freshly trashed playground for gorillas.

That last one helped him catch a whore-snuffing roughneck from Morgan City. Man developed a sudden taste for single malt Scotch after one kill. Left the bottle. Left a partial print. Stupid move. Good eye for single malt, though.

And then, there was the Big M — motive, a word bandied about on all the TV cop and courtroom shows. Which wasn't much of a distinguishing variable at all, at least in Cider's mind. Somebody wanted somebody else dead, a primal urge as old as the serpent and the garden. He saw it as a separate thing, an entity unto itself, something with its own power, logic and mobility, leaving its own pattern and signature. The rationale the killer attached to this ancient lust didn't much matter to him — jealousy, greed, revenge or kicks — except as a marker on the path to a collar or an endlessly open file in his drawer.

How a killer killed mattered more to Cider. Each individual had a murderous style, a deadly rhythm that kicked off the low, humming vibrations of his own internal tuning fork. Like a sodbuster seeking water with a divining rod, Cider trusted those vibes.

He trusted something else as well — what the victims told him in wide-eyed death, what he saw as he squatted on his bootheels and gazed into a set of sightless lenses, searching for a shard of image, a sense of the horror of this life's last moments or the utter unknowing surprise of having the plug yanked out violently, without warning or time to flinch or record a thought of what was happening.

Sometimes, the eyes told him nothing. At other times, a great deal, silently passing him information that would rise from his innards as he worked a case, causing the tuning fork to vibrate at a faster frequency, clicking confusion into clear focus.

It used to drive Cortez crazy. At the crime scene, he'd snicker or blow his breath in exasperation, like a stable nag anxious to head back to the barn and reluctant to clop another few yards up a well-worn trail. Over the ritual post-scene meal at an all-night Mex cafe off Westheimer, Cortez would sop up his *huevos con chorizo* with a corn tortilla and quiz him loudly, sweat from the hot sauce beading up on his bullet-shaped bald head.

What the hell d'ya see in a pair of dead eyes, breed? What d'ya think they can tell ya that a forensics report can't? You know, you keep up this Injun mystic shit and they're gonna bounce you from the department on a psycho. They talk about you downtown all the time — fuckin' Apache half-breed redneck motherfucker communin' with his murder victims. Captain asked me about it the other day. What the fuck m' I s'posed to say? Nah, he don't do that Cap. He just cleans their teeth and straightens their collars so they'll look good for the autopsy.

Cider smiled at the memory of Cortez, his mouth stuffed, yellow-brown goop dripping from a gnawed tortilla and smearing his close-cropped mustache, nagging him, aiming for a rise and getting nothing but an arched eyebrow and a jet of cigarette smoke. He never corrected Cortez about his Indian heritage — his grandfather was a Comanche shaman, not Apache. Not that Cortez would know the difference. Nor did he ever tell his partner that another voice snickered and nagged, the voice of his long-dead redneck daddy, a roustabout from Wink, that rowdiest of West Texas oil towns. In his mind and in his dreams, he and daddy would argue back and forth about the value of communing with the dead, daddy punctuating his points with a dollop of tobacco juice from the cut plug he fed into his face. Or twisting a well-chewed King Edward on his lip.

Too late to tell Cortez he had a confederate in his nagging. Too late to tell him anything — he was dead seven years, killed in the Hill Country near the mouth of the world's sixth-largest bat cave by a psycho black hit man with an Uzi and a bad toupee. The same psycho planted three slugs in Cider's chest and shoulder, smashing bone and giving him something besides his knees to gauge a coming change in the weather.

A rogue pee-eye from Dallas, an ex-homicide cop named Burch, put a Third Eye in the psycho's forehead with a Colt 1911, saving Cider and the state the trouble of having to track down and burn the killer. Up until the psycho showed up to ruin their day in a cave-side ambush, Cider, Cortez and four local deputies had been trailing Burch and a crazy blonde from Tennessee, chasing the two runaways because they were the main suspects in four murders.

A real shithole of a case — everybody was a dirtbag, from Burch to the victims, including an old-line Dallas crime *patron*, a Houston lawyer who fronted for a gang of border narcos and a mahogany-bodied woman who was the main mama of the gang's chieftain, a red-headed crazoid named T-Roy Bonafacio.

Nobody got the Big Needle. Everybody wound up dead, even one of Burch's ex-wives, brought along to talk Burch out of any stand off, killed at the cave by the psycho, along with Cortez and the four deputies. Everybody dead or long gone. Everybody except Cider and Burch, who was cleared by the Tennessee blonde before she disappeared.

Cider wanted somebody to pay, either by his hand or the state's, but couldn't do anything from a hospital bed with holes in his chest and shoulder. And when he got out, there was only Burch, obviously a patsy in this game, not a player.

No matter how loathsome and tempting a target Burch looked, pride wouldn't let Cider drop the hammer on him no matter how much he wanted vengeance, no matter how much he wanted somebody's head on a spike for his partner's death, no matter how much he hated Burch for being alive when Cortez was dead. And that was all it boiled down to — Cider wanted payback; all he got was air, bad memories and an augmented ability to gauge changes in the weather with body parts.

He swung his dark-brown LTD into a new condo complex off Post Oak Road, cruising past the open wrought-iron gate and the wall of freshly mortared brick, rolling toward the parked patrol cars with their flashing rack of lights and past the gawking residents in their shorts, nightgowns and other forms of hastily thrown-on garments. There was no pre-game mix of dread and anticipation, just the heavy weight of more of the same he had already seen too many times pressing down on his soul.

Stepping out of his car, he saw a blue he recognized from his old patrol days — a guy named Horton, thicker, grayer and more weathered than he remembered but still possessing the good street cop's ability to fight indifference and cynicism with the narrow professional's pride in doing the job right and tolerating nothing slack. The crime scene was secure. The other blues were outside the yellow plastic police line. Nobody was inside the victim's apartment, messing up the carpet with cigarette ash and boot mud, picking up ashtrays or framed pictures, pocketing cash or other loose valuables.

"A real wall-painter, this one. Got blood spattered clear up to the ceiling in the bedroom. Blood tracks in the bathroom and the hallway, too."

"Got a make on the victim?"

"Yeah. Arthur Lexington Yates. Male Caucasian. DOB 5/24/48. Five-nine. Two-fifty — that's being kind. Fucker ain't seen that weight since Nixon. Brown hair — what there is of it. Brown eyes. Beard."

"A citizen or a player?"

"Carpet salesman by day. Player by night. Got a sheet longer than a roll of paper towels. Drug-related mostly. Some strong-arm work. A shitload of fencing beefs. A chop shop roust, looks like. Did trey-of-a-seven at Huntsville for one of the stolen properties."

"This wouldn't be Hoghead Yates would it? One of Manny Ruiz's crew?"

"Glad to see you plainclothes fellas tryin' to stay on top of things but we need to catch you up."

"Christ, ol' Hoghead. Damn. I nailed him for stapling a grocer's hand to a butcher block one time. Fucker walked when the grocer had a sudden crisis of faith in our legal system."

"He moved up in the world before he bought it. Word is he went from running Manny's supply routes to doing the same for another outfit."

"How'd Manny like that?"

"Not worth a shit but he couldn't do much about it. Not without getting himself dead."

"By who — the other outfit? Who the fuck are they?"

"Not sure but they got some juice. Enough to keep our late buddy out of Manny's gunsights and themselves out of ours. Until now."

"Hmmm. Guess the Mexican standoff is over. Was Hog still running the same game — carpets and coke?"

"Yeah, far as I know. Or carpets and horse. Whatever was sellin'. Getcha a good price on a nice shag in puke green and a brick of China white rolled up inside, how 'bout it?"

Cider coughed up a dry laugh. Like a horse shying away from the starting gate, he wanted to stay with Horton and not go into that apartment.

"M.E. here yet?"

"Naw, she's crosstown workin' another 11-44."

"She?"

"Yew bet. Lucille Bates. She of the big tits and big ass. Wish I could get her to ride my Johnson again."

Cider chuckled. He and Lucille played a few rounds of mattress roulette back in his younger days.

"The crosstown look to be a 187?"

Horton nodded.

"Lucille will be a while. Might as well go in and take a peek. These the blues that took the call?"

"Yeah, those two. Hill and Martinez. Kids. Pumpin' iron all the time. Wearin' them fuckin' biker gloves. I hate that shit."

Horton dug a pouch of Red Man out of his back pocket.

"You still chew?"

"Naw. That stuff's too stout for me anymore. Gave it up when I gave up softball. Gotta save my knees and gums for old age. I cheat every once in a while but only with the tamer stuff."

Horton nodded as he stuffed leaf into his jaw.

"Tell Lucille to call me when she's done here."

Horton nodded again, ducked his head to the right and shot a thick stream of brown into the curbside grass. Cider walked over to the two young blues. Both were linebacker big — bulging pecs, flaring lats, biceps like bocce balls, all stretching the fabric of crisply pressed uniforms. Both wore their hair in the modified brush cut favored by suburban metalheads, Hill's blond, Martinez's black. They had the rolling swagger of jocks and lifelong ironheads, free-weight addicts who thought the true path to exalted street cop status ran in the same direction as the ability to outmuscle and intimidate anybody, from the dirtbags to broken-down homicide lieutenants.

They crowded close, leaning in as they answered his questions in flat, uninterested tones, rolling their heads, flexing their arms and shoulders, hulking well inside his personal comfort zone but just short of truly getting in his face. He could smell Aramis riding over the musk of fresh sweat, Wrigley's Spearmint skating on top of breath soured by coffee, onions and the copper penny-and-sweat sock scent dredged up from the lungs by a quick session of iron just before roll call.

He quickly ran them through the traps. Call at zero-one-thirty-two. Complaint about loud music from a unit at the back of the complex. Party out of hand, the caller said, a resident named Deterling, William J., 204 Bayou Laplace Court.

Hill took the call. Rolled up at zero-one-forty-three. Heard the music well before he got to the rear of the complex. Lights on, windows open on the only occupied condo in the unit, the last one built in the complex. Second-floor residence. Saw nobody on the balcony or moving across the windows. Saw no crowd of cars that would indicate a party going on.

Called for backup. Martinez answered. Rolled up at zero-one-fifty-four.

Hill took the lead. Martinez covered. Cider could see them, combat-flexed, pistols drawn, hoping for some action. Covered the four rooms and the balcony. Noted the body. Couldn't miss it — more than 300 pounds of blubber hanging by a web packing strap from a ceiling beam.

Checked for signs of life. None. Secured the premises and called for a supervisor — Horton. Zero-two-eighteen.

Always a line to walk here. You want the main picture but you also want to go in fresh and ready to let it all come to you, not primed to lean the wrong way by what another man just saw. Grab the barest details, the key stuff, the fleeting items that were gone by the time you got there but might have hung around for a blue to see, smell or feel. Jot 'em down. Get on in there. Filter out the opinions and the bustin'-for-detective slant that some blues always tried to trot out.

"I seen a lot of shit, L.T. — crackheads blowin' each other up and shit, gangbangers and drive-bys — but lemme tell ya, this is some kinda different, this is some kind of serious," said Hill, nodding sagely.

Martinez leaned in — Cider could feel his breath on his cheek: "Thas' right, L.T. — whoever done this was into some mainline pissoff. Lotta anger workin' that room. You get on the trail of who done this, you wanna take him out first time you see him."

Hill kept nodding, his massive arms folded across his chest.

"You can't ever tell with this psycho shit. I mean, wait'll you see the burn holes in this guy's chest."

"Burn marks — cigarette?"

"Naw, bigger than that. Now like I was sayin', you can't . . ."

"Holes or tracks?"

"What?"

Martinez cut in: "Tracks, L.T. Bigger than holes."

"Thanks. Any burn smell as you came in?"

"Hard to tell. Windows were wide open and the guy shit all over the place. Puked too. That's what hit you when you walked in. That and the dead smell — the blood, you know."

"Yeah, I know."

Hill watched this exchange with impatience.

"Fuck the smell, L.T. Focus on the fucker who did this. Might be a serial guy. Might be a jealous lover. Might be one of those gay-bob things that got outta hand. I mean, look at that damn rig he's hangin' from."

Cider flipped his notebook closed and pocketed it, snapping a sharp look that Hill didn't see. Damned if he'd deal with a dumbass iron pumper like this; sorry the Chicano blue had to, at least for this shift. Wishing he had accepted Horton's offer of Red Man, he pulled out a small tin of Skoal Wintergreen, popped the top and shoved two fingers of scented black tobacco into the pocket between his molars and his cheek.

Jes' a pinch between cheek and gum for reeeeel tobacco pleasure, Walt Garrison used to say. Fuck you, Walt — lost five large on your bowlegged cowboy ass when you couldn't convert a third-and-two at Cleveland more than a few years back.

His jaw worked the tobacco absently as he tried to lasso his wandering mind and get it cinched up for the job ahead. He looked at his right hand and saw the tin of snuff, then glanced up and offered it to the two young blues.

Martinez reached for a pinch, his fingers mincing delicately, like a matron holding a bone china teacup. He sighed a thanks as the tobacco settled in. Cider moved the tin toward Hill, but this blue screwed up his nose like a kid getting a whiff of a fresh dog turd.

"Thought all you studhoss muscleheads dipped. Goes with the steroids and wearin' your baseball caps backwards."

Martinez laughed. Hill glared.

"You sayin' I got this pumped doin' `roids, L.T.? 'Cause guess again — hate that kind of shortcut. Shows no respect for the body. Hate that stuff too . . ."

A full-muscled point to the Skoal tin.

". . . rips the shit out of your gums, L.T. Man your age should think about that. Think about keepin' his teeth. Think about crossin' guys bigger and younger than he is too."

Cider concentrated on twisting the top back on the tin, feeling the slow burn flare white across his brain. He pocketed the tin then stepped up close to Hill, close enough for a hoarse whisper.

"When you got a brain that's smaller than your balls, son, you don't tell another man what to think. When you're too much of a peckerhead to recognize a possible clue, you don't flap your jaws about what's important. And when all you got is a bunch of muscle, you don't throw down on an old fuck like me who can still make you shit through your teeth. Are we reaching a level of communication and understanding here?"

Hill shrugged: "You got the rank, L.T."

"Fuck that too, asshole. Any time you want to make it citizen-to-citizen, drop on by. And let's drop that L.T. bullshit boys — it's lieutenant. I didn't serve in Nam and neither did you. I hate it when everybody and their brother tosses I Corps jargon around like they all did time in country when they didn't. Cheapens the coinage of respect."

Cider stepped back and smiled like a carney barker welcoming a mark into the fat lady's tent. Hill was rigid with anger. Martinez kept his distance, eyeing both men.

"Now, I'm gonna tell you why I was so in'ersted in the smell factor — it might tell me whether they did him here or brought him from someplace else."

"Why would you think that?"

"Too little time between the first call about the noise and your roll up. Maybe that means somethin', maybe it means the neighbors waited a long time before they called, maybe it just took a while for them to notice the noise."

Martinez: "Guy who called it in — Deterling — said he didn't notice the noise until after he flipped his TV off and went to bed. Said he tried to ignore it and go to sleep but couldn't."

"Neighbors see anything else?"

"Nah — guy's kinda isolated back here. Only one livin' in these new units. Only one they could get to buy after real estate went south, I guess. Deterling said the builder's gone belly up and folks are worried about bein' left holdin' the bag."

"No cars seen goin' in or out?"

"Nah. There's a back entrance the builder uses. You can just make it out that way, beyond the lights."

Cider followed Martinez' line of point. He couldn't see what the blue wanted him to see but he did note the wide gulf of darkness between the rear units and their well-lit walkways and parking slots and the faint line of street lamps that marked the path of a side road that fed into Post Oak. He gauged the distance at a half-mile.

"Good enough."

He could feel Hill's stare and met it with his own. Hill broke first.

"Be seein' ya, boys."

His knees creaked as he started up the stairs — reminders of his ancient sacrifice at the god-a-mighty altar of Texas high school football. He ducked under the yellow plastic police line and stepped inside. The techs weren't here yet either.

All the lights were blazing -- flipped on by the blues as they came in. Standard condo drywall — white walls and a stippled ceiling, a fan with three fluted lamps curving from its centerline, glowing underneath slowly spinning blades. A Leroy Neiman print, the one of Joe Willie Namath at his gimpy-kneed finest, hung above the mantle of a gas fireplace on his left. On his right, an arched opening above a long pine bar gave a full view of a galley-style kitchen, all brushed stainless, butcher block and oak veneer cabinets. A rack of wine glasses hung above the bar, light winking and bending through the polished clearness.

His gaze lingered on these few signs of order as he snapped latex gloves over his hands, reluctant to rove over and register the chaos in the center of the room — the ripped cushions of the burgundy-colored sofa, easy chair and ottoman, the grayish stuffing bursting out of ragged slashes in the fake leather; the splintered coffee table and smashed terracotta table lamps, reddish-brown shards scattered over the sharp tines of wood; the long vertical frame holding the matte finished print of a Vargas girl, her impossibly perfect breasts and legs and inner thighs draped and molded by a gauzy Roman toga, her come-hither eyes taking in the full sweep of the upended room as a breeze from the fan flipped the frame back and forth on its hidden wall hinges, covering and uncovering an open wall safe.

Cider picked his way through the wreckage and peered into the safe. Empty. He turned and spotted a broken and upended Punjabi urn, potting soil pouring from the lip and the largest cracks in its thick casing, one stream of dirt emerging from the mouth of a trumpeting elephant enameled on the side of one of the biggest broken bits. Dirt and wood chips trailed across the floor, pointing toward the roots of a ficus tree — a few hours ago firmly centered in the urn, now just another piece of carnage at the scene of a homicide.

Something bothered him about the urn and the dirt. The tree had been ripped out and the urn cracked open, but most of the potting soil was still inside. Not so thorough. A top-shelf pro would have combed through all of the dirt. Which might mean the place was tossed for window dressing. Or it might mean they started on the urn first then found the safe while sifting through the dirt and found what they wanted inside. But the safe was open not blown, meaning they had the combo.

How?

Get ahead of the curve, dumbass — either they had it from some insider before they walked in the door or they burned it out of ol' Hoghead wherever else they put the screws to him.

Well, hey daddy, wondered when you'd wander into my thoughts.

The old roughneck sumbitch stood there in the middle of his mind's eye, rolling a King Edward Imperial in his mouth, oily coveralls and short-rimmed hard hat tilted back on the same coal-black thatch of hair that would never die, just turn pure and shocking white as he rolled into his sixties and on toward death.

Someplace else, that seems pretty obvious. But why drag his ass back here, wreck the joint, then ice poor pitiful Hoghead?

Get it in gear, buddyrow — even you ain't this stupid. This ain't no murder for the sport of it, this here is a callin' card deal.

Too much trouble just to announce a gentleman caller, daddy, these boys are serious and seriously lookin' for somethin'.

True enough maybe, son — true enough. And maybe they found it in that there wallbox buddyrow, but they leavin' sign for somebody too.

And it ain't me is it, daddy?

No, son — they know you'll see it but this ain't your mail.

Good talkin' to you, daddy, but I gotta get on in there and look at the message these boys left.

You do that, son — don't envy you your job. Not ay-tall. And I never could stand watchin' you stare into their eyes.

Now daddy, don't start.

I know, son — we'll talk about that some other time.

The blood trail smeared its way down the narrow hallway with the wood parquet floor that ran from the front room toward the master bedroom, passing the tan-tiled bathroom with the glass brick window, the raised garden tub and the bright splash of vomit and blood that fanned across the doorway. It was as if they were herding Hoghead back toward the bedroom, decided to cut him along the way and Hoghead answered back by puking up his dinner.

The drywall was badly dented about midway down the hallway, the floor gouged and scarred. A struggle here. Cider pulled a penlight out of his coat pocket and ran it around the dished-in edges of the dent, searching for hair, a scrap of skin or blood.

Nada. Have the techs check it anyway.

Near the dent the wall was marked by something black that skidded across the white surface — a belt or black leather coat maybe. He flashed the light along the floor, hunting for a careless footprint in the blood. If there was going to be a slip up, it would be here, where Hoghead tried to make his last stand.

Nada y no mas.

He kept the flash on the floor, stepping gingerly on the few clear areas of flooring as he slowly moved forward, like a rookie angler on the slippery rocks of a trout stream.

A glint on the floor to his left. He had to lean forward, penlight in mouth, one arm bracing the wall to prevent a header into the blood, reaching with the other. He palmed a small, thick, broken circle of silver. Looked like jewelry of some sort. But not the gold that Hoghead favored.

He flashed a mental image of the last time he saw the man — four or five gold chains nestled in the chest hair curling out of an open silk shirt the color of heavily creamed coffee, complemented by a thick-linked bhat bracelet on one wrist and a Rolex on the other. All gold, gold, gold in the maximum carat range, baby — gunning for that wiseguy chic of overkill cool.

No silver, baby. Shit no. None of that cheap stuff. Chicks don't dig it. Like it, Ciderman? Get it for ya' wholesale, fresh from them kikes on Jewry Row in Nuevo Jerk City. Get it, Ciderman — Jewry Row?

Got it, Hoghead. But not as bad as you, baby. He dropped the silver into a glassine evidence bag he slipped in his pocket. He flashed the penlight around, searching for shiny mates.

Nada again. Shit.

Gotta tell ya' Hog, not much of a last stand. Won't go down as no private Alamo Mission kind of thing. Just one broken circle of jeweler's silver, a black skid mark on the wall and a dent in the drywall.

He stepped into the bedroom and was hit by the smell of blood and feces. A younger cop, one less scarred and calloused by burnout and experience, might have been blindsided by the gore, might have become addled and unfocused, might even have lost his dinner.

Not Cider. Not ever. Not at his first homicide scene. Not at his first trip to the morgue. Not since the all-night party during his rookie year on the force that earned him his nickname, when he drank too much applejack and puked enough to last a lifetime in front of most of the Third Precinct dayshift.

The sights and smells of the crime scene were mere data to him, no matter how grim. He noted their shape, their composition. His mind recorded this fresh input. Smears of red and brown marked the walls, highlighted by a jet of arterial blood that reached the ceiling. The room looked like a pack of wild dogs had ripped through it — smashed picture frames, splintered drawers, a shattered mirror, scattered piles of clothing, an upended mattress and box springs, the foam core yanked through rips in the quilted cover.

And slowly spinning above it all, like a pig hoisted up on block and tackle for gutting and skinning, Hoghead's nude body, his gut cascading in triple welts of fat, red and brown streaks drying on his body, burnt circles of flesh spotting his groin, his wattled nipples and the soles of his feet.

Cider pulled over an upended chair, dragging it to a spot underneath the rotating corpse. The body hung from wide, thick webbing, the kind used to secure packing crates in a moving van. The straps crisscrossed the chest, then intersected in a D-ring just behind the sagging shoulders, then ran up to a heavy and tastefully varnished timber in the bleached blonde wood so favored by the trendy interior decorators. Pickled is what they call it, seemed like, with mirrored ceiling squares edging along the wood.

Seemed like ol' Hog had gone to quite a bit of expense to put in this overhead gear just above his bed. The perfect setup for one of those pleasure swings from the Xandria Collection or those wholesale purveyors of sex toys from Carrboro, North Carolina, Adam & Eve. But this was heavy-duty gear, strong enough to handle ol' Hog without ripping open an unintentional skylight. Maybe ol' Hog liked 'em just as tons o' fun as he was. Maybe ol' Hog liked to sling himself in this bulked-up pleasure rig.

Standing close to the body, placing a gloved hand on the dangling left arm to stop the spin, Cider checked out the burn marks. Too big to be cigarettes. Not gory or deep enough to be a poker or branding iron. Looked like something electric — a cattle prod or battery-and-cable rig. Something on the wire about that. Something from another case maybe. He couldn't remember but made a note to check case files back at the office.

Move on. Move on. Check it all out. Take it all in. Everything was important. Even the tiny moles that dotted the folds of fat in Hog's neck. Even the sweaty ringlets of hair that rimmed his bald dome and curled down his neck, joining the thick animal pelt that covered his back, matted now with quickly drying blood. Even the two broken fingers on the Hogman's right hand — the index and middle digits taking a sharp right at the second knuckle and overlapping the last two fingers.

He picked up the hand and held it close, the penlight's steady beam locked onto two ripped fingernails. Well, well Hog. Might have to upgrade your last stand a bit. Underneath the ripped nails were ragged strips of flesh and what looked like hair. Something for the techs after all.

Hoghead's head and neck hung forward. A glistening sheet of blood, draped over the body's left shoulder like a Hermes scarf, cascaded from the side of Hog's neck, its source dead-centered on the carotid. That's how they finally snuffed his lights. And that would explain the firehose pattern of blood on the wall. But that wasn't what caught Cider's attention; what drew his eye was the thick slurry of saliva and blood that rimmed the lips and glossed over the stubble of Hog's chin. Cider reached up and opened the lifeless mouth, clicking on the penlight to look inside.

No tongue. Just a neat, surgically cut stub where a tongue should be. And a mouthful of quickly drying blood and saliva. That scratched the certainty that they burned Hog someplace else, then brought him here to kill him. No tongue. No screams. No reason to crank the stereo to max decibels. Until giddy-up time.

Yep, daddy. Like you said. A calling card. A message for somebody.

Cider stepped down and straddled the chair, craning his neck so he could look into Hoghead's dead and clouded eyes.

Who's the message for, Hog? What's all this supposed to say to somebody?

Cider stared into the dead man's eyes, losing the minutes and his sense of place. Bubbling through the clouded lenses, floating down from a hanging head to his steady gaze, were the screams that Hoghead Yates couldn't scream. That and nothing else.

"Hey — L.T. Loo-ten-ant? Where you at? The techs are here."

It was the Chicano blue — Martinez. Cider stood up, his knees crackling.

"In here, *vato*. Tell `em to watch the blood in the hallway. And tell `em not to spill their cookies at the smell."

He waited for two techs to enter the room, told them to pay particular attention to Hog's right hand and left them to their business.

Cider Jones never spilled his cookies.

NINE

Nobody ever gave Jason Willard Crowe a nickname. Nobody called him Jace, nobody hung him with that Texas mark of manhood and hailed him by his initials. Nobody ever got that close.

Not his father or mother. Not his coaches or teammates. Not his wives, including the lovely and ever-volatile Savannah. Not his rich ex-father-in-law, the legendary Lon Quantrell, a man who could make the earth open up and give him sweet crude, a man who could make bankers smile and the financial markets purr, a man who could make a Texas governor bend over and beg to be cornholed again because it was such a pleasure to service such a personable and politically generous businessman.

Behind the flash of Crowe's irresistible smile there was a hardness that most didn't notice, encountered only by the persistent, the competitive or the love-crazed. Behind the gold flecks that brightened the hazel eyes, back where someone really had to be looking to find it, was a deep and abiding coldness, mirthless as a power saw, mean only in its lack of compassion.

Teammates sometimes saw it surface in the heat of a game, in the huddle, an icy laser at a hapless tackle who blew a block or a receiver who ran the wrong pattern, targets who were broken and useless to him, not to be trusted or used when it was all hanging by only the spring in his legs and the strength of that right arm.

There was the fullback who fumbled early in a Quad-A title game; when the coach called that boy's number on fourth-and-goal and his team trailing by five, Crowe ignored him, called a bootleg and scored himself.

Later that same game, a blitzing linebacker blew through the pocket, slamming a forearm into Crowe's face, knocking out three front teeth. But not before Crowe threw a rope of spiraling brown leather that split the numbers of a streaking split end for another six. Spitting teeth and blood, Crowe lined his team up for a two-point play and ran over that linebacker to score again, gashing the opponent's leg with his spikes and spitting blood in the boy's face.

But meanness wasn't what you saw in that deep pocket Jason Crowe liked to keep hidden because meanness wasn't a central motivation. It was just a tool to be used along with cruelty, sweetness, smooth talk or a well-executed seduction, not an end unto itself. You might see a flash of mean coming through the gold flecks of his eyes just like you might see a flash of kindness or carnal intent.

Mean wasn't what turned his crank. He never killed cats as a kid or slapped his wives around or abused a partner or hired hand just because he could and it gave him a thrill. There was something else sitting in the closely guarded recesses of those brilliant eyes, shadowed by a shock of thick, razor-cut black hair, dead straight and shiny.

What you saw was the relentless calculation of a computerized spread sheet and the whirring precision of a machine that couldn't love or forgive. If you ever got in that deep.

Few did.

The machine was in high gear at this moment, restless and frantic. The computer was zipping through a worrisome program, searching for a solution. Don't overheat. Don't crash. Run through the loop one more time, clipping the binaries and the if-thens, triple-checking the unwanted answer. And run through it again. All while steering a mustard-colored Mercedes 250 SL through a mid-morning jam in downtown Monterrey, a cellular phone jammed to his right ear.

". . . that transfer cannot be accomplished, Señor Goldschmidt. There are not enough assets in the account to . . ."

"Are you sure you have the right number? Let me read it to you again — Two-zero-zero-four-eight-five-zero-zero-nine-dash-three-four-one-one-dash-L-as-in-Lima-P-as-in-Papa."

"Correct. We have the right account. But I am showing a balance of only $7,000 U.S. at this time."

"Can you check and see if a deposit of $500,000 U.S. cleared?"

"It did. Ten days ago. The last of three deposits. Then we show a withdrawal for wire transfer by you four days ago."

"That's impossible. I didn't call you then."

"Our records show that you did. The proper access codes were given. The party asked for the correct officer in the sequence you established with Señor Montelban. And the faxed request for the wire transfer appeared to be in order."

"Let me speak with Señor Montelban."

"I am afraid he is not at the bank right now, Señor Goldschmidt."

Jason Willard Crowe was seized by sudden ripping clarity.

The bitch has my money!

She knows which Dominican bank to call. She knows the codes, the account numbers, the right officer to ask for, the right things to say to him and the proper electronic handshake.

The bitch has my money!

Not all of it but an icy and righteous one-point-five mil, lifted from those technologically innocent-but-deadly gentlemen from New Orleans. A lamentable loss of capital but a far more disturbing disruption of the carefully structured system of false identities, codes, accounts and instructions scattered from Houston, across the Caribbean, down through Central America and bending back to Mexico. A shadow network established during the days he was pulling the strings of international finance for the greaseballs, a fast track set down for just this moment and just this purpose — a quick transfer of thirty million, much of it long buried from skimmed accounts, some of it still quivering from the fresh sting he engineered three weeks ago, back when the y'ats thought they were doing him a favor by staging his death and spiriting him out of the country.

The bitch has my money! She has access to my system!

He didn't waste time wondering how. That was easy — she pried her way into his PowerBook, he supposed, and copied all the codes, numbers and names on a diskette.

Clever girl.

She got past the passwords, the maze of false files he set up and discovered the data sprinkled in the middle of a dummy spreadsheet for a company that didn't exist. But who told her why this was important, who gave her the clue that these numbers and codes dealt with the most vulnerable point in the whole operation?

The Dominican bank was the junction of the scheme, the place where he was funneling money squirreled away in dozens of old accounts, parking it there until he could shuffle the stash into a score of bright and shiny new accounts waiting in Switzerland, Singapore, Turks and Caicos, Luxembourg, Hong Kong and Macau. Because this was the transfer point and his plan demanded speed, it was the one place where his exposure was the greatest and he needed the most security. He thought he had wired up everything. Everything except that damn PowerBook.

And his damn wife. She wasn't a tech-head; she could barely operate a Krups coffeemaker. She damn sure wasn't a hacker. She had to be playing ball with someone, playing along, screwing the tech-savvy patsy until she could screw them over.

For being stupid enough to write down anything concerning this key aspect of the plan, he allowed himself a small measure of anger and self-loathing, then shrugged it all off like a blindside sack on second-and-eight.

Focus on the next play. Forget the mistake — it was the price you paid for haste, complexity, an addiction to laptops and an inability to memorize the figures you can so easily manipulate.

The machine stopped whirring. He became calm. His path was clear, open and obvious, despite the catastrophe, as choreographed and automatic as the jukes and shifts on a broken field scramble out of the pocket. He downshifted into the old sixth sense of a jock, where everything slows and there is all the time in the world to make the right move.

He remembered an old lesson, one from the worn text of the athlete and the warrior. There is simplicity in crisis; chaos and chance often narrow the options and make the choices easy, even if they are dangerous and unsavory. The cool competitor knows this and accepts it.

Athletic cool had already come in handy once in the past three months, back when the feds and his coke-head yupster investors, burned and angry, started to close in, endangering his continued ability to drive to the club and complete a round of golf, threatening him, a prized asset of the greaseballs, and his continued liberty to do their bidding.

When the dogs started yapping, he kept thinking: Not now! Not now! Too soon! Then the cool kicked in. He downshifted. He concentrated on the action, modifying his game plan to meet the fresh threat of the playing field, setting up a new system to move the cash faster. Helped the y'ats stage his own death. Just walked away from everything he owned. And pulled it off without a hitch, like scoring six standing up.

Now a new threat. From his wife. A blitzing linebacker, a conniving wife with her hand on his money — what's the difference? Downshift and deal with the challenge. Do it. Crowe knew he needed to go back to Houston.

But not before keeping an appointment. At an exclusive hair salon, frequented only by the rich and reclusive. For a special `do

— yes, indeed. He wanted a new look — a brush cut and a gray dye job. Hair just shy of a military crop, more like something you'd see cruising through a leather bar. Something for the sporting rump ranger. Something to match the blue contacts. Maybe a moustache. Maybe not. He guided the Mercedes up a broad tree-lined avenue that wound past the iron gates and thick walls of Monterrey's most expensive villas.

A new look. Do this, then go to Houston. For two reasons — money from the sale of the coke and smack he hoisted from the y'ats and to smoke out his wife, to find out just how far she had penetrated his system, whether she knew the end destination of his cash, a quarter of which was still in the upper end of the pipeline, awaiting transfer to the new accounts.

He knew he would have to drastically alter his appearance to make this move. He knew Houston would be crawling with people looking to clip him quick — wiseguys homegrown and from New Orleans, cops crooked and straight, cowboys hired by angry investors in his broken oil and gas deals, freelance talent that sniffed blood in the water.

And whatever allies the Savannah had mustered. Of course, he would have to kill her but that gave him no special thrill. She shared his bed for four years when she wasn't wandering, and a body like Savannah's was a terrible thing to turn cold.

TEN

Burch heard the scream before he could push the door of his pickup open against the humid blanket of Houston heat. And again before he could swing his battered legs toward the pavement and reach inside the wear-shined linen of his Yugoslavian sport coat to thumb the catch off the tooled cowhide El Paso Saddlery shoulder rig that held his Colt.

The sound came from a window two floors up, from a brick-faced brace of townhouses cushioned by moss-draped oak trees and sealed from the rush of traffic down Kirby by two blocks of side street and a wall of wrought iron, concrete and more brick. And an electric gate with a card key that he didn't have.

This was Savannah's hiding place. No doubt. The address matched the one given him by Consuela Martin, her old Dallas running mate, and the screams sounded like they were coming from what could be her unit.

Burch glanced up and down the street and saw no traffic. No helpful residents rolling toward home to let him in. And he saw no cars moving toward the gate from inside.

Only one choice — vault the gate, bad knees, belly and all. He groaned at the thought even as his legs started the choppy steps that he hoped would give him enough momentum to jump and reach a cross bar about seven feet up. If he could do that and if he could clamber up the scrolled and scalloped ironwork that fanned across the bottom two-thirds of the gate in a Big Easy fleur-de-lis pattern, then he might be able to bull his way up and over. If his snakeskin boots didn't slip. And if more than two decades of Luckies and bourbon didn't make this a check his heart couldn't cash.

His first attempt started with such promise. A jump that only a black bear or some other lumbering field beast could love. But it grabbed him enough air to get both hands wrapped around the crossbar. He wedged his boots between the gate's iron scrolls and started muscling himself toward the top. The slick sole of one boot slipped, shifting his weight to the left, the momentum tearing his off-hand away from the bar — the start of a heavy fall on his blue-jeaned ass, a jolt he could feel through the roof of his mouth and the top of his brain pan.

On the way to the superheated driveway apron, a spike of iron caught his right sleeve, ripping the Tito-era linen at the armpit and in a jagged slash from elbow to wrist. That same spike raked the Colt from his holster, sending the gun clattering across rough-finished concrete. His left hand broke the fall and was sanded bloody and raw by the same concrete that was ruining what was left of the worn bluing on his pistol.

"Goddam, cockbite, motherfucker, Christamighty shit . . ."

His hand felt like it was hot-wired to a car battery and plugged into a gas station air pump. He could taste the jolt of his fall on the tongue. Blood too. He tried to stand and his left knee locked up, a sliver of cartilage from the old football wars slipping into something it shouldn't, like a barroom lech nailing married strange with a husband working the swing shift at Texas Instruments — when hubby wasn't sitting two stools away. He sat up in the middle of the apron and started kneading his knee, trying to work out the chip, cocking his ear for screams. Silence. Not good. Not good at all.

"C'mon goddamit. Get the fuck out of there you little piece of shit."

He didn't hear the Saab until its grille was about a foot away from his right ear and the driver tapped the Swedish horn twice. His heart lurched as he spun away from the noise, sprawling across the concrete to grab his Colt, the sudden motion causing the chip to pop out of his knee.

"Would you please move!"

Her hair was streaked with tinting the color of butterscotch. Bangs cutting just above the eyebrows. Locks as straight and thick as a show horse's mane, shoulder-length and pulled back, sunglasses sitting just so on a crown of hair, just where the bangs fell forward and the rest swept back.

She didn't see the Colt in his hand. She just saw a hulking, bald-headed guy in jeans, sunglasses and a cheap jacket with a torn sleeve. Well below her on life's economic ladder. Obviously. Just look at the jacket. And look at those boots. Snakeskin. Of the gaudy, belly-cut and brightly dyed style seen in border bars and Telephone Road icehouses. Worn by a man who is definitely not *Tejano* chic. Ugly, in the way, and too slow and stupid to get up and off the hot concrete. Too dumb to recognize class and scurry from its path.

She tapped the horn again. Longer this time. He stepped to the side and she started to put the car in gear, assuming he was getting out of her way. He wasn't. Quicker than she thought possible, he was by the driver's window, the Colt holstered, a thick hand wrapped around the arm she had perched atop the door, grabbing her halfway between her elbow and the thin bracelet of Navajo silver that Bryce bought her in Santa Fe.

"If you blow that horn one more time lady, I'm gonna snap that steering wheel off the column and wrap it around your rich girl neck. Your plastic surgeon won't like that worth a damn, will he?"

"Let go of me! Who the hell do you think you are?"

"I'm a man in quick need of getting in your damn little fortress there because a friend of mine has been screaming her head off, I've fallen off that damn gate and I can't get my fat ass up and over."

"Who is your friend?"

"Savannah Crowe."

Burch saw her wrinkle her nose slightly in the manner of someone too polite to mention a fart but too wrapped up in the scorekeeping of society to let it go unnoticed.

"I take it you two don't fuck the same tennis pro."

"You son of a bitch, she doesn't live in this complex! Now let me go!"

The scream reached their ears just as he figured out where the butterscotch queen kept her card key — on the passenger-side visor. He swiped for it with his left hand just as she popped the clutch, stalling the Saab, but not before the door post slammed him in the rib cage and the car dragged him about six feet from where he was standing. His grip never broke from her left arm. His head got wedged between her neck and her tits — implants by the feel of their insistent uprightness on his chin.

Two sets of screams filled his ears — one near, one far. Butterscotch started beating on him with her fists. He planted his feet on the concrete again and pushed himself out of the tight spot between her body and the steering wheel, his face rising into hers, matching her bared teeth grimace with the redneck glare that used to scare the scumbags in East Dallas, banking on the chili and onions he had for lunch and the bile rising in his throat to give him the worst breath of the day since he woke up.

"Shut the fuck up, lady. Shut up or I'm gonna breathe on you some more."

She started to scream again when he heard the boom of a shotgun and felt the shock of the buckshot as it shattered the front window, showering them both with pellets of safety glass. He pushed himself free of the window, palming the card key, reaching for the Colt and pushing Butterscotch across the center console.

"Stay the hell down!"

He spun toward the rear of the car, his mind's eye snapping an image of a stocky, dark-skinned man aiming from a second-floor balcony. The shotgun boomed again, the buckshot wanging into the polished green paint of the driver's door, right where he had been just a second before. He could hear the chilling *shiiing-shiiing* of the shooter working the pump action, plunging another shell into the chamber as he racked his first round into the Colt.

Two shots. Assume the sportsman's plug is out of the tube magazine, giving the shooter at least five rounds instead of the three a quail hunter can legally carry. Hell, assume the shooter's got a riot pump with an extended magazine, giving him eight packages of lovely buckshot to play with.

Useless math. Just assume the guy has to be cooled out *muy pronto* so a certain bald-headed pee-eye can get his ass in where its pimply self can do something to save his client's hind end.

Burch was crouched below the door line on the passenger side of the Saab. Butterscotch was wailing: "Jesus, Jesus, Jesus, Jesus — make it stop."

Blood from his left hand was making a sticky mess of the Colt's rubber grip. His knees were screaming from the discomfort of the crouch. His thighs were tightening toward a cramp.

Move fast, move fast, shithead. If there're two on the move up there, they'll soon be down here to flank and waste your sorry ass. If there's only the one on the balcony, covering for whatever's happening inside, it's even odds that won't be offered for long.

He put the Colt down by his left boot. He peeled off his jacket, grunting with the effort of keeping his body out of the line of fire. He flicked the jacket up and out, like popping a fresh sheet over a bed, tossing the coat like a matador's cape onto the hood of the Saab with his right hand, palming the Colt with his left and rising above the roof of the car, praying to the whiskey gods his sucker's play would draw the shooter's eye.

As he flattened into a shooting stance, bringing the sights of the Colt onto the shooter's body, his mind registered a small item — the trick didn't work. The barrel of the shotgun, big as the mouth of a cannon, was pointing right at him. He squeezed off two quick rounds, figuring this would be the last act in a bumpy and checkered career, assuming he was a dead man, the thought icing his nerves instead of making him flinch.

The shotgun boomed at the same instant his Colt roared through its first round, filling his ears with sound. The buckshot wanged into the roof of the Saab, less than a foot from his left elbow. The luck of a blind pig and the miss was his acorn.

Everything was moving slow. The shooter working the pump. Burch drawing his bead. The slow spin of a spent shell, yellow against the black of the shotgun. The sound of two pieces of machined brass, hot Corbon casings from his Colt, bouncing across the trunk of the Saab. The bright yellow splinters where two 230-grain hollow points smacked into the rail of the balcony — Flying Ashtrays that missed their mark. The shooter swinging the shotgun out and down, pointing at Burch.

Blooming into the Novak combat sights of Burch's Colt, the red-and-black checkered shirt of the shooter. He ignored the black hole pointed at his head and squeezed off four more shots, sending the Flying Ashtrays downrange.

The shotgun boomed again but the barrel was jerking up and to the shooter's right, the buckshot whickering into the trees limbs above and behind Burch, the shooter slamming into the glass door of the balcony, a slug shattering the window next to that door, another thunking into the reddish-brown wood of the condo's outer wall.

Burch kept the Saab between himself and the balcony as he walked toward the gate and the card slot. Two rounds left in the Colt. Two spare magazines in the shoulder rig's ammo holder, dangling under his left armpit.

He kept scanning the upper-floor windows and the wooden stairway to the second floor as he slapped in the card and the gate started humming and rattling its way open.

Two rounds left. He pocketed the card and grabbed a full magazine, shucking the one in the Colt and slapping the fresh one home. The smashed window next to the balcony door, black and backlit by the late afternoon sun, was his biggest worry. Perfect place for shooter Number Two to set up shop. He kept the Colt pointed that way as he moved across the grass as quickly as heft and bad knees would let him.

The stairs. He hated the stairs. Any kind. Particularly the metal sort used for fire escapes, the ones with the diamond-patterned stipples. Like the one his partner was walking up, gun in hand, the night he got gunned down by the *compadre* of a dead border *narco* named Teddy Roy Bonafacio. Gunned while Burch was watching, helpless with a shotgun in his hand and the naked body of a curvy young *Chicana* blocking his line of covering fire.

And here he was, gun in hand, a Colt 1911 instead of his partner's Smith & Wesson revolver in .44 Special, walking up a set of stairs. Wood instead of iron. But a damn set of stairs. Climbing toward an open door.

He couldn't see shit beyond the threshold. Nothing but black, just a dark hole as he lumbered up, sure he was walking right into a waiting gun barrel. He kept moving, his eyes shifting through the quadrants of the door's darkness, banking on the ability of peripheral vision to pick up movement no matter how dimly lit.

His ears were cocked for the slightest sound. He could hear the buzz of traffic on Kirby, the sobs of Ol' Butterscotch and the clank of the gate as it slammed shut, cutting the silence that always follows gunfire and a killing.

He entered the room in a rush, his boots skidding slightly in the thick tan carpeting, his gun tracking through a three-quarter turn, taking in a living room where barnyard animals would feel at home, free to root through the upturned furniture, the ripped cushions, the shattered dishes and potted plants.

Lots of earth tones for the dirt and stuffing to rest upon. Lots of tasteful umbers and siennas and ochers. Kind of Santa Fe-ish. But not too fadishly Southwestern. Done before northern New Mexico became a net exporter of style. A couple of O'Keefe skull prints hung on the walls.

He could feel his gun hand swell against the Pachmayr grip. He shifted to his off-hand, his right. Not a big problem. He always was a half-assed lefty, with one foot or hand hanging loosely in the majority world of the right handed, the other tugging him into the space of the twisted and temporally different.

Should have been a full-blown lefty. Would have been except for that day in first grade, when Miss Smythe, all bouffant and creamy skin and high-rising tits and tears on the playground the day John Kennedy's brains got blown out ten miles from their school, noticed him holding that long, yellow Eberhard Faber No. 2 in his left hand and said to him: *You don't want to be different from the other children, do you?*

Different — he wasn't sure what that meant but the tone of his teacher's voice told him he didn't want to be that. He shifted the pencil to his right and suffered lousy penmanship for the rest of his life. His first bad experience listening to a woman whose tits caught his eye.

A half-assed lefty. Bat left. Throw right. Best moves to the left on a football field. From a right-handed stance. Athletically confused, one coached called him. And not truly ambidextrous. But able to shoot a Colt with either hand. He felt his body ease behind the new gun hand, his weight shifting, his feet shifting in mid-shuffle as he crabbed his way down a hallway that was half in sunlight from a skylight at his end, half in shadow down by a closed bedroom door.

Muffled thumping from the other side. Like a headboard

banging against the wall of a no-tell motel. Or somebody getting their head staved in. He hopped into a short run, ignoring the pain in his knee and hand, gathering himself for the jarring impact of his shoulder smacking into a hollow-bodied bedroom door. His left shoulder, of course.

It took two tries. The door splintered at the lock and he tumbled into the bedroom, sprawling across the foot of the bed, drawing a mouthful of rose-colored satin and a faceful of matching quilt comforter as he slid to a halt just inches from the painted toes of bound-and-gagged Savannah Devlin Crowe.

A spin to the left. In a crouch. Gun up as he turned and covered the room. Three steps to an open bathroom door. Nothing. Steps to the closet. Nothing but clothes and shoes. Savannah's eyes following him through every move. Savannah's head banging into the wall. He stepped to her side and grabbed an end of the duct tape that had gagged her screams, popping it off her mouth with a quick yank.

"Shee-it, that hurt, you fuckin' cocksucker! You enjoyed that, didn't you, you peckerhead shitbird!"

"A hero's welcome, lover — I expected no less."

"Ain't nothin' but a sandwich, bud. And in your case shit on rye."

"Why the head bangin', darlin'? You're starting to knock the veneer off that classy broad act of yours. Bang another time or two and you'll be talkin' real up holler. All ready to call the hogs to slop."

"Fuck off, Big Boy. If you'd been here two days ago like I asked you to be, that cowboy wouldn't have barged in like he did. And I was bangin' my head so the cops would know I was in here and some dumbass rookie wouldn't walk in and blow me away. Instead, I get you sprawlin' across the bed like some spastic muffdiver."

"Hey Irish — all the muscle in the world ain't gonna keep you from getting clipped in your girlfriend's condo. I thought you said you were gonna get out of town. Instead, I find you hangin' out near the Rice campus. Probably blowin' up Kirby in a convertible, wavin' to the frat rats, stoppin' to get ribs at Goode Company's."

"You know I'm a vegetarian, lover."

"Ah, the rich girl's purr is back in your voice. You must want something."

"Untied?"

"Naw — you look natural that way. Safe, too."

"Goddam your ass, Eddie! Get your fat-bellied self over here and untie me! If you don't right now, I swear to God I'm gonna kick your balls from here to Dallas when I get free."

Burch picked up a pillow and jammed it into her face.

"Chew this while I check out your visitor."

Burch eased through the glass door and stepped onto the narrow balcony. The shooter was slouched to his right, his black boots, pointy-toed and spangled with the chains and silver caps favored by Austin rockers like Joe Ely and *Tejano* toughs found on any barrio corner, were splayed toward Burch.

The torso was half in and half out of the shattered balcony window, the geometric sharpness of the shirt's red-and-black checks blurred by blood from two chest wounds. The shotgun rested against the balcony's wooden railing, upright and steady, just beyond the shooter's lifeless outstretched hand, as if put there with care.

Dead meat. Burch bent down to check for a pulse at the neck out of habit. Nothing. He rolled the body's right hip toward him and pulled out a thick black biker's wallet, joined to the belt by a short chain. A grand in cash. A license with peeling laminate. Roberto Guzman Delgado. DOB 2/01/69.

Young and cheap. Cowboy, probably — low-level freelance talent. Emphasis on low-level. Not on talent. Sent by a low-level player. Or an amateur pissed enough to go for a hired gun but not connected enough to hire the McCoy. He pocketed half the money, put the rest in the wallet and put it back on the dead man's hip.

More trouble where this one came from. And from other places. From other people able to hire far better gunhands than this one. Burch felt a sudden tug of fatigue. In seventeen years on the Dallas police force, he had killed four times. As a pee-eye, five times, including a black hitman in the Hill Country just outside of Mason, Texas. That one still rode with him — a shot to the forehead, the Third Eye, unblinking and powder-grimed, just below the toupee, slamming the hit man's head into the bat guano and the flesh-eating beetles that lived in the filth.

And now, Roberto Guzman Delgado. Number nine in his nightmare parade. Less than nightmares, these days. More like unwelcome visitors that shook him out of uneasy sleep. Not that scary, really but still unfriendly. Any night now, ol' Roberto would come to call. Terminated by two Flying Ashtrays from a Colt that was new two decades ago, back when Roberto was in grade school and Burch first got his detective's shield.

He slowly dropped the hammer on the semi-automatic and holstered it, the gun's weight restoring a sense of balance. He rose from his crouch, his gaze shifting to the driveway below. The green Saab still sat there, engine stalled, driver's side door open now but the driver still inside. He could see the shattered windshield and the gouged metal where the buckshot struck, quicksilver on a shade from the forest. He could hear Butterscotch sobbing. He could see her legs splayed on the concrete driveway, too weak to let her walk.

Out on Kirby, the backbeat hum of traffic carried a new tone — sirens. He could see flashing lights turn onto the tree-lined side street that would lead them to this spot. He stood still, his hands on the rail, watching them roll up, knowing they would be on the muscle, guns drawn, juices flowing.

He was no longer one of them. He wasn't even a citizen — theirs to serve and protect. He was a pee-eye. On foreign turf. And that was one rung lower than a wiseguy, one rung above a total lowlife.

At least he wasn't automatically planted at the foot of the cop's narrow and cynically colored ladder of humanity — an asshole.

Worst word a cop could say of somebody. A label applied with a smirk, a stone face or totally unmasked venom, its target the sudden bearer of a ticket to the street blue's extra-nasty chamber of hell.

Cops were quick to pass out such tickets. But usually for good reason. Something that wasn't in the legal codes, something entirely rooted in interaction and instinct, a person's vibes and a cop's gut. What somebody says underneath what they say. The pause or the look before they answer a question. The whiff of wrong or right they give.

Burch knew he wouldn't get flagged with an asshole ticket unless he did something stupid or provocative. He knew he'd have to earn that special shade of damnation — really work at pissing them off to slip his boot heels completely off the ladder. But he also knew this was something well within the scope of his meager people skills.

The first cruiser whipped into the driveway entrance, nosing forward heavily as the driver hit the brakes hard. Showtime, Double E. Time to be rock steady and earn that blood money, wherever it came from.

Maybe they'd be in a good mood. Maybe they wouldn't be steamed at having to clean up a bloody mess left on their doorstep by a Dallas pee-eye.

Maybe. But not likely. Not likely at all. And he'd still have to stick his hands in the air and have some blue with terminal halitosis get in his face and rip the Colt out of his shoulder holster.

His left leg started to shake. His left hand felt like something you could dribble on hardwood.

He felt like shit. And knew he looked even worse.

ELEVEN

Cider Jones thought nothing could surprise him. Nothing seen on the job. Nothing seen while off-duty. And damn sure nothing that rolled through his imagination while awake or asleep.

But the last sight he expected to see as he walked into the homicide bullpen was Ed Earl Burch, slumped, torn and gripping a mug of black coffee like his life depended on it, sitting beside the desk of Jack Grunwald, giving monotone answers to Grunwald's questions. It caused the cop's mask to slip a little — a slight tightening of the jaw, a small uptick in the brightness of the eyes. Nothing a citizen would notice. Everything a cop would. Or an ex-cop.

Burch was looking right at him. Noticed Cider before Cider saw him. Noticed Cider's slip too, damn his ass. And knew that Cider was surprised and unhappy — unhappy to see him, unhappy to be caught unaware. Points to the pee-eye, grayer, balder and heavier than he last saw him, out by that Hill Country bat cave, leaning over him, wrapping a compress around his shattered shoulder and gaping chest wound, draping his dead partner's jacket over the bandages to keep him warm.

Cider Jones didn't feel gratitude. Not then. Not for the bandages. And not for the ex-cop's courtesy of not allowing his crazy Tennessee honey to finish him off and leave no witness. A seething anger sliced through his pain; he wanted Burch dead or hung with a Murder One rap, guilty or not.

But he drew air. Zilch. Zippo. Bradford PA.

Guilty or not, Burch was a wrong guy in Cider's book, the man metaphysically responsible for Perez's death. And now the sumbitch was drinking coffee in his office, talking to Numbnuts Grunwald, a cop doing the zombie rhumba toward a twenty while sporting the worst closure rate in the department. And the bastard caught him when the small tells of surprise slipped across his face.

Huge ball droppage, as one of the young studhosses would say. Cider behind in the count.

Swing for the fences, cabron. Perez whispering in his ear. The voice of a dead partner.

Cider slapped his briefcase flat on his desk, startling Grunwald. Burch sipped his coffee, keeping his eyes level on Cider, the lids half closed behind the glasses, the orbs lightless but bloodshot, giving nothing away, not even the gotcha-buddy of a few seconds ago.

"Damn it to hell Cider, you sure do make an entry."

"Oughta start screenin' the scumbags we let in this office, Jack. You're not careful, you wind up scratchin' under the armpits and the crotch and start sniffin' the air like something died under your desk."

"You know this ol' boy?"

"We got a bit of history."

"Care to tell me about him? He shot the shit outta some *Tejano* gunhand out by Rice. Nice part of town. Just off Kirby. Too damn nice for a shootout between barrio lowlife and shitkickers. Usually save that for Telephone Road. Not these two — buckshot and .45 slugs scattered through the Spanish moss and into some rich gal's Saab."

"Any collaterals?"

Cider winced inside as he heard himself use this phrase. He

hated all the tough-guy military slang infiltrating the cop's patois — collateral damage, another word for innocent bystanders caught in the cross-fire; neutralized, another word for blown away. Even some of the Marine jargon that was as inspired and twisted as any Corps lifer — fragged, meaning assigned to some shit duty, not booby-trapped to death in an I Corps latrine; brain fart, as in a dumb idea; goat grope, as in things or a situation in minor disarray; Boy Howdy, as in a surprising fuckup or an unexpected bonus.

As in: Ain't that a great big Boy Howdy. As in the correct response to Grunwald telling him that no bystanders were hit in a firefight where nine rounds were exchanged. Surprise! Nobody else got iced! Well ain't that a great big Boy Howdy! Yew bet!

But even this was RoboCop bullshit in Cider's mind, another corrosive way to keep distance between your job and your innards. A moral dilemma for the cop. Humor — a great cushiony mitt for the nasty short hops of the blue's field of reality — could also fry the circuit of a cop's sense of ethics and responsibility. Too close a margin, cushioned by too little humor, and the cop gets early burnout; too far, buffered by one too many tasteless jokes that reinforce the notion that all citizens except your parents are lowlifes — and you better check Mom's yellow sheet again — you get the Rodney King tapes and one-liners about *Gorillas in the Mist*.

"Real fine. Bad enough we got this Dallas asshole poppin' our lowlifes for us. Don't need him nailin' citizens, too. Although if we don't boot his fat butt back to Cowboyland, just plain folks will start turnin' up dead too."

"Sounds like the voice of experience."

"Yessir, it is. Remember Perez and that bat cave where him, me and them yokel deputies got all shot up? This here's the pile of shit that drew all the flies in that deal."

"I'll be damned. And here I thought he was just some no-account shamus that needed his pistol yanked before he hurt somebody we give a shit about."

Grunwald slid his chair back and gave Burch his best hard guy glare. Which made Burch almost spit a laugh into his coffee. Instead, Burch fought to maintain the half-lidded deadness in his eyes.

"What's the deal?"

"Claims he's got a client. Says his client was screaming when he drove up to the townhouse. Says he was tryin' to get in the gate of the complex when the gunhand threw down on him with a 12-gauge pump. Mossberg. Extended magazine. Fucker blew the hell out a rich gal's Saab tryin' to blow up our Mr. Burch's shit. Burch got lucky. Six shots from a Colt that oughta be used as a boat anchor. Two rang the *Tejano's* bell."

"Who's the shooter?"

"Punk named Delgado. Street tough. Graduated to low-grade muscle stuff. Freelancer from what I could get from the Barrio Boys. *Tejano*, though. Definitely not a *cholo*. Cockroach killer boots with silver tips and chains, fancy and tight jeans. No chinos. No plaid shirt buttoned at the neck."

Like spore or migrating cancer, gangbangers from El Lay were bringing their style east to Phoenix, Denver, Kansas City, Chicago, Houston, Atlanta or anyplace else that had a surplus of dead-ended project kids and a heavy population of blacks and Hispanics. Sometimes local toughs adopted the West Coast style; sometimes a crew moved in and converted an instant roster of local disciples.

Houston's gang squad had two turfs to check — the black projects and the barrio — and sported two sticks of detectives with two nicknames, the Ghetto Boys, the Barrio Boys. Not very cute or clever — barely a pun. And the Barrio Boys had two styles to juggle — the *cholos*, with their plaid flannel shirts and bandanas, and *Tejanos*, countrified toughs in pointy-toed boots and crisp Resistol straws.

"Asshole here have his papers in order — carry permit, pee-eye ticket and all?"

"All in order."

"More than we can say for his clothes. Who's the client?"

"Oh, you'll like this one — Savannah Crowe. She of the lately fried husband. She of the husband's pissed off clientele looking to peel somebody's hide because their money's gone and so is hubby."

"I'll want to see paper on that."

"Already on your desk."

"Real fine. Where's little missy now?"

"Door Number Four. Soon to be in the company of counsel."

"And what type of slick suit will we be dealing with today?"

"Ah — definitely shittin' in tall cotton there. One of Mr. Haynes' associates."

"The Racehorse sending in one of his colts? Hmmmmm. Upscale company. Were the DeGuerin boys busy?"

"Hey, you know what happens when Waco fever strikes. You get used to cults and Fibby infernos and incinerated true believers and their children, what's the wife of an extra-crispy investment counselor to you?"

Cider was bored by the banter but kept at it because something was worming into his brain and a top cover of talk would keep it inching forward into his consciousness. Something about the body fried in the Beemer and ol' Hoghead twisting from his bedroom ceiling. The style and the vibes — that's what was causing Cider's tuning fork to hum. He wasn't quite dialed into its frequency so he let Grunwald's chatter wash over him, hosing away the debris between understanding and the main truth that was beginning to emerge.

Grunwald was rolling, serving up quips in couplets and triplets. Chat, backtalk, banter — it was the balm of the bullpen. And Grunwald could really spread its healing grace. He was a lousy cop but a great saloon talker, at his best when it came to snappy exchanges, one liners and *bon mots* at the bar or coffee machine. Cider used to love mixing it up with him or Perez — the insults, the slams, the switchbacks and other rhetorical turns. But lots of things went stale when Perez got zapped.

"Any time you boys want to stop pretendin' I ain't here, lemme know. I'll be in the crapper dumpin' all this good coffee you keep in stock."

Burch shifted in his chair, starting to rise, feeling the chips in his knees start to grind.

"Keep your butt seated, asshole. We'll let you know when you can take a shit."

Burch stood up. He'd heard the magic word. Asshole. He figured he couldn't make anything worse by flipping his tie at the last Houston homicide detective he ever wanted to ever see.

Damn — thought this guy went out on a medical. Got the shit shot out of him outside of that cave. Burch shuddered as he turned, fighting off a glimpse of his ex-wife's corpse, white-skinned and losing heat, lying in the rocks with the bodies of four sheriff deputies, this Houston guy and his dead partner, a bald-headed Mex with a pencil moustache.

He chased that vision with a standard benediction from Louie's — it just doesn't matter. Repeat as necessary. Repeat because it was a True Fact — one of the Racehorse's colts would be along shortly to back everybody down. And he did feel a case of the drizzles coming on. Stress loosens the bowels. And his shit definitely felt weak and watery.

A face, red and distorted, rushed into his vision, blowing hot breath and causing him to blink in surprise.

"You will sit your ass down until I tell you to stand or I will sit it down for you. And that'd just be so fine by me. Are we communicating here, mister?"

Burch stopped blinking and met the stare of Cider Jones.

"I didn't kill your partner, son. A shitheel black scumbag did. And he killed my ex-wife. Remember that? Remember, son?"

The two men stood inches apart, staring each other down. Burch could feel the other man begin to soften, his anger running out of him. He stepped around the detective and headed toward the can.

Behind Door Number Four, Savannah Crowe sat at the short end of a metal table, away from the door, smoking a Benson & Hedges Menthol and using the long pearl-coated nail of her left index finger to pick a line of duct tape adhesive from the corner of her mouth.

Her cheeks and lips were still tender from Burch ripping the tape from her face. She was still pissed. Waiting three hours and some long change in a police interrogation room didn't improve her humor. She nursed her anger, keeping it over a low heat, saving it for whatever showdown would occur in this place.

She was a woman used to outflanking anybody with intelligence, cunning, a flash of raw sexuality and a hint of barely bridled anger. The last was a highly successful weapon in the society of the polite, the stupid and the spoiled she found herself in these last five years.

In that arena, most opponents recoiled at the threat of seeing the Celt and the Slav in her, served up hot and raw, spilling all over the nice table linen and tea service. It was something that went way beyond the pouting antics of a rich girl accustomed to abusing the help, proven when she backhanded a debutante twice in the middle of Cafe Annie one winter Wednesday night after a catty insult, then dumped a plate full of free range chicken tarragon and polenta over the woman's raw silk suit and broke the china over her tight cap of black curls.

Screaming and crying. Stares from startled patrons. Waiters and artfully slinky hostesses, vested and clad in variations of black, scrambling to the rescue. Savannah pulled out a cigarette, jetted smoke through her nostrils and signaled the bar for the check.

She stood up, leaned close to the clear red glaze dripping off the woman's ear and said: "Never mistake me for the hired help, sugar.

And never mistake the power your husband has for your own. It's my husband who works for your husband, making him more money for you to spend. I'm not part of the package."

Jason loved her notoriety: "You're my nuclear deterrent." She added violent marquee value as the explosive wife of the financial genius who pumped out his own musk of sex-and-drugs-and-rock 'n roll, a combined cachet that helped lure more clients from the coke-and-daddy's-oil-royalties set. The woman's husband dropped Jason after the Cafe Annie dustup, pulling out of a limited partnership, losing principal and a hunk of a prospective tax write-off. But four other investors jumped onto the bandwagon, attracted by her violent buzz and the idea of having a financial advisor who could service their portfolios and their nostrils.

What worked while wading among the Houston hipsters might not play in front of a homicide cop and an ex-lover with an up-close memory of her moves. Eddie used to laugh at her flaring anger. Or get a hard-on and want to fuck. She'd spout off and maybe slap him; he'd grab her and want to take her immediately — in a restaurant, on the highway, on a conference table, in a doorway. When nothing else seemed to arouse him, her anger would, a tool she sometimes used to jumpstart a dull rack session or a boring dinner.

She doubted if a flash of anger would get Eddie addled and easily influenced today. She doubted if he was buying anything she had to sell. And the first detective she saw seemed too stupid to react to anything other than a sugar-dusted donut. Or a vacuum lip lock from a hooker. She heard another voice beyond the door, deep, loud and commanding. Not a tone one would associate with air kisses and the cocaine sniffles.

With this audience, anger would be a backbeat, an undertone. Let the attorney take the lead. If he got here anytime soon. Let him do the talking, springing her and Eddie and getting them back to the business of staying low.

New digs would be the first order; it was stupid to stay at a girlfriend's. She knew that now — knew it before Delgado showed up. But she liked being right on the edge. Staying totally out of sight would have bored her silly and made her pace and growl like a caged leopard. Lying low, but still being exposed enough to grab kept her juices flowing, kept her connected to the action. She needed that — as much as sex or a cup of coffee in the morning. But she couldn't let that impulse ruin her. Too much was at stake — about thirty million too much, if the file in Jason's computer was accurate.

A safe house first. Keeping Big Boy in place and under control was the second priority. She couldn't afford to have him play the loose cannon; she couldn't afford to piss him off and have him walk away. And she didn't think a seduction would make him a passive player. He had to feel like he was something other than a human shield for her; she had to sell him a story that put him in a starring role.

The door opened. Cider Jones stepped in, scowling at a file he was juggling back into his left hand, careful to keep the coffee mug in his right hand level.

"Miz' Crowe."

Savannah nodded, stubbing out her cigarette.

Cider sat down, still reading, sipping his coffee, grimacing at its heat or its taste. She couldn't tell until he blew into the mug. He kept her waiting, taking another loud sip.

"Something I don't get to see these days — a man slurping his morning coffee."

"It's almost six, ma'am."

"Morning for you, isn't it? You're the late shift."

Cider nodded, taking another sip, turning a page in the file.

"You know, here's something interesting — says here when the blues showed up at your door with news your husband had been killed, you said `The bastard left me holding the bag.' Or words to that effect."

"I believe I used the word `cocksucker.' "

"I'll take your word, ma'am. Hardly the tears of a freshly made widow."

"My husband and I took a pragmatic approach to marriage. We were partners — in business and bed. Very little room for sentiment in our relationship."

"Strictly business?"

"To put it in different words."

"What bag were you holding?"

"As I've explained before — I knew my husband was in trouble with his investments. I knew people were upset with him, upset about their losses, angry because they felt they had been misled. Some would find his death a questionable occurrence. Some would see it as a staged event. Others would take it at face value. Either way, they'd be coming after me for their money. And some wouldn't be very nice about it."

"Badasses among the young and the restless?"

"Not all of my husband's clients were yupsters."

"That so? What sort of nasties were on the client list?"

"My husband had other things on his plate that I had no part of."

"Some friends down Cali way?"

"You're not very imaginative."

"I heard you liked that in a man."

"My likes and dislikes aren't on the table right now. To answer your question — my husband compartmentalized his business. There were the partnership deals on oil and gas that I was involved in, particularly in the recruiting of clients. Then there were other deals in which I played no part."

"You had no clue what he was doing?"

"Clues and guesses are just that."

"Care to elaborate?"

"No."

"Guy by the name of Hoghead Yates mean anything to you?"

"Fat guy with lots of gold chains?"

"The same. So, you do know some of your husband's seedier associates."

"Knowing him doesn't mean knowing what he was up to."

"Pity. Sure enough is. Mr. Yates wound up twisting from the ceiling with his tongue cut out and some of the same burn marks we found on what was left of that crispy critter found in your husband's car."

Savannah grimaced.

"Thought he was fried."

"Pretty much. But there was enough of him left so we could tell he'd been tortured before he was iced. Musta knew something someone else wanted to know. Burn marks from battery cables. Same as on Hoghead."

"A stylistic connection."

"Exactly."

"Which doesn't bring things any closer to me."

"If you want to whistle through the graveyard that way, I'll listen to the tune and tell you it's pretty. But let me also tell you this lady — if they're doin' this to their friends, think what they may do to you. This cowboy Delgado wasn't one of the nasty boys. He was low-rent talent who got lucky and found you before they did."

Savannah said nothing. Her smoke filled the silence. Cider let it stretch for a few more seconds.

"So I take it you weren't surprised when it turned out he wasn't the guy who got fried in his car."

"Only in a tactical sense. I didn't think he had that sort of gruesome theatrics in him."

"So you think he staged this by himself."

"I don't know."

"What do you think?"

Savannah paused, then looked at Cider.

"No."

"Think he's got it in him to cut somebody's tongue out?"

"Same answer."

"I'm hearing that tune again, Mrs. Crowe. You whistle it pretty."

"Look, bud — my husband played up pretend connections with wiseguys and Columbians to give himself this dangerous aura. It was mostly for show, something to sell the yuppie suckers. Like I said, he had some side deals with some unsavory types but I don't think for a minute they ever saw him as a serious player."

"You still believe that? After that scene out by the Intercontinental? After gettin' trussed up by that *Tejano* gunhand?"

No answer. A knock on the door. It opened and a tall red-headed man with freckles, a tennis tan and a light gray suit strolled in. The colt of Racehorse Haynes. At hour four of the proceedings. With the look of Up East prep run through nothing but pure Ivy League and a round of GQ ads.

And an accent that was as West Texas as a Saturday night dance at The Post out in Marathon, an outdoor tradition since the Apache wars and the days when Black Jack Pershing chased Pancho Villa, an under-the-stars event where the sheriff still asked the men to take off their hats to twirl with the ladies.

"I'm afraid I'm gonna have to put this cozy little chat on a more formal basis, detective."

"It's lieutenant. And Mrs. Crowe doesn't seem to mind answering a few gentle questions about her missing husband, counselor."

"I'm sure she doesn't but I do when her counsel isn't present."

"Which would be the proper stance if Mrs. Crowe was being charged but she's not, so what's the point of having somebody hold her hand? Good Kee-rist Jesus counselor, I'm talking to her as victim of a crime, not a suspect."

"You're not the only lawman in town who has an interest in my client, detective. As you know from that file you're reading, her husband is wanted for questioning in the death of that John Doe found burned to a crisp in Mr. Crowe's car out by the Intercontinental and she's being pressed by various other investigative agencies about her husband's investment counseling affairs and his alleged associations with certain people you folks seem to regard in less than a favorable light."

"So she's a lady wading chest deep in shit and you figure I'm just another lawdog interested in pushing her head under."

"Your words, not mine, detective. Let's cut to it — we both know if you can rope her, you'll ride her."

The lawyer sat down, pulling a small tape recorder out of his jacket pocket, clicking the Record button.

"This is Barton Phillips, attorney for Mrs. Savannah Crowe, at a homicide interrogation at Third Precinct. Present in the room is Mrs. Crowe and Lieutenant . . ."

Phillips clicked the recorder off.

"Forgot my manners. Need to get your name, detective."

Cider flipped his file onto the table in disgust, shooting his eyes toward the ceiling and crossing himself.

"Since we're getting so formal, I might as well say grace first. God is Great, God is Good . . ."

"Glad you thought of lunch, detective."

"It's lieutenant, son. Get it right on that recorder of yours."

"It's why I carry the little sucker. Now how 'bout the name that hangs behind the title."

"Willis Quanah Jones."

"As in Quanah Parker?"

"The same. A historian and a legal eagle. Real fine."

A click of the recorder.

". . . Lt. Willis Quanah Jones was asking Mrs. Crowe questions when I arrived about the circumstances of her husband's disappearance . . ."

"Able to hear through solid glass — got yourself a good lawyer Mrs. Crowe. Talks kinda country though for his looks. Must be hangin' around some of the Racehorse's seedier clients."

Phillips put the recorder on the table.

"I'm assuming Mr. Burch is also not being charged."

"A premature assumption, counselor."

"Oh? It's a matter of self-defense — a private investigator coming to the rescue of a client under assault. A witness who will testify that the dead man fired the first shots. And a statement by Mrs. Crowe about the assault on her person."

"Burch was carrying a concealed weapon."

"Thin beer, detective. This is Texas and he's got the proper permits. And we have a signed agreement between Mr. Burch and Mrs. Crowe that states he is an operative in her employ."

"Not in yours?"

"No. A personal service contract between my client and Mr. Burch. She preferred it that way."

"Papers I assume we can see. Along with copies of that proper weapons permit. You folks move fast. Didn't think Burch was here much longer than a day."

"Full service firm, detective."

"Yeah. And I run a full interrogation shop, counselor. Hope you got a few of them microcassettes around. It's gonna be awhile before Mrs. Crowe quits answerin' my questions. And then we've got Mr. Burch."

"We're here to cooperate, detective. After all — she's a victim in this."

"It's lieutenant, son. Get it right."

TWELVE

Two men sat at a rear table in a small cantina in the rust-bucket heart of the Ship Channel barrio, smack on the raggedy border between the old Second Ward and Magnolia Park. It was a white-washed stucco building with loud letters in yellow, orange and black announcing *La Gloria Josefina — Comida y Bebida*, a brave declaration staking out a dilapidated corner of commerce in one of Houston's carelessly scattered pockets of Latino poverty.

One of the men was an Anglo with gray hair in a brush cut. He wore a dark blue Gore-Tex rain jacket and tan slacks. The other was Mexican, short and heavyset. He wore jeans and a Roper shirt with broad gray and red stripes that cut diagonally across his thick chest and cannonball belly.

A crisp Resistol straw, crown side down to preserve the crease of the brim, sat in front of the Mexican. Next to the hat, a Motorola cellular phone, the old-style column of gray plastic with the thick rubbery antenna, as much a sign of modern macho as a knife or a pearl-handled pistol.

The Anglo had a pair of mismatched pickets standing a thin line of watch over his side of the table — a tall bottle of Tecate and a short shot of Dos Reales tequila.

The place was empty and closed. Lunch was long over. Dinner was two hours away. The phone chirped. The Mexican swept the column into one thick hand, holding the other palm up toward the Anglo.

"*Momento, por favor.*" Into the phone: "*Háblame.*"

Long seconds of listening. Single Spanish words of reply. Silence and tension. The Anglo, watchful behind a face glazed smooth of any tics or tells, took a sip of the aged tequila, blowing through his teeth before taking a cold swig of Tecate.

"*Bien. Gracias, hombre.*"

The Mexican rang off, centering the phone in front of him with a thunk. He smiled and allowed himself a small chuckle.

"My friend, it always amazes me the results you can get by putting a little money on the street."

"Honey beats sulfur. And a kick in the balls. Particularly when it's somebody else's money."

"*Es verdad, hombre.*"

The Mexican turned his head toward the kitchen door.

"*Josefina! Dos tequilas, por favor! Añejo para mí y para el hombre. Y una Carta Blanca para mí.*"

An old woman, brown, broad and leathery, banged through the swinging kitchen door and waddled toward the small bar tucked into the right rear corner of the room.

The two men sat quietly until she served them and padded back to the kitchen, each taking sips of tequila and cold beer.

"Well?"

"It's as you thought. You remember Chuy Reynaldo? He put up some money on that powder deal that went sour when you left here. He wanted his money back. Or how do the Anglos say it — a pound of flesh? That's it. A pound of flesh. He figured your wife could give him one or the other so he sent Delgado."

"One of the many badgering poor Savannah since I've been gone."

"*Si.* One of the many. But not one of the worst. You know of the Hoghead Yates?"

116

"Yes."

"His tongue cut out, hanging from his ceiling like a slab of beef, burn marks all over his body — a thing you wouldn't want to happen to an enemy, much less a friend."

The Mexican gazed at the Anglo, looking for a reaction. The only thing he got was the surface glaze of those eyes made blue by tinted contact lenses. Color didn't matter, it was like looking at a man wearing smoky-dark shades. No idea what was going on inside. If anything. Complete cover.

"It happens."

"Not every day, hombre. Not even in our circles. This is something you read about in Columbia. Or Miami. Not here."

"Try New Orleans. That's who did our friend Mr. Yates. He was the only one from our little circle they ever met. Remember that."

"What did he know — where you are at?"

"*Nada.* His usefulness came to an end some months ago. I paid him off. He was out of the loop."

"New Orleans isn't your only worry, hombre. You have other badasses after you. And they are all putting out some serious money and some serious players. If my bank account wasn't enjoying such a nice injection of your money, I might join them myself."

The Anglo grinned.

"I'd hate to have to kill you, my friend. It would end a profitable business association that is about to enter its most fruitful phase."

"I'm not one of your rich clients, my friend, leaning over the plate, licking his chops because of the promise of future riches. Let us make one thing clear — your money buys my neutrality and certain of my services. That's it. You pull through this thing and we can do business again, it will make me happy because I truly like you."

"And I you, *mi carnal.*"

The Mexican chuckled.

"Remember, hombre — even Cain killed Abel."

"I didn't know you were religious. Thought your people were old-line *Juaristas,* priest killers and church burners."

"I'm of a more cautious nature — I place bets on the red and the black."

The Anglo chuckled.

"Bien, hombre. Now we know where we both stand with each other. Tell me what I need to know."

"The Delgado thing was very unfortunate. Your wife had no idea who was looking for you and had no idea that people thought she was the key to finding their money and other valuables. She apparently thought those rich kids and some hard-ass businessmen were the biggest threats."

"Nah. Savannah isn't stupid. She knew she was at risk. And she liked it. It revs her up. She's an action junkie. Hooked on danger worse that a crackhead."

The Mexican shrugged.

"Tal vez, hombre. She is your wife. All I know is that she was staying at the home of a friend down by the Rice campus when Delgado found her. Hardly a hideout. Now she takes things much more seriously. She's gone underground and hired some muscle. She also has the Racehorse Haynes as a lawyer."

"Shit. Bitch always did have expensive tastes. Racehorse huh? Enjoying a big hunk of my money as a retainer."

"Si."

"Who's the muscle?"

"Never heard of him before. He's not a local. He's not connected. Some Anglo from Dallas. Used to be a cop up there."

"Got a name?"

"Si — Ed Earl Burch. A name only the mother of an Anglo could come up with."

The Anglo shook his head and ran a hand across the thick gray brush of his hair.

"Ah, sweet Savannah. Buys her men with money and a whiff of that cunt of hers. Then cuts their balls off. And gets them to like it too."

"You know this man?"

"Not really. I know of him. He used to be her boyfriend. *Un amante.* She must be paying him well. Or fucking him. Or both."

The Mexican said nothing.

"What else do you have?"

"Odds and ends. The homicide shit who caught the Delgado shooting has a hard-on for your wife's old boyfriend. Cider Jones — *muy mal y loco,* speaks to the dead, looks in their eyes for guidance. His grandmother was *una bruja,* a witch. Or his grandfather was a shaman. I forget which."

"Interesting. Do you have an in with him?"

"No. Not really. Not unless you have something to trade with him, like dirt on this cowboy from Dallas."

"Why's he got the hard-on for Burch?"

"Something to do with the death of a partner. One of us — Perez."

"What about Burch?"

"Nothing much. People I know in Dallas say he's strictly a small-timer but I would guess you know this already. My cousin works in the bar where he hangs out. Burch is always in there, hanging out with *los borrachos.*"

"Anybody we know?"

"No. Nobody connected. Cops and lawyers and politicos wet their beaks in that place. Oh — I forgot. My cousin says Burch is close to this one guy. *Dios mia* — the name. Like son of bitch — Kru-ko-vitch! You say the wife knows nothing about the computer? Well this one does. He is a *periodista* — a writer — but my cousin says he is also a computer devil. What do they call them? Si, a hacker."

"When did Savannah hire Burch?"

"Well — the hombre just blew into town two days ago but my cousin says one of the bartenders was bitching about Burch the other day. Stiffed him on a tip or something. The bartender said Burch was a stupid bastard, working for some cunt down in Houston. Said Burch and this Kru-ko-vitch were in there together, working on one of those small computers. My cousin said the bartender laughed about who Burch was working for. Said Burch was always a sucker for women and would be back to drown his sorrows — he'd pour him cheap liquor and charge him the price for good stuff."

"The man has friends."

"Si. Friends who think highly of him."

"So Burch and his buddy were in this bar, working on a computer. Did your cousin say what they were working on?"

"Si. They were talking about you, my friend."

"Your cousin is a goldmine. Make sure he is paid well for his information. Do we know where my lovely wife is hiding?"

"That is taking more time."

The Mexican handed over a small scrap of paper with numbers scrawled in pencil.

"Call this in an hour. They will give you the place."

"Who is they?"

"Someone with somebody inside the department."

"Who?"

"Someone I do business with but not one of my people."

"And they will give me an address?"

"Si."

"Forgive me, my friend, but this smells like a set up."

"Hombre — if I wanted to hand you over to somebody you'd already be bound and gagged."

The Anglo smiled and gunned the last of his tequila.

"*Es verdad*. My thanks for your help. Now, the last of the matters between us. Is my little transaction still on?"

"For tomorrow night."

"Who are the buyers?"

"Hombre — I can't tell you that. Let us say that they appreciate quality merchandise at a bargain price and have no fear of prior claims on the goods they buy."

"Good. I'm getting damn little for that product and that much high-quality carbon. But I'm in a hurry."

"Traveling money?"

"Operating funds. The money doesn't matter so much though. I just hate giving up anything I have my hands on because of some unexpected tactical difficulties."

"That's pride, my friend. It could cost you your life."

"Maybe. I prefer to think of it as grace under pressure. I'm not going to cut and run. I'll improvise and salvage what I can. I've had to rearrange many things since I became aware that my lovely wife has access to all of my financial matters."

"This is a serious game, hombre."

"I'm a serious player."

The two men stared at each other. Seconds of silence broken by the sound of two stacks of $100 bills slapped on the table.

"A commission for that last nugget of information — about Burch's friend. Make sure your cousin gets a cut."

The Mexican reached for the stacks and riffled the bills with a thick thumb, eyes on the money.

"*Bien, hombre.* Good luck with your hunt. I look forward to doing business with you when you get to the other side of your journey."

The Anglo nodded and headed toward the back door of the cantina. The Mexican watched him leave. As the door swung shut, he reached for the cellular phone, punching the 'Talk' button and the eleven digits of a long-distance number. He heard a click as the other party picked up the line.

"Talk to me . . ."

He never got the chance. A slug from a silenced Smith & Wesson

686 smashed into his right biceps, sending the phone flying across the cantina, spinning him out of his chair. The pain was white and hot, gluing his tongue to the roof of his mouth. No words. No screams. No curses. All he could do was hold out the hand of his undamaged arm in silent supplication.

No mercy. The second slug smashed into his forehead, giving him a Third Eye that would be as unblinking and lifeless as the other two. Brains and blood blew out the back of his skull, splattering across the oilcloth of the table behind him. His legs kicked out, knocking a chair across the floor. His body fell with a heavy thud.

Josefina banged through the door. The Anglo turned and pumped three slugs into her head and chest. Her body banged back through the way it came but didn't clear the doorway.

The Anglo walked across the room and picked up the cellular phone.

"Wrong number."

"What? Carlos?"

"Wrong number. The party you want no longer lives here."

"What? Crowe, is that you?"

"I'm sorry, we have a bad connection."

"You are a dead man, my friend."

"Not right now."

He clicked off the phone and wiped it clean with a bandana. He stepped to the table and wiped his shot glass and beer bottle. He pocketed the stacks of money and moved to the side of the Mexican.

A final round into the mouth. A message for the loose-of-tongue. Whispered words to a corpse: "A change of plans, hombre. New buyers for my wares. Your services are no longer needed."

He walked to the body of the old woman, straddling her, reaching down to push two fingers into the side of her neck.

No pulse. No hurry to reload.

THIRTEEN

"He's in Houston."

"You got a place?"

"We know where he was. He's starting to leave his own body count."

"Interesting. Where was he?"

"Some shithole in the Ship Channel barrio."

An address. Scrawled on a notepad.

"The wife?"

"A small hang-up there. Some cowboy went gunning for her. She's taken a dive. Hired some muscle, too."

"Who would that be?"

"Fella name of Burch. From Dallas. Ex-cop. A nobody."

"A new player, guy. One you don't know too much about."

"One you don't have to worry about."

"Easy for you to say. One question. What brings Crowe to town?"

"The same thing that brings you there. His wife. Our merchandise."

"I've got an extra item on my list."

"Oh?"

"Him."

"Of course."

"I'm worried, guy."

"About what?"

"A pigeon that flushes too easy. I'm assuming he's here to move his merchandise but why not do it from a distance? Why expose yourself? Why not do it by remote control? Push a button, guy. Get your money."

"He must figure his support is blown. And after your little overture, that's the right way to figure. You've flushed him, now take him out."

"He's the extra item on my list."

"X him out. Get our goods."

"It's what you pay me for."

The line clicked dead in his ear. Louis, lost in thought, stared at the phone and the pressboard night table with the teak veneer. Jack, bulky and stuffed into a padded armchair meant for Jazzercise addicts, shifted in his seat, re-crossed his thick legs and eyed his partner and boyhood friend.

Louis fingered the long gouge mark that ran from his sideburns to his jowls — a weeping groove left by the late Hoghead Yates. He flexed his back, feeling the tight knot where Hoghead had hip-checked him into the hallway wall.

A grimace. Sloppy work. Not in control. Too much muscle and not enough finesse. Too much work for too little information. A big bloody message, though. One anybody could read. But a broken silver bracelet in the bargain. One of Louis' favorites. Cuban links. Broken and a hunk of it missing.

Bad news. Flesh samples and a piece of personal jewelry left on the scene. Bad business. Definitely minor league.

Yates knew damn little about Crowe. Didn't know his movements or machinations. Bad intelligence from New Orleans said Yates was a still one of Crowe's key players; dialing him up on the battery cables proved he had been cut loose and left out of the loop.

New Orleans also blew this latest set up. He and Jack sat in this hotel room, smoking too many cancer sticks, listening to the rattle and roar of the Gulf Freeway, waiting for a call and an address. They sat because it was easy — get a call, get Crowe, get to the goods. Take out the players who bought the goods.

A straight line. A play that wouldn't alarm those Italianate fellows in New Orleans. Maintaining the pose as the loyal foot soldier. Until the right time for the right move.

The call came. Too late — the setup man dead, the quarry on the loose out there in that great big wide-sweeping world where anybody can hide for as long as they want to. Until they get stupid or full of pride or drawn to danger. Or broke and in need of a quick injection of cash. Or grabbed by the need to inflict some painful revenge.

Crowe wasn't stupid. And he wasn't addicted to danger — that deadly sin rode in the soul of his crazy wife. What would bring a man back to the first place anyone would look for him? Three words turned in Louis' mind. Money. Pride. Revenge.

He lit up a Kent with an old Ronson Varaflame butane. Silver plated. With a diamond check pattern etched into the sides. New Orleans was oh-for-two; wrong about Yates, unable to deliver Crowe or his wife on a platter.

And the set-up man was dead — Carlos Benitez, the best independent fence in Houston, an old Crowe associate, the only one canny enough and mercenary enough to move hot goods wearing the greaseball brand. Xed out. Extry dead, as one of Louis' cracker prison buddies used to say.

It meant Crowe wasn't using his old Mexican network; at least he wasn't using anybody brown known to New Orleans or anybody connected in Houston. And that meant the passive act had to be dropped; Louis knew he had to start making his own moves to find Crowe, the wife and the goods.

Louis took a deep drag on his Kent. Exhaled smoke. A three-word mantra.

Money. Pride. Revenge.

They were no closer to Crowe and getting their hands on the coke, the China white and those diamonds. And whatever else Crowe had skimmed from the boys from New Orleans.

Turn around the assumptions. Maybe Crowe and his wife aren't partners. Maybe there was a double-cross. Maybe she's got her hand on his money. And his balls. Maybe Crowe was more jock than Yuppie. Maybe a dose of macho won't let him let his wife get away with pulling a deal on him. Maybe he wants some payback along with his money.

"We gotta do a rethink, guy."

"On what?"

"On why this guy's back in town and why he isn't using his old connections."

"Why?"

"He just iced his best shot for moving the goods."

"That we know about."

"That New Orleans knows about. New Orleans is way behind the curve on this one, Jack. We can't sit and wait for a phone call. We gotta hit the street, guy, and come up with our own line on Crowe."

"What else is New Orleans wrong about?"

"Question of the day, guy. If they've been wrong about who he's connected with, they may be wrong about everything else. Like being partners with his wife. Like just being some Yuppie ex-jock with a good mind for figures and a taste for small-time larceny."

"Never underestimate someone who kills somebody."

"Quote of the day, guy. Quote of the day. We been underestimating the shit out of this Crowe. New Orleans, too. Time we quit doin' that, guy. Gotta start beatin' our own bushes."

"What about this new player?"

"Cop from Dallas. New Orleans says he's a nobody."

"New Orleans won't have to face a bullet from this asshole."

"I think we're gonna have to make a couple of calls to the Big D."

"I can handle that. Know some good people up there. From the old Campisi outfit."

"You do that, guy. And do it quick. I got a guy I gotta see crosstown."

"Certain cop friend of ours?"

Louis smiled around the new Kent on his lip.

"Could be, guy. Could be."

"One question, Louis."

"What's that?"

"Is New Orleans on the button about anything?"

"One thing and one thing only."

"The wife?"

"Bingo. We find her, we find him. And we get the goods."

"How d'you figger?"

"He's here to kill her. After he makes a sale. Business first. Then pleasure."

"We play it that way, the goods will be gone."

"We get him, we get who he did business with. We also get something much bigger."

"And what would that be — a trip to Disneyworld?"

Louis smiled, stood and shot the cuffs of his pearl gray shirt, the one with the monogram on the pocket and the black bone buttons.

"A pot of long green, guy. A much bigger pot than New Orleans would ever let us dip our beaks into."

FOURTEEN

Burch woke up and felt her eyes on him, icy and green, like a cougar sizing up a mule deer from a perch in the desert rocks. He groaned. As he did every morning. From the pain of prematurely arthritic knees, an ankle full of bone chips that rattled like a fishing lure, an elbow that occasionally locked up with a wafer of loose cartilage and a wrist that was shattered in a car wreck fifteen years gone and hit him with dull pulses of discomfort that provided a nice backbeat to the sharper notes played by earlier injuries from the gridiron and other youthful obsessions.

He groaned for another reason — terminal stupidity.

Louie, that ancient saloon seer, was right. He'd never learn. Show him a good woman and a lady from a lower hell. He'd pick the one who would wreck his life — every time. And he couldn't blame his dick. Ol' John Henry wasn't at fault. No sir. It was a sickness. An addiction to emotional pain. An automatic overdrive on his hormones, an override on his survival instincts. And one day it might just kill his fat ass.

Maybe today.

He rolled toward the nightstand and groaned again. A bottle of Maker's Mark poked its red-waxed neck from underneath the tilted shade of the lamp, a few inches of amber left near the bottom. Next to that, two juice glasses with dregs of whiskey and water that was once ice, the unholstered Colt with its worn bluing and fresh scrapes, an extra magazine of slugs both jacketed and hollow point, a pack of Luckies, his Zippo.

A crooked white stick to the lips. The snicking sound of metal. Rowel on flint. Flame. Blue smoke deep into the lungs. A lid snapped shut. Another groan.

"In pain, lover? Got a hangover head?"

"Still doing a systems check. We did what I assume we did, right?"

"Umm."

"How were we?"

"I was fabulous. You provided adequate service."

"I was a reluctant partner."

"You were a drunk lover. But then again, so was I. We used to be at our best that way, remember?"

"I remember a lot of things about us, Slick."

"Don't ruin the morning, Big Boy."

"Didn't know you were sentimental."

"I'm not. I just want to fuck you again. It helps if I'm thinking good thoughts."

"Didn't know that mattered."

"It doesn't."

Her fingers were on his cock. It stirred and rose. Her mouth followed. He watched, taking a final drag on the Lucky and tossing it into the thin liquid layer at the bottom of one of the glasses. Her wild curls spilled across his belly.

He sat up slowly and pulled her toward him. Her long legs slid along his flanks, scissoring him with her knees. His cock slid into her cunt. Seated, she leaned forward and tongued his mouth. He leaned back on the heels of his hands and let her ride.

"Ahhhh, baby — I missed having you inside me."

Burch said nothing. He didn't dare. He stayed quiet and picked up the pace of his upward thrusts. When something this bad for you feels this good, silence is the only hope for salvation. Like an unspoken prayer from a man doomed to always repeat his mistakes.

They were at the home of an old friend, a man named Jennings. An ex-Army intelligence officer, one who didn't live up to the derogatory letter of that old Groucho Marx line. A freelance journalist with work appearing regularly in *Esquire*, *Texas Monthly*, *Outdoor*, *Playboy*, *Field & Stream*, *American Handgunner* and just about any other rag that valued the same manly male myth pumped out by aging Hemingway devotees like McGuane and Harrison. A sometime security consultant who was still as sharp with a .45 as he was a nine iron.

In his younger days, when he still had hair and didn't have a belly that plowed ahead of him like the prow of a broad-beamed icebreaker, Jennings dialed up Charlie on field telephones and dropped true believers from choppers hovering above the Delta.

Before that, he played icy counter-spook games in Berlin, back when there was a Wall and not long after an American president, soon to be dead, could draw roars of approval for calling himself a pastry instead of what he meant to call himself — a citizen of that divided city. Back when two world views were still locked in a remorseless yet ritualistic struggle, one where brutality and cunning were equally valued. Along with a high church reverence for the perverted rules of the game — a chess game for death artists in priestly raiment.

Jennings was a man who still loved all the tools of his old trade, electronic or violent, brain-driven or muscle-bound. He still loved to keep a hand in, no matter how small the stakes or large the risk. As long as it didn't get in the way of working on his short game, hunting for the perfect chicken-fried steak or settling in with his nightly fix of Armagnac and a pricey double corona.

He still kept a network of nasty friends, inside and outside of the game. Some were cold-eyed muscle. Some were romantics, pretenders and wannabes who never would be. Others could punch up a full dossier with the touch of a button. Or have somebody iced with a coded word. And more than a few were part of the Saigon Mafia, what law-enforcement types referred to as a criminal element well-wormed into the heart of the community of Vietnamese expatriates who live along Bellaire Boulevard in the southwest pocket of the city.

Bellaire wasn't Tu Do Street and Houston lacked Saigon's fetid colonial decadence, but an old 'Nam hand like Jennings could still wheel his way off the 610, find a bowl of tongue-scorching *bún bo Hue*, a cold bottle of 33 and an old ARVN acquaintance working the shady and lucrative side of life.

Jennings looked like Friar Tuck, with a fringe beard and a glint of evil merriment in his blue eyes, and could always be counted on to hide the fragile nuggets of his true self in a thick layer of highly believable half-truths, amusing images, bawdy turns of phrase, clever truisms and total fabrications.

About women. About war. About golf games and family. About whether he was an heir or a po' boy. About the insignificance of both. About Faustian bouts of drinking and feasting. About long military fasts in the cold or tropic wet. About politicians and saints. Even about death. Delivered with the weary, story-telling touch of a veteran boulevardier. Shuffled and reshuffled, according to audience and need.

Sometimes Burch would call the bluff. Always between the two of them. Never in front of others. It's all cover, Jennings would say with a shrug. Except for the stories that appeared under his byline. Those he told straight and well, with the familiar, from-the-shoulder tone of two men taking measure of each other with midnight long past and with deep whiskies in hand. Which was the only other place where he used no cover and stepped into the open in honest, naked friendship.

Male bonding say the libbers, the sensitive males, the pop psychologists and the psychic emasculators of both sexes, with a dismissive sneer, a shrug of self-mockery or a slight smile of amused contempt. But after Burch's first divorce, the one that left him gutted and howling in sleepless pain deep into the night, it was Jennings who called him twice a week and listened to him wail in anguish. Not any of his closer acquaintances from the force. Not any of the people with whom he regularly hoisted a glass at Louie's, male or female.

Only Jennings. And Louie — but only at closing, when Burch, isolated all night in the smoky crowd by his pain and bitter drunkenness, was still on a stool, still hoisting Maker's to his lips. Louie's loyalties came from commerce and saloon camaraderie — a friendship with a regular patron, loyalty to Burch's contribution to his bottom line. Jennings' came from only one place.

They first met in Germany, when Burch was serving with an armored outfit near the Fulda Gap. And again when Burch was a cop in Dallas. Jennings came up to do a piece for *Texas Monthly* about the son of a prominent investment banker who was garroted in the bathtub by his gay lover, an artist and crystal meth addict who was once the father's lover as well. Burch had caught the case and chased down the killer in Toronto, slamming him to the floor of an art gallery off of Yonge Street with a forearm shiver that would have made his old line coach proud.

But he had also managed to piss off the father, a well-connected disciple of that establishment discipline known as the Dallas Way. A suspension. The lover arrested during the course of that suspension. At his own expense. Cold shoulders from his superiors. Extra embarrassment for the father. A scandal aired and a demotion from the Dallas Way hierarchy. Another black mark in Burch's long skid out of the department. Another angle for Jennings' story.

Ironclad loyalty was the coin of Jennings' friendship, given freely and expected in return. That and a willingness to open a vein for a friend. One overseas phone call from the Racehorse's office and the three-bedroom condo was Burch's for the using, overlooking the long green fairway of the seventh hole at Champion's Golf Club, an old-style duffers-only-no-tennis string of links on the northwest side of town. Within view of the clubhouse that Jack Burke and Jimmy Demaret built. A costly and cushiony clue that one of Jennings' cover stories might indeed be fact — an heir to the Piggly-Wiggly grocery chain fortune.

Another clue — a pair of rare Colt Walkers, the massive, black-powdered sidearm of the Texas Rangers, worth as heavy an amount of change as Jennings would ever care to ask. Assuming he ever would. He wouldn't.

One phone call also gave Burch some extra muscle — two of Jennings' security confederates, a slight, bald-headed, lisping man named Carl and a hulking Cuban black named Benito.

"You got it," Jennings said, his voice a murmur and a rumble, flowing from the phone, giving everything the tone of a terrible secret, a warning washed in brandy and smoke. "You'll like the boys, Double E. Just do what they say and take no prisoners."

Jennings was in Scotland working a month-long tour of the ancient greens and fairways, wedging side trips to the Côte d'Azur, Paris and Venice between courses. He gave him a fast warning about his client, knowing Burch would hear it, use it but not walk away from the case because of it.

"I know you'll be stupid enough to fuck this bitch so I won't waste much talk on that but you need to know you're in a much bigger game than she'll ever tell you. Her old man took something from the ginzos and they don't take kindly to that. My guess is she's either a partner with him or has her hands on what he stole."

"Hell — we don't even know if Crowe is still alive."

"*You* don't. Everybody else seems to know he's still among us.

Cops included. I suggest you catch up fast."

"Cops know that crispy critter ain't Crowe. That don't make him alive."

"You can't afford to think that way. Assume every player is on the board unless you knock 'em down personal."

"So what has a little bird told you the stakes are — money, drugs or what?"

"Drugs and diamonds is the word. But who gives a fuck? You don't take from these people unless you take big enough to buy yourself a new life far, far away from them. And in my book, you can't take enough to do that."

"Your advice, counselor?"

"She's gonna use you as a shield until she gets what she wants. Then she's either gonna toss you to whatever wolves are on her heels or dust you like she did before. But know this — you won't be left standin' this time. It'll be terminal."

"So I oughta do her before she does me. But take the goods first."

"Nossir. What you ought to do is take a long walk clear the fuck away from all this. Real quick. Failing that — find out her game, blow her brains out and leave it all on a silver platter for the ginzos except for a finder's fee."

"Assuming she's trying to pull all of this off and isn't just trying to keep from getting splashed in the fallout. She's got all manner of people after her who are pissed at Crowe. On both sides of the law."

"You tell yourself what you want to. But you're gettin' played like a fish again."

"Probably so."

"Look — don't pout. All I'm sayin' is play heads up or take a walk. You got the boys for four days and my place for as long as you want. Just give me a couple of hours to set it up."

"Thanks, bud."

"*Nada y nada.* Keep it low."

The two bodyguards moved like wraiths through the condo, both wearing Beretta 92s underneath loose-fitting tropical shirts, one always on watch while the other took care of mundane necessities like groceries or laundry. Quiet and unobtrusive. Quick and low-volumed explanations, cloaked in the tones of consultations about maintaining the perimeter, staying off the phone and staying out of sight.

Sonic sensors on the outside, miniature versions of the devices the Border Patrol uses along America's no-man's-land. Motion sensors on the inside. Installed by the owner, a man who loves his toys. With friends who feel the same way. The boys brought cellular phones with scramblers. Night scopes. Detectors for bugs. And a neat little black box that could read whether a window was being beamed with a laser listening device.

Burch was old fashioned. He drew particular comfort from the boys' more conventional stores. Scoped Mini-14s, the favored long gun of the Klan and survivalists, stacked in a corner of the living room. Shotguns in the kitchen, the den and each bedroom — Ithaca pumps with extended magazines. Total pros. Made him feel like a lurching amateur. And as safe as a freshly diapered baby.

Surrounded by all that professional security, Burch felt a surge of confidence. It gave him the energy he needed to work on Savannah the first day they hit the condo, with Carl and Benito gliding through the background, making sure their backs were watched.

"That husband of yours — alive or dead? Or a little bit of both?"

"Don't be cute. You know what the cops say."

"They say that body in the car ain't him. That don't make him alive."

"What are you saying — that I killed his sorry ass?"

"Or somebody else, after he made his cute little getaway."

"That's a novel thought."

"Can't get it out of my mind that he might be dead and all this is just a scramble over what he left behind. So which way is it?"

"Could be either way. It almost doesn't matter — people are coming at me, assuming I'm either in on his play or know where to get my hands on what he left behind when he got fried."

"Poor baby. Ever'body pickin' on you."

She shot him a glare, green anger on ice.

"Won't work, Slick. Seen the act before. So let me ask it again — is your beloved, Jason Willard Crowe, the late great or just late for supper?"

"You know I hate it when you go redneck on me."

"Well this ol' redneck wants to know what the game is and who all the players are. We know about Mr. Delgado. And I believe we have to contend with some gentlemen from New Orleans. And that wild card, your husband."

"I know the sumbitch didn't die in that car and I think he's alive now."

"What're we playin' for, darlin' — table stakes?"

"This isn't a poker game, Big Boy."

"I know. It's what you call your True Life. With all its serious rules and such."

"You're getting philosophical on me and you haven't even had a drink yet."

"We can cure that right quick."

The bottle of Maker's Mark still had some amber nectar. Juice glasses flanked the bottle like battle-weary pawns. He tossed watery remains from one and poured himself a four-finger eye-opener. Neat. No ice.

"I figure it this way, Slick. You're either partnered up with hubby and just takin' the heat for him until his deal is squared up or you've got a hand on what he's got and are squeezin' away."

"You think too much."

"Never in my life. But I'm thinkin' right aren't I?"

"What's your point?"

"My point is this — you've got a new partner."

"That would be you."

Burch nodded, taking a sip of whiskey.

"True enough, maybe."

Savannah slapped her knee, laughed and said: "It's a waitin' game, sugar."

"I can wait with the best of 'em."

"Just make sure there's somethin' good to make the wait worth your while."

"Feel somethin' on your hand?"

She glanced at her right hand, then looked his way with the cocked head of a curious dog.

"No — what the hell are you talkin' about?"

"Your hand. You don't feel anything on it?"

"Eddie, your mind must be fried. I don't feel a damn thing on my hand except my skin."

"You should feel somethin' else there too."

"Like what?"

"Like my hand. Right there in the same pocket you got your hand. Waitin' on that money to come in. Waitin' to grab a share so there's somethin' good to make all of this worth my while."

He said that with swagger in his voice, buoyed by bourbon and smart patter. But that feeling was gone now, shattered by his romp with Savannah and the sure knowledge of his vulnerability and lack of control. Puppet time again. With all strings attached.

After their morning session, Savannah hopped into the shower. Burch waited until she was through then did the same. When he stepped back into the bedroom, one towel around his belly and another to rub the water out of his hair and beard, she was snapping shut the lid of an IBM ThinkPad and snicking a phone line out of a portable modem.

She had a look of shock on her face, one that froze out his sharp words and angry scowl.

"You stupid whore, you just gave us up if you tapped into a data line you regularly use."

"It's gone."

"You understand me, Irish?"

"It's gone, Big Boy. It was there yesterday. Today it's gone."

"What're you talkin' about?"

His hand was on her shoulder. She was staring at the towel around his belly but not really seeing it.

"Money."

"You're not making sense."

She shot him a sharp look.

"Quit bein' as stupid as you look."

"Quit bein' a bitch and tell me what you're talking about."

"That pocket we both had our hands in? It's empty now. Nothin' there but your skin and mine."

"You can tell that with a computer?"

"Wonderful technology. Makes a nice little electronic mousetrap with the spring set and the cheese in place."

"He's onto you right? He's moved the money where you can't get it."

She snorted and shook her head with the weary disgust a smart sixth grader reserves for a classmate bound for Vo Tech.

"I never could get it. But a friend could. He's a wizard when it comes to computers. We just had to wait for Jason to move it to a place where we could put our hands on it."

"Who's this computer wizard? Knowing you, he's a special kind of friend. How many times did you have to fuck him before he'd do what you want?"

"You shouldn't be jealous, Big Boy — I'm fucking you now and will again any time John Henry's ready."

Burch ignored the carnal bait and focused on the money.

"Let me get this straight — you and the computer whiz were set up to grab the money as Crowe moved it from Point A to Point B."

"Whenever Jason was ready to move it."

"How much did you grab before hubby got wise?"

"Enough. But I want it all."

"Don't we all, darlin'. Me, you, your husband. And those gentlemen from New Orleans."

A knock on the bedroom door. Benito with a cellular phone in his hand. One murmured word: "Jennings."

Burch stepped into the hall and matched Benito's hushed volume with his own murmur.

"Hombre — we're moving. *La señora* has used the phone and somebody could do a trace."

Benito nodded.

"*Claro.*"

Burch took the phone in hand.

"What?"

"You're in a good mood. I take it the flesh was weak."

"I hate it when your crystal ball is in gear."

A pause. The sound of static.

"Your boy is in town."

"Crowe?"

"The same."

"Where?"

"Some Asian gentlemen I know say he's doing business with one of their associates."

"Old friends?"

"Comrades-in-arms. From our follies in Southeast Asia."

"Why?"

"Moving product."

"Why take the risk?"

"Good question. He's a new player to these people. They don't know him. Haven't done business with him."

"His normal channels are blown."

"Be my guess."

"A certainty. Wifey broke into his little computer deal. Nice little system of automatic wire transfers to overseas accounts."

"Remote control. File and forget. I take it he's figured out that she's tapped the system."

"You got it. So we'll be putting fresh sheets on your bed."

"Hmmmm. Thoughtful. But risky."

"No choice. Wifey's been tapping databases from here."

"The boys know a place. Stash her. Do your hunting."

"Bet on it. Your friends give you a name?"

Jennings gave it to him. Not in the accent of a true Texan, but in the voice of a man who used to speak Vietnamese for a living. It was a voice the bar girls on Tu Do Street used to hear, full of lust and good humor.

And it was the last thing a true believer heard before getting hurled from a hovering chopper.

FIFTEEN

The bar is long, dark and cool in the early afternoon before the Happy Hour rush, washed in the smell of stale beer, Pine Sol and fresh-brewed coffee.

Light from the narrow frosted panes of glass flanking both sides of the front door slants down the sharp left-right turn patrons must make to enter the main room. The glare flashes across dozens of framed charcoal sketches of Louie's favorite regulars — the locally famous and insane, the hard-chargers and fast-laners, the steady boozers and saloon sports, the motel Romeos and Juliets and the railside philosophers.

Burch's portrait, drawn by the light of the cigarette machine on the short end of the bar, is the first one on the left, on the bottom row. His likeness looks badly bloated and hungover. Charcoaled in the wake of his first divorce, it is photographic in detail.

Krukovitch's sketch, capturing his ironic and angry expression, hangs on the opposite corner of the top row. Drawn in the wake of his third collection of columns — *Jangled Mutterings, Confused Complaints* — it has the dapper air of a dust jacket photo.

The hip monarchist himself sits at the end of the bar farthest from the door, the short end where Louie holds court in the choice hours that cut toward midnight and away from the post-work rush. It is Monday. Krukovitch is pounding out his column — a rant against Ross Perot. Little Hutch huffs in from the kitchen, muscling three cases of Old Style in bottles.

"Hey, Kruk."

No answer. The clack of the laptop keyboard. Hutch pitches a damp bar rag at the columnist, hitting him just above his wire-framed glasses. A startled look, a twitch of annoyance, a smile.

"Now, dammit, I told you to rap sharply on the top of my head when you wanted my attention."

"I'm too lazy. Listen — I gotta run some errands. Be gone an hour. Any deliveries — just sign the boss's name."

"Got it."

Krukovitch turns back to the laptop, his smile lamping out like a candle flame pinched between two wet fingers. A fast forward of the minutes — ten, maybe twenty. A clacking keyboard. A sip of coffee. A quick hit from a smoldering Carlton. A face so intensely focused on the glowing screen that two men — one from the kitchen, one from the front door — step to within four feet of the columnist and he still isn't aware of their presence.

A throat clears. That startled look — one part deer-in-the-headlamps, one part outraged Lutheran uncle caught cheating at cards.

"Good Christ! You scared the shit out of me!"

No response.

"The bar's closed right now if you're looking for a drink. If you've got some business that needs taking care of, Hutch said he'll be right back."

The one closest to Krukovitch, the one who walked in the front door, smiles. He is a squat, olive-skinned man with the trunk and arms of a wrestler, the belly of a lifelong beer-and-shot artist and a head that is pinched like a worn-out pillow and too small for his torso. His wiry hair is frosted with grey and hangs over eyes that are wet and brown and docile, like a rabbit or a deer. His voice is nicotine spilling over a cold bar of lead.

"That's nice. But we'd like a beer now."

Krukovitch glances from the wrestler to the other man — tall, thin and black, wearing a blue windbreaker, baggy jeans and a Detroit Tigers baseball cap. He wears octagonal-shaped wire frames over amber eyes that flash in the low saloon light.

"Like I said, the bar's closed right now."

"Tha' right? You in here. You somebody special?"

Krukovitch tries to laugh. It sounds like someone gargling with cotton and gravel. He shakes his head.

"No — nobody special. Just somebody who puts half his paycheck into this place every week. Some folks call me a regular."

No smiles now. Dull, flat stares — Bunny Eyes' not so wet and friendly. Closer to him. Crowding in. Well inside his always jangled comfort zone.

"Guys. Look. I'm just babysitting until the bartender gets back."

"You too good to get us a beer?"

"It's not that. I don't work here and the place isn't open for business."

The black man leans forward. The soft rasp of his voice heightens Krukovitch's fear.

"Open. Not open. Doesn't matter to us. We're here for business an' you're the only one here, so I guess you'll have to do."

Krukovitch slides his stool back and stands again, hands up and palms outward, edging backward to give himself some room. A huge hard hand stops him, gripping the back of his neck. Another hand grabs his left arm, levering it down and pinning it against his back, quick and brutal, causing his breath to blow from his lungs in a sharp protest of pain.

Face slams into the rolled edge of the bar. Red gushes from a shattered nose. Glasses star with shattering lines. The wire frame twists. The left temple pops, falling to the floor, the left lens sticking to a bloody cheek, the right lens digging into the source of the flow, a new ridge of bone and cartilage riding just below ripped skin.

"Damn, he howls like a baby."

"Must not like your gentle ways."

"You got a beef with the way I treat you?"

Knee to the groin. Body knifing over the knee. New and far sharper pain, causing his guts to freefall like an elevator with a severed cable and his bile to rocket upward in the opposite direction, a coffee-colored spray on the grimy floor.

"Watch my shoes, man! You little shit, you puked on my shoes!"

Head slap. Sparks, pain and blurred colors.

"Fuck your shoes, man. Take care of business."

The thin black man takes Krukovitch's face in his hands, peering at the damage. A sympathetic cluck of the tongue. A sad look. A touch of sugar on the sandpaper. A good act.

"We got to clean this man up."

A bar rag to the face.

"Got to get this blood and this puke off the man so he can talk to us."

Face blurry, black and close. Then nothing, vision closes with pain and tears.

"You wanna talk to us, don't you? `Course you do. You see? Man wants to talk. Gonna tell us what we want to know, right? Not gonna just tell us what we want to hear."

"Man can't talk. Somethin' happened to his face."

"You should know. But you're wrong about this guy, man. He'll talk now. He likes us. He wants to be cooperative."

"Ask him a question."

"Now?"

"He's not getting any prettier standing here."

"Him? He's not standin' at all. He's leanin' on you."

"Ask him."

Hands cup the face. A black blur through tears.

"We hear you're a computer wiz, man. We hear you know everythin' there is to know about them boxes. Make `em dance and sing. That right?"

"He's not listenin'."

Head slap. Stars and strobes.

"He hears, man. He just can't talk."

"Ask him again."

"Man — I need you to listen or my boy here will keep hurtin' you. You the computer wizard, right? You know what to do and how to do, right? Nod for me, man. Nod. It's important."

Hands cup the face. A nod from Krukovitch.

"There you go, now. See? I told you. We've got one cooperative muthafuckah on our hands."

"Get on with it."

"Gettin' there, my man. Gettin' there."

Hands cup the face. The black blur gets closer. Krukovitch can make out a nose, ears and eyes, haloed by bar light.

"You know a guy we know, right? Comes in here all the time. Guy name Burch. You and him are tight, right?"

A strangling noise. A moan through snot and blood. A nod.

"Good man. See that? Man's really cooperatin' now. Talkin' to us."

"Quit clownin'."

"No clown in this bar `cept you. We gave him the stick, now we got to give him some sweet, show him we not all badass. Now pay attention to this next question, my man. Since you know this fella Burch, since you so tight with him, you know his lady friends, right?"

A nod.

"Good. You remember Savannah Crowe, right? Savannah? You know her real good, right?"

A single shake of the head.

"Now don't be jerkin' me around. If you tight with Burch, you know his ladies and you know this particular lady."

Another shake. A mumbling string of words.

"What? What you tryin' to say?"

A hack. A string of spit and blood.

"Not well."

"What? You gonna sick up again?"

"No."

A pause for the pain. A series of short breaths.

"Know her but not well. Don't like her."

"Why not — she a looker. Very fly. Very fine."

"Fucked over my buddy. She's a cunt."

A laugh from the wrestler: "Man, they're all cunts, even a man's mother."

A frown from the thin black: "Not my mama." The black turns back to Krukovitch.

"If she's such a shit — if she jobbed your buddy so bad — why he work for her again?"

"Burch's a stupid shit. He needs money."

"So it's okay by him if she's a cunt and fucks him over as long as the money is right."

"Guess so."

"We talkin' about a shared value system here? Buddies who see things the same way when it comes to women and money?"

A shake. Several more. A tighter grip around the neck. A blurry orb of white moves into Krukovitch's field of vision.

"I think my man here's exactly right. I think shared values are exactly what we're talkin' about. Your buddy jumps to her tune again because the money's right and the pussy's wet and tight. Only natural for you to do the same. Work a little of that computer magic for her in return for some long green and a touch of Mister Fun in the joy box. We communicatin' here?"

"Wrong. Hate the bitch. Wouldn't fuck her with your dick. Warned Burch off. Wouldn't listen."

"Buddies help buddies, right? And a guy who wrote the book on how to break into computers would do a favor for a buddy, right? Or a buddy's client. Right?"

"No. Helped Burch do a Nexus check. On the husband. That's it."

"Friends of ours think different. They think you and Burch are helping the little missus. They see you as the guy who helped the missus crack into a computer and grab somethin' that didn't belong to her."

Hand up, palm out. Pain wave recedes. Brief return of the scowling focus of Krukovitch's barroom debating form.

"That doesn't make any sense. I'm Burch's friend, not hers. She's bad news for him or anybody. Even me. You guys are proof of that. I'm not even involved in this deal and I'm still getting my ass kicked by pros. Burch is my friend but he's on his own with this one. I told him that before he left."

A look passes between the hired muscle.

A shrug from the thin black man.

"Man makes sense. You know her rep."

A roll of the eyes from the wrestler. A look of expectation from Krukovitch — the nervous high school rhetoric ace waiting on approval from the head master.

"No sale, Jack."

A fist to the stomach. Another body fold. More bile on the floor and any shoe leather that gets in the way. Blackout on the edges of sight. The body jerks upward, feet leaving the floor. Hard hands vice each armpit, leveraging the lift, leaving a swelling and bloody face dangling inches from the wrestler's upturned mug.

"I think you're holdin' out on us. Now listen — I'm not nice like my friend. I'd just as soon snap your neck as keep talkin' to you. But my friend, he's cultured, he's refined. He believes in keeping the channels of diplomacy open. Me — talk's cheap and you don't have enough money for my time. Myself — I see you as helpin' your buddy and that bitch get their hands on somethin' that belongs to some people who want it back."

A shake of the head.

"I'm tired of dealin' with you."

Feet slap-slam to the floor. Legs buckle. Body spins to the pull of the wrestler's right arm. Bloody and pointed chin in a massive hand. Quick twist to the right, head snapping beyond ninety degrees. A loud pop of the neck.

Body slides to the floor, legs and arms jerking, eyes sightless and bulging. Strong smells — urine and feces — float upward.

"Christ, I hate this part — that stink."

"Man, I can't believe you. You fuckin' waste the guy just when we get him talkin'. Then you complain about the odor. Make up your mind — you dainty or you a stone cold killer?"

"Try me an' see, Jim."

"Ain't no Jim here, muthafucka. Just a stupid ass usin' his muscle when finesse was workin'.

"Wastin' our time, Jack. He wasn't gonna talk. He was stallin'."

"You wrong, man. Fucker wasn't in on it. I could feel it. We had him dancin' just right between sugar and the stick. And you break his neck for nothin'. Not what a pro would do."

"Shut the fuck up and grab that box of his. We gotta split."

"What we need this for? We know he wasn't in on it."

"No, we don't know. We're muscle. We do as we're told. We get his laptop. We already got his files and computer from home. We give it to Ivan the Brain and he tells our people whether our friend here was doin' what we know he was."

"Wastin' him was doin' what we told to do?"

"Hey — they said leave a callin' card."

"Messin' him up did that."

"I gotta live in this town. You don't. Can't afford to have somebody pointing a finger at me."

"You keep shit like this up and you won't be livin' here long. You won't be livin' at all."

"Shut the fuck up an' get moving."

SIXTEEN

Burch elbowed his way through the river of people flowing up and down the main concourse of the Astrodome, the harsh overhead lights flashing off the clothes and jewelry of a crowd wading deep in full-blown rodeo chic

Earrings dangled under sprayed-stiff piles of Big Hair, necklaces of turquoise or onyx or carnelian nestled in deep cleavage, coin-sized conchos on belts cinched above the packed hips of tight Wranglers, pearl speed snaps flashed on shirts with flames blooming across the chest or aqua-on-purple-on-black Aztec symbols only a bubba could love. Golden blouses with ruffles and shoulder cutouts shimmered in harsh fluorescent light, plate-sized buckles rode above the crotch of men both beer-bellied and whippet thin, silvery bands accented black bullrider hats riding low across eyes challenging, drunk, happy, pissed-off, wary and sometimes all of the above.

There was the soft luster of buffed animal skin. Cowhide and snake, ostrich and kangaroo. Boots, vests and jackets fringed or vented. No glow from Burch's scuffed ensemble — snakeskin boots with small tears marring the dull reptile pattern, a well-worn leather blazer that used to be jet black, but was now striated with brown-edged cracks. It used to have a full complement of buttons but was still full cut enough to cover a Colt holstered in a shoulder rig. Too hot for the weather, too shabby for the company but the best he could do now that his Tito-era linen jacket was ripped beyond repair.

Tito's dead and so's his country. There ain't no Yugo in the Yugo anymore — damn good start to a honky-tonk tune.

Yessir, punch it up on the ol' jukebox. A tune with an international conscience, complete with pedal steels and twin fiddles backing up words about a country shattered by ethnic hatreds and ancient religious conflicts and that everlasting lust men have for killing each other. A real weeper in two-four time. A timeless classic right up there with "Faded Love."

And the Yugo, that car without a country — lemme tell ya friend, that's just a bad automotive mistake most people would rather forget.

Dead dictators, Balkan wars, Communist clunkers and dreams of jukebox glory. Burch shook this line of thought out of his head as he navigated, one hand gently parting the wave of people, tapping a shoulder or cupping a strange arm, the other holding a warm Frito pie, a greasy Texana marvel of fairgrounds, high school football games and rodeo arenas, second only to the corny dog in health-threatening tastiness.

A simple delicacy — open a bag of Fritos, from the side, not the top. Only Fritos would do. No substitutes, nothing by Golden Flake. And the thin chips only, not the wide ones made to scoop bean dip. Ladle a couple of dollops of chili into the bag. Homemade was best, Wolf Brand if it had to be canned. Never Hormel or Dinty Moore. Deadly in salt and fat content — nothing but gristle, lard and a little corn meal. Grab a spoon and dig in. Good and good for you. Yew bet.

Burch popped out on the far side of the flow and headed for a beam in the hallway wall, a niche where he could lean a shoulder, munch his goodies and watch what needed watching. A cold Coke would be nice. An icy Pearl would be better. Burch had neither.

From his post, he had a clear view of a concession stand about twenty yards down on the opposite side of the crowded concourse. Two long tables covered in heavy red cloth patterned with scattered prints of horseshoes, bucking broncs, snorting bulls and lean cowboys. Folded T-shirts and stacks of gimme caps lined the tabletop. A tall hinged exhibit rack loomed behind the table, draped with caps, hangered T-shirts and cheap straw cowboy hats.

Two Vietnamese girls and an older woman waited on customers. A Vietnamese man, rail thin and weathered with a jet-black razor-cut pompadour and half-moon spectacles, sat to the side closest to Burch in a folding metal chair, his face in three-quarters profile to Burch's line of sight, pointed the opposite way, eyes down, reading a newspaper.

The man matched Jennings' description. A sign above the souvenirs gave final confirmation, Vu Nguyen Thanh Enterprises. All Burch had to do was watch, hope the man kept reading his paper and pray one thing happened and another didn't — Crowe showed up but didn't see Burch before Burch spotted him.

The question of why Crowe would run the deadly risk of returning to Houston, where too many players serious and small wanted him dead, nagged at Burch until he kicked it around with Jennings. The semi-retired spook had a ready answer — Savannah's electronic larceny wrecked Crowe's pipeline of long green. He was on the run and needed a quick injection of cash from product cached in Houston and, save for those icy diamonds, not that easy to transport.

Crowe also needed new buyers, players who weren't tied to New Orleans or the Mexican cartels and weren't dancing in the conga line of killers who wanted to snuff out his candle. Vu Nguyen Thanh fit the bill. Jennings knew Thanh in South Vietnam as a pilot who flew ground support missions in rugged Able Dog Skyraiders and rose through the ranks to become a trusted hatchet man for the cowboy flyboy who served as premier and vice president of the doomed republic, Nguyen Cao Ky.

Like most ex-pat Vietnamese gangsters, Thanh was fiercely unaffiliated with anybody but his own kind. He also saw himself as a patriot and serious businessman, not a racketeer.

Jennings' take:

Thanh thinks he's a goddam Swiss banker, open to doing business with anybody but the fuckin' Chinese — a long history of bad blood between the Chinks and the Viets. Hate each other long time. Don't let that banker shit fool you, son. Thanh's a killer, likes to use a blade. Turning your back on him will get you dead, muy pronto.

Burch thought there was another reason for Crowe's risky return to Houston — pride. It was the pure arrogance of an ex-jock who wanted to impose his talented will on his opponents one more time by suddenly shifting course and scoring on a broken-field run. Throw in the blind conceit of a man who always thought he was the smartest guy in the room because he usually was. Crowe came back to Houston just to prove he could.

That left one more question Burch didn't need help from Jennings to answer — why take a run at Crowe? Because the arrogant Jason Willard Crowe was exposed and vulnerable. Because it offered another chance to grab up more of Crowe's cash. And it offered another opportunity to wreck Crowe's money pipeline, leaving him weak and wide open to the killers on his trail and unable to come after Burch and his feckless client and lover. Jennings would call that "neutralizing the threat by proxy" and pat him on the back with a chuckle.

Standing at the edge of the concourse, Burch felt slightly naked and exposed. One-man stakeouts — the textbooks pegged them as extremely difficult to maintain. Too easy to be spotted, too many exits and options to cover, too little time to stay in one place before you become as obvious as a dog turd floating in a rich man's swimming pool.

The smell of the chili took his mind off these tactical troubles.

He spooned up a Frito-studded lump of reddish-brown goo, triggering instant salivation at the anticipation of another bite. Two, then three followed. Always the total pro, Burch kept his mouth happy and his eyes on the subject. His brain noting the number of pages the man carefully turned and smoothed -- five — and the taste and texture of each bite — crunchy grease with a slight backbite of dry fire that held the promise of later returns elsewhere in his digestive pipeline.

He finished the Frito pie and belched. He checked his watch — thirty minutes until the Grand Entry of the Houston Livestock Show and Rodeo, a youngster on the rodeo circuit compared to granddaddies like Cheyenne and Calgary, but a big-money event that cowboys clawed each other up to enter. A hot ride here could earn a cowboy ten or twenty large and mean the difference between breaking even on a year of driving and flying to 150 rodeos around the country and putting some money in the bank for that dream ranch.

Thirty minutes until the crowd in the concourse started heading toward their seats, thinning the thick cover between him and Thanh. Burch was in a good spot for a man eating a snack — a ledge with napkin holders, condiments and the predictable number of crushed cups and crumpled wrappers started five feet from where he stood and ran the twenty feet between him and the snack stand opposite Thanh's souvenir operation, an overflowing trash can was between him and the ledge. But when the crowd disappeared, he would have to move.

The thin and leathery Mr. Thanh kept reading. A large man with the shoulders of a linebacker and the up-on-the-balls-of-the-feet stride of a third baseman passed by the stand, his back to Burch. Closer to Burch, a woman with shoulder-length red hair, a "Luv ya Blue" t-shirt from the Oilers' glory days, skin full of freckles and the carriage and bearing of an Afghan hound, brought her baby carriage to a sudden halt, causing an instant diversion in the hallway's current of humanity, a change in stasis accompanied by curses, collisions, spilled beer and some deft sidestepping.

The baby was howling, maybe from hunger, maybe from a damp diaper or lack of sleep or the fear of being crushed by a crowd of duded up strangers. Burch couldn't tell, the mother didn't seem to know and the baby couldn't say. The mother seemed flustered. Instead of steering the carriage to the side of the hallway, where she could tend to her child and not be jostled by the traffic, she dropped her rose-colored quilt bag of baby supplies and her brown leather shoulder bag with the nickeled sliver conchos and long fringes right where she stood.

She bent over her child, unsnapping a powder blue jumper, pulling the top of the diaper forward and leaning in to do a quick nasal inspection. She grimaced, shook her head then reached into the quilt bag for a fresh diaper.

Burch managed to keep most of his attention focused on Thanh, still reading his newspaper. The sports section now, keeping him just as unaware as the mother doing her diaper drill ten feet away.

Thanh folded the paper, then pointed to the tall stacks of T-shirts, issuing quick orders to the women working the stand — quietly, while remaining in his seat, calmly puffing a cigarillo stuck on the end of an ebonite holder with a thin gold band.

Burch cursed himself silently for letting his attention stray. He never saw Thanh fuss with the dark stick of tobacco and the elegant holder, the flame of a lighter or match didn't catch his eye. Not good. And there was strong need to get a whole lot better. Right away. No time for distractions.

The crowd was starting to thin. Grand Entry was now fifteen minutes away — all flags and glitter, flashing lights and galloping horses, cowgirls with muscled haunches in tight denim, cowboys with tight lips and fancy-tooled chaps flipping to the motion of their mounts. Booming music and bombast from the rodeo announcer — part carney barker, part play-by-play man and pace setter, a mouthpiece who could make, break or get in the way of a show with the timing of his patter and the smoothness of his delivery. The good ones were like a just-right dash of Tabasco; the bad ones made you think of an alarm clock someone forgot to turn off.

Burch shook his head and cursed again. A wandering mind was a quick ticket to the land of the hurt or the dead. And a man his size in one place this long might find that ticket faster than he could think about it. He had to move. His choices were poor. Few spots offered the combination of clean sight line, position out of Thanh's field of vision and plausible explanation for being there. But with the Frito pie out of hand and into his belly, he could no longer pose as the snacking rodeo redneck, greasing up for the contest to come.

Sometimes events make up a man's mind. Burch felt a presence at his left elbow, slightly to his rear, just out of the edge of his vision. His hand eased into his jacket until it rested on the grip of the Colt.

"Easy, hoss. Just a friend here not a baddie. Course a baddie would have you all wrapped and ribboned right now, but that ain't me. A friend sent me — a friend I am."

Sam I am.

The phrase leapt into Burch's mind from the books he used to read his young nephews.

Sam I am.

I sure do like green eggs and ham.

"My friends don't talk as much as you do, pard. Or nearly as fast."

The man laughed. The sound was thin and horsey.

In a combo move that was more fluid than his bearish body could usually pull off, Burch turned his head, smiled like he was seeing a long-lost friend, hooked his right leg behind and between the other man's legs, draped his right arm around the stranger's thin shoulders and jammed the snout of the Colt into the left rear ridge of the man's ribcage, thumbing the safety off, careful to keep the gun shielded by his jacket, the wall and the man's body.

"Dammit, that hurts."

" 'Sposed to do that. You got two seconds to tell me who the hell you are or I'm gonna smack your face into this steel beam here and walk away."

"You won't do that, mister. It'll draw the attention of that Asian gentleman over there you been watchin' for the last fifteen minutes. And that special someone you hope will show up — fella by the name of Crowe that's married to that old girlfriend of yours. You make too fast a move, it'll draw looks from people you hope ain't lookin' this way and it'll upset that delicacy you just wolfed down — gotta give a Frito pie a chance to settle."

"So you noticed my dining habits and know about Jason Willard Crowe. I'm not impressed — any shithead in Texas knows how to order up a Frito pie and every wiseguy and cowboy from here to New Orleans has got Mister Crowe's name on their lips. And I've been in town long enough and have made enough noise for those same shitheads to pick up a line on me and my lamentable track record of love."

"Who's talkin' too much now?"

"It's infectious. Like watchin' somebody yawn. I'm gettin' tired of this buddy-buddy pose — who the hell are you and who sent you? And make it quick, bud — this Colt's cocked and my hand's startin' to twitch."

"Jennings. You know him, right? Round fellow with a beard and a taste for golf, Cuban cigars and women about a quarter century younger than himself. Spooky type fella — and I don't mean Casper the Friendly Ghost-type of spook neither."

"Nice talk. No sale. Jennings is a man about town. If you know about me you know about him."

"Try this on for size, pard. Jennings said to remind you to stop carrying a torch for your first ex. Belle — and I don't mean ding-dong. She ripped your heart out and he doesn't want to hear you crying across a long-distance phone line at four in the ay-yem. That's a quote, bubba."

Burch looked at the man — under six feet; thin and bony in the body and face; the grey-white pallor of too many cigarettes, too little exercise and too many all-nighters; a greasy, swept-back wedge of thick black hair that looked like it was drawn by a cartoonist's hand; acne scars along the jawline; the grey Oriental eyes of a husky.

Or a wolf.

Beta division. Definitely not Alpha. A shifty follower. One that had to be watched. Not the type of guy a friend would send to watch another friend's back. Unless there was nobody else to send. Jennings was only a part-time player these days — maybe he had a limited roster of true badasses he could tap. The two guys guarding Savannah — Carl and Benito — were A-Listers. No doubt.

"So you've talked to Jim Jennings. Caught him at the clubhouse at St. Andrews, right?"

"Other way around."

"You were at St. Andrew's?"

"Don't be a horse's ass. He reached out and touched me."

"Jennings must be slipping. Time was he wouldn't say a word to a guy like you let alone put you to work. Man needs a good personnel manager."

"And you need somebody to watch your back. You're stretched thin here messin' with some serious folks. I'm here to help but I'm gettin' strong-armed by the guy I'm s'posed to help. I'm gonna give you two choices — we quit this bullshit, work together and catch this fuck Crowe or we create a scene that blows the deal all together."

"Out of the goodness of your heart, right?"

"Out of the green of a retainer fee and a cut of the spoils. Word is Crowe wants to move horse, flake and some hard glitter."

"Word is that's New Orleans product, greaseball property."

"This is Houston. And the zips don't give a fuck about no Eye-tal-yans in the Big Easy."

Burch relaxed his grip and eased the pistol away from the man's ribcage. Using the man's body for cover, he thumbed on the safety and holstered the Colt. The wolf smiled.

"We got a deal?"

"We got a stalemate. I don't know you, I don't trust you and if you turn the wrong way I'll waste you."

"Jennings said you were a hardass."

"True enough. What's your name?"

"You can call me Joe."

"How `bout I call you Mr. Slick."

"Fine by me."

"Okay, Mr. Slick, I'm gonna put you to work. Move on down the hall there and buy a soda and something to eat. Post up on the far side of that stand like you're havin' a snack and watchin' the world go by. Look at your watch a lot. Like you're waitin' on someone. I'm gonna cross over and watch you. If our friend makes a move, bend over like you dropped something on your shoe. I'll move up."

"Done."

"First, I'm gonna check our backtrail. You'll be able to see me post up when I get back."

Burch didn't like this new development. But on a tactical level it solved the problem of doing a one-man stakeout. Working with another player — partner didn't apply — lowered the odds of exposure. It also allowed him the necessary luxury of checking his own back — a gamble, considering he didn't trust Mr. Slick and didn't know if or when Crowe would try to connect with Thanh.

He spun on his underslung cowboy heels and walked away from Mr. Slick and Thanh's concession stand, scanning the concourse crowd as he plowed into its sluggish current. If he was quick and lucky — and someone was careless — he might catch an averted eye, a missed step, a dodgy move. Or something instinctively familiar. A large man in a burgundy windbreaker caught his eye. Big but sure-footed. Like a cat. Or a linebacker. Or a third baseman. Like someone he had seen before. Just a few minutes earlier. The man was ducking into the men's room.

Burch didn't follow. He scanned ahead. Sometimes you caught someone looking at nothing, blank eyes and a blank face hoping his eyes would pass on by.

There. On the wall to his left. Leaning in the opening of a short semi-dark hallway at the top of steps that led to a janitor's closet. A man in a tan safari jacket, with thinning salt-and-pepper hair and a thick chin that jutted from his jaw like the heavy prow of an icebreaker. A man trying real hard not to look his way after spending the past ten or twenty minutes doing that very thing.

Burch didn't waste a step. He muscled his bulk through the crowd and walked straight into the man's face. Until he was a foot away, the man kept looking into the blank nowhere, refusing to train his eyes on Burch. And that was fine by Burch. He slammed a shoulder into the man's chest and a knee into his groin. The man doubled over with a loud grunt and Burch threw a leathery forearm into his face.

Momentum carried them deep into the darker section of hallway. Burch spun the man around and slapped his face into the wall, grabbing the man's right arm and pinning the wrist up between the shoulder blades, drawing a sharp yelp of pain. He parked a fist in the man's kidneys. Twice. That seemed to shut down all resistance.

With his right leg and boot, he spread the other man's legs and kicked his feet back so he was forced to lean into the wall. With his free hand, he patted the man down, drawing a Ruger 9 mm in matte chrome from a Galco slide holster and a pair of handcuffs. He pocketed the pistol and opened the cuffs, ratcheting them tight to the right wrist and then the left.

"You makin' a big fuckin' mistake, asshole."

"Hmm — talks like a cop. Let's see if you are one."

Burch reached inside the man's jacket. Nothing. He tapped around the front of his tooled leather belt, feeling for the badge some of Texas' cowboy lawmen liked to sport next to their handcuff holders or spare magazines. Nothing.

A wallet wedged into the back pocket of tight jeans. A license, credit cards, some cash, some business cards, a carry permit and an ID. Buchalter, Gerald Dwayne, DOB 10/17/51, Houston address. The ID was from the Harris County Sheriff's Department. A reserve deputy. Which meant this guy could be anything from a rent-a-cop, badge groupie or high school chum of the sheriff to a rung well up the ladder past private investigator, up there to the spot reserved for the serious muscle of a city's major players, maybe one of the sheriff's heavier patrons or campaign contributors or maybe just somebody rich enough to buy some official sanction for their goons.

Gerry D. didn't have the smell of particularly heavy talent. But you never knew. Burch thumbed a business card into view — white with two lines of black Helvetica type. Buchalter's name and three-word kicker: Antiques And Collectibles. Nice touch.

"Gettin' to be a rough business, your trade. Didn't know you needed a piece and some cuffs to go to an auction. Tell me somethin' Gerry — got somethin' in a nice faux Louis XIV?"

"Funny man. You're about to find out how funny life can get."

"Not from you, fuckhead."

He muscled Buchalter down the stairs. He pinned Buchalter against a metal door with black stenciled letters: Janitor. It was locked.

"What the fuck is this?"

"Talk time."

"Ain't talkin' to you."

"The hell you ain't. Lemme tell you somethin', son. I think you're lightweight talent nobody gives a damn about. I think you're just cannon fodder, a free agent hired by guys who don't care how many players they lose as long as they got their bases covered. Am I gettin' warm?"

"Fuck off."

Another fist to the kidneys.

"I don't have time for this. Who you workin' for — wiseguys or some rich fuck Crowe ripped off?"

Through clenched teeth Buchalter spat: *"Chingada su madre, cabron."*

"My, my — the man speaks a little Tex-Mex."

Burch clucked his tongue, kicked the man's feet out from under him and slammed his face to the floor. He leaned over to whisper in Gerald Dwayne Buchalter's ear.

"My mother's dead, needledick, so I'm particularly sensitive to folks makin' crude remarks about her. One more time — who's paying your fare?"

"Nobody you'd know. Just one of the little folks Crowe ripped off."

"Bullshit. Little folks don't hire muscle or pee-eyes or whatever the fuck you want to call yourself. Little folks don't stumble on a trail this warm unless they're lucky."

"Always been that. Until now."

"Your luck's still holdin'. You ran into me instead of a badass who would've killed you on the spot."

Buchalter, face still kissing the floor, snorted a laugh laced with pain.

"Funny thing about little folks — they can get you just as dead as your regular badass. And seems like everybody wants a piece of this Crowe fella — little folks, badasses, wiseguys. Regular feeding frenzy you got yourself into. You picked me off but there's a dozen other guys playin' the same game. Could be here tonight."

A thought flashed through Burch's mind. *He was watching me, tailing me, not Thanh. He's been on my trail, not Crowe's.*

Burch ran through the places he had been since leaving Jennings' condo that morning — a gun shop on Bissonnet to buy fresh rounds for the Colt; the Racehorse's office to chat up Barton Phillips, the youngster handling Savannah's case; lunch at a Vietnamese joint south of downtown to talk with one of Jennings' contacts about Brother Thanh; a bank for some cash.

Who put this guy on my tail — the colt shyster, Jennings' Oriental buddy or somebody else, one of those little people he's blathering about?

Burch took a shot.

"You tell Barton Phillips I don't need no babysitter — got one already."

Buchalter laughed.

"Right thought, wrong party, handsome. Some folks do want to keep you healthy until they can get Crowe dead though. After that, I wouldn't give you long odds."

Didn't answer my question, asshole. Did tell me you only had eyes for me. And we'll just keep those eyes down here, thank you very much.

Burch unbuckled Buchalter's belt, ran it through his arms and the pipe of a handrail then buckled it snug. He pulled out his bandana and stuffed it in Buchalter's mouth. Then he clubbed him across the back of his skull with his own pistol. Buchalter sagged toward the floor, held by his belt and the guardrail. Burch didn't like his look and wet two fingers, holding them under Buchalter's nostrils. Breath.

"Sorry `bout that."

Burch waved the man a salute and started up the stairway.

Time, son. Time and other players. A linebacker. A third baseman. In burgundy. Could be, son. Could be. Saw him twice. Be nice to brace him once. No time, son. No time.

He knew it would take him ten minutes to take a full turn around the concourse. He knew it was ten minutes he didn't have. He had already wasted five minutes taking care of this problem. He couldn't afford to press his bet. He headed back toward Mr. Slick and Mr. Vu Nguyen Thanh.

He walked straight to a spot where Mr. Slick could see him while staying out of sight of the concession stand. Mr. Slick moved toward him, growing very theatrical, pointing to his watch then spreading his arms in mock aggravation.

"Where the fuck have you been, Charley? You're late and the show's done started."

"Charley?"

"Nice touch, right?"

Mr. Slick was right about the show. Burch could hear the rodeo announcer crank his way through the Grand Entry buildup — *the Tradition, the Cowboy Way, the Excitement, the Wild West, the By-God Americanness of This Time-Honored Spectacle, Buffalo Bill Cody and the Line That Goes Through These Cowboys and Cowgirls Who Are About To Put It All On The Line For You! And now, ladies and gentlemen, will you please stand up for our National Anthem.*

No mention of Manifest Destiny or Wounded Knee. Nothing about the shyster promoters who regularly ripped off the cowboys during rodeo's infancy, back at the turn of the century when rodeo was more of a Wild West circus than a sporting event. Nothing about a hard ride for a short dollar. Even today, in the time of popular madness about all things Country & Western and weekly exposure on ESPN and other cable outlets, the average utility infielder made three times as much money as this year's All-Around Cowboy champ.

"Bout time you got back. Where you been?"

"Checkin' our backs."

"Must've been something out there. You been gone a while."

"One player. Bound, gagged and dreaming."

"Damaged goods?"

"Slightly."

"Anybody else back there?"

"Maybe so. Big guy. Burgundy jacket. Moves like a cat. Didn't have time to check."

"If big man is a player, your move on the other guy was a calling card."

"No shit. But this game's getting too crowded. Thought I'd thin the herd a little."

Mr. Slick nodded.

"What's been happening here?"

"You're about to find out."

Burch turned his head slightly, just enough to put Thanh and the concession stand in the correcting curve of his glasses. A young Vietnamese man, in his twenties with spiky hair, a green Baylor sweatshirt, ripped and faded Levis and black Justins with silver toe caps and ankle chains, walked up to his elder and whispered in his ear.

"That's twice that boy's been here. He ain't workin' behind the counter and he ain't bringin' in stock."

"Setting the table for the meet."

"Be my guess."

Burch's estimation of Mr. Slick went up a notch. The man stayed put and saw things straight. He knew the moves. This didn't make him trustworthy but it did make him a tactical pleasure to work with. It reminded Burch of his days as a Dallas cop, working with guys he didn't particularly like. Two pros could find common ground in the street smarts of the beat cop and share the satisfaction of working well in harness, even if one chewed tobacco and drank bourbon and the other hated the Cowboys and did crochet in his off hours.

One difference between those days and today — Burch was walking on the same dark side of the law as his quarry, looking to take down a man to take his money. He could tell himself he was protecting his client. He could kid himself with the scent of the quarry and its familiar vibes from the days when he wore a badge. But that didn't alter the path he was walking and its intended destination — Crowe and his purse.

Thanh stood up and gave a command to the younger Vietnamese. The younger man nodded his head and turned to leave. Crowd noise rose to a roar, the announcer's voice booming over its peak. People in the hallway stopped in mid-stride, glancing toward the portals and the arena beyond.

"Take the youngster. See where he goes. I'll stick with the bossman."

"You got it."

Burch watched Mr. Slick move into the thin hallway traffic. He was quick — by Burch's side one second, in the middle of the concourse the next. He walked straight past Thanh's stand. He didn't hesitate. He didn't try to put bodies between himself and the subject. With posture and gait, he sold himself as Joe Citizen, just another rodeo fan looking for his section in the stands. Or the men's room.

Another roar. Barebacks or saddle broncs. Rough and crowd-pleasing. But not the roughest. That would be bullriding. And bulls were last. That's when the place would really rock.

Thanh was reaching under the table, his eyes on his business, when Mr. Slick passed. He pulled out a battered gray Samsonite briefcase, plopped it on the table, popped the latches and pulled out a business envelope made of heavy paper the color of bright burley tobacco. Too thin for lots of cash. Thick enough for a downpayment — a bona fide.

The main money would be someplace else. So would the product. An educated guess. The best Burch could do on the fly.

The envelope told Burch one thing — Mr. Vu Nguyen Thanh wasn't going to do this deal by remote control. He was going to do it up close and personal. And that meant Burch hadn't fucked up by siccing Mr. Slick on the youngster. Burch was rolling sixes and sevens, his street instincts carrying him along with ease and rhythm.

Thanh eased behind the women working the stand and slipped

from behind the table. Burch let him look around. The man headed in the opposite direction from the youngster, walking toward Burch.

Burch stayed put, gambling Thanh was doing the same thing he had done. Checking his back. Watching for watchers. He pulled out a pack of Luckies and fired one with the Zippo, giving him a reason for standing there, hoping no one called him for smoking in a public place where it was forbidden by the tyranny of health Nazis. He waited for Thanh to double back, riding that groove of certainty that comes when the street moves run full tide, overriding the conscious mind.

Rising noise that plummeted suddenly, bottoming with a collective note of concern. A cowboy slammed into the dirt just a few seconds into the ride was Burch's guess.

Thanh was out of sight. The Lucky burned his throat and burned toward his knuckles. Doubt started to eat at his certainty.

Easy, hoss. Stay in the groove. Stay put.

Burch looked at the smoke from the Lucky, watching it stream toward the ceiling. It was the perfect pose, a reflex. When he brought his eyes back to the center of the hallway, there was Thanh, moving briskly, with confidence, with business on his mind.

From the curtains behind Thanh's stand stepped a second young Vietnamese man, stocky and sporting black jeans and a black sports coat with thickly padded shoulders and a loose-enough drape to cover the hardware Burch assumed was riding near an armpit.

Jesus. Never saw that fucker. We're blown.

The second youngster joined Thanh in the hallway, smiled, shook his head and gave him a gliding, palms-down gesture straight out of a ZZ Top video.

Thank you, Jesus. You're in the chute now, son. Ride it out.

Burch blew out a smoke-laced breath, dropped the Lucky and ground it out with a twist of his boot. He let the two Asians move toward the first bend in the hallway. He stepped into the flow and trailed along.

He could see them ahead, one eye on them, one eye on making his way past the people in the hall. The Ruger he took from Buchalter, still in his jacket pocket, thumped against his hip as he walked. The arena crowd buzzed — a low thrum that marked the time between rides. The announcer started a bit with a rodeo clown, playing straight man to the clown's obvious punch lines. The sound hit Burch full, then faint, depending on whether he was passing a portal or walking along a solid bulkhead.

The two Asians cut out of the flow and down a side staircase. Burch eyed the people milling and standing near the cut in the wall that opened onto the staircase. He sidled his way past two drunk roughnecks in gimme caps that advertised drilling equipment and thought about easing the Colt out of its holster. He decided not to and hit the staircase. On the wall to the left of the opening, a sign said: Contestants, Concessionaires.

Burch was neither. But he could turn on the good-ol'-boy and bullshit his way past most rent-a-cops, parking lot guards and uniformed flunkies. On a good day. Just like this.

At the end of a hallway walled with concrete block painted the puke yellow of high schools and hospitals, two tables were drawn together with a narrow opening between them. Four middle-aged women, two at each table, sat in folding metal chairs. In front and behind each table stood a guard — Lone Star Security on the shoulder patches, pot-bellies curving over pistol belts and billy clubs.

Milling around either side of this barrier were cowboys with numbered squares pinned to loud print shirts, along with stockmen, friends and hangers-on. He saw Thanh and the younger man disappear behind a bend on the other side of the tables.

Burch picked a young blond-headed competitor wearing a three-digit number, bat-wing chaps, a straw Resistol with a George Strait San Antone roll and crease and the bored look athletes use to cover the butterflies.

"Howdy. You up soon?"

"Naw. I'm in the slack."

"Rough stock or timed?"

"Roper. Calves and team."

"Oh — good deal. You know Bill Huber?"

"Yew bet."

"I owe him some money. I don't suppose you could get me through here."

The cowboy rubbed his jaw and spat on the floor. For a second, Burch thought he had blown it.

"Yew bet."

They walked up to the table. The cowboy arched a thumb at Burch and said: "He's with me." The guards nodded in unison. They passed on through and walked toward the dirt, noise, smells, portable corrals and pawing stock common to the backside of any rodeo. Glaring lights that made you squint. Noise that jacked your blood pressure, made you sweat and made it tough to hear the spoken word.

"'Preciate this. Been awhile since I've been on this side of the chutes."

"My pleasure, mister. Ever cowboy up?"

"No. Too rough for me. Football was my poison. My cousins rode a lot. Real regulars at Mesquite. Didn't do the circuit much. Too busy working the ranch. Real cow hands. I helped them out. Hung around the chutes. Drove the truck. Warmed up their mounts. That kind of thing."

"Mesquite. That's Dallas. Never been there. Heard it's kind of a cocktail party with bulls and broncs as chasers."

"That would be Mesquite. Every Friday night. Great place to get throwed. In and out of the ring. Where you from?"

"Wyoming."

"Got a name?"

"Name's Ken Archer."

Burch shook Archer's hand and gave his real name.

"Tell me somethin', Mr. Burch. You don't really know Bill Huber at all, do you?"

"No, Ken. Not really. Only met him once. At Pocatello. Seemed like a real nice fella."

"Thought so. Ol' Bill don't loan nobody any money that don't ride the circuit."

"Guess you want to know what I'm up to."

"None of my business, mister."

"`Preciate you seein' it that way."

"Yew bet."

Archer tapped the brim of his hat in salute and peeled away from Burch. They parted just behind the corrals holding the rough stock — a series of pens divided by metal pipes that held the bulls and broncs. The dirt was a clumpy, chocolate brown clay-based mixture that covered the concrete he was standing on and the long ramp that sloped between the stands to the heat, humidity and parked stock trailers outside the Dome.

No Thanh. No Asian gunsel in black. No flunky in a green Baylor sweatshirt. No Mr. Slick. No joy, as the jet jocks say. At any angel. Just blue sky and no contrails.

Burch didn't worry. At his eleven o'clock, there was a Pace Arrow RV with a large sign advertising it as headquarters for the Professional Rodeo Cowboys Association, the big league sanctioning body of the sport. At his two o'clock, there was a long red snack trailer with a round Coca-Cola sign centered at the top of its facade. Asian faces worked the counter, serving free cups of Col. Pemberton's Atlanta-grown elixir to the cowboys. In between the two was a short ramp leading to locker rooms. On a metal door to the right side of the ramp was another one of those convenient signs that said: Concessionaires. His gut told him Thanh and his lethal youngsters were behind that door.

The arena was at his eight o'clock. A clown was working a

routine with a donkey and a rubber chicken. Burch couldn't remember the punch line. At his seven, the rough stock chutes — snorting broncs, frantic stockmen, tense riders and cowboys perched like crows on the catwalks and cross beams. At his nine ran a broad pathway between the stands and the arena rail, a link between the rough stock chutes where Burch stood and the chutes for the timed events — bulldogging, calf roping and team roping.

Burch leaned on the cross-pipe of the corral, ignoring the proximity of a dozing brindle-colored bull with the wheelbase of a milk truck, a dropped horn with the curve of a Gurkha fighting knife and the floppy hump that marked him as a Brahma. You could ignore something this big and deadly but you could never lose the feel of sleeping nastiness just inches away from your back.

The feeling braced Burch and relaxed him at the same time. Made him more alert. He enjoyed it. To his left, along the rail, the hardboys of rodeo, the bullriders, flexed, stretched and worked their rigging with rosin. Impossibly small and young-looking, they were gearing up nerve and muscle for the night's finale, short rides on a ton and a half of slobbering meanness. Some rides shorter than others. Or deadlier. Lane Frost's last turn at Cheyenne still burned the collective rodeo memory. A horn to the heart. A dead cowboy in the dirt.

All testosterone and tension up on that stretch of the rail. Rolling necks and eyes. Furious concentration on small items and tiny, practiced gestures. Hard glares for those inside and outside their circle. The pre-game smell of fear that any ex-jock can recognize.

For those faddish folk just surfing the curl of the cowboy craze, this is the Main Event. They may not know how hard it is to rope and ride. They might not appreciate the subtle combination of power and finesse shown by a bulldogger or the flashing skill of a calf roper. But they could plug into the current pumping out of this socket. Sure as hell. It holds the thrill of primal power. The promise of violence and blood. And the strong hint of death.

Big Money could smell the waves of ozone rippling from this electric connection. So could television. Big Action emphasized; the subtler cowboy arts downplayed; rodeo seen through a distorted lens; heroes made out of men ballsy enough to ride a bull but utterly clueless about ranching, cattle, riding and roping. Hanging around his cousins at the Mesquite rodeo, Burch often heard them dismiss the competition with this phrase: "Aw, he ain't what you'd call a real ranch hand — he's just one of them rodeo cowboys." Bravery with the bulls was no guarantee a man could be trusted to cinch up a saddle tight enough not to fall off.

Even the cowboys buy into the distortion, lusting after the cash that is finally flowing into rodeo, cussing the corny clown acts, the kiddy events and the long delays between events. It is a pace ill-suited for the camera's eye, they say, one that harkens back to county fairs, roundups and rodeo's roots in the unique, workaday skills demanded of those who work cattle and its status as the only sport to rise out of a laborer's duties. Rodeo's got to leave the past in the past, they say. Rodeo's got to get modern.

Leaning on the rail of a corral at the Astrodome with a few tons of rough stock at his back, Burch didn't feel the need to defend the tradition of rodeo. He felt at home, at ease among people girding themselves for a hard, hard sport. But he knew he had to move. To his rear, sitting in a spot that was tucked next to the mouth of the ramp he just passed through, was a horse trailer with its rear doors open, an awning propped up over the back and an old man shoveling manure and soiled hay out of the stalls. Burch walked over.

"Need some help?"

"No sir. Got her covered."

"Mind if I perch myself here?"

The old man stopped his work. He leveled a look at Burch.

"What's your business, son?"

"I need a clear view of that door and that snack stand."

"You the law?"

"Used to be. Kind of now. Been trailin' some Vietnamese gentlemen."

"Well you just missed two of `em. Young guy in black and that older one with the cigarette holder. Must think he's F-D-goddam-R. Went through that door over there. Slopes been goin' in and out of there all night like a bunch of ants. Don't like the looks of them sumbitches. Didn't kill enough of `em when we were over there if you ask me. Have a seat."

The old man gestured at a stack of overturned feed buckets in the shadow of the awning. Burch spotted a gimme cap on a hook just inside the door. He grabbed it — a sweat-stained red number with Carnation Feed scripted in white across the front — slapped it on his head and sat down. A small change in profile.

The old man went back to work. And didn't say another word.

SEVENTEEN

For most people, on the majority of the days that make up their lives, the world is a chaotic place that assaults them as they struggle to get to work, feed the kids, find love or seek out a quiet place to turn it all off and breathe an unharried breath. Too many choices, too much feedback, too many snarling dogs and snappish humans.

All this just on the days when true disaster doesn't strike — a car wreck that kills your spouse, a tornado that threshes your house into matchsticks and lost memories, a child molester wearing the cloak of a trusted coach striking your brood, a gangbanger deciding your head would make an excellent target while he rides down a traffic-clogged interstate and decides to practice using the new gun he just stole.

But there are times when the world narrows down to an essence or a simplicity — the sure cut of a running back as a hole opens up in a line of thudding bodies, the moment a buck steps into the crosshairs and a hunter squeezes the trigger or lets the arrow fly, the first shot in a firefight, the defenseless afterglow of an orgasm that lets love pierce a hardened heart.

For Burch, the world became a suddenly narrow place when he spotted the flash of a green Baylor sweatshirt heading down the locker room ramp. Two cowboys obscured his vision. They parted and Burch could see that the sweatshirt was on the body of the first young Vietnamese kid he saw at Thanh's T-shirt stand. The youngster was leading a tall, trim gray-haired man with a deep-water tan, a military haircut and the wounded stride of an ex-jock with bad knees.

Burch was still in the shadow of the awning. He pushed away panic and the desire for sudden movement. He pushed away this thought: *Where's Mr. Slick?*

He fought very hard to sit still and watch. Before he walked into the arena, he'd been in the groove and felt the calm that instinctive sureness brings. While he was leaning against the corral, feeling the tension of the bullriders and the napping malevolence of the bull, he'd been alert and relaxed.

But sitting at the back end of this horse trailer, with the rise and fall of the crowd noise and the nagging desire to see what was happening in the center of the arena, out there in the dirt, beyond the pennants, banners and cowboys who perched on the superstructure of pipes and catwalks above the chutes, Burch became antsy. He couldn't find a place to rest his hands. He couldn't find a position that didn't hurt his butt. A thin ridge of plastic cut into each ass cheek.

Burch forced himself to become very still. The man with the gray brush cut was Crowe. No doubt. Now that his quarry was in sight, he wanted to leap out and kill it. Or tackle it — a full-bore, hat-on-hat hit, a total pancake. He was fighting old cop and ballplayer instincts and even older fight-or-flight reflexes that man has carried since emerging from the primal ooze. See the perp, nail him. See the ballcarrier, drill him. See the prey, kill it. See the predator, run.

To get Crowe's money, Burch had to get Crowe. To get Crowe, he had to be patient. He had to wait. While the deal went down behind the closed door and the roar of the rodeo crowd thrummed through his bones and left him jangled and edgy.

The barrel racers were running: Hard-charging women with wild eyes, thick-muscled thighs and teeth clamped around braided leather quirts, thundering into the arena on fast cow ponies. Speed, power and finesse from their mounts. A dirt dance around the barrels. A flat-out sprint through the spaces in between. Not that Burch could see them. The omnipotent voice of the announcer gave Burch an update he couldn't avoid. The images running through Burch's mind turned the peg on his wired nerves.

Burch did what the techno-cops call a risk assessment. A threat analysis. Keep it simple for the redneck challenged — Who the hell can shoot your ass?

A sure bet was the youngster in Baylor colors — a pistol in the waistband covered by that oversized sweatshirt. At least one gun behind the door with Thanh if the youngster in the stylish black jacket was there. Crowe would also be packing. But not the ever-elegant Thanh; he wouldn't soil his manicured hands with clunky hardware. He would get close with his blade and go for the throat. Or the back. Two main players and a skeletal supporting cast. In a very public place that gave comfort to both of them.

That strengthened Burch's hunch about the envelope Thanh took from the briefcase. Burch imagined the rest of the set up. Thanh handing the envelope to Crowe with a sheaf of cash inside; Crowe giving Thanh a sample of the goods. A ritual and prelude to the real deal, a trade of bona fides that symbolized shared risk.

Burch figured the product was elsewhere and so was most of the money. Crowe and Thanh would go to the product and money to complete the transaction face to face. Very risky for Crowe but he needed his hands on the cash. Now.

Burch didn't know if he could tail them all the way to the trade and didn't know how much cash he could scoop up if he did. Didn't matter. He did know he could be a human wrecking ball, smashing Crowe's emergency pipeline and leaving that arrogant asshole naked and alone against that killer conga line. It would have to do.

Sudden darkness. The Astrodome in a blitz blackout. Burch's heart lurched. He felt the tilting pitch of vertigo. Laser lights flashed and stabbed the stands. Like tracer in a firefight. Strobes stuttered. The announcer started a rumbling intro, his voice booming the bass notes. Crowd noise ratcheted up to jet turbine level.

Bulls and the snuff-dipping samurai who ride them. He worried about losing his quarry in the dark. He rose from his seat and edged toward the corral, straining to see the door closed on the deal going down between Crowe and Thanh. He pitched the borrowed cap onto the pile of overturned feed buckets.

Bulls banged the pipes. Burch jumped then steadied himself. Stockmen cussed as they coaxed bulls from the pens and into the narrow alleyways that circled left and right and led to the rear of the chutes. Working his way toward the door, Burch felt this action more than he saw it — lighter space where darker bulk stood just a second before, the shadowy dodge of the stockman, the zapping sound of a cattle prod, the smell of burned hide and hair. And fresh bullshit — a natural form of protest.

Burch stood at the last angle of the corral, the corner closest to the door. The lasers stopped. So did the announcer's voice. The crowd noise fell to a long yammer and a constant buzz, one part beehive, the other part jackhammer.

Strong spotlights flooded the chutes and the first quarter of the ring. The glare blinded Burch — a garish white that struck the chopped up dirt, the mounted pickup men, the red-and-white barrel and the two clown-suited bullfighters, one sitting on top of the barrel, the other in the feet-apart stance of a linebacker, standing on the balls of his feet, hands dangling between his thighs, about five yards in front of the first gate that was about to boom open with the twisting bulk of a bull and rider.

He felt buck naked and exposed. The chute gate clanged like a car clipping a guardrail. The crowd noise pierced his ears and bored into his chest. He moved forward and to his right to get out of the light, glancing to his left and the center of the arena.

Quick snapshots in shadows and glare.

The brindle bull, rump high in the air, shit smearing its butt, tongue out and slobber flying as it twists its head upward and to the right, trying to hook a horn into the rider. An overmatched cowboy in a white shirt with a blue flame across the chest, already behind the curve, black hat flying forward, head snapping back, out of synch and one buck away from a drilling in the dirt.

Burch veers toward the Coke stand, his face toward the door, letting his light-shocked eyes pick up the grays and blacks of the shadows again. The door opens. Two figures fill the brightened frame. Burch reaches inside his jacket and clears the Colt, thumbing off the safety and easing into a two-handed grip and a combat shuffle.

An empty doorway. Two new figures in the frame. A flash of brushy gray tops the one to Burch's left. He steps forward slowly, shifting his head so his peripheral vision can pick up the first two figures — the young guns, in a black trapezoid between the glare of the arena and the light from the door and the Coke stand.

Two more steps. His eyes pick up the young guns. One is heading toward the locker room ramp. The other faces the pens. Twenty yards between him and them. Crowe and Thanh step through the door.

An opening.

Speed, shadows and glare. More noise than Burch can stand, noise that thrums through his chest and makes him open and close his mouth as if his jaw hinge is stuck.

Ten yards. Now five.

Two far figures starting to turn toward him. Two near figures catching the pause and shift of their guardians. A half turn from the older men. Burch, out of the shuffle and in full stride, clubbing Thanh with the Colt, catching him just above and behind the left ear, dropping him like a month's worth of laundry on a rainy Sunday.

A body slam into Crowe. A grunt of pain. A chop to his gun hand. A bright piece of metal in the dirt. The Colt shoved against Crowe's temple. A hammerlock around his throat.

"Don't move, asshole. Call off the dogs."

"Not mine to call off, asshole."

"Do it."

"Fuck off, needledick. They don't give a shit about me. You just clocked the guy that cuts their checks."

The young guns split to Burch's right and left, closing the distance, making it harder to cover them both. Burch points the Colt at Thanh's head. A sudden stop. Freeze frame for five while the rodeo world flowed around them — the white brightness of the arena, the cascading crowd noise, a pack of cowboys and cowgirls, all hats and arena jackets, stepping from the Coke stand and flowing around the two guns.

The freeze frame melts.

Movement at Burch's feet — Thanh shifting from collapsed heap to the hands and knees stance of a crawling baby. A glance from Burch. A shift and a slight involuntary easing of the hammerlock. A hard elbow into Burch's gut. A turn and Crowe's open hand slamming into Burch's chin, snapping his head back, breaking his grip, shoving him back.

The young guns, moving fast, fanning their pistols toward Burch. Thanh up and in Burch's face, blade in hand. Crowe breaking away, bending toward his gun in the dirt. Burch fending off a knife thrust with his left arm, swinging the Colt toward Thanh's body, stepping in and under the rush.

White flashes and sharp cracks. Slugs slapping into Thanh's back, lead from the young guns, slamming his body into Burch. Burch catching the body with his right shoulder, aiming for Baylor green that his eyes see only as a lighter shade of gray.

Two booming rounds from the Colt, bass notes cutting through the river roar from the stands. Baylor down in the dirt. Another crack and flash from the young gun in black. Hot pain stabbing the right forearm. The Colt up and over the back of Thanh with his left hand. Sights center on the rush of black leather.

Two loud bass notes, slamming a duo of Flying Ashtrays into the black center of the body. Arms, head and legs fly forward, curling around the chest and abdomen. Mouth flashes a full oval of surprise. A sliding seat in the dirt. The body topples to the right.

Lights and the rise and fall of oohs, aaahs, whistles, hoots and yells, tracking the arena action, not the sideshow behind the chutes. Movement in the corral. Not bulls. Not broncs. No hatted stockmen. A stumbling unfamiliarity to the motion. A flash of brushy gray and a figure perched on the second set of pipes, backlit by the arena glare.

A grimace through the pain from his right arm. Boots on pipe. Burch up and over. Pushing through rumps, horns and hooves. A rolling eye. A snort. A bellow. Dodgy steps. A whack on the rump. A smack on the snout. The smell of piss and shit. Slogging through slop.

A shout from a stockman. Broncs in the next pen, heads bobbing, bodies cutting and weaving. Crowe in the middle, picking his way past the moving stock. Burch with boots on pipe, hauling himself up to the top.

A pop and a flash of white from Crowe's right hand. A sizzling sound zipping near Burch's left ear. A clumsy fall into the next pen. Pain in arm and knee, shooting into the roof of his mouth. Hooves and hocks, up close and way too personal. Snorts, whinnies and the sweet-rot smell of horse.

Crowe already clambering over the far rail, pulling himself onto the catwalk just behind the chutes. A cowboy's hand on Crowe's arm. A pistol in the cowboy's face. The cowboy backing off, hands in the air. Burch slamming through the broncs, bouncing and stumbling, short of breath, blood pounding in his ears, muffling the sound from the stands.

The last rail of pipes. Cowboys looking down from their perch on the catwalk. Cowboys looking at Crowe, clambering over an active chute. Suspended motion — a gloved hand left unwrapped, a cowbell left dangling and unsecured, a rider's concentration broken. Looks of fear, confusion, anger.

Burch. Boots on pipe.

"You can't come up here, mister. We got a rodeo goin'."

"Let'm up."

"Hell no."

"Let'm up. He's after that other sumbitch."

"You law, mister?"

A nod from Burch. Gloved hands pulling him up to the catwalk.

"Git that sorry bastard. Sumbitch stuck a damn pistol in my face."

A familiar face. Archer. The roper from Wyoming. Confusion for Burch. A roper behind the rough stock chutes. An oddity. Ropers belong at the other end of the arena. Behind the second set of chutes. A flash of memory — Archer in the slack, his turn won't come until after the bulls. Archer takes Burch's arm, turns and yells.

"Let'm through, boys. Let'm through."

"We got a rider goin' out there, Ken. Can't do it."

"Let the man through."

To his left, a chute bangs open. Bull and rider slam into the ring. A parting of cowboys on the catwalk. Helping hands. Burch stumbling across an active chute, stepping on pipe, then bullflesh, then pipe, bending down to steady himself.

To his right, at the far edge of his vision, a big man in burgundy bulls his way toward the small gate cowboys use to exit the arena after their ride. Linebacker. Third baseman. Third time's the charm. A player.

A quick look into the glare. Bull twisting. Rider snapping forward. Crowe to the right, dodging. Burch over the gate, thudding down on the thick chopped-up clay. Eye to rump with a bull the color of a Siamese cat, the size of a runaway pickup. Rushing bulk. Clay and shit strike Burch in the face.

Burch cuts left, looks for Crowe. Crowe heads for the clown in the barrel, the sides banded with chipped red-and-white paint. A pickup man spurs his horse toward Crowe. Crowe points the pistol. The pickup man reins in but blocks Crowe's path.

Five yards. No breath. Lungs searing. Gray on the edge of the vision. Ears feel packed with cotton stuffing. Burch barrels into Crowe. Pistols fly to the dirt. So does a fat rectangle of brown paper. Burch on top, clawing his way up Crowe's body, fighting to pin an arm or make a face eat sand and clods of clay.

Crowe twists. A knee to Burch's groin. A forearm shot to the chest. Burch rolls, staggers to his feet. Crowe is up, grabbing for his pistol. The envelope is between them. A yell from the right. The big man in burgundy, in the arena, arm rigid and pointing at Burch, aims a chrome-plated revolver. Linebacker. Third baseman. I'm dead.

Four quick pops. Four dark blossoms on the big man's chest. He pitches forward, dropping his gun. Crowe and Burch frozen in place.

Fast-rolling bulk to Burch's right. A rush. The sound of hooves. The split-second awareness a ballplayer gets when he is about to get blindsided.

The hit. The smacking sound of horn on bone. Burch airborne. Flying to his left. Vision jarred and blurred.

No noise. No glare. Just black.

EIGHTEEN

The room had that quick and final hush, like the sudden silence after a car wreck — before the sirens and the cries of pain, just after the echoes of tires and grinding metal die somewhere above in the air.

You could listen to it and learn. Cider Jones did, stepping through the front door of a small bungalow built in the Craftsman style — low-browed lintel, stone cairns bracing the roof of the porch, twin dormers with windows dark and dead, a driveway snaking from the street and toward a cracked concrete apron in back. The bare-dirt backyard downhill from the house to a border of scrub oak, thick brush and a molasses-colored slough.

The house sat on a no-hope dead-ender west of the whizzing traffic clipping along Fidelity Street and south of Jacinto City, isolated from the rest of what used to be a robust enclave of steel mill workers and Ship Channel dock hands.

The green sign on the corner said Kerr Street and Cider knew its history — a partner from his days as a blue grew up here and used to talk fondly of bubba daddies, grimy and sweat-stained, coming home to doughy wives and packs of children. It used to be a place where everybody knew who got too drunk on Saturday night and slapped their wives around and who slipped out to the icehouses on Holland Avenue and slept around while hubby pulled a graveyard shift.

Kerr Street was new Asian immigrants now — Cambodians mostly, refugees from Khmer Rouge genocide. Bent and broken Anglos too poor to move away. And the odd biker or two.

It would be a lie to call it a neighborhood.

But it wouldn't be much of a stretch to see it as a great place to get lost in, an urban rat's nest where nobody cared who came and went and everybody kept to themselves. Unless you were a threat to them and theirs.

Cider stood at the front edge of a tidy, threadbare living room, boots on scarred, clean-swept hardwood, left hand on the arm of a well-worn couch covered in a dull, scratchy fabric of black-and-red plaid. The couch served as a divide between the living room and the wall of the front bedroom, forming an alley that ran from the front door, past the open archway to the kitchen and on to the hallway that led to the back of the house.

He looked at a man who would no longer be a threat to anybody. Or their kin.

The body sprawled across a large rug with a machine-woven Navajo blanket pattern in the same colors as the couch. Pistol near an upturned right hand, watch on the underside of the wrist, pilot style. Head toward Cider, angled away from his right boot. Trunk and legs cutting a rough diagonal across the rug.

Face up.

Or what was left of a face. The lower jaw was blown away. A bloody maw under a bald pate. Close range. Shotgun blast. Buckshot or a deer slug. A one-shot kill. Splatters of blood and bone on one of the front windows and the far corner of the front wall. In that same corner, a matte-chrome Mini-14 leaned in the angle just below the splatters. Blood darkened the rug's lighter-shaded panels.

Which put the shooter in the narrow, hardwood alley in front of Cider and to his left. Cider listened and slowed his breathing. He panned his gaze from the body to the spot where the shooter stood.

It happened in his mind's eye:

A quick spin to a sound or a sense, gun up, but not quick enough; the head shot and the metallic shiiing-shiiing of a fresh round racked into a riot pump; the turn toward the second target moving up the hallway from the back of the house.

A spin by the shooter. A full ninety degrees to the left. Two shots down the hallway. Quick strides on the hardwood. Another fresh round in the chamber. No movement from the target. No need to break the sudden hush.

Which would put a second body in the shadows of the hallway, heels toward him, head pointed toward the bathroom and back bedroom.

"There's a second stiff back in that hallway, lieutenant."

A blue by his elbow.

"I know. Make sure the techs and the M.E. are on the way. And give me some room, okay? I'll get back to you in a bit."

"You bet."

This was one of the many ways he missed Cortez. His partner had a knack for chatting up blues, getting the scene-setting information from the ones who caught the call while keeping them out of Cider's face. Now that he worked alone, Cider couldn't indulge his mystic side without keeping part of himself rooted in reality. And he couldn't be so focused on his inner visions that he forgot his manners and came off like an asshole to fellow officers.

Usually he talked to the blues before he entered a crime scene, clearing his real-world decks. But he was out of synch on this one, his internal tuning fork vibrating before he hit the door. He knew he was already in that special place that flowed from his Comanche ancestry, a private zone of the spirit where the eyes of the dead told him things and ghostly zephyrs gave him clear mental images of recent violence.

Cider forced the blue and memories of his dead partner out of his mind, filing the details for later. He felt himself float back into the zone. He edged around the couch and into the alley, hunting for a light switch when he reached the lip of the hallway.

Dim light — a forty-watter instead of a hundred. No smoke — Cortez was dead and so were his cigs. A body already in his mind's eye. A black man, heavily muscled across the chest and through the arms — Aaron Neville without the gris-gris bag, the ear cuff, the mole on the forehead or the sweet, soulful voice. The body had something the New Orleans singer would never want — a pair of bloody blossoms, lung high.

Gun still in the shoulder holster. Caught flat-footed. Time enough to get a surprised look on the face and get blown back down the hallway.

His mind's eye:

Black man heading down the hallway, his back to the shooter. Single blast from a shotgun, kill shot taking down bald guy in the living room. Time enough for a turnaround. Two rounds to the chest.

Cider went into a squat, gazing into the dead man's empty eyes. In the zone. Diving into the sightless stare. The eyes held him. The eyes and what they told him.

Threat. Vigil. Calm and quiet. Confidence. Everything covered. Looking outward, not inward. Electric shock. The unexpected.

A voice: Who you serve is who kills you. Who you shield is who cuts you down.

"Hey — Lt. Jones — the techs are here."

The blue. In the open doorway. Cider snapped out of the zone. He noticed the flashing lights of a marked unit, framed by the door, for the first time.

"Thanks. Hey — I forgot my manners. What's your name?"

"Bondurant."

Real world details from the blue:

An anonymous call. Gunfire. Address given. This blue in a solo unit. A two-man unit as backup. Tense silence. Careful approach. An open back door. Nobody home but two stiffs. Scene secured. Two backup blues canvassing the neighborhood. Nobody stepping forward.

Real world details he didn't need to be told:

Two dead men expecting trouble. But not from the quarter where the killer came. Packing heat in shoulder holsters. Other weapons within easy reach. A Mini-14 with a thirty-round banana mag and flash suppressor — a handy, close-quarters weapon that was no longer street legal, thanks to Slick Willy and the Assault Weapons Ban. And on the shelves of a bookcase built into one living room wall, the glowing red lights of electronics that didn't look like stereo equipment to him. Sensor monitors, maybe. And a night scope, definitely.

Cider's head was down. The blue cleared his throat. Cider didn't look up.

"Thanks for your help."

"You bet."

Cider didn't see the blue shake his head in disgust. He was listening to a voice repeat a two-sentence message:

Who you serve is who kills you. Who you shield is who cuts you down.

NINETEEN

Her brain felt like cabbage force-fed into the whirring blades of a food processor, the high electric noise plummeting into a choked baritone as metal cuts into the pile of pale vegetation, then rising again as the resistance is overwhelmed and the shredding is consummated, automatic and well beyond the control of anyone who should want to suddenly stop it and make things whole again.

The roar of a shotgun in her ear. A sudden spasm of nerves and muscle. A fight to keep the car on the road.

She saw a flashing image of the swift, sure hands of one of those PBS chefs, deftly making a Cuisinart do its humming dance. On her gray matter, her nerves and all those neurons, synapses and electrochemical neurotransmitters that drive any animal's machine.

Julia Child as Vishnu the Destroyer. Graham Kerr as Old Scratch. Justin Wilson as Cerberus. But this wasn't an amusing PBS half hour with the fatass Joo-stan and his red suspenders and overcooked Cajun act or the tittering wit of the Galloping Gourmet. Not that the repackaged, health-conscious and teetotaling version of that over-the-top Aussie made her laugh anymore. He was a better act as a drunk. And what was on her tongue definitely didn't have the taste of the best blackened piece of life experience she ever put in her mouth. I-gar-ron-tee you d'at, Joo-stan.

The shotgun's roar. A smaller flinch. No loss of motor skills or automotive control. Eddie's voice in her ear:

What this is, Slick, is a hard dose of what you call your True Life. You get your expectations reversed, your plans ripped and tattered. You get snapped back from your dreams and delusions and nice, neat blueprints and have to look at something mean right in its bloodshot eyes. You do sumthin' stupid or bad then have to deal with it straight up. No chaser. Scary bidness, this True Life, Slick. There ain't no channel selector. There ain't no on-off switch. And there ain't no instant replay.

Sad Eddie the sucker. So willing to be used. So easy for her to use. A sorry loser with the saloon sport's gift of twirling world-weary phrases around painfully obvious facts. A tiger in the sack, despite his gut and gray hairs. But life as an aging studhoss wasn't making him any wiser or smarter. His heart still followed his cock, setting him up for the easy falls most men his age were able to avoid.

Savannah's rules: Good sex can be found on any bar rail or street corner. Killer sex doesn't mean True Love. And being able to deliver and receive world-class rack time doesn't make you a Good Person or a desirable Life Partner. Sex is a weapon or a tool. And sometimes it's just pure, nasty fun.

But Eddie's phrases sure fit this deal. Wherever the hell he was right now. Hopefully lost and clueless about her present location. Maybe dead if he crossed her loving husband. Surely dead if he joined up with her again; a partner didn't fit in her life view of wealth, sun and sand. And a fat, bald defrocked homicide detective wasn't enough to shield her from Jason Willard Crowe now that her husband was wise to her moves so early in the game. What's a speed bump to a Mack truck running full bore? She shivered and replayed a sad sucker's words.

Your True Life. No channel selector. No on-off switch. No instant replay.

Just the sound of a shotgun in her mind — like Uncle Milo in a duck blind down home. Just copper pennies and old sweat socks on her tongue and an endless feeling that her master controls had been sliced and diced beyond recognition, hashed into coleslaw by the high fear she felt while cooped up with Carl and Benito. Fear and the sure conviction that Crowe had suddenly gained control of a game designed by her but mastered by him. The clock wouldn't run out and the gun wouldn't sound until he found her and killed her.

He was relentless. And cold. Colder than bare feet left too long on the stony bottom of a rushing mountain creek. Once that thrilled her; she fancied that her fire would melt his ice pack and cause him to turn from the track traced by his will to the one deftly drawn by her. He was a just a man. And every man who got in close quarters with her did what she wanted.

Eventually.

And eventually she took what she wanted and left them in the dirt — long before they were wise to her, long before they were tired of her addicting ways. In bed, in a bar, in everyday life. In all the ways she was fiery and intoxicating and kept men wanting more than she would ever give.

Except this man. Her husband. Her destroyer — a mirror icy and dark that forced her to look inward at what she feared the most. Down deep where the nasties crawl and fly about, the psychic snakes and gargoyles, the towering shadows of things a person tries to forget but cannot — Uncle Milo's cooing voice and his fingers sliding inside the waistband of her Quick Draw McGraw pajamas; a stab of pain in the dark; the bottomless shame; the shouts, crashes and thumps of dad and mom too drunk and too locked into their nightly love-hate dance to notice what was happening to their daughter; the unquenchable urge to get even and prove her worth by besting men.

In business, in banter, in bed. Or with a shotgun in the early morning mist, at the raggedy edge where a farmer's field and the woods meet. And they thought Uncle Milo died in a hunting accident, from a shot fired by mistake through the fog.

No mistake. A dead uncle. But it didn't even the score or kill her need to constantly prove her worth. That she always had to do. To keep the snakes and gargoyles in their cages. To stay out of the shadows of those locked away memories. To keep herself in the sunshine, whole and untouched by the men whose lives she entered and the chaos she left in her wake.

Then she met Jason Willard Crowe. Sex, drugs, money and a high-wire lifestyle. Standing toe-to-toe with the biggest challenge she ever met in a man, one she was stubbornly confident she could overcome. She would outlast him. She would wear him down. That's what she always thought. Until she realized she never would. Until it dawned on her that she was the one whose psychic defenses were slowly eroding, exposing those nasty psychological innards.

She knew she had to get away. And she knew she had to beat Crowe at something, best him somehow. Take his money and take him at his own game. That would leave him in the dust like the others. That would give her a hunk of his power. And cold cash was far tastier than eating the heart of the vanquished.

It was so smooth and easy. She knew he was running a big scam of some sort. She saw him spending a lot of time on his laptop. She knew that he saw her as a techno-peasant who took little interest in the whispery electronics of computers. To keep him thinking that way, she kept up her constant barrage of barbed comments about the cyber-slaves of the Information Age, about the master surfers of the Internet not knowing how to have a face-to-face conversation in a cafe, about the emasculating nature of machines and technology.

"That computer's making you a eunuch."

He would smile and say: "It's making me money. And you know how hard I get at the thought of money."

"That doesn't do me much good."

"It would if you'd bring your mouth and cunt over here."

"Why? You've got that little gray machine. Stick it there, hon. Get a hum job."

A head slap before sex. Rough and raw in the rack. As it always was between them. Part of the plan to keep him lulled. Along with standard firefights over money, drugs and the latest recruits for his nose candy and limited partnership service. No sweetness and light. That would make him suspicious.

The next step was also smooth and easy. A girlfriend with a brother who was a grad student at Rice, a hacking wizard with a trust fund, a grunge wardrobe full of plaid flannels, ripped jeans and Phillies Blunt T-shirts, a wedge of lank blond hair that hung over his left eye and was cut razor close on his neck, a roll-out-of-bed-and-roll-one lust for high-powered Texas tea. A cover story that was perfect because it was the truth — a need to leave Jason, a need to find his hidden assets. The hushed excitement of a conspiracy.

She slipped the brother backup diskettes from her husband's laptop. She found the numbers to data lines Jason regularly dialed up. Both gave the brother the toehold he needed to penetrate her husband's computerized world and find out what he was up to.

What he found was a shock to them both. She assumed it would be stock and commodity trades. It was much bigger. Millions instead of thousands. A systematic flow from American accounts to a rat's nest of offshore depositories, screened by a series of business entities with unrelated names — Antilles Ex-Im, Ltd.; Zaxxon Exploration, Inc.; West Texas Leather & Boot; Westheimer Realty; Tres Hombres Enterprises.

And the weak point. The Dominican account. Easily accessed by the hacker.

He was easily kept on a leash.

He didn't want money — he had scads of old oil and ranch bucks rolling in from the trust fund. He grooved on the technical challenge and the illicit nature of their little venture. And he was glassy-eyed about fucking her. He had a long, thin cock and loved for her to grease it up with Vaseline and let him slide it into her ass. He would pump hard, his breath hissing with each thrust.

Just before he came, he would cry out: "Say hello. Say hello. Say hello. Say hello."

Like a parrot on a Key West lampost.

Then, as he pulled out and shot semen on the cheeks of her ass: "There it is. There it is. There it issssss . . ."

She could see his cock, twitching with a life of its own, arcing out below the fish-white muscles of his belly, rising toward the falling wave of his greasy hair. She could hear him hissing above and behind her. She eased into the feeling, flowing with the erotic image and sound memory, letting it work on the blown fuses of her circuitry and crowd out the flashing hands of those TV chefs and that high fear that made her gag on the taste of pennies and socks.

A shotgun roar. The *shiiing-shiiing* of pumping metal. Carl's face. Then pulp. Benito. Rushing toward her. Then sailing back, leaving his "Oh!" of surprise like a string of black holes in the hallway. Uncle Milo, rising out of the mist. Then gone. A roar. A scream. Her scream.

Horns blowing, sound rising and falling in a real-life Doppler demonstration. Her head snapped around. Her eyes darted toward the mirror. She took several deep breaths, exhaling fully.

The car drifted into the slow lane. Eyes searching for a place to pull off. The parking lot of a machine shop — broken concrete in front of a rust-pocked Quonset hut, a single lamp casting weak light on the corner nearest the door.

She wheeled the car into the lot, wincing as the tires crunched over shards of glass. A pop as loud as a pistol shot. A bottle busted by steel-belteds. Spasmed muscles and a stab of the foot on the brake pedal, juddering the car to a nose-down stop.

Head in hands, eyes closed.

"Jesus, girl — get a fucking grip on yourself."

The door yanked open. A warm, wet blast of air overcoming the refrigerated interior, steaming the car windows. Her head jerked back by the hair.

"How `ya doin', miss. Mind if I drive?"

A broad round face. The smell of wet leather. A flash of silver. Fists slam into the side of her face and head. Another roar. Pain, this time. Then black nothing.

TWENTY

It hurt to scratch his nose. When he tried to shift his weight from one cheek of his ass to the other, it felt like God was trying to filet his guts from his ribcage. He didn't bother trying to smile.

The right side of his face was hot and swollen, his right eye partially shut. His right shoulder was heavily bandaged. When he moved, he felt something grinding under the gauze, felt it in his teeth and his skull. It triggered a spiraling wave of nausea.

He was awake but groggy, unaware of ever being out, slowly realizing he was feeling pain through several wavy layers of pharmaceutical protection that distanced his brain from the sources of hurt, blunting their sharp rebukes when he moved the wrong way. Which every way seemed to be.

The light was institutionally harsh. It hurt his eyes in the way rays from a fluorescent tube always do.

The room was painted a custardy yellow, a color common to hospitals and college dorms. Since night school was the closest Burch ever got to college and those sessions were more than fifteen years in his past, back when he used to wear a detective's badge in Dallas, he figured he was in a hospital. But the narcotics made that deduction a tiresome bit of mental lifting.

He had the morphine slows, which was fine by him. Moving fast only brought on pain. And pain just made it tough for him to get comfortable on this rock-hard hospital bed. He wished somebody would turn off that light above his head. He wished that somebody would be whoever was talking to him at that moment, saying something he couldn't quite understand, in a voice coming from a place he couldn't see without turning his body.

He listened but the words didn't make any sense. They drifted in and out, like a bedside radio turned on low after midnight, picking up a wavering signal bouncing in from half a continent away.

Something popped in his head. The signal became clear and strong.

". . . you're fallin' and there ain't no net for you now. Whistlin' right on through the clouds and down toward that hard, hard earth. Ain't a friend in sight to catch you this time. No sir. No Racehorse. No colt of his. Gotta hand it to you though. Sure picked a splashy way to fuck up — shootin' up the Astrodome in the middle of a rodeo. In front of God and everybody and an arena full of bullriders. Couldn't have fucked yourself any worse if you'd pissed on the Alamo Mission . . ."

Burch wished he could switch stations. He couldn't. The voice played on. Like a sermon your grandmother listened to every Sunday. Just before she sent half her money to the preacher who owned the static-laced voice.

". . . got to give you style points for your shootin' eye, too. Dusted those slants. With that Colt, too. Must have that thing tuned pretty tight to shoot that good with. Sure ain't no GI Colt you're carryin'. Army sidearms used to rattle worse than my goddam knee — that's gospel . . ."

Burch couldn't stand it. He clenched his jaw and rolled toward the voice. Its owner sat in the corner nearest his right shoulder, in the shadows beyond the arc of the light above Burch's head.

"Do me a favor, Slick — shut the fuck up."

A laugh from the voice.

"You back with the livin', huh? Good. Good. You need to relax. Save your strength. Now where was I? Oh yeah . . ."

Burch moaned.

"Man who can shoot is still somebody in this state. That's a savin' grace. Particularly if he shoots somebody who isn't too popular. Which applies big time in your case, maybe the only lucky thing you got goin'. Everybody hates those boat folks from Vietnam. Everybody — bubbas, blacks, Mexes. Helps that they shot you too. Hell, it helps that they shot their own boss. How'd ya' arrange that? Got them to shoot their own boss. I can hear the Racehorse argue it now: `Ladies and gen'lemen of the jury, my client is the injured party here. People were tryin' to kill him . . .' "

"Who the fuck are you?"

"Aw, you know me. You know me real good. You wrapped me up nice and warm with my dead partner's jacket one time. You remember. Out by that bat cave in the Hill Country. Me shot up by that big spade with the high squeaky voice who killed your ex wife. Killed my partner too. Been blamin' you for that one. Blamin' you for years, son. Wanted to see you get the Big Needle for that. Not right of me, maybe. But somebody ought to pay for Cortez."

"Someone did, shithead. The spade."

"Aw, that don't count. Guys like that are forces of nature. Like tornadoes. Like hurricanes. Evil does what it's gonna do, son. And you can't pin the blame on evil any more than you can a hurricane. Naw, you got to get below the surface of things. Get to the cause of the matter — the thing that puts stuff into play. The who that puts evil into play. And in that case, it was you and that crazy Tennessee blonde. You were the cause. You two were the damn catalyst. Not the spade."

Floating up through the haze of hospital narcotics, Burch saw an image — Carla Sue Cantrell, the crazy Tennessee blonde, a big .45 in her tiny hand, pointed at his head the first time they met. Carla Sue, with that North Dallas snooty-girl accent dropping into the flat slap and twang of a pure up-holler grit when she got pissed or enthusiastic about something. Or when she was about to kill somebody.

Which she did. Quite often during their run across Texas and into Mexico seven years ago, gunning for a half-Mex, half-oil-field-trash drug lord named Teddy Roy Bonafacio who had killed her uncle, outrunning the law and T-Roy's hired guns. She blew T-Roy down with a clipful of slugs from his Colt to keep that sorry bastard from slicing Burch's heart out of his chest.

Saw her one more time, down on the border, in the Big Bend country. He was in trouble again and she helped him climb out of it, killing a few *hombres* what needed killing. She also left him with a bittersweet memory. Hadn't seen her since.

Carla Sue's image floated into a slow fade, like smoke curling from a Lucky. Burch was back in the hospital room, but lost. The voice was silent. Burch looked at the wheeled tray poised above his lap and saw his Zippo and a fresh pack of Luckies. He reached for the smokes and winced, the pain holding his hand in mid-air, halfway from its destination.

"You want a cig? I'll do that."

An arm and a hand reaching. A Lucky on his lip. Flame and smoke. The head and body above and behind him, out of his field of vision. Burch blew out a stream of smoke and rested his head on the pillow.

"Now that I study it, you may not be in as bad a shape as I said you were. Might be that you're double lucky. I mean, you got folks shootin' at you, with close to twenty thousand witnesses and just about ever' champion rodeo cowboy you can name to back up your story."

"That's one bit of luck."

"There's more. When I got to the `Dome and saw that leather jacket of yours, I 'bout creamed. Thought I could peg you to this real gristly murder I got in my case file. Killer left a streak of leather on a hallway wall. Black skid mark. Like he got bodyslammed then slid along the wall. You got a black leather jacket. And it's skinned up pretty good."

"So I'm the perfect match. How come I'm not in double lockdown right now."

"You don't wear silver."

"What?"

"No silver. Killer wears silver. Left a piece of bracelet on the floor. What the silversmiths call Cuban links."

"The bitch could sure shoot."

"What? The blonde?"

Burch didn't answer. His mind was on that bittersweet memory.

"Are you talkin' about that blonde? Where is she now? What happened to her?"

"She liked to kill people. But only people who crossed her or got in her way. Enjoyed blowin' those types right on down. Satisfied her. She wanted to kill you. For a reason. One you don't want to look at."

A long pause. A wait for Burch to continue his line of thought. Burch was drifting in and out of the drug clouds. Lucidity was waiting in the clear air. His mind was trailing through gauzy streams of cotton.

"So she was kill-crazy and you were runnin' with her, which made you just as dirty as her. You two were sides of the same coin. Didn't matter who pulled the trigger."

Burch broke out of the clouds. He managed his first good look at the owner of the other voice in the room. He wasn't surprised — vultures always circled the halt and the lame. And a badge-wearing bird always found it easier to peck at a prisoner than fly after prey that was still on the run.

"For a dude who's managed to keep hold of his detective's shield, you're pretty fuckin' single-minded. Subtleties, Slick. Pay attention to them."

"Feelin' good enough to get up on your hind legs and do a little growlin', huh? Good. Glad to see you up on the muscle. You'll need that attitude to carry you through the meat grinder. You know, I'm gonna sit back and enjoy this. Just might go out and buy me one of them expensive cigars and blow blue smoke at the ceilin' and watch."

"That would make you a voyeur. Or fat-assed brass. Or maybe you're a yard bitch. Maybe you like to watch all the studhosses carve each other up for your amusement. Thought you were a front-liner, a grunt. Thought you could swing the lead."

"You're gettin' overheated. Might need to call nursey in here to give you another shot of sweetness and light. Cool you down."

"You're right. You need to shut me up. You need me quiet before I say somethin' you don't want to hear."

"I'm all ears. You say what you got to say. I'm like a priest. I'll listen to any man's confession. Even a shitheel like yours."

"No confession, lieutenant. Just another hard nugget of what you call your True Life. Involves that crazy blonde you keep tryin' to wrap around my neck seven years after the fact. Drives a man crazy to keep obsessin' about somethin' bad like that. Keeps him from livin' life. Keeps him from lookin' at things he'd rather not look at."

"You got a point to this?"

"You bet. You want to hang me so bad for your partner's death you're missin' some true facts. You're like a buck in rut. All in a rush to fuck somethin'. Subtlety just blows right past you. I told you that blonde liked to kill people. But only people who got in her way. Or harmed her and them close to her. You just see it as kill crazy. You want to demonize her. And me. You got to or else you got to stop and think and look at stuff you don't want to. Well, you're missin' the point about her. She wanted to kill you because you brought that psycho shitheel to our doorstep and almost got us killed. She wanted to kill you because you got my ex-wife killed.

And she liked my ex-wife. Liked her more than she liked me. She wanted you off the board because you were standin' in the way of squarin' things for her uncle."

"Glad to see you stand up for your lady. Make her a paragon of virtue. But you sound like a true believer. One of them Branch Davidians. You'da been perfect for that bunker in Waco. Right there at the side of ol' David Koresh and all the other crispy critters. Lemme tell you somethin' one more time. She was a stone killer and you got her stink all over you."

"You keep seein' it that way, lieutenant. Roll it around in your mind like brandy in a snifter. Hold it close like a lover. Bet it keeps you warm at night. Bet it keeps the creepy-crawlers back in the shadows. Must be what keeps you from thinkin' about what you need to think about."

"And you're going to reveal that grand truth any time now, aren't you?"

"Not that it will do any good. But it's what any cop needs to know when his partner gets blown away. It's what I had to learn when mine got gunned down."

"Can we speed things up a little bit? I'm not ready for a Sermon on the Mount."

"And you're not ready for much of anything else, either. But you're going to hear this from me one more time, then I'm gonna quit wasting my breath on you. One — I didn't kill your partner. The spade did. This stuff about me bein' a catalytic converter for evil is a bunch of bullshit. We were all in the whirl of what was goin' down back then. Some of us got killed — your partner, my ex-wife. Grief for everybody. Blame to go all around. I've swallowed what's due me for my wife gettin' killed. She didn't deserve it. She wasn't part of what was goin' down. She just got sucked in. Sucked in because she used to be my wife and my trail led you to her. Had to chew up that knowledge and move on. Had to chew up me blamin' you for gettin' her killed, too. But the main thing was chewin' up that guilt I was directing at me. You got the same thing for your partner's death. But you haven't taken the first bite of that in seven years. It's what every cop feels when his partner gets killed — he's dead because I didn't watch his back. He's gone because I wasn't good enough, didn't see things I should have, didn't move quick enough when the deal went down."

"Nice sermon, preacher. I'll put a buck in the collection box on my way out."

"Chew on it, Slick. Chew on it. Swallow and shit it out the other side. Then move on."

A beefy face zoomed close into Burch's field of vision. Lank, dark hair, Indian black and straight; a pock-marked jawline.

"Chew on this, son. Another wad of grief and guilt for you. Your best buddy got killed up in Dallas yesterday."

"What the fuck are you talkin' about?"

"Boy name Krukovitch. You know him well. Somebody walked into a bar, beat the shit out of him and broke his neck. No witnesses. A nasty way to die. My money is on it bein' connected to you and your client."

"Might not be. Dallas can be a badass place."

"Who's hangin' onto fantasy now?"

Burch knew it was the right call. Knew it in his gut. Knew it was connected to Savannah and her ride, a course he had eagerly joined. His stomach churned with nausea that had nothing to do with bruises and broken bones.

"One more piece of joyful noise. Your client? She's flown the coop. Left that little safe house you had her stashed in. Left two bodies behind, too. The thin bald guy and the black Cuban. Deader 'n hell. With a shotgun. Very messy."

Burch said nothing. Cider Jones was standing by the door, looking back at Burch.

"That makes it three people, son. Four, counting Delgado. And the slants make *numeros cinco y seis*. We won't count the elegant Mr.

Thanh since his boys done him in. Still makes a pretty hefty bill — six stiffs charged to your account. One of 'em a close friend. Two others iced by a client. Enough for any man to chew on."

Burch said nothing. He took a last drag on his Lucky then snapped his arm forward, flicking the burning butt toward the big cop in the doorway. It struck Jones in the forehead then fell down the front of his shirt, spreading sparks over the lapels of his jacket.

Burch grimaced in pain, his eyes too watery with tears to witness the accuracy of his shot. The cop barked out a brittle, reflexive laugh, the kind a jock uses to put down an opponent's best shot. He patted out the cigarette cinders burning the front of his jacket, his eyes narrowed on Burch.

"I'll get nursey now. You look like a man in some pain. You could use a shot of something."

TWENTY-ONE

You could blame a jokester for the name of this place. Or a land speculator looking to lure some unwary buyers. Or maybe a booster with grand visions of a future metropolis. But to call it Eagle Pass was to give it a sense of soaring, geographic grandeur that this gritty little South Texas river town never did have and never would.

The name brings to mind raptors on the wing, spiraling in the updrafts above a great sandstone cliff, flying over a rock gateway through the mountains. Particularly when an Anglo lets the original Spanish roll off his tongue — *Paso del Aguila.*

It sounds grand and sweeping, wind-swept, vast and noble. The reality is far different — broken, scrubby land full of mesquite, live oak, *huajilla* and cat's claw, with barely discernable folds, ancient and small ridgelines leading down to the Rio Grande.

Hardly mountains. Barely hills. No daunting cliffs. Just a shallow cut for a river running north to south, a vertical divide between two countries, bordered by worn shoulders covered in gravel, sloping down to a broad brown back of slow-moving water. And miles of uninterrupted horizon, west and south into Mexico, east and north into Texas. Desolate, not noble.

The eagles the first Spanish and Indian inhabitants saw were nesting in the tops of low-slung pecan trees. But Eagle Roost is hardly a Chamber of Commerce drawing card. Not even in Spanish

— *Nido del Aguila*. It is a contradiction. A shit-spattered perch for avian grandeur.

For Anglos, the problem is partly one of linguistic ambiguity. In Spanish, *paso* can mean a pass through the mountains. Or it can simply mean a pathway from one place to the other. Or the gait of a man or horse. Or a place where something or somebody dwelled. In this case, the original settlers probably meant the phrase to indicate, "place where you see a bunch of eagles flying 'round."

But there is also the matter of a hijacked name. When old Spanish conquistadors like Domingo Ramon or Pedro de Rivera saw the birds that Eagle Pass is named for, they weren't in Texas and they weren't standing on the banks of the Rio Grande. They were looking at a ford about thirty miles west in Mexico, on the old military road between Guerrero and Monclova Viejo, at a crossing of the Rio Escondido. That was the true *Paso del Aguila*.

The place where Eagle Pass now sits had a different name — *Paso del Adjuntos*, path of the alternates, another name capturing that wonderful Spanish linguistic ambiguity, using a word that could mean a business associate, an assistant professor or the aide to a professional. Instead, the word christened a smuggler's route. After Texas broke away from Mexico, the Mexican government prohibited trade with the new republic. But black market trafficking continued between San Antonio and Mexican villages along the Rio Grande, the traders using this new, alternate crossing that ran north of the old Camino Real and its ford near Guerrero.

The true purpose of this *paso* created a problem. Calling it Pathway of the Smugglers would be an insult to the nobility of those who used the route and would bring an unwelcome bit of publicity. Truth-in-advertising was about as useful as a neon sign over a lovers' lane. And in this case, it might lead to a killing. Or a visit from the *federales*. Better to leave it vague and call the people who used this route associates and their pathway the same. That's the way the logic ran. After all, one of them was probably one of us.

As with most things *Tejano,* this sensible arrangement was upset by an Anglo. After the Mexican War, a Texas militia commander set up an observation post here in 1848, filing dispatches with an Eagle Pass dateline. He praised the place as a natural spot for a thriving town. His dispatches never mentioned any smuggling. Or any eagles.

The commander's name was John Veatch. He was the jokester with the grand dreams. The name stuck.

So did the sense of a place flying under false colors — a fantasy trumped up by Anglo land hustlers and civic dreamers, a fabrication that did little to cover the truth of a haven for outcasts and outlaws. It was a town plagued by marauding Indians, peopled by rustlers, killers, slave hunters, cashiered soldiers and prospectors who failed to make it to California.

Other Anglos were filled with the nightmares and bitterness of battle. At the end of the Civil War, Confederate Gen. Joe Shelby bivouacked an unbowed brigade of the Army of the Trans-Mississippi near the town on his way to offer his services to Maximilian, the Mexican emperor. As his troops splashed across the river, Shelby paused to bury the brigade's battle banner beneath the water — one Lost Cause drowned in defeat and sadness, another rapidly pursued in futility. Through the 1880s, a bandit named King Fisher dominated the town and Maverick County until a pair of Texas Rangers shut him down.

Across the river from this home to dreamers, schemers and outlaws sits a Mexican twin with an unambiguous name. In English or in Spanish. *Piedras Negras.* Black Rocks. As in coal. Originally a garrison town, later the roost of an uprooted Seminole raider named Wild Cat, it bore a name that wasn't stolen from someplace else, one that wasn't meant to hustle the unwary outsider, a name that played off the low-quality seam that started near the surface just east of Eagle Pass and ran west, dipping under the river and the streets of the Mexican town, angling deeper into the earth as it journeyed several miles into the interior.

Coal built both towns, made them more than just dusty cattle villages, particularly after the completion of the Southern Pacific railroad. German engineers built the mines. Mexican labor brought it out of the ground. Until the early 1920s, the decline of the steam engine and a slow slide into far tougher economic straits.

That changed with the heavy industrialization of northern Mexico, driven by the rise of the *maquiladora* factories on the south side of the river. This created new interest in coal too dirty to burn in U.S. power plants but acceptable for the less-stringent environmental standards of Mexican generators, namely a big belching complex about thirty miles southwest of Piedras Negras.

It is an interest rich in irony, crystal-perfect as an example of how modern-day growth along *la frontera* has reversed the pecking order between towns like El Paso and Juarez, Brownsville and Matamoros, Eagle Pass and Piedras Negras.

By the early '90s, the Mexican tail wagged the Anglo dog. Growth in Mexico — cancerous and chaotic in Ciudad Juarez and Matamoros; calmer, more controllable and less culturally devastating in Piedras Negras or Ciudad Acuna — created an economic dependency on the north side of the river that Anglos in El Paso or Brownsville didn't like to admit, preferring to mask their reliance with rhetoric about closely knit trans-border partnerships that they say make the national boundary irrelevant.

This is a clever rap, rooted in the prickly cultural and economic history of the border, a place unto itself, a scar rather than a boundary, pulsing and always open, never quite healed, a land that is neither fully American nor completely Mexican, a gritty outlaw zone that is disparaged and orphaned by the mainstream of both countries. It is stubborn territory, where the Anglo and the Hispanic have clashed, collided and imperfectly intertwined, forming tighter bonds than the outsider expects and the stereotypical symbols of the white rancher and the Mexican ranch hand allow one to see.

But talk doesn't cover the reality of American cities leaning on the Mexican towns they once looked down upon as one-stop shops for trinkets, cheap booze and young whores.

This changed relationship can be seen with a casual pass through both towns — the threadbare weariness of Eagle Pass, a town wearing the worn, hopeless smile of the owner of a roadside souvenir stand overlooked by too many travelers; the trim, self-contained bustle of Piedras Negras, a town that looks well-fed and prosperous but not overwhelmed by growth, its tidy square, ancient cathedral and narrow streets testimony to a place still firmly rooted in a Mexican identity that hasn't been shouldered aside by a blast of the worst America has to offer, like it has in the honking, fast-food hurly burly of Juarez and Matamoros.

Cullen Mueller passed these reminders of the new relationship between Mexico and America every day but didn't think about them. Not on most mornings. And not today. Not with the worries he had on his mind.

Sipping coffee out of a lidded Dallas Cowboy travel cup, punching the Seek button on the Sony radio-CD player of his black Chevy Suburban, he settled for music blaring from Piedras' top station, which billed itself as the Rancheria of the Airways.

But he barely noticed it.

Tooling away from his house on Seco Creek and down US 277 toward the heart of Eagle Pass, Mueller, a short barrel-chested man with a bass-boat tan and the sharp-eyed squint of a card player, usually eyed the sky and gauged the weather's impact on fishing. Usually, he had the taste memory of the sharp, savory bite of his customary breakfast burrito at the front of his brain. *Cabrito* and kidney, slapped on a fresh-baked tortilla at a little street-side stand on Main.

But on this morning, with the warmth and caffeine of the coffee shifting him through the gears of an escalating day, he wasn't focused on breakfast or his ever-present fish lust. And he was even less aware of the weather and what was rushing past his open window, his arm resting on the cold metal ledge, the breeze ripping past the Rolex on his wrist, riffling the hair that led to a carefully folded-back shirt sleeve of perfect white.

His thoughts were whirring around a single matter with two opposing consequences — the collapse of the Mexican peso. It was a joy and a worry to Cullen Mueller.

A joy because it chopped his overhead by more than a third, meaning his company's dollars bought more of everything for less at the *maquiladora* factory they ran on the southeast side of Piedras Negras, more labor, more electricity, more water, more heat.

A joy because it made it easier to meet the bottom line his stateside partners expected him to meet. They were lazy, greedy bastards who rarely bothered to cross over to see his operation and expected him to come to them for a monthly accounting.

A joy because it meant it cost less to keep Marta, his mistress, an ill-tempered, narrow-hipped woman with a spectacular chest and the sharp, copper cheeks of an Indian. Her flat, one floor above the tight passage of Avenida Xiocotencatl, was cheaper. So was the silver she loved to wear on her wrists, fingers and neck.

But Mueller, whose German ancestors came to Texas with the first land companies of the 1830s, knew these were short-term highs. The peso's sudden collapse caused him panic for reasons that stretched beyond the horizon of the rising day, out there beyond the bottom-line pain the crisis was giving the standup members of the Eagle Pass Lions Club.

Underneath the syrupy patter that sweetened his hustle, below the endless line of "Hey, pards" and "amigos" he passed out to contacts like a dentist giving Chiclets to a balky child with a bad tooth, Mueller could give a shit about the griping of shop owners who saw their steady stream of Mexican customers instantly dry up. He heard that lament every other day over lunch at the Charcoal Grill or La Fiesta and nodded gravely, feigning concern, doling out a squeeze on the bicep and a "Hang tough, pard," but not caring that Mexicans weren't buying as many groceries or blue jeans as they used to.

Some of his luncheon companions, always in danger of going under because of the town's stagnant economy, would go bust this time. It happened before, the last time the peso collapsed in the early '80s. To him it meant the absence of two or three familiar faces at the table, two or three fewer names you called on for a round of golf or a run up to Amistad, the big international reservoir above Del Rio, for a day of fishing. No problem — they would be replaced by new players. Sooner or later. When the free-fall stopped and the economy smoothed out at whatever new level it chose to flow.

His eye was on bigger worries than the loss of a lunch or golf *compadre,* troubles that caused him to fidget in his seat, pick the twill fabric of his tan Riata slacks out of his crotch and pop his ultra-dark aviator shades down his nose so he could check the mirror image for the sweep of his carefully combed and lacquered hair up and over ruddy and spreading baldness. Sandy brown strands over brick red skin, testimony to a long day on the big reservoir.

The obvious worry was the long-term impact the peso collapse would have on Mexican economic policies and the country's lurching movement toward free markets and easier access for foreign capital, meaning the dreaded *Los Gringos.* This was a huge factor for anyone doing business on that side of the border.

He remembered a history lesson he didn't learn in school, one passed to him by an aunt long dead, a trim, cultured Mexican woman married to his favorite uncle, who was also dead. She told him of the strong pull of the Revolution and its tendency to punish any Mexican politician who strayed too far toward capitalism and the appearance of economic servitude to the hated gringos. It happened before; it would happen again.

"Mexico doesn't forget," she said. "The politician who fails to remember *La Revolucion* will be rudely reminded of its lessons."

He remembered the last collapse a decade ago. It triggered a crisis of confidence — the Mexican government, mindful of the Revolution's hard memory, halted their tentative steps toward open markets. Americans new to the *maquila* game pulled up stakes and the stateside businesses that relied on *maquilas* for parts and subassemblies looked elsewhere for suppliers, turning to companies located on more stable ground.

Sorry son, we like your product and the job you do but we need to know this stuff will be there for us and you can get it to us on time. Too shaky down there. Like doing business in a bed of quicksand. Not worth the worry. Call us back when things get calm.

Mueller and his partners barely survived that mid-'80s dive. They scrambled around to find new customers for the extruded plastic parts they could crank out of their factory, turning to firms in Texas, New Mexico and Arizona, finding companies accustomed to cutting deals in Mexico and unfazed by the country's fluctuating economy.

This was tough sledding in a Texas doubled over from the triple body shot of the oil and real estate bust and the savings and loan collapse, but they did okay with firms in the other states. As one crusty owner of a Deming, New Mexico, electrical components company told him: "Hell, my daddy started doin' business down there in 1901. Got shot at by a bunch of *Villistas*. Unless you tell me ol' Pancho's come back from the dead and is knockin' on your door, I ain't worried."

Prophetic words given the Zedillo government's decision to send in the troops against Subcommandante Marcos and the Zapatista rebels in Chiapas state, a tough-guy gesture meant to soothe the nerves of investors in the massive Mexican bailout, mainly the U.S. government, the International Monetary Fund and assorted Wall Street types. A dicey move for any Mexican politician, fraught with the risk of appearing to be the gunhand for gringo money interests. But there you had it — the *federales* and rebels shooting at each other again. Far from the border but too close to Mexico's violent, revolutionary past for Mueller's comfort.

Mueller's mind wasn't eased by Zedillo's sudden reversal — a halt to the military operation and a request that the rebels reopen negotiations. More talk. With Subcommandante Marcos, the pipe-smoking son of the middle class whose identity had been revealed by an informer and whose romantic reputation was dogged by the rumor he might be receiving massive subsidies from the CIA.

Mueller heard these rumors in the *bodegas* in Piedras. Bundles of fifty-peso notes bandied about by the Zapatistas in Chiapas. Subcommandante Marcos as a front for the CIA, bidding to undermine the party that had ruled Mexico for six decades, the *Partido de Revolution Institucional,* the PRI, a corrupt and doddering dinosaur ripe for toppling. Hopes that voters would rush to the more business-oriented *Partido Authentico Nacional,* the PAN, a group that would cut a more favorable deal with American capitalists.

Crazy talk but seductively logical. And the fireworks could resume at any time. Unless you were a gunrunner or a mortician, revolution was no place for a capitalist. At least, not a small-timer like Mueller. Another reason for long-term worries.

Mueller also had to juggle the interests of that special client, the one his partners knew nothing about, the one who just wanted a flat one-for-one return on the money pumped across the border then back again and occasionally asked him to handle a little cross-river shipping problem.

That special client gave him his biggest worries but filled his pockets with enough jingle to afford the Rolex, the new Suburban and the Ranger bass boat with the 200-horsepower Yamaha In-Line Four that made it an aquatic rocket. Tired of grubbing for customers during the bust, Mueller had been willing to listen to a smooth-talking friend of a business acquaintance, a man who called himself Mr. Stabler and walked with the cocky limp of an ex-jock, a man who said he needed help servicing a group of businessmen with a special problem that would earn him a steady stream of cash into the account of his choice if he helped solve it.

It had been easy pickin's — money in, dummied-up supply bills and service contracts and order forms, money back out, minus a handsome handling charge, of course. Screw the small dips in the exchange rate; with a steady flow, the little ups and downs evened out.

The smooth talker didn't seem to care. They phoned each other regularly and sometimes he dropped down for a visit, flying his own Beech Baron into the municipal airport. He took the smoothie to Piedras and the Restaurante Moderne on Allende — he and Marta and a friend of Marta's to put on the smoothie's arm. They ate and drank and the smoothie told him the special client was very happy. But he didn't trust a man stupid, arrogant or vain enough to pick the last name of a left-handed pro quarterback as a *nom de guerre*. He made it a point to make himself known to the contacts in New Orleans and backchannel a relationship with them. Call it insurance.

Smoothie dealt him the cash on a biweekly basis. He checked with New Orleans on the same basis. This new money gave his business a stronger foundation and kept those parasitic partners off his back. It also put him in the bar and restaurant business in Piedras Negras, the perfect complement to the wash-and-wear service he was already giving.

The shipping deals were even easier; a package slipped into goods headed north, a truck number called in to a New Orleans number from a payphone next to a Shamrock convenience store in El Indio. Sometimes a call to meet a truck bringing supplies and a special package from the states.

Smoothness until a few weeks ago. Then the smoothie stopped calling; fresh money quit rolling in. And he got a midnight visit from two rude dudes with thick y'at accents fresh from Metarie — bull-necked, big-bellied guys who looked like they muscled crates and drums for a living and didn't give a shit about what went down their gullets or how much whiskey or light lager they used to wash it down. His wife and son weren't home; they were visiting her folks in Houston.

The dudes jerked him out of bed and smacked him around. But they didn't kill him. Only because he was able to show them the money that hit his accounts before the smoothie disappeared was still in play.

He was lucky. But he was also pocketing the payoff of playing it smart. The insurance policy kept him alive. Alive and dented. Alive and working a direct relationship with New Orleans. No more backchannels. No middleman to entertain.

Smoothness again until the peso collapsed. Then he had to work like a madman to get the client's cash back over the border before a third of its value vanished in the free-fall. They didn't mind the little dips but they'd kill him two or three times if he didn't cover their backsides on this one. He was still smoothie's recruit, not theirs. And it was clear they wanted to kill smoothie in the worst way and didn't care who they took out along the way.

That's why a Ruger .357 in matte chrome rode in the map pocket of the driver's side door and a blued Smith & Wesson in the same caliber nestled in his tooled leather briefcase with two speed loaders full of jacketed hollow point. Right next to the Toshiba laptop and portable modem. He was watching his back for the smooth talker, too.

He recovered most of the money. New Orleans seemed satisfied with his accounting but told him they were shutting down the laundry for a while. A setback. Another key business partner spooked by Mexico's instability. Back to where he was at the time of the last collapse. But better than being dead. And there was still the promise of special shipments that required his familiar touch.

His stomach rumbled as he turned onto Main. Burrito time. He pulled into the dirt lot of Flaco's *taqueria* and ordered his usual. Two of them, gobbled as he rolled down toward the checkpoint leading to the Puente Internacional, a slow crawl cross the river and around the welcoming arc of shops and the park that fronted the cathedral. Faster rolling out Abasolo to the crosstown cut on Avenida Torreon, which became Calle Zaragoza and led him to a long two-story blue stucco building at the end of Calle Monclova.

The sign above the entrance said Dos Republicas Fabricar Plastico. Inside, the hum of machinery and the sharp sweet smell of plastic resins, powerful despite the sweep of chilled early morning air from the factory's ventilation fans. The first shift was in high gear, making harnesses for the wiring systems of vans and light trucks and housings and mounting brackets for the fans on a cooling system of a portable generator.

He spoke to Luis Aguilar, the shift foreman, then headed for his office at the rear of the second floor with a list of logistical problems to iron out, burping up a bit of *cabrito* and kidney as he climbed the stairs, huffing with exertion.

"Got to hit the treadmill, son. Just got to."

He patted his belly and ducked into his office. Phone and paperwork. Trying to unknot a supply problem and hustle up a new customer or three. Two or three more cups of coffee. Lost in thought.

The cellphone on the left corner of his desk chirped — one of the old-style Motorola columns that all the business machos carried, slapping them upright on the table at lunch or happy hour like so many phallic silos. Used to be pistols. Now you muscled up with an electronic device that peeped like a parakeet. A sign of modern times.

The cellphone chirped again. His private number. Mistress or wife. One of his fishing or golf buddies. But not New Orleans. Definitely not New Orleans. That would be insecure. Their calls came to one of his cafes or bars. Another chirp. He punched the Talk button and slipped into an informal, but guarded tone that was different from his brusque business style.

"*Bueno.*"

"Why haven't you called today?"

A sharp, accusatory tone. No pouting. Marta, leading as she always did with a slap instead of sugar.

"*Vida mia*, I've been buried under a ton of work."

"I don't care about that — it's almost 11 and I haven't heard from you. Are you coming over to take me to lunch or did you plan to just pop over for a quick fuck?"

"I plan on doing both. And neither one that quickly."

"Humph — mister big-time businessman. Always in a hurry. Always trying to do too much at once. And never doing anything the right way."

"Look, I've about got things squared away. Some jokers are supposed to call me around noon about a new order. So look for me around one."

"One my time."

"*Si, mi vida.* Your time, not Texas time."

"It would help if you lived over here so I wouldn't have to worry about time differences with Texas."

He said nothing.

"Instead of being with me, you live over there with that fat cow of a wife and I sleep alone."

"I don't have time to get into this right now."

"Hah! You never do. And you won't until it's too late."

Bait in front of his nose, like the blade of a spinner flashing past a big lunker. He knew there was a hook there. He bit anyway.

"What's that supposed to mean? You tired of not having to pay the rent? You bored with toolin' down to Mexico City or up to San Antone with me? You rather be flat-backin' college boys from a crib in Boys' Town?"

"Jódase en el hocico, pendejo! Comer mierda y besar mi culo . . ."

He listened to this long tear of Spanish profanity, waiting for her to pause and catch her breath.

"See you at one. Be ready."

He punched the Off button and gingerly placed the cellphone back in its recharging cradle. It wouldn't chirp again. Not because of her. She would be there when he pulled up.

He was certain. She bitched and cussed him thoroughly at every opportunity and he never failed to take advantage of an opportunity to ignite her rage. But they had been together four years and enjoyed the same things — fucking, fine dining, dancing, travel to cities far enough to be away from home, but not so far as to be totally out of touch with what was familiar. That meant cities in the Southwest, Central America and the interior of Mexico, but not New York or San Francisco or Kingston, Jamaica. His wife was stuck in the groove between Eagle Pass and Houston and welcomed the fact he didn't press her to take business trips with him. Which he did on a frequent basis to cover his cards.

His wife did like to fish, so he took her along occasionally. Marta didn't fish and ridiculed him for wounding poor water creatures with sharp hooks, warning him he would come back to earth as a bass that would be endlessly jerked out of its hiding place, hounded by hell's own anglers.

Sex bound them together. Marta loved to suck his cock and would start unzipping his trousers before he had a chance to clear the door of her flat. He loved to fuck her from behind in the shower, with hot water pounding his chest and her back, soaking the place where their bodies merged.

Marta had talents outside of the bedroom, ballroom and dining hall. She was a meticulous bookkeeper, with the soul of a hard-nosed supply sergeant. When he cut the deal with smoothie and bought into a small string of bars and cafes, Marta took over ordering supplies and making sure the bartenders and managers didn't rip him off too badly. She banked the daily take, skimming some for herself, he assumed, and handing a cut over to him for walk-around money. She also tended the books — the legal ones. The off-book accounting he handled himself.

They would huddle at her apartment and go over her handwritten ledgers. He would enter her numbers in the spreadsheet of his laptop. After lunch. Before sex. If they could wait that long. Most times, they couldn't. Marta would bring the ledgers into bed and spread them across the scattered sheets and pillows. He would sit cross-legged and naked with the Toshiba on his bare thighs. Sometimes, Marta would reach under the laptop and stroke him to hardness.

Mueller could feel his cock start to stir as he thought about Marta, her coarse curls, the flat sharp planes of her face, her broad nose and full lips. Her nipples stood out from her breasts like the cherry top of a cop car from the 40s, tall, bullet-headed cylinders the color of oxblood. Their bases would whiten when he clenched them between his teeth and pulled back, dragging a throaty moan from her mouth, open and huffing hot puffs of air in time to the thrust of his hips and cock.

He checked his watch. Almost noon. His call didn't come in until quarter past. It was a waste of time — three strangers blathering to him on a conference call where individual words were wiped out by static or the talker's distance from the speaker phone. Lots of bold noise. Lots of qualifiers. One message shot through the static — these guys were taking their business elsewhere and didn't have the cojones to tell him so directly.

The call ended with false promises. He shook his head in disgust and checked his watch. Quarter till. He would be late. She would be mad. Bad for their luncheon conversation. Good for siesta sex. He grabbed the cellphone, tossed it in his briefcase and gunned the Suburban across town.

Traffic crawled. He drummed his fingers on the dashboard,

feeling his tension rise. She wasn't at the curb. He didn't expect her to be. She would be upstairs, fuming, practicing her glare of impatience. A firefight over lunch, he thought. He eased the Suburban onto the sidewalk and tapped the horn twice. He crooked his neck to look up at her window. No waving hand, no quick pop of the head. He tapped the horn again then waited. Nothing.

He checked the side-mirror for traffic then popped open his door, sliding out and grabbing the briefcase as his boots hit the street. He glanced at the Ruger nestled in the map pocket of the door, metal swathed in mustard-colored silicone cloth. The gun's dull gleam jostled a small germ of doubt that wasn't fast enough to catch up with his hurried consciousness.

Her door. His key. Two steps inside. A third. Nobody home. Cold metal jammed into his temple. An arm around his throat, jerking him backwards and on the back of his heels. A leg thrust between his legs, bracing him in this helpless position.

"Welcome, Cully. You're late. Marta was pacing the floor when I got here. Bad manners to keep a lady like this waiting. Felt sorry for her and had her take a load off."

"Where is she, man? What have you done to her?"

"Now, now, Cully — calm yourself. We're all friends here. We've broken bread together, sipped wine, laughed at each others' jokes. Hell, I've even fucked some of Marta's best friends. The last thing I'd want to do is hurt Marta."

"Where is she?"

"Right where you like her, son. In bed. I took the liberty of using certain carnal accessories to keep her there. Nothing harmful of course. The same silk scarves and handcuffs she keeps in her nightstand for you. I assume she uses them on you. Does she? Or are they for some other Anglo studhoss?"

"Piss off, Crowe."

Mueller felt Crowe's arm tighten across his throat, the biceps cutting his airway. He started to gag.

"Now, be nice. Keep things friendly. I've had a very long night and a very long morning and I'm in too filthy a mood to ask for anything twice. Be a good boy and drop that briefcase on the floor. Very good."

Mueller coughed twice then tried to talk. He coughed again. His voice was raspy.

"You are a crazy bastard for coming here, man. New Orleans wants you real dead, real quick."

"Yes, and you'd like to be the one who gives them what they want, right? That'd square you up just perfect with those wop bastards, wouldn't it? Put you solid on their side and wash away the taint of being associated with me."

"You got me wrong."

"Really? I think I underestimated you all along. You're still alive, aren't you? I assume some gentlemen from the Pelican State dropped in shortly after I disappeared. Normally they'd bounce you off the walls, hook you up to some nasty electrical device, get the information they want out of you then snap your neck for you. But you're still walkin' and talkin' and fuckin' ol' Marta here. That tells me you were smart enough to get friendly with New Orleans behind my back."

Mueller said nothing. He let Crowe muscle him across the living room of Marta's flat and dump him hard on a ladder-back chair. Crowe pinned his arms behind one of the slats then bound them together with electrical cord. Next came his legs.

Crowe rose up from his work and stretched toward the ceiling, hands at the small of his back, moaning slightly as he rolled his head from side to side.

"What's wrong with you?"

"Bus ride — twenty hours."

"A man like you on the Gray Dog. I don't see it."

A stare and a tight smile: "Reversal of fortune."

Long seconds of silence. Crowe's eyes on Mueller, flat and

assessing, sensors taking in the data and giving no feedback. A nod from Crowe and a break in the silence.

"You helped yourself by doing that."

"Doing what?"

"Talking to New Orleans direct."

"I know."

"You helped me, too."

"How's that?"

"Gave them a false sense of confidence. Made them think they had my action monitored. Made it easier for me to sucker them."

"Glad to be of service."

"And your service hasn't ended. I'd say it's just beginning."

Crowe bent over and picked up the briefcase. He fished out a sheaf of bills — just under six hundred in Jeffersons and Lincolns, cash that would carry Mueller across the next two weeks of lunches, golf matches and fishing runs.

"This will come in handy."

"Don't tell me a man with your talent is running short of long green."

"A short-term liquidity problem, nicely solved by your donation."

"Can I get a receipt? My tax man insists."

"What happened to the trust between us?"

"That disappeared when two guys from Metarie showed up at my door."

"I see your point."

Crowe continued his inspection of the briefcase. Mueller, growing more anxious by the second, tried to fill the silence.

"Nice haircut."

"You don't think it's a little too butch?"

"Wouldn't know about any of that fag stuff, bud."

"But you do know first-class computer equipment. This Toshiba's a jewel. Hayes modem. Very nice. Knew you'd have it with you. And what's this? A wheelgun?"

Crowe held up the Smith.

"For me?"

Mueller shrugged.

"I don't take it personally. Particularly since it isn't pointed at me."

Crowe shoved the Smith into his waistband then took the Toshiba to the dining room table and wired it to the modem. He brought the cellphone over to Mueller.

"You're going to take a trip. At least, that's what you're going to tell your wife. And your foreman. Make it someplace you have to be for two or three days. Say El Paso. Tell me which speed-dial to hit."

Crowe punched the buttons he was told to punch. He listened then put the phone to Mueller's ear — the answering machine at home.

"Hi, hon — I've got to tool up to El Paso to meet some boys who want to toss some business my way. I'll check in. Love ya. Bye."

"Oh, that was very good. Very, very good, son. Put you on Broadway with an act like that. But then again, you get lots of practice lyin' to her so you can be with ol' Marta, doncha?"

Mueller fed the same lines to Luis. Without the "hon" and the "love ya." Luis laughed and teased him about taking a two-day siesta with Marta. Mueller: "Ya got me, *hombre*. See you in two."

Crowe had another task for him — setting up the Toshiba and modem. Mueller walked him through it. Crowe wrote the commands on a small notebook he pulled out of the breast pocket of his tan sportsman's vest, the kind photographers like to wear.

Crowe punched the keyboard while standing at the table, pausing only to ask Mueller an operational question or two. The modem screeched. Crowe rattled the keyboard again. He broke the connection, stretched to his full height and shot Mueller a wink and a dry chuckle.

"Fan mail. Got to keep my public amused."

Crowe stepped into the bedroom. Mueller heard two sharp metallic barks, like sheetrock being tacked up with a nail gun. Panic filled him and he tried to stand up, toppling himself and the chair to the floor. His face was flat on the clean-swept tile, his eyes facing the bedroom door. Crowe filled the doorframe.

"Marta! Marta!"

Three more metallic barks.

"She can't hear you anymore, son. And you couldn't answer even if she could."

Five pieces of brass in his pocket. Wires and two boxes of plastic — one flat and rectangular, the other the shape of two columns of Saltines strapped back-to-back — stuffed into a tooled briefcase that belonged to a dead man. A quick move out the door and a vehicle that was too redneck for his tastes but a fitting mode of transport for his next destination.

He saw it in his mind — a white chapel and high desert mountains, a place of sanctity and grace, isolation and abandonment. Perfect for prayer and spiritual renewal.

Or a killing.

TWENTY-TWO

Fuck Humphrey Bogart.

Fuck the Maltese Falcon and all the movie dialogue William Faulkner, that overwrought Mississippi drunk, lifted wholesale from Hammett's book.

And double-fuck to the line that when a man's partner gets killed you do something, anything, whether you liked him or not. Even the score, Bogie said with a sneer, or the entire brotherhood of detectivedom will fall off the face of the earth and civilization will slip into a new Dark Age made more sinister by the lights of perverted science.

"Naw, son — Bogie didn't say all that. That last part — the part about science perverts — that was that British fucker. Churchill. The guy with the cigar and the V-for-Victory sign. Neville Churchill."

"Who the fuck are you?"

"I'm the shitass drivin' this car and keepin' your fat sorry self just a foot or so outside the long reach of Brother John Law."

"Slow down, Slick. I gotta puke."

"Told you not to suck down that whiskey so fast. It don't mix with hospital food and pharmaceuticals."

Too late. Head out the window. Brownish-yellow bile spewed into the slipstream, streaking the white flank of a '72 Cutlass convertible. A gallon from the gullet. An eternity hanging over the side. Each long retch shooting pain through his damaged shoulder, his face, his ribcage.

Head back behind the windscreen. Skull slapped firmly into the red suede headrest. Whorehouse plush. Sleeve across the lips. Eyes up, watching the fuzzy halo tracks of the streetlamps rushing through the humid air above his head.

"Arrrrrrrrrrgggggggh! Ahhhhhhhhhhhhyeeeeech! Goddam — I haven't done that since junior high."

"Waste of good whiskey."

"Howzat?"

"Didn't stay inside of you long enough to get you drunk enough to pass out. Now I got to listen to more of your craziness. And you fucked up the detailing on my car."

Whiskey bottle in the passenger's hand. A long pull — clear air bubbling through the brown.

"Ahhhhwhoooooooo, that hurts!"

A long racking cough.

"Leave that whiskey be, bud. Don't want you sickin' up all over my tuck and roll. Gotta hit the carwash as it is."

"Bill the Racehorse, Slick. He'll pay for it."

"Yeah — and stick you with another jolt of his hourly rate. He already owns your soul as it is."

"He'll have to get in line. Three or four of his Dallas brethren hold paper on me already. And I don't care how much of a badass he is in court, he can't get something from me my ex-wives have already spent."

Another pull. Shorter this time. Fewer bubbles in the brown. Less brown to bubble. The physics of bourbon.

"Life gets simple, Slick."

"Explain that one to me."

"Life gets simple when the pressure's on. Our choices are easy and obvious. Find the bad girl. Find the bad guy. Take 'em down. Or take 'em out."

"You're forgetting a few details. We don't know where missy is. Or hubby the finance king. No clue at all on missy — just two of Jim Tom's friends blown away. And the only thing from hubby is some fuckin' fax to the Racehorse's office."

"Nice poetry in that message. `For Burch: A brown donkey. A dead horse. A white chapel. Where the mountains clash and the miners used to be.' Nice and neat."

"You sound like a man who can read between the lines."

"I sound like a man whose memory isn't completely shot. It's an invitation. To a place I took his wife back when I was fuckin' her. All that's missin' is the time and a place to leave the RSVP."

"Donkeys, a dead horse and a chapel. What's that about?"

"There's a chapel down Mexico way, just over the river. You can see a range of mountains called the Sierra del Burro. Foothills, really. Drawfed by the Sierra del Carmens. Some other mountains called the Sierra del Caballo Muerto — Dead Horse Mountains."

"Sounds grim."

"It's in the middle of some grim country. Down below the Big Bend. Grim but stunning, if you go for starkness. It's like the skin's been peeled back and you can see the earth's ribcage down there."

"You sound like you like that country."

No words. A nod.

"So we know why we're gettin' the invite, don't we?"

"Naw. Not really. I used to fuck his wife and I did try to take him down in the middle of the Astrodome but that ain't enough to make a smart man want to kill you. Not when you've got bigger enemies than a broken-down pee-eye after your ass."

"Check the glove box."

"What?"

"The glove box."

He popped the latch and peered inside. On top of the maps, manuals and unpaid parking tickets that live inside every car's glove compartment sat a fat, long manila envelope, bound with clear tape.

He pulled it from its resting place and slapped it on his thigh.

"Heavy. Got some throw-weight to it."

"That it do."

"Where'd it come from?"

"That bull did ring your bell, didn't he? Your buddy, Mr. Crowe, dropped that in the middle of the ring. Cowboy buddy of yours handed it to me. Figured you was owed a finder's fee."

"How much inside of this thing?"

"Fifty large."

"How much did you take before sealin' it back up?"

The driver shot him a hurt look.

"Not a red cent, son. Figured I'd wait on you to be generous."

"You might wait a long time, Slick."

The driver snorted then looked at his passenger, a bearded, bleary-eyed man with a swollen jaw and a lump of gauze and bandage around his shoulder.

"You're holdin' the reason you've made his Most Wanted list. You took his money. He wants to take you. Easy enough to see."

Another pull. No answer. Just thoughts. Crowe gone rogue, maddened by a scheme gone bad, wanting to take out everybody who tripped him up. As good a reason as any.

"What I can't figure is why the Racehorse was so keen to spring you and why that hard-on cop let you walk so easy. I mean, hell — that bull banged you up pretty bad. And Detective Jones hates you a whole lot."

"One word — motivation. The Racehorse figures I'm one motivated motherfucker since I'm in debt up to my tits and there's a bunch of bodies on my conscious. Including a good friend. I'll go further than any hired hand."

He shot a look at the driver, one eye closed, the other bloodshot and evil beneath a shaggy eyebrow.

"As for our buddy, the Ciderman — well, a different kind of motivation moves him. He wants to throw me in the meat grinder, hoping I come out as a hunk of sausage on the other side."

"Why's he hate you?"

"He thinks I got his partner killed."

"Partners. Jee-zus, I should have guessed. Brings us back round to that Bogart thing."

"It does, Slick."

Another pull.

"Arrrrrgggggh. Fuck Bogart."

"You keep sayin' that. Why?"

"Fuck Bogie and all that partner crap. Fuck Hammett and Faulkner. Fuck Churchill, too. And it's Winston, goddam it, not Neville."

"All right, Winston. Fuck him and fuck them. Answer me why?"

Another pull. The answer bubbling through the brown, unspoken but loud in Burch's brain:

Because a friend is more than a partner. And a friend doesn't let a friend get dead. Not without doing something. Anything. To even the score.

TWENTY-THREE

Jack is dead.

Simple and certain, the thought came to him as his eyes scanned the road ahead.

He felt nothing. He kept driving. The thought would rise up and cross his consciousness, like a highway sign caught in the headlights. Then it would disappear. Into the darkness of his mind and memory.

He kept driving. South by southwest.

Jack is dead.

Then nothing. He should feel something; they went back a long way. The Irish Channel. Angola. He didn't. He couldn't even recall what Jack looked like, beyond the man's hulking bulk and dark, greasy hair. And the cool, ferocious power of big muscle in action.

But that was memory, impressions and quick-frozen images. Not emotion. He didn't feel a thing.

Jack is dead. He never came back after leaving their Houston motel to roust some of Crowe's dead Mexican partner's crew and never called. He always checked in — always — but this time he didn't.

Louis drove to the motel and cruised past the aftermath of fatal gunsmoke — flashing blue lights, a meat wagon, a body bag wheeled out on a gurney. He felt an icy dagger in his chest and just knew.

Jack is dead.

Louis shrugged off the loss and kept driving, looping them well south of San Antonio and sticking to farm-to-market and secondary blacktop before angling north toward Piedras Negras.

Somewhere deep in Dimmit County, after dark hours of solitary back road cruising broken only by the lights of the occasional town, he pulled over onto the gravel shoulder and waited for a semi to roar past so he could swing across the blacktop and creep the car behind the dark hulk of a boarded up service station.

Grit carried in the truck's wake slapped the windows and fenders, shaking the springs and shocks once, like a shopper too broke to buy a discount mattress and glad to take that fact out on something, anything handy, particularly the very thing beyond the reach of a thin and naked wallet.

He eased onto the cracked concrete apron, his headlights playing over the rusted bolts of the pumpless island, and parked behind the building. He stepped out and stretched, flexing his arms and shoulders, pulling his sweaty shirt from his back, letting the air play over the moisture. He took a Maglite out of the pocket of his loose-fitting black trousers and walked toward the rear of the automobile, his hand tracing its flank.

The car was old Detroit iron, a '76 Malibu Classic, a two-door that was once a glossy burgundy rolling off the showroom floor, but was now a faded shade that could be called deep russet, on the uptown side of primer red. The engine was a remanufactured 350 V-8, GM's best of the era. The body was bondo-ed but sturdy. The tires used and recapped but still deep in the tread and even in the wear. Not a bad pickup for a grand and change on the southside of San Antonio. In and out of a body shop. Cash and carry. Thirty minutes. Maybe less.

That was the easy part. Transferring his cargo was far trickier. Rental car parked in the cool bowels of a parking deck next to the Riverwalk, near a wall and a heavy concrete cylinder, away from the security cameras. A long wait until the six o'clock rush of office workers and evening shoppers and strollers was over and the cool of the night hush gave him time and cover to make his move.

One trunk open. A fast move with a vial, a syringe and a slender needle. Not his old kit. Modern-day throwaways. Two trunks open. A dead lift with lots of leg, just like the old days under the big iron of the prison gym. A shoulder carry. Big load. Lots of sweat. Lots of time to cool down — later, on the highway, with the windows wide open to the thick night air.

No sweat now, standing on the side of the road on the drag-ass end of a long night's drive, with cool pitch darkness receiving the first faint brushes of daylight, a change felt more than seen, picked up on the edge of vision rather than the center of eyesight.

He pulled out his silver cigarette case and put a Camel Wide on his lip. He lit it with the Varaflame and blew smoke, then walked to the rear of the car.

Trunk open. Flashlight on a supine form. A shake. Two shakes. A moan, muffled by tape. The smell of urine. Not unexpected. Another shake. Muttered profanity. The thud of a foot kicked against carpeted metal. More profanity. Signs of life. A reach and a sharp pull, greeted by a yelp of pain.

"You motherfucker! You fuckin' enjoyed that, didn't you, you piece of shit! Bet you get off on smackin' women around and tyin' 'em up. Makes you feel like a big man, in control. Makes up for that little dick the world laughs at you for . . ."

The words skidded to a sudden stop at the distinctive sound of a switchblade snicking open. Gleaming metal arcing downward.

"You smell like horse piss. Climb out of there when you can and clean up."

"I can't move. I can't feel my legs."

"That will change. Sit up."

"I can't."

"I said, sit up!"

230

He grabbed her by the collar and pulled her into a sitting position. She yelped like a dog. He slapped her twice, then bent down to put his face within inches of hers.

"You smell like piss. Here. Clean yourself up. Get dressed."

A milk jug half filled with water. Thunked into the well of the trunk. A towel, faded jeans, a black buckaroo shirt with white piping and pearl speed snaps. Thrown into her lap in a tight ball. From the bag she had in the car when he grabbed her. Clothes and an IBM ThinkPad with modem and a Nokia cellphone. Standard issue for the rising yuppie. And a Beretta 9 mm, the full-sized version adopted by the American military. Optional equipment, opted for only by yuppies taking a wild walk where they didn't belong.

"Turn around."

"Fuck off and get dressed."

He took a deep drag on the Camel Wide, eyes on her, watching her clamber out of the trunk, laughing softly when she banged her ankle bone on the bumper.

"Quit laughin' you shit, and help me stand up."

"You look like you gettin' along awright."

"No thanks to you."

"You right about that. No thanks to me."

She stood awkwardly, shimmying out of soiled jeans and a blue cotton blouse, shucking panties, but locking an angry stare on him the whole time. She was barefoot, flesh on gravel, and it was clear that the stone was cutting the bottoms of her feet. But she didn't try to shift or hip hop; she stood her ground, shaking her wild bronze locks, splashing water on her thighs, bush and ass, stepping into the fresh clothes, taking her eyes off him only when she bent forward to rub water on her calves.

He slammed the trunk lid. She jumped and yelped again. He laughed.

"Twitchy young thing, aren't you, sugar?"

"Don't sugar me, you sumbitch. Takes more than cheap tricks and slaps to scare me."

"Not tryin' to scare you, missy. Just messin' 'round 'cause I'm bored."

"Sweet talk won't cut it either, bud."

"For someone who's so self-assured, you talk too soon and too much. If you'd shut up and quit baring your teeth for a second you might learn why you're not dead. Yet."

"I already know the answer to that question. I'm fishbait, baby. You need me to get to my husband."

He laughed and flipped the cigarette into the darkness. A red cartwheel, a splash of sparks.

"There's more than one reason, sugar. Again — you talk too soon and too much. Shut up and listen. There's an art to doing that. Too few of us learn it."

"Including you."

He laughed.

"Including me. You know, technology is a wonderful thing. Our leaders keep telling us that, blabbing on about this Internet thing and doing your grocery shopping with your television set. It's amazing stuff. It overwhelms a simple man like me. But about a year ago, I figured I better dive on into this hi-tech world or get left behind. Took a night course down at UNO."

"Where would that be?"

Her voice dripped with disdain. His answer was rolled in a thick, y'at accent.

"N'awlins, sugar. Jazz n' boo-dan n' Pat O'Brien's n' the Cafe Du Monde for cawfee n' beignets in the moh'nin. The Big Easy, sugar. `Cept nobody I know who lives there calls it that. Kinda like nobody in San Francisco calls it Frisco. Just the tourists."

"Is there a point to this yarn?"

"Yeah, there's a point. That course taught me how to drive a computer. Apple and PCs. Gave me enough knowledge to peek into that laptop of yours. Did it at a cafe up the road about three hours ago, back when you wuz in bye-bye land. Interestin' stuff in there, sugar. Truly."

He held his hand up in the scout's salute.

"I might make a suggestion though. If you gonna have passwords for your laptop and AOL, you ought not scrawl them in the address book in your purse where any jerk can find it. Good thing it was an upright citizen like myself cruisin' through your e-mail instead of some hacker fuck."

"Are you enjoying yourself?"

"Immensely. Your husband says hello."

"What?"

"You heard me. Himself. Jason Willard Crowe. Speaking to us through the ether. Dropped a thoughtful little note asking us to visit him at a place about five hours from here. Actually, the note was for you. It was sweet. Something about desert and destiny."

"My husband's a jock and a financier, not a poet."

"He's a dead man runnin' up a blind alley."

"Oh? He seems real alive so far. Alive enough to leave e-mail."

"Which isn't the smartest play I've ever seen."

They stared at each other. He shifted gears.

"Got to hand it to ya. People think you got a pussy inside them jeans ain't thinkin' right. Ya got balls. Takes 'em to take out two pros like you did back at that safe house. And you got 'em, sugar. Big brass ones. Big enough to want to take me out as soon as you can. Think I hear 'em clankin' right now."

"Why don't you quit comparin' me to Mario Cuomo and tell me what you think you found in my little computer."

"A suggestion that we have more in common than you might think."

"And what would that be?"

"Call it a shared objective."

"I'll call it a bunch of bullshit. The only thing we have in common is the gravel we're both standing on."

He laughed and pulled out the cigarette case. He pulled out another Camel Wide and tapped it on the flat silver. When it was lit, he jetted smoke and pointed to her with the index and middle fingers of his right hand, the white cylinder of tobacco vised between them.

"You don't listen. It's a failing of people who think they're smarter than they really are."

He closed the distance between them before she could react. He slapped her twice then caught her arm when she tried to swing at his face.

"Like I said. Balls. But no brains. Maybe the phenobarbital scrambled your smarts a little. Put a little tarnish on that brass. Could that be it? You're smart when you don't have Class C narcotics washing around your bloodstream? Hmmm? What'cha say, sugar?"

She said nothing. He shoved her so she took an involuntary seat on the trunk lid. Then he stepped between her splayed out legs and grabbed both arms, leaning close.

"Let's wrap this up because we still have some serious road time in front of us. We both want the same thing — the money, honey. The greenbacks your husband ripped off some gentlemen associates of mine back in N'awlins."

"You're their catchdog. Go fetch what they lost and bring it back. Get a pat on the head and a biscuit for your trouble, right, bud?"

"That was the game plan."

"So it's like I said before. I'm fish bait and you're just followin' orders like a good little Nazi."

"You still talk too much and too soon."

"You keep sayin' that but I don't hear anything to make me think different. I mean, they own you don't they?"

"So you say. So they think."

"So it is."

"Maybe not. Been hired muscle for these gentlemen for years. Always efficient. Always loyal. But I've decided to play this one for me, not them. I'm a free agent. Undeclared."

"Why tell me this?"

"To suggest to you that it might be in your best interest to play ball with me instead of whack me at the first opportunity. To show you that there is a mutual interest here. To highlight the idea that the only way we're going to get our hands on what your husband's got is to team up and outsmart him."

"Plus, you need me as bait."

"There's that, too. I need a new partner though."

"A partner?"

"Yeah."

"Why?"

"I lost my old one."

"And you want me to take his place? How stupid do you think I am?"

"You're lookin' at the wrong side of the coin, sugar. It's how smart I think you are that matters."

"You want me to believe we'll be partners, playin' halvsies, instead of you leavin' me with a bullet in the back of the head out there in the desert when you no longer need my services. That's about it, isn't it?"

"It's as good an offer as you're gonna get, sugar. Get in the car."

She walked to the passenger side and stared at him across the roof. He caught her look and returned it.

"What?"

"Just wonderin'."

"Wonderin' what?"

"If I'll have to fuck you before I have to kill you."

He laughed, his cheeks rising up and making quarter-moon slits out of his eyes.

"Never can tell, sugar. Never can tell."

TWENTY-FOUR

Safe in the rat hole. Beer in hand. Pistol on the table.

A new set of wheels outside in the searing heat. A new band of the color spectrum shot through his brush-cut hair. Dark brown. Like a cow patty.

No chestnut highlights. No bounce or shine. Flat. Like the weathered finish of his new ride — a `71 Chevy C-10 pickup.

Crowe stood in front of a wheezing air conditioner, naked and dripping from a cold water shower, rolling the cold bottle across his forehead, enjoying the blast of air that hit his chest. His left hand dropped across his left thigh, fingers spreading the flesh so he could examine the red teeth marks that stung to the touch.

Marta. Hand on his cock, lips pouting in the promise of a blowjob that she hoped would buy time, her sudden strike blocked by a turn of his hip and leg. And a forearm shot to the face that snapped her head back and knocked her senseless. But not before her teeth sunk into the flesh of his thigh. Deep. That earned her three silenced slugs to the brain when he stepped back into the bedroom after trussing up Mueller.

Too bad. She had been a sweet, wild fuck, all too willing to let him backdoor Mueller anytime he flew into town. Which was more often than Mueller ever knew. His cock stirred at the thought of her. He looked down as it hardened. Down boy. No time for you.

Marta wouldn't leave his mind. His cock continued to rise. It would be nice to have her here now, nice to step up and take her from behind, her hands on the window frame, the cool blast of the air conditioner playing over their mutual heat. Nice, but a complication he couldn't afford.

He had known that before he knocked on her door. And she had known something bad was about to go down as soon as he walked into her apartment. He was smiling and full of charm, his mind made up and his motives hidden behind a friendly mask, but he saw that she sensed a vibe he couldn't suppress. He saw her fear and turned on a brighter smile, letting a hint of lust cross his face. She played along. More than played. Her tongue entered his mouth, fierce and hungry. She led him into her bedroom and unbuckled his jeans. And tried to bite his cock in half.

He wondered if that was her plan of attack or if she had tried to use sex as a form of denial, a sensual way to lose track of danger and stubbornly ignore its existence. Even as you fucked it. Or started to and lost your nerve. An interesting mental exercise. And it helped deflate his hard-on.

Too bad. For him and her. His mind turned to another woman. His wife. The lovely and treacherous Savannah. That's how she sees herself; that's how she'd love to be introduced in a novel or a prime-time soap. And why not? She was a looker and about as trustworthy as a cat in heat.

Always scheming. And if a man let her ravenous hunger for sex and wildly unpredictable demeanor blind him, he was easy meat. If he fell in love he was a walking dead man. He had dodged all of those traps. But she had taken his money anyway. He didn't bother to ask why. The answer was easy — he was a man in a hurry to get long gone, harried by bigger predators who occupied his attention, shoving her into the background of his consciousness, the ground clutter of his warning net.

He thought about this with cool detachment. He allowed

himself a chuckle about his stupidity and her brazen moves. He had to hand it to her — she kept her play covered, allowing him to think he was duping her, finding a computer wizard to crack his system, siphoning his money quietly from the most vulnerable point in his complex web of accounts.

He laughed again. Out loud. Head back. But not at his own foolishness. Lovely and treacherous Savannah would have a moment of surprise and shock once she learned where he was right now. A moment only, because she had tremendous mental balance, on par with a cat's physical ability to right itself in mid air.

He imagined her keying up his electronic message, her quick mind overcoming any fear or dread and instantly figuring out where he was and what led him here. He imagined the small measure of self-recrimination she would feed herself, the bitter taste of knowing that he had used information she had fed him during another attempt to gain access to his icy spiritual innards, the knowledge that he had sidestepped her again and was always above her, out of reach, beyond her control.

Savannah had revealed this place to him in an attempt to make him jealous about an old lover. The white chapel. The abandoned mining town. The stark spines of the Sierra del Carmens and the Santiagos. The desolate beauty of the Big Bend country, where the Rio Grande came roaring through canyons named Santa Elena and Boquillas, where vestigial outriders from the Rocky Mountains, running a course from northwest to southeast, collided with the forgotten cousins of eastern mountains, lumbering from northeast to southwest.

Savannah was struck by the isolation. He heard the awe that shaded her voice and his ears pricked. At the time, he was looking for a backdoor, an outpost for his own operations, a transit point for business conducted outside the realm of New Orleans. A perfect place for the discreet movement of small shipments. On an irregular basis. To powder the noses of his clients.

It was prime. He could fly himself into a long dirt airstrip at Stillwell's Crossing, where an old mining engineer and prospector was trying to turn the abandoned headquarters of a mining company into a hunting lodge and base for outback trips into Old Mexico. He could have the run of the place as long as it wasn't deer season. Best of all, New Orleans money paid for these side trips, short diversions from the main business of checking on his string of *maquila* operators, of which Mueller was one of five.

When he visited Stillwell's Crossing, he passed himself off as a writer seeking isolation, spending long hours talking with Curt Danko, the bearded, bear-like proprietor who spent his youth packing into the Sierra del Carmens, searching for signs of gold and silver ore.

Curt drove him across the river in a heavily dented yellow Ford F-150, rattling across the single-lane bridge and past the sullen customs guards, grinding through washed-out sections of gravel road, past the boarded-up barracks where the miners once lived and the rust-pocked graders and dump trucks of the old machine shop, up onto the plateau where the white chapel kept to its solitary self, above the wreckage and remains of a thriving place now dead, standing apart from a carcass picked over by the scavenging villagers of La Linda.

By his second trip, Crowe was driving himself over the river in Curt's pickup. By his third trip, Crowe had made the proper contacts and spread the right amount of *la mordita* to those who required it. By his fourth trip, he was packing out small packages of powder deep into his duffel bag. But he only made three more runs with cargo, his instincts assigning a different value to the isolation of this place, a different role in plans that were still gestating in his unconscious.

He kept up the contacts, especially a man named Enrique Salazar, advising this local *patron* how to smooth out his delivery routes to *El Norte* and how to invest his profits. He played to the man's greed, his ambition to make his little village as important and feared as Ojinaga, an outlaw town opposite Presidio where gunfights between rival drug lords were a common thing and a *narcotraficante* named Pablo Acosta controlled the action until he was gunned down in the late '80s.

Slow and easy, *jefe*. Slow and easy. Take little bites. Until you are strong enough to take them. Slow and easy. Don't make a move until I'm just a memory.

Crowe didn't whisper that last line in Salazar's ear, but his counsel of caution seemed to take. And he kept spreading his money around, buying friendship and time.

He was also buying a rat hole. An escape hatch. A small two-room shack in the foothills above La Linda. A small network of eyes and ears on both sides of the river; the cousins, nephews and sons of Enrique Salazar, a man unknown to his regular contacts. In Houston. And New Orleans.

Money bought Crowe the right to slip on down here without question, with little notice, into friendly arms. As friendly as the face on a hundred dollar bill.

He smiled and took another tug of beer, enjoying the cold, bitter bite of Mexican brew done in the old German style. Bohemia. In the brown bottle. None of the airy nothingness found in a clear bottle of Corona or Sol. And none of the low-cal blandness of American beers, calibrated to eliminate all the sharp differences of bitter and sweet that once distinguished the product of different breweries.

He hated the sameness of the big American brands. Not out of any romantic sense of Old World craftsmanship but out of resentment of a choice denied him, a calculation made for him, without his say. He had equal contempt for the microbrewery movement and its scheming play on America's unquenchable lust for a past that never was.

Another pull. Bottle almost empty. A swig or two left. He checked his reverie about beer.

He listened to the hum of the gas motor that doubled as water pump and generator. He stepped away from the air conditioner and picked up the pistol. One of Mueller's .357s. The Smith. He swung out the cylinder and emptied the six long rounds onto the table. Winchester Silvertips. He dry fired the gun several times, from full cock and in double action.

A grunt of satisfaction. He preferred semi-automatics but this would do. The trigger pull was smooth and glassy. The heft and balance made for a natural fit in his palm. He slipped the hollow-points back into the cylinder and carefully placed the pistol back on the table.

A loud, burring noise caused him to reach for the pistol. He relaxed and walked over to a squat and battered rotary phone sitting on a scarred pine counter, the clapper in its bell clearly bent, causing it to sound more like a rattlesnake than a ring.

"*Bueno.*"

"Señor Salazar sends his greetings and wonders whether you'd care to dine with us tonight."

"Tell *el jefe* that nothing would give me greater pleasure. Tell him I will come with a gift and a favor to ask."

"I will."

"*Gracias.*"

"*Por nada, señor. Por nada.*"

He hung up the phone and reached for the leather briefcase resting on a straight-backed wooden chair. The briefcase was richly tooled with an acorn and leaf pattern, like a saddle, with straps running out and down from the center of nickeled silver conchos to buckles made of the same metal.

He reached inside and pulled out a leather pouch the size of a quart Ziploc bag. Inside that bag was another pouch made of chamois, a thick trifold. Crowe opened the chamois and shook free a glittering slide of ice blue flash. Diamonds.

He counted ten stones. A gift. Better than money. For a bigger favor than mere friendship could buy.

TWENTY-FIVE

He smiled through a blast of cigarette smoke and cleared his head with an icy gulp of bourbon. Krukovitch's face ballooned in front of his, scowling and gesturing with a Carlton burning between the index and middle fingers of his right hand.

They were sitting at the amen corner of Louie's bar, at the short end by the cigarette machine, a step or so from the men's room. The holiest of holy for the hardest regulars, down where the boss hung out.

Burch was facing the long straight line of the bar's run toward the front door. Kruk was in the first seat of that line, canted toward him, the padded shoulders of his jacket cutting a diagonal that connected the liquor bottles on the bar's back wall with the smoky noise coming from the tables in the main room.

"Is there any woman you haven't called Slick?"

"No. I call them all that. Saves me remembering their names."

"I have this image of a trial. You're charged with a long list of the normal male cruelties toward women — churlish indifference, random betrayal, non-stop roguery. You're in the dock, seated on top of a Harley. And one by one, all the women who you've called Slick are marched in by the prosecutor. And one by one, they rise up in the witness stand, point at you and say, 'There he is! That's him! The man who called me Slick. That's the brute right there. He took something from me and never came back for seconds! He never even called.'"

He smiled through the cigarette smoke and took another gulp of bourbon. Krukovitch sat in front of him, saying Slick over and over again, like a dust-covered needle skipping across a vinyl record, the word clicking out of his mouth like a cricket's chirp. There was a startled look on Krukovitch's face; he was suddenly aware of the fact that he couldn't stop saying Slick. He froze. The startled look turned into fear and wide-eyed panic, like a man realizing a piece of meat was wedged in his throat.

Burch kept smiling through the smoke, sipping bourbon. Krukovitch's hands flew to his throat. His face turned purple. His eyes bulged behind his Trotsky-style glasses. "Slick" croaked from his lips.

Burch thought of the sound of a crow or raven and kept smiling. His glass was empty. Krukovitch uttered his nickname for Everywoman then pitched backward on his barstool, tipping over, crashing to the floor. No motion. No sound.

Burch smiled and rattled the cubes in his empty glass. Sean stepped over and poured him another. Smoke from Krukovitch's Carlton rose from his stilled right hand.

"He didn't leave a tip."

"Don't worry, you're covered."

"There's a woman down there says she knows you."

Burch peered down the length of the bar and saw the long black curls of his third ex-wife, the dead one, the one killed outside the world's sixth largest bat cave by a psycho shitheel with a bad toupee.

"Yeah. I know her. Name's Slick. Buy her a drink. On me."

"She says she doesn't have time and neither do you. She says its time for you to go. With her. To her place."

Sean leered: "Lucky dog. She's choice."

Burch reared back in horror.

"Not me, pal. Not now. Life is good. Buy her a drink. I'll slip out the back door."

Burch tried to slide out of his barstool but couldn't. He tried again but was frozen in place. He felt a cold clamp on his knee. Krukovitch. Rising up from the floor. Still croaking out a single word.

"Slick."

A jolting thump and the feeling of a pounding heart trying to wedge its way up and out of his throat snapped Burch into the dark consciousness of a lumpy king-sized bed and a room that wasn't his own. He had no idea where he was but knew it was better than where he'd just been.

He felt frightened and unmoored. His head throbbed to the familiar beat of too much whiskey taken too fast or for too long. Pain also pulsed from his ribcage and his bandaged shoulder. He felt the gauze and his mind flashed up an image of the Astrodome and the thick orange-brown dirt and clay of the rodeo ring.

He groped for his glasses and waited for his heart to wind down and settle back into its customary lodgings. His handicapped eyes started finding their way through the dark, picking out the slight differences in coal and onyx that told his brain where a chair or dresser might be, maybe a standup lamp, its shade looking like a black pyramid floating in a field of lighter gray.

His pulse slowed. His fear didn't. He sensed something his eyes couldn't see, a dark form in the far corner of the room. He listened hard, heard nothing but felt a presence. He moved his hand back to the small table where he found his glasses, moving his fingers slowly across the surface, bumping a cold glass and the base of a lamp, searching for the cool checkered comfort of his Colt.

He eased the pistol out of its leather holster and thumbed off the safety. The sound rang out like a carpenter striking a nail. It made the room very quiet.

A whisper from the corner.

"Whatever you do, don't start blastin'. I'm a friend here."

"Stay real still, Slick. I have no idea who the fuck you are or where the fuck I am."

"Stayin' still, big man. Like a corpse."

Burch kept the pistol centered on the dark form and reached for the table lamp. Its light made him wince. Blinking in the corner with a dirty beige blanket drawn up around his neck was a thin, pallid man with thick greasy hair and gray wolfish eyes. Burch drew a blank, then a sudden memory — the Astrodome, the backup Jennings sent.

"Mr. Slick. Sorry to disturb your slumber."

"'Bout time your memory came around. You been wallowin' around in a whiskey and Percodan fog for about two days now."

"It happens when you live the night life."

"It happens when you get the shit kicked out of you and are too sorry to take care of yourself."

"You my nurse?"

"I've been your life line for about six days now, son. You remember that big sumbitch that was fixin' to take you out at the Astrodome?"

A quick image flashed — a hulking man in burgundy with a chrome-plated revolver pointed his way.

Linebacker. Third baseman. I'm dead.

Chest blooms and the big man fell down.

The image died.

"You look like a man what's remembered where he left his car keys. Guess them hospital opiates haven't totally fried your mind."

"So, you covered me. That was your job."

"Yep."

Burch eased down the hammer and put the Colt back in its holster. The phone rang, startling both men.

"Who the hell is this?"

"Good mornin' to you too, Sunshine. This is Ed Earl Burch's room, right?"

"Right."

"And I am speakin' to Ed Earl Burch his ownsef, right?"

"As rain. Who the fuck are you?"

"Just who in the fuck do you think would be callin' you from Alpine, Tex-ass, at four in the ay-yem?"

"Some shitass guitar maker who thinks he's a cowboy, most likely."

Laughter on the other end of the line. Rich and raspy. From the throat of Wesley "Spider" Throckmorton, god of the hand-crafted electric guitar, axe-maker and customizer for everybody from Eric Clapton to Junior Brown, the Texas retro honky-tonker who paid homage to Ernest Tubb with a wickedly hybrid instrument that was half Stratocaster and half Hawaiian lap steel.

When Throckmorton wasn't making semi-hollow-bodied guitars known for their mellow sound and lightning action, he was riding with the top hands of ranches like the O2, the o6, the Paisano and the Gage Holland, whoever needed an extra and more-than-passable cowhand. And when he wasn't doing that he was dodging the odd natural occurrence, like the earthquake that struck two days before, while Burch and Mr. Slick were wheeling in from the Houston.

"Have to tell you this one — Junior was in here when we had our little shake n' bake, pickin' up his new guit-steel. We were headin' out to this little bar where he was goin' to sit in with some boys I pick with. I was changin' my shirt and the thing hit. Well, I thought a truck had hit the front of the shop or a train had derailed. I come back out and there's Junior, splayed out like a cat cornered by a dog, protectin' that new guit-steel, yellin', 'Earthquake! Earthquake!' I damn near laughed my ass off."

"I hate to cut in on a good story but what the hell you callin' back so early for?"

"It's late for me, son. I'm gettin' set to ride out with some of the boys from the O2. Chasin' strays down along the river. Be gone most of the day so it's catch you now or catch you never."

"Need to see you, son. And not be seen doin' it. Catch my drift?"

"Sure do. Shady shamus stuff, huh?"

"Shady enough. Don't want anything nasty to get splashed up on you but I could use a hand."

"You remember how to get out to the place?"

"Sure do."

"Be there after sundown. Should be back by then. I'll tell Rhonda to expect you."

"They's two of us."

"Always is with you. Still like 'em dark and difficult?"

"Not a *muchacha* this time. An *hombre*. Backup."

"Hmmm. Sounds serious."

"It is. I wouldn't mention me to anyone."

"Not even Nita?"

Burch winced. Nita Rodriguez Wyatt was Rhonda Throckmorton's best friend, the ex-wife of one of Sid Richardson's heirs, spending his money and living in his house in Alpine, riding high among the artists, cowboys, river rats and hard-eyed merchants who did whatever they had to do to keep living in a land that either made a body break and run or stay until death came knocking.

A handsome woman, taller and heavier than most of the *Tejanas* who struck sparks with him. She liked aged tequila straight from the bottle and favored heavy coin-grade silver with a patina that gave off a subtle glow against her brown throat, cascading black curls and the waist of her flared, calf-length skirts.

She liked silver almost as much as she enjoyed giving long, bawdy replays of her sexual exploits. Usually at a crowded bar, her eyes roving for the next conquest as she bragged about the last. Sometimes with the partner present in a roomful of people. Like she did about three years back after they had spent three days of serious rack time together and stepped out for a small dinner at the Rancho Throckmorton, home of a converted chicken shack known as the Coop de Ville.

If asked about her, Burch would have to say, "We've met." And hope he could leave it at that. Knowing no one would. Particularly Nita.

"Whatever you do, Slick, don't breathe a word of me to Nita. Might as well send up a flare to the bad boys."

"A cryin' shame. She'd be mighty glad to see you."

"That's what I'm afraid of. Glad is one of the things she has plenty to spare. A loud mouth is the other."

"There is that. Care to clue me in on how I can help?"

"Gettin' me on the other side of the river. Through backcountry. Need to get down around La Linda."

"I believe we can help you there."

"Knew you could. See ya for supper, Slick."

"You bet."

Burch reached across his body to hang up the phone, wincing with pain.

"What's the plan?"

"Sleep. And more sleep. We're four hours out and don't have to be there 'til sundown."

"Who was that on the other end?"

"A man I have to see about a horse."

Mr. Slick nodded, settled back then rose up again, his eyes open wide.

"A horse? Is that how we're getting across?"

"You bet."

"The hell it is — I don't ride."

"Then you don't go."

"The hell I don't. You won't make it five feet without me holdin' your hand, dolin' out them little painkillers you need to get you on down the line. Besides, I'm the man what's watchin' your back."

"My back ain't what's on your mind."

"A man can juggle two thoughts at once, can't he?"

TWENTY-SIX

He wasn't that hard to seduce. He was easy, she thought. And not all that bad in the rack for a guy with a belly and soft rounded shoulders. His prick never went down and his tongue traveled back and forth across her body, driving her up and down the orgasm roller coaster as much as she drove him.

And his hands and arms, roped with muscle, kept pulling her to him, turning her back and forth, spreading her open for another thrust. Or another bite from his hungry mouth.

No seashells and balloons. Nothing tender. Just firecrackers, loud grunts and cries, lots of muscle and slapping flesh. And the musky scent of wet slick sex.

It was hot and she needed it. But it was too easy and she knew it bought her nothing from this man. Not even a chance to escape while he slept. She took the dive into pleasure-induced exhaustion, not him. As she rose back into consciousness, blinking back the blur of sleep, he was wide-eyed and in her face, his cock hard and insistent, pushing her open and into a punishing rhythm that caused the bed's rickety box frame to squeal like the hinges of a screen door caught in a wind storm.

She watched him take a sponge bath at the sink, his eyes on her image in the mirror, the matte-chrome Taurus within easy reach on top of the toilet tank near his right hip. He shaved then brushed his teeth, never moving his eyes. She stared back, trying to take his measure, trying to find a chink, a hint of weakness, stupidity or overconfidence, a sign of the strutting rooster most men become after a bout of carnal sport.

Nothing.

He stepped into his outfit for the day. Black pleated trousers, grey shirt and the Taurus tucked into a slim inside-the-belt holster centered at the small of the back. Silver watchband snapped shut. Silver ring twisted onto the finger.

"A little overdressed for cattle country, aren'tcha, mister man?"

"Why is it every time a woman fucks a man she wants to redo his wardrobe?"

"Sorry to be such a cliché."

"You could care less. So could I."

He filled a plastic cup with water then popped the safety cap on a drugstore bottle, shaking free two black capsules. Downed with a gulp, a smack of the lips.

"Got a heavy pedal foot on those pills, don'cha?"

The tight smile. Lips pulled back across clenched teeth, cheeks moving upward. But no mirth showing in the eyes. Nothing there. Just the stare of an animal. With chemically widened pupils.

"Showtime pretty soon, sugar. You know it. I know it. Mother's little helpers keep me up and alert. Helps me keep one step ahead of you."

"I'm not the one you need to have a step on."

"A man in my position needs to keep a step ahead of everybody. Those he can see. Those he can't. And people that aren't even up on the radar screen yet. Up and alert is the only way to be."

"Didn't need anything to keep that cock of yours up and alert."

Another tight smile.

"It helps when you have some inspiration."

"I didn't think you noticed."

"I did. But you're wastin' the sweet talk, missy. Take your shower and let's get gone."

She stepped into the bathroom, checking for windows that weren't there. Just tile, a stall and a toilet. No tub. No escape. She let the hot water jet across her body, scrubbing hard as she thought. The sting of the spray made her relax, letting the thoughts flow out, leaving her mind blank.

Jeans, scuffed Justins and the black buckaroo shirt, the armpits sweetened with a spray of Opium. A glance at him, fiddling with a high-dollar fountain pen marled with a whorled pattern of gray and black. Waterman or Mont Blanc. Maybe a Parker. A touch of prep school that didn't fit his y'at accent.

"Very nice. A little out of place — for you and this neck of the woods. But very nice."

The tight smile. Amusement lighting up the half-closed eyes.

"You like this little item, missy?"

"On an accountant. Or a banker. Maybe a lawyer. But not you."

"It's a tool of my trade."

"You draw up insurance policies on the side?"

The smile and a laugh, dry and serious. Dead eyes. Quick movement behind her and to the right, his left hip bending her back, his left arm muscling across her shoulder and throat, his left hand clutching her chin, forcing her head to arc up toward the ceiling. A sharp cold point pushing into the right side of her neck.

"You're late on your premium, sugar."

He kicked out her legs and spun her to the floor. The impact jarred her vision. When it cleared, she saw him standing above her with a smirk on his face. In one hand was the body of the pen. In the other was the top, a top with an ugly gray spike of steel extending from it.

"Not just an accessory. A tool of my trade. Understand?"

"More than I need to."

"Good. Let's go get a bite to eat, huh, sugar?"

She nodded and picked herself up, a thought crossing her mind. She watched him reach into his jacket and park the decorated spike in an inside pocket.

His cock started to spurt, filling her mouth. His left hand slipped from her curls, his right hand still kneaded breasts hanging through an open shirt. His head was back, eyes locked on the frayed fabric just inches from his hair, his mouth open and echoing a loud groaning blasphemy.

"Jee-zus Chriiiist . . ."

It was the last thing he ever saw or said. She rose from his lap, her left hand lancing toward the side of his neck. His groan turned into a scream then a sucking noise. His right arm crushed her to his chest, his hand searching for her neck.

He collapsed, his weight driving her back toward his open fly. A jet of blood coated her hair, her face, her neck. She pushed herself free, her hand snaking up to the thick coat of wetness. She looked at the pen top sticking from his neck, its fancy design covered.

He never felt that casual bump at the cafe. He never felt her hand inside his jacket pocket. He never saw her palm the pen top as she took his cock into her mouth.

"Check out the tools of my trade, asshole."

TWENTY-SEVEN

The rump of the horse in front of his was flecked with sweat, its muscular movement giving him the focus for a long stretch of self-hypnosis. He needed it to keep himself riding upright on the bright rim of pain this jaunt through rough border country was shooting through his battered shoulder and taped and tender ribcage.

It didn't help much. But it beat getting another narcotic jolt from Mr. Slick and becoming so zombified that he fell out of the saddle. Pride wouldn't let him do that. Not in front of these *vaquero compadres* of Spider the Guitar King.

His mount was a big-chested sorrel gelding named Shorty. A bit of cowboy humor in that name since Shorty was bigger than most cowponies, more than sixteen hands tall with the longer legs and heavier build that suggested some extra thoroughbred or gaited saddlebred blood in his veins. Which made Shorty a smoother trail horse that still had plenty of cow sense, the kind they used to breed for the ranch foreman or owner who needed to cover a lot of ground in a day's time without getting pummeled by the gait of a short-coupled quarter horse. This was fine by Burch.

The two *vaqueros* were named Silva and Dag, short for Dagoberto. They were cousins out of a long line of Mexican cowhands, flashier and crueler with their mounts than their Anglo counterparts, a threadbare haughtiness to the set of their sweat-stained hats, the way they wore their worn jeans and chaps, their upright riding styles and the touch of tarnished silver on their oil-colored saddles.

Silva was thin, tan and mustached, quick and lithe. Dag was shorter, stockier and darker. Both rode roan cowponies; Silva's had a white blaze between its eyes. Both were hands for the O2, one of the big spreads, once part of the A.S. Gage empire but now owned by a big Back East corporation that ran a line of freighters and tankers, made luncheon meats, mined kaolin and treated the ranch as much as a tax write-off as a working cattle operation.

They left Spider's rancho around three, bouncing down off the main road and onto a rutted cow trail that ran along the north bank toward La Linda. They tacked up and slipped over the river in the early morning darkness, letting the icy water slide up and over horse bellies and human thighs, clenching their teeth against the chattering chill as the wind hit their wetness on the other bank.

It would take them a day's ride to get close enough to the old mining town to scope it out, a backcountry cut through what was once part of Villa's domain, home to bandits and smugglers, rustlers and prospectors — and *candaleria* workers, harvesters of the spiky desert plant that yielded a rich wax coveted for its polishing luster.

Forbidding country, rough, arid and isolated. But sparsely majestic and not deserted. Hippy river rats lived upstream in Terlingua and Lajitas. Inside the Big Bend National Park were ghost communities like Solis, La Clocha and San Vincente, now the primitive campsites for the hardy backpacker or river rafter. And on the other side of the river, Boquillas del Carmen, a tourist stop for rafters looking for a cold beer after a run through the rapids, a haven for smugglers who sprung to life in the dark hours.

There weren't many roads, just a dirt-and-gravel track that ran between La Linda and Boquillas, hugging the south bank of the river. They stayed clear of it, using old cattle and smuggling trails that crisscrossed the promontories that high-walled the Santa Elena, Mariscal and Boquillas canyons, then laced their way down to flatter country that ran between these rocky spines.

The last of the winter rains was still fresh on the land, brightening the dull desert browns and grays with bursts of olives, ochers, reds and yellows, darkening the rocky outcroppings with moisture. The tangy creosote odor of the greasewood was strong in the air — the scent of telephone poles after a thunderstorm. A damp chill hung across their shoulders and seeped into their lungs as they rode.

Burch fumbled in his pockets for Luckies and his Zippo. Shorty's ears pricked up at the snickering metal sound of the lighter, head rising and alert, then slowly lowering.

It hurt to suck down the first lungful of smoke but Burch did it anyway. Twice. Three times.

He pulled up to the side of the trail and waited for Mr. Slick to catch up, careful not to spur his horse into the cat's claw and Spanish dagger that reached out from the sides of the narrow sand track.

Mr. Slick was riding a barrel-bodied bay mare named Sue Bee. Because she was slow but would sting you with a quick deep bite if you didn't keep an eye open while picking stones and mud out of her hooves or cinching up a saddle tighter than she liked.

"You seem to be handlin' this."

"Hate it like sin itself, son. Need another pill?"

"Hell, no. I'm enjoyin' the pain."

"That would make you a masochist."

"So they say."

"What's the plan?"

"Well, the boys say we'll ride up into the heat of the day, find some shade, then take it a little farther in the evening and hole up and dry camp it from midnight till dawn. Keeps us out of the way of any *narcotraficantes* wanderin' around that time of night."

"They with us all the way?"

"Naw, Slick. They'll get us close in then they split. We'll have to take it from there by ourselves."

"Can we trust 'em?"

"Spider does. Too late to ask that question now."

"Do we know where we're goin'?"

"Yeah. A little white chapel."

"It's been a long time since I went to church."

Burch laughed then looked down to study the scarred stock of a Winchester lever-action carbine, a short-barreled weapon in .44 Magnum resting in a leather scabbard laced to the left side of his saddle, a brush gun chambered in pistol caliber that looked like something Jimmy Stewart or Chuck Connors would carry. Good for work just beyond shotgun and pistol range, with the same knockdown power as the cannon Dirty Harry carried. But it didn't have legs long enough to really reach out and touch someone, like you could with a .308 with the heavy Krieger barrel and the 10x scope, the kind that FBI sniper used up on Caribou Ridge, Idaho, to kill the wife of white separatist Randy Wayne Weaver. The press got it wrong when they hung the Ruby Ridge tag on this infamous standoff, but it became the legend that everybody printed instead of the fact.

Burch didn't have a .308. He had this stubby little frontier brush gun. And the Colt. That was all.

It would have to do.

He spurred his horse into line behind Mr. Slick and Sue Bee, running the image of that white chapel through his mind.

In truth, he had little more than a mental postcard to go on. Silva and Dag had cousins living in La Linda. They spoke of a gringo who came and went sporadically, enjoying the protection of a local *patron* named Salazar, a man with grand designs but little proof he was able to project his power beyond the boundaries of the village.

The gringo hadn't been seen in several months. And the cousins had no idea where he holed up when he did visit — abandoned shacks, huts and small houses were scattered through the foothills, the foresaken hopes of miners trying to build homes outside the company barracks, which were also empty, their innards scavenged, their windows broken and gaping.

The chapel and Salazar. That's all Burch had to go on. Like his Colt and that pistol-calibered carbine, they would have to do.

TWENTY-EIGHT

Cider Jones was two hours too late and couldn't decide whether this was bad luck or just the very thing he intended all along.

The cop in him doggedly wanted to nail the woman and wrap up the hit man — scumbags who killed citizens living on his turf, during his watch. Didn't matter that the victims were scumbags themselves, like the Hoghead, twisting naked and dead from the exposed beam of his Houston apartment.

Never did matter — Cider took their killers off the board, avenging them with all the passion of a spreadsheet program.

Until now.

Wrestling with somethin' else though, ain't ya, son?

You bet, daddy.

He shook the chaw-and-chew image of his dead daddy out of his mind. But not the point he made. Something else was muscling aside the automatic cop instincts. A desire to sit back and let this one play out — no arrest, no court, no attorneys, no judge and jury. Pulling for a deadly ending for everybody involved — Burch, the bastard he blamed for the death of his partner; that killer cunt girlfriend of his; her crazy-cool husband; this back-in-black New Orleans muscle.

He kicked Burch loose to let this happen but the old instincts slapped at his soul, making him work the trail, tracking the girl, picking up where she had been strong-armed by the hit man, figuring out who the hell he was and how the hell he fit into this puzzle box, factoring in the New Orleans greaseballs and their panicky and murderous attempts to find Crowe and get back their fuckin' gelt. And extract their measure of revenge.

Beautiful, one side of his mind told the other. Let `em all kill each other. Very dead. Very soon. Just watch it all go down. The only tricky part — making sure Burch, bashed up and shaky, drugs slowing down his driving demons, made it to the ball in time for the last dance.

Burch didn't let him down; he didn't let drugs or pain get in the way of whatever revenge siren was singing in his head. Cider had him tabbed, lurching toward the Big Bend country and the border, his mind always on the bald-headed pee-eye, his bile readily rising at the memory of his dead partner and the man he blamed for that death.

When he allowed himself a gut check, he was amazed at how strongly he reacted to someone he would normally dismiss as a dirtbag. A fallen cop, no doubt crooked. Someone beneath contempt, certainly unworthy of any emotional capital. But the thought of Burch burned him deep. And it went well beyond the death of his partner.

He's your double, son.

Shut up, daddy.

Think about it. He's what you would be if you had the same fall from grace. And you wonder if you'da handled it as well as he has. Or fucked it up even worse.

Right.

He didn't kill your partner but you hate him like he did. He didn't kill you even though he should have and had the chance. You wonder if you'da done the same, been as mindful of doing the right thing in the same circumstances. You'll always wonder if you're as good as he is even though you still have your badge and he doesn't.

Sure, daddy.

Don't listen to me but I'm right. You hate this man because he's just like you but he doesn't have a rule book to live by anymore. Just what his gut tells him is right. Sometimes he fucks up. Sometimes he doesn't. And you don't know if you could live that way, without something in black and white telling you what to do.

Take a hike, daddy.

Cider followed the trail of the hit man and the girl — headed in the same direction. More or less. It was a big state. With lots of ways to get to the same place. They were splitting the difference between Laredo and Del Rio, then running north through Dimmit County and Carrizo Springs with the border on their western flank.

He slipped in behind them, easy and loose. He told himself nothing was different, that he was working the case — cool and slow, confident he'd nail them. Eventually. Once the deal went down. His dead daddy laughed and spat spiritual Red Man in the dust of his mind.

You can fool yourself, son. You can't con me. I changed your diapers. I know you better than you know yourself.

To prove the voice in his head wrong, Cider pushed to close the gap, acting on a report that the hit man and girl were spotted at a motel near Del Rio, telling himself — and daddy dead man — he'd pop the both of them on sight. With cuffs, not bullets.

Late by two hours. Rolled up on a still-working crime scene southeast of Dryden but the action was winding down, the body already moved to the Terrell County morgue in Sanderson, forty miles away from the two-lane blacktop where the corpse was found stretched out next to the tire tracks of a car long gone.

"Looks like the boy paid the ultimate price for a little roadside sin."

The speaker was the sheriff's chief deputy — the pro behind the pol. A short man, whippet-thin, decked out in tan cavalry twill and a Stetson straw with a cattleman's crease. A small circled star on his chest. No holster, no hog leg. No other talismans of authority. Just a sharp, all-knowing, black-eyed glare from a pockmarked face slashed by a thin, trim moustache.

"Who found him?"

"Rancher heading into town — fella named Roy Booker. Family's been in this county since Villa was playin' hide-n-seek with Black Jack Pershing."

"Solid citizen?"

"You bet. No motive there. So — I take it you know who our friend is and why he's dead in my county with his fly open and his cock out."

Cider told it flat and fast. New Orleans muscle after a wayward one of their own. Wifey of the wanted one the probable killer. The bodies in Houston both left behind. He told it all — except for Burch and a lust for revenge rattled by hospital pharmaceuticals.

The deputy, Hicks — his daddy's name and genetically inherited acne, his Mexican mama's eyes and olive skin — stared at him the way a cop stares at street scum, bolstered by the barely disguised disgust country folks have for city slicks.

"Been doggin' 'em long?"

"About three days."

"Long leash."

Cider shot the deputy a sharp look. No question mark riding on it. Both men knew what the deputy meant.

"You want to say it plain?"

"Not much point is there? You're a big-city homicide *hombre*. Not some hayseed *rurale*. You don't stake a lead to the meat for a bunch of killings in your backyard unless you got a reason."

Cider said nothing. He could feel his dead daddy stirring in the back of his mind, snickering softly, shifting his chaw before hacking a glob of juice into the dirt.

Got ya, son.

Shut up, daddy.

261

"You got your reasons but you'll forgive me if I don't like 'em worth a shit. You runnin' a long leash on these two means I got a killin' on my books. Mine. Don't matter we know who the victim is and don't give much of a damn he's dead. Don't matter that we know who did it. Don't even matter that you'll run down this killer bitch. What matters is I got a mess I gotta clean up. Thanks to how you're playin' this deal. I got questions to answer from people I don't want askin'. Chief among them is this shitheel bubba I got for a boss. Man thinks it's 1870 all over again and he can get away with hatin' Meskins while smilin' and ignorin' 'em. Thinks he can forget most everybody in this county has some brown runnin' in their blood. Him too. Man hates me a whole lot. Knows I'll have his job come next election. Knows the old-time deal between the bubbas and the *patrons* is about over. Knows the next sheriff will be a *Tejano* not so beholdin' to the old guard and he wants to make sure it's anybody but me."

Hicks quit talking and turned his hard eyes toward the long nowhere of road that ran toward the border. The heat was starting to rise, the night wind dying down, the light filling in the shadows of the broken and blasted country south and west of the Dryden — parched arroyos, sun-shattered rock, dry creek beds that were wet only in winter, sand the ancient color of something long dead, fit to grow only what had the power to punish someone foolish enough to walk its surface. Like the stunted Spanish dagger waiting to slash the flesh of horse or man.

The squawk of the radio in the deputy's cruiser broke the moment. Hicks walked over, reached through the rolled-down driver's window and snaked the mike to his lips, looping the chord over and past the wheel with a practiced flip of his hand. He talked with his back toward Cider.

Cider walked over to the roadside sand where the hitman's body was found, squatting by the edge of a rough rectangle of yellow police tape that staked out where a deadman's blood made a dark streak that was drying fast in the heat. No eyes to look into. Nothing to tell him anything other than the marks of a body roughly spun out of the front seat of car, landing face down, dead toes gouging the soil as they bounced to a rest.

He stood up, his knees cracking in protest. He walked over to his gunmetal gray LTD, reached through the open driver's window and dug a Motorola cellular out of his briefcase, glancing at the numbers scrawled on a business card taped to the back of the clunky plastic unit. Never could remember the access code.

No signal. No surprise. Not this deep in the West Texas outback.

He'd have to wait and hit the next sun-blasted small town and hunt down a pay phone. Strictly old school. And that was fine by Cider, who used to rely on his dead partner, Cortez, to keep track of the latest technological wizardry, but now had to fend for himself.

A few hours back, he hit the outskirts of Comstock and dove into the lot of a darkened Shamrock gas station with a Southwestern Bell pay phone hanging on the whitewashed cinderblock side of the building, shielded by an battered and open-faced aluminum box.

He reached his contact with the Rangers and got an update on the loose tail they were running on Burch, his good buddy. Holed up in a strip motel on the outskirts of Alpine for two days. Calls to a local who built custom guitars and rode hard with the big outfits that still ran cattle through unforgiving country. Saddled up to be border bound. Lost in the miles and miles of deserted ranchland that ran south toward the river.

Lost and impossible to track. Unless the trackers also saddled up. No need. Cider and the Rangers knew where Burch was headed. A little white chapel. And a date with someone everybody wanted to see dead.

Cider needed to get gone and call the Rangers about this latest killing. He waved to Hicks.

"Headed to the morgue."

Hicks nodded and started to turn away. He stopped.

"Gonna shorten that leash?"

"No."

"Bodies are gonna pile up."

"Not on our side of the river."

Cider cranked up his car, heading for a long gaze into the eyes of a dead killer from New Orleans. And a hunting lodge with a clear view of a little white chapel above a blasted little Mexican mining town called La Linda.

He was no longer a cop. He was a watcher now, unhappy with his choice but no longer listening to the snickering voice of the dead man in his head.

TWENTY-NINE

The easy part was the action. The play.

Rolling out of the pocket with a ton or so of grunting, screaming beef clawing toward you, eager to slam your body into the turf before you could see a friendly color curling into the clear and dart the ball between the numbers. Cutting loose on a man holding a gun on you in that sliver of a second before he had the chance to do the same to you. Pulling the string on a complex series of international wire transfers that bled enough money from New Orleans wise guys to leave you set for life.

Cool and loose. Finding that quiet zone in the middle of a howling storm of fear and chaos. For Crowe, a dose of icy calm was automatic, something he didn't have to tap into or conjure up. It came naturally, slowing the rush of action into a half-speed freeze frame, keeping his gears meshed and lubed while others ground the teeth off theirs. He stayed centered. On the field, that was more important than arm strength and foot speed. In the game he was playing now, it was bigger than an eye for all the angles and a brain that was accustomed to being five moves in front of most players.

He knew Burch would come. He also knew the people Burch was likely to call on to get to La Linda. His relationship with Salazar bought him this information, courtesy of Salazar's network of cousins and brothers and in-laws and gunhands, people who worked on both sides of the river, who had friends and relatives working the sprawling Anglo ranches of the Big Bend, who would get a call if someone saw a bearded burly Texan nosing around Marathon or Alpine or Marfa.

But he would have to wait. And that was the hard part, the part that was toughest for him to learn and practice. It had been that way during his days as a jock — the physical part came easy, the mental part took discipline and a degree of cold-cured willfulness. Subdue the impulse to push and hurry the action; have the patience to let the action come to you and master the art of slowing down time, splitting the seconds into subseconds, hanging in calm detachment in the face of that bellowing stampede.

The wait. He hated it. But with machine-like precision he had mastered its art and made the act look easy.

The diamonds cinched the relationship with Salazar, binding the Mexican tighter to Crowe, buying his loyalty with the promise of more rewards to come as their relationship deepened and blossomed. With all that ice, Crowe was telling Salazar that now was the time, now was the moment to step forward and start making the moves that would make him a new king among border *narcotraficantes*. Crowe was confident that Salazar had his eye on the long game, the promise of a profitable and steadily maturing alliance instead of the quick hit for easy money. Helping Crowe wrap up some unfinished business from up north was the first step along that road.

Dinner at Casa Salazar had been *borracho y teatro*, part theater, part drunken revelry, a hearty mixture of both. *Cabrito a la frontera* — kid goat, spitted vertically like meat for a gyro, cooked by the indirect heat of mesquite coals. Lots of mescal, tequila's poorer cousin, made from different varieties of the agave plant, distilled only once, not twice, bottled with the worm floating along the bottom. It was rawer stuff, akin to iron jack, the once-distilled sugar cane brew poor islanders drank because they couldn't afford rum.

Crowe sat on Salazar's left, giving him a profiled view of the patriarch's silver pompadour, sharp nose and acne-pocked face. Cesar, the eldest son, sat on his father's right, his sharp Indian features framed by a flowing moustache and black hair swept back in a thick wave. Other sons and their wives and girlfriends perched on benches that flanked the long table. As they ate and drank, Crowe and Salazar spoke the notes of the elaborate overture of courtesies, oaths of everlasting friendship and compliments that precede any Mexican business negotiation. Underneath the smiles and bold declarations were nuances and inflections there for the reading by the careful negotiator.

Crowe enjoyed these exchanges. They annoyed most Americans new to doing business in Mexico. But Crowe appreciated the style and substance of such formalities; it slowed things down to waltz time, adding a degree of freeze to his naturally icy calm and was an essential part of the deal, with its own rules and nuggets of communication. It was a tool of the trade; the inpatient gringo plunged through them at his peril.

At the end of their duet, Salazar's voice dropped and his brow furrowed.

"My friend, you have been away from us for quite some time, but I have kept your counsel close to my heart and have remained patient despite some developments that have created opportunity for me and my family. I have done this out of respect for your counsel . . ."

A pause here and a glance at Cesar.

". . . and despite the urgings of those close to me to move now and fill the gap that has been created by a few recent tragedies."

"Don Enrique, your waiting is over. I've executed a plan that gives me the freedom and the money to launch the venture you and I have talked about. I appreciate your patience and the patience and loyalty of your son, Cesar."

A pause and a nod toward Cesar, whose face was smooth and

stone-like, his dark eyes hooded as he focused on the table in front of him. Crowe knew he would have to kill Cesar someday; he could feel that electric certainty flowing from the younger Salazar. But he also knew he would be finished with his business and long gone before that day came.

"I've made mention of a small problem that troubled me. I now consider it solved, thanks to your generosity, and the way clear for our partnership to fully flower and bear fruit. To set this journey on a proper course, I give you these."

Crowe cleared a space on the table between himself and Salazar. He pulled the pouch out of his pocket and poured the diamonds onto the scarred, stained wood, the stones catching the light from the fluted brass ceiling lamp and the torchieres spaced along the walls of the dining room.

Salazar smiled then laughed. He grabbed Crowe's forearms in both of his hands, hardened by decades of work and far larger than the rest of his thin body. They had a bone crushing power, matched by the look in Salazar's eyes, a look that told Crowe that this man wasn't a fool and would do what it took to be the biggest *narcotraficante* in the region.

"We are going to be very rich and very powerful men, you and I. They will know us in Mexico City. And in Washington. And they will fear us, the politicians and their lackeys."

He spit on the floor.

"It will be like the days when Villa rode this country."

This startled Crowe.

"You look surprised, my friend. You didn't think of me as a political animal did you?"

"I've always tried to keep my politics and my business separate, Don Enrique."

"Ah, but a man must always mind his politics as well as his business. It is his passion and his motivation. Otherwise, the money is just money."

A true believer, thought Crowe. A man who sees himself as the next Villa, riding again against the *Colorados* and the *Hacendados*.

"Don't you worry about politics getting in the way of business?"

Salazar laughed.

"In what way, my friend? Politics is business! Business is politics! It has always been so. What worries you?"

"A high profile. A name that is known to too many people."

"What is wrong with that?"

"I like to work in the dark."

Salazar laughed again.

"Then do so, my friend. I like the spotlight. I want my name known."

Crowe was walking a line that was growing thinner the more he talked. But if he let the matter drop Salazar might tumble to the idea that his game had a much shorter clock on it.

"And that's the way it will be, Don Enrique. I will be your silent partner. In the dark. Out there in the shadows. But let me ask this — don't you fear your government?"

"My friend, my government knows how to do business. But it is a government that may not be in business much longer. Mexico is changing, my friend. And the old ways of doing business and the old masters, the PRI *caciques*, they're losing their grip. Look at Chiapas. It can happen here."

"Revolution is bad for the businessman."

"Only for you gringo capitalists, depending on the NAFTA and all those PRI promises. For a man like me, chaos brings opportunity."

Crowe nodded, smiled and raised his glass.

"To chaos and opportunity, Don Enrique."

Salazar laughed, met the toast then called out for music. Four men — two of them old, two of them young — walked out, guitars strapped to their bellies. One of the old men wore a *bajo sexto*, the 12-stringed guitar that made the player look like he was giving birth to the topside of a '58 Caddy coupe. They launched into the old *rancheras* and *corridos* of the border, vintage story songs about legends like Joaquin Murrieta, the border bandit, and Gregorio Cortez, the man who led the Texas Rangers on a long chase through the Lower Rio Grande border country after killing an Anglo sheriff who shot his brother while questioning him about a stolen horse.

The voices were high and hoarse, filling the songs with yelps and cries of pain and the sweet aching harmony of lost loves and injustices unavenged. Then came the *rancheras,* the *redovas* and the fast drinking songs, tunes like "Por To Mujer" and "Y Andale" that begged the feet to dance. Salazar took the hand of his eldest daughter, Elena, the widow, her husband killed while chasing cattle up a rocky box canyon. The father spun her about, his boots thudding into the heavy wooden floor like horse hoofs banging against the wall of a stall.

Cesar and the other sons and cousins waltzed out their wives and girlfriends, flanking their patriarch and his daughter and spinning to the music. The men called to the singers as they danced with their women. The sound of boot leather and old wood added a fat line of rhythm to the old tunes, the songs of Villa, the music of *La Revolucion.*

Crowe sat alone at the table, sipping mescal, the poor man's spirit. At least it wasn't *pulque* or *sotol*, he thought. At least his association with this Villa worshiper would be a short one.

Too bad.

A wild ride into the Chihuahuan desert appealed to his athletic spirit. Action. Blurry and fast. Beat the devil and his disciples. And make another fortune to pile on top of the one stolen from the wiseguys of New Orleans.

Ballsy but not part of the plan.

Too bad.

He tossed down the mescal and took out a Te Amo Toro, a thick cigar with a rough brown wrapper, clipping the end with a pocketknife and firing the tobacco with a kitchen match. He felt eyes on him and looked up, catching the runaway stare of a young woman with a jet of black falling across her sharp Indian face. She wore a loose white blouse and a long dark peasant skirt that failed to hide the fullness of her figure. Her face was turned away in embarrassment so she didn't see him stand and walk toward her, his face smiling around his cigar, smoke trailing in his wake.

"*Vamos a bailar.*"

"I'm sorry, señor but I don't dance very well."

"You'll do fine. Dance with me."

He grabbed her hand and pulled her onto the floor, pushing past the dancing couples, clearing a space with size and smoke. He pulled her close, caught the pace of the music and moved them to it. He spun her out and away, then danced in a circle around her, his boots slamming the floor, his hands clapping to the beat, his teeth clenched around the cigar in a tense smile. He caught her eye and held it. She shook her hair and stared back.

The others hooted, laughed and applauded, led by Salazar. Cesar stood and stared.

"So this *gringo* knows more than just money. He knows our food, our mescal, our music."

"*Claro*, he knows our dance and wants to know our women."

"How is that different from any other *gringo*?"

"It isn't."

Crowe ignored the comments and finished the dance, his eyes on the woman. The song ended and he bent forward in a deep bow, his hand holding hers.

"Gracias."

"*Por nada, señor. Por nada.*"

He looked up. Salazar was still smiling. Cesar was not. A small man stepped up to Salazar and handed him a cellular phone, whispering in the ear of his *patron*. Salazar spoke into the phone, listened, asked two short questions then punched the Off button and handed the phone back to his the small man.

"Señor, that was a call from north of the river. Seems my nephews are entertaining an acquaintance of yours."

"Is she tall, blonde and bad tempered?"

"They said she curses like a *vaquero*."

"That would be my wife."

THIRTY

"You're a needle-dick bastard."

"Nice to see you too, Savannah. I see travel makes you an unhappy camper."

"I don't see you exactly going first class either, handsome."

"No. I've had to improvise."

"Is that what you call running for your life?"

"Things aren't that desperate."

"Oh no? What do you call this little shack here — the Mojado Hilton?"

"This is my little hidey-hole. My briar patch."

"B'rer Rabbit never had such a butch haircut. Makes you look like bait for rough trade. Better watch it — some of these Mex cowhands may be tired of fucking cattle. Might give you a whirl."

"Savannah, you're turning into a cliché. I expect you to mount a better attack on my manhood than some tired old homo jibe. Oldest trick in the book."

"All this cross-country rambling has turned me into a cliché, hon."

"Too bad. I've found the back roads refreshing. Your little siphoning job caused me a moment or two of discomfort but no big train wreck. Actually, it was kind of bracing. Forced me to do a little broken-field running, making things up on the fly. Exhilarating.

Brought me up to a fine edge. Which is the right way to be when facing someone as strong as you."

"Sell it someplace else, lover. Your last ballgame was fifteen years ago and honey, your legs are long gone."

"You're right. No timeouts or huddles in this game is there? No clock. No ref."

"And no chance for a trick play, bud. I've seen all your moves."

"Not all of them, Savannah. You're here aren't you? And I've got you."

"So what? We were gonna collide into each other one way or the other, on your terms or mine, so having the upper hand really doesn't matter that much."

"It does to you. You've been dying to ace me out for a long time. I'm the one you can't beat and it's killing you. It will kill you yet."

"If you just wanted me dead, I'd already have a bullet in my brain. But I got somethin' that's yours and you want it back. I got you, mister. Took a hunk out of your hide. Made you take a tumble. Little ol' me. And you can't stand it."

"A small thing. Like tripping on a sidewalk crack. Annoying but not cataclysmic. How much did you take off me?"

"What?"

"How much did you clip me for?"

"You don't know?"

"I can guess but it's kind of like trying to gauge how much water somebody scooped out of a moving stream."

"What do you mean?"

"Think of my system as a river. Or an irrigation ditch. I know how much I put in. I know how much I should get on the other side once the stream runs its course. But I don't know when you put your bucket in the stream. Or how many times. And the stream was still running when I tumbled to your play."

"Don't you keep an eye on things?"

"It was automatic. Standing orders for transfers from one bank to the next, one account to another, one currency to another. Once money in one account reached a certain level, it went to the next. You tapped the big pool, the one before that money really disappeared into thin air, out there where nobody could trace it, not the wise guys, not the U.S. government, not General Motors or Chase Manhattan, not even the Pope. It was also the only place in the pipeline that gave me quick access. Which made it the weak point."

"Five."

"Really? That's all?"

"That's all. Stung you, though."

"Just a slap in the face, darling. Hit me at a bad time, though. When I needed to move fast. But I still got my reflexes."

Crowe smiled and bounced on the balls of his feet like a boxer. Savannah gave him a bored look.

"What I have a hard time believing is you getting mixed up with a loser like Burch again. Although I understand it — it was your way to get next to that computer wiz friend of his, Krukovitch. But still . . ."

"What the fuck are you talkin' about, lover? Krukovitch isn't a player in this. And Burch was the only muscle I could trust after you skipped town and left me holding all that bad paper from your clients."

"So who helped you hack into my system? You have trouble with a Krups coffee machine let alone a software program. Of course, I gave you a real edge by being stupid enough to leave my laptop around but you needed somebody to crack that for you."

"Kindness of strangers, lover. Kindness of strangers."

"Blanche would be proud. But knowing you, whoever it was wasn't a stranger for too long. How many times did you have to fuck him before he was eating out of your hand?"

"It only takes one time."

"Not for me, sugar. All the times in the world between us and

I'm still eating food out of my own bowl. Sorry to hear about Krukovitch, though."

"Why?"

"I guessed wrong. So did the greaseballs."

"Guessed wrong about what, him being involved in this?"

"You bet. The goombahs had him killed. Before one of my associates could get next to him."

"Jesus. He was Eddie's best friend."

"I know. Gives your boy Burch some strong motivation. Reason to hate both you and me. And the goombahs. But New Orleans is a long way away — we're the only ones right in front of him now. I doubt your Mr. Burch will take a discriminating view. I doubt he'll give much of a damn who actually had his best friend killed. He'll take it out on whoever he can get his gun sights on."

"You're right. He's slow and dumb but if he gets close he'll drop payback on us both."

"I'm counting on that. It's a new game, Savannah. My game. And the five mil doesn't matter. Think of it as table stakes. An ante."

"Where's this game gonna be played, lover? In that little white church?"

"I knew you'd appreciate that touch."

"You know, Eddie gunning for us both gives us a reason to be partners."

"Not a chance, honey. Not a chance."

"Why don't you tie me up someplace else, then? This chair is too hard."

"You sound like Goldilocks. But this ain't a fairy tale."

"C'mon, lover. At least tie me up where I'll be comfortable."

"Like the bed?"

"That's a start. Like old times. C'mon. Tie me up in bed. It might be fun. For both of us."

"Not a chance, Savannah. I'd rather yank my pud with a cactus glove."

"Needle-dick bastard."

THIRTY-ONE

Burch saw the smoky predawn mist snake through the draws leading down to the river, thought of a place half a continent away from here and felt the faraway pain of his dead daddy gallop up into his throat.

Rulon Edward "Bill" Burch died four months after his seventy-fifth birthday, wasted by weeks in the hospital and years of a hateful disease that ate away his memory and storytelling wit and withered his workingman's body into a shuffling spindle. Near the end, the best housepainter in Coppell, when sober, didn't know his only son, wouldn't speak to his only wife and called his only daughter by his wife's name.

In those last days, with his wrists tied to keep him from jerking the IV lines out of his arms and the food tube out of his nose, his hazel eyes would widen in anger and his big horsey head would stubbornly swing away whenever mama leaned in close to tell him she loved him and was glad he was still alive. At the very end, when he coded in the recovery room after doctors cut a hole in his stomach and inserted a food tube, he revived just long enough to ask the nurse to let him die. Then he was gone.

She buried him in a peach-colored blazer, an off-white shirt and a navy tie peppered with daisies and other flowers. With his blotched, parchment-thin skin and shrunken features, he looked like an old light-skinned Negro waiter, ready to serve double bourbons and scotches at the clubhouse to the fat white money and its frat-rat sons, white folks slicked back and sleek after eighteen holes and a long hot shower.

Resting in his copper-colored casket, daddy didn't look like the man who could knock back bourbon and beer at the American Legion hall all night and knock out flawless trim work with a blinding hangover in the still heat of day, squinting through sweat and the smoke curling up from a Lucky on his lip. He didn't look like the man who could make you laugh with long-winded country tales or stop you dead with a wild and murderous glare. And he sure didn't look like the young man barely out of his teens who stood his ground with an M1 Garand in the frozen wasteland of Korea, firing clip after pinging clip of .30-06 at the endless horde of screaming, bugle-blowing Chinese charging the thin G.I. line night after flare-lit night.

That man died long before the gaunt figure in the casket did. And when mama leaned in to tell him she loved him one last time, the stubborn fire was gone, his eyes were closed and he didn't turn away. It was fine for mama but it stabbed Burch badly with the hard truth that he had put a lot of distance between himself and his father's long slow decline, widening a gap he would never be able to close.

Daddy's final resting place was the third deck of an above-ground burial vault out near Farmers Branch, at the back end of a cemetery far from his home in the North Carolina mountains, miles away from the graves of his father and mother and two younger sisters who could backsass him until he was tongue-tied in anger, then stand back and sweetly call him by the Christian name no one called him — Rulon — and ask why his face was so red and he was stuttering so badly.

Burch stood beside his mama as the preacher said all the proper words that made her cry and didn't feel a thing except for the wide rivulet of sweat that ran down his back and into the crack of his ass, causing the fabric of his dark gray polyester blend suit to stick to his skin.

The service ended and one of his ex-wives stepped forward to hug his neck. She was the second ex, the cocktail waitress he married between the one who tore up his heart and the one who got killed by the spade hit man with the high-pitched voice. This ex only stayed with him for three months. She never spoke to him after the divorce but loved his daddy and would flirt with him whenever he answered the phone when she called mama, who stayed friends with all his exes. He was surprised to see her but it was only a surface reaction. Nothing else rose up to break through his numbness.

A week after the funeral, after paying the undertaker and the hospital and carting mama down to the lawyer's office so he could send the will to probate court, Burch drove for two days to the little hamlet outside Asheville where his daddy, Korean War veteran, grandson of a Klansman and the great-nephew of a hanging judge, grew up.

He walked what was left of the family homestead with his cousin George, a stumpy version of himself, cursed with the same belly, bald head, big eyes and beard as Burch, but about a half foot closer to the ground.

It was a full-blown redneck kind of a day, one that started well before sunup but well after George's usual wakeup hour. Burch remembered the year daddy got laid off from the refinery down in Texas City and moved the family back to North Carolina, settling into the old homeplace where Burch's grandfather, Judson Earl Burch, still lived. It was a rambling house built of pegged poplar, with a pepperbox entrance and a long porch running down the front wall.

George would wake up with his daddy Gus, who would rise at 3 a.m. to fix a breakfast of eggs, ham and red-eye gravy then call down to the Burch house.

"Unc' Bill, you up yet?"

"No, George — just who in the hell do you think is talkin' to you?"

"Be down for breakfast."

By the time his daddy pulled on his trousers and headed to the kitchen barefoot to light the wood stove, George would be banging through the pepperbox door, wondering what was on the menu for his second breakfast.

Burch's time with his cousin wound through a silent rising light and a stand at the end of a sloping field of green, waiting for the smoky mist to rise out of the hollows and a groundhog to pop up into the crosshairs of his cousin's varmint rifle, a stainless steel, bolt-action Ruger .223 with the 10x scope and the dull grey plastic stock. That same half-light mist was rising in front of him now, thousands of miles from the lush green mountains of daddy's kin, with the sharper-spined peaks of the stark grey Sierra del Carmens as a backdrop. The memories rose to mind along with the mist.

So did the remembered hours with his cousin — a huge roadhouse breakfast of eggs, flapjacks, grits, ham and coffee; a session in an old man's garden, baiting Hav-A-Heart traps with grape jelly for the raccoons that were tearing up the corn and lettuce; an hour shoveling sawdust into a small trailer for another old man to use in his garden.

It ended with a brush-busting walk along the line of the six acres that remained in the Burch family name, digging through the ruins of an old springhead that watered cows through the Depression years, spending a half hour picking ripe blackberries from a snake haven of thorny vines that was in the same spot where he and mama picked berries four decades before, back when he was five and the tiny pump house his father built over the wellhead he had drilled for his own daddy was shiny and white and seemed as big as the weathered outhouse behind the old homeplace.

A doublewide stood where the old house used to be. The land

belonged to somebody else. The pump house, splintered and stripped of shingles, was the only sign of his daddy's hand on what was left of family land.

Burch felt something move from his guts up into his chest and his eyes burned with hatred toward the white trash trailer violating the space where his grandpa used to sit in the shade, a dog at his feet, drawing stick figures in ink on the brim and crown of a cheap fedora.

But that moment passed quickly. They picked up the free and easy talk that had carried them through morning, joking the way only two middle-aged men who had seen a lot and were comfortable with each other will do. They picked berries until their hands were stained, then George took him home, gave him a shot of homemade blackberry wine, let him shower and walked him to his rig for the ride back to Texas.

"Been too long, son. Seems like we only see each other at funerals."

"Yeah. Maybe I'll make it back for deer season."

They both knew that wouldn't happen.

His legs and back were sore but he felt clean, fresh and buoyant from the shower and his time in the close, high land of his kinfolk, moving through a working Saturday with his cousin. There was that brief, dark moment at the old homeplace, but it passed quickly.

Maybe he had said all his goodbyes to daddy through the five-year decline of the Alzheimer's, he thought. Maybe all he would feel was relief — that his mother wouldn't have to burn herself out trying to take care of a man angry about her trying to keep him alive, that his daddy didn't have to spend any more time locked in his mind like a graybar lifer, that he wouldn't have to feel so damn guilty about not pitching in any more than he did.

What rode through the front of his mind wasn't grief or guilt. It was the dawn mist, the humped ridgeline and the keening note that sang through his blood in the ancient, Highlander key, reminding him it didn't matter he was born in the flatlands of Texas, that he and his daddy were of mountain stock and for a short time that he was stepping through the land in which his people were born to live.

He headed west on I-40, pointed toward Knoxville, pushing his rig up through the hairpin mountain turns, punching up a college FM station playing bluegrass.

He listened to Bill Monroe blaze through three of his standards, including "Blue Moon of Kentucky" and "Walls of Time," the old man's plaintive wail drawing a tighter line through the Celtic call that was already stirring in his chest. Whipping through a long set of downhill curves, he nodded his head in time to the Stanley Brothers' "Rank Stranger," barely noting the high-banked gravel of the runaway truck ramp that flashed past his window.

Then J.D. Crowe, Tony Rice and Doyle Lawson sang "Model Church," a song about an old man talking to the soul of his dead wife, telling her about finding a place of worship that "had the old-time ring." The singing was accompanied only by a lightly strummed guitar and a standup bass, the lyrics carried by the tight harmony of the three men, recounting the old man's joy at finding comfort in a church that made him feel like "some wrecked marine who gets a glimpse of shore."

The string in his chest broke and a black ball of grief rose up from his stomach and into his throat. Tears blurred his vision and he heard a strangled cry fill the cab of his rig, drowning out the song. He bawled all the way down the backside of the mountain pass. Cars and tractor-trailer rigs roared past, horns blaring. He howled for his daddy, barely able to see the road, never touching the brakes, not giving much of a damn if he flew off the four-lane.

When he got down to a flatter stretch of highway, he turned off at the first exit and pulled into the gravel lot of a barbecue restaurant called The Pig Pit. He pulled out a bandana, blowing his nose and wiping the clear trail of tears and mucous from his beard and moustache.

This is how it hits you, he thought. Not beside the casket, looking down at the dead body of your daddy. Not when an ex-wife hugs your neck at the graveside service and whispers her regrets. Not even when your own mama breaks down and sobs out her misery. You get nailed after a glorious redneck day with a cousin, rambling over the land of your father and his ancestors, the place of all the old family myths and experiences, your heart broken open by a bluegrass song your daddy didn't even know while roaring down a mountain that doesn't care if you live or die.

And it hits you two years later, sitting stiff and sore on a brushy slope a mile south of the Rio Grande, watching mist that triggers memories. Of his dead daddy. And a dead friend, a death Burch knew would bring him another painful reckoning.

They were in a cold camp that gave them a good view of the river, the town of La Linda, the thin iron bridge that crossed back to Texas and the short-browed and narrow mesa that rose above the sand and brush of the steep banks. In the center of this higher ground stood the white chapel, wood-framed and isolated from the abandoned mining company barracks, the wrecked and scavenged dump trucks and bulldozers of the motor pool and the hump-shouldered adobe huts of the town.

Burch swept the vista with a pair of Bushnell pocket binoculars. He was alone with Mr. Slick, their horses tied to a picket line and hobbled in a brushy draw behind and below their vantage point.

Dag and Silva were gone, their guide job done, their unwillingness to play any other role made clear on the other side of the river. Which was fine by Burch. This was his play. He didn't even want Mr. Slick along but needed at least one gunhand who wasn't hobbled by busted ribs and a taped-up shoulder. And while he was thankful for their expert escort, he didn't trust the vaquero cousins — hell, he barely trusted Mr. Slick — and moved their stakeout a half mile from the place Dag and Silva put them to a place he spotted in the falling light of yesterday's hideout.

For breakfast, they had PowerBars, the modern-day substitute for beef jerky. Just as tough to chew. And not nearly as tasty. Washed down with canteen water chilled by night air that did nothing to wipe out the gritty alkaline taste. The pain Burch felt in the saddle was doubled by a night on cold rocky ground. It hurt him to glass the chapel and town. He did it anyway, careful to cup his hand over the top of the lenses to keep the rising light from bouncing off his optics, flashing a signal to anybody who might be watching for a watcher.

"You want a pill?"

"Naw. What I want is a cigarette."

"So fire one up."

"Not a good idea. This ain't the city — smoke can be seen and smelled by country folk."

"Got some Levi Garrett in my bag. If you care for some."

"That'll work. Didn't know you chewed."

"I don't. Not unless I'm on a job. Country folks aren't the only people who can see or smell smoke from a stakeout."

Burch grinned then caught the pouch of chewing tobacco Mr. Slick tossed his way, clutching it awkwardly to his chest. He settled a ball of stringing tobacco between cheek and gum then glassed the chapel again.

With his eyes on the chapel, he heard a twig snap somewhere behind him and a hiss from human lips. He turned his head, binoculars still frozen in front of where his face used to be and saw the blurry movement of Mr. Slick reaching for his Remington pump. Three shots roared across their little camp, blowing Mr. Slick off his spread bedroll and across the saddle he had used for a pillow.

"Don't make the same mistake as your friend, señor."

"Wouldn't dream of it."

"Keep your hands where they can be seen."

He felt someone step up behind him. Two someones. They gripped him under the armpits and jerked him to his feet. He yelled out in pain and one of the someones slapped him across the face.

"You sound like a woman, señor."

"You would too if you had some busted ribs and a banged up shoulder."

"Hombre, now you sound like an old man who is better off in a warm bed than out here in the cold."

Burch was forced to turn toward the voice. The man was tall but big-bellied with long black hair tied back in a ponytail. A blue bandana, folded into a tie-wide strip, ran across his broad dull-copper forehead. The man had a Beretta 9 mm in his left hand — the gun that killed Mr. Slick. He flashed a smile above a black goatee — gold teeth up front.

"That was a good trick, moving from where Dag and Silva put you. We found you anyway. Took us some time wandering around in the dark but then we heard your snores."

"That was my partner, the fella you just killed."

"No, señor. It was you. We were close enough to tell."

"Which would make you part Apache."

The man shrugged.

"Who can tell? We were quiet enough to slip up on you. If you want to tell yourself only someone with Indian blood could do that, be my guest."

"I'd love to jaw at you some more about whether you're that good or whether I'm just a fuckup but I'm in some pain here. Had a bull throw me across a rodeo ring."

"Si, we heard of your exploits."

"So I'm famous on this side of the border. That will make you a big man by killing me."

"Kill you? Oh no, señor, I don't need to kill you to prove I'm a man. Killing you would be like killing a fly. A little thing. Of no importance to me. *Mi patron* has another plan for you."

The man jerked his head with a silent order. Hands shoved him forward. Pain shot through his ribs as he took his first step. His football knees were stiff and throbbing. The man led, then Burch, then his two escorts. A fourth followed, stringing Sue Bee and Shorty.

It was a long, slow, twisting walk down from the slope-side camp, down across a brush-filled arroyo, then up a hen-scratched switchback trail that scrabbled up the loose and gravelly face of the little mesa.

At the top, there was a clear view of the white chapel, pure against the Sierra del Carmens. The chapel door was open. Standing in the door was a man.

Jason Willard Crowe.

THIRTY-TWO

"Thank you my friends, for escorting my guest to this private little service. Tie him up in that empty chair and then leave us please, to worship in peace."

The sanctuary walls were whitewashed plaster, stained rust and tan by years of water flowing from a leaky roof. The pews, rough, unstained and backless, were pushed together toward the back, clearing a space in front of the altar that had been used as living quarters by squatters, with a fire pit in the center and a pile of mattresses to the left of the Madonna statute standing on a rough-hewn wooden wall bracket.

The strong smell of urine — animal and human — rode an undercurrent of mold, must and rat droppings. Between the fire pit and the altar sat a trussed up and angry Savannah, eyes glaring, head tossing like a wild mustang, curls flying around her face.

The boys eased him into the chair facing her with the care of nursing home attendants. Which meant his ribs sent his brain only a modest signal of pain, matched by the alarm his shoulder sent when they bent back his arms to tie them to the rungs of the ladderback. Then they filed out, nodding to Crowe, who answered with a curt little wave and a muttered "Gracias."

Crowe walked toward them smiling, his eyes cold and vacant. Burch had seen this look many times on many different kinds of street scum and prison alumni. He knew what it meant — a man ready to deal out death, just moments away from flipping that first lethal card on the table. He kept his eyes level on Crowe's face and gave him nothing.

Savannah's eyes were locked on her husband, a man she had an overwhelming and pathological need to best, a man who was so familiar to her when they played the same side of the same game on all those chumps up in Houston. She either ignored the message of Crowe's look or didn't know its language because it had never before been directed at her.

She was in her full-blown bitch mode, spitting fire like the first time Burch saw her at Louie's, ready to chop down another big dumb male despite the ropes binding her to a ladderback chair.

"Got your little tableau set out just like you want, doncha lover? And what does it prove — that you're in charge? Not on your life. It proves I got you, scrambled your plans and made you come to me. Hear that? Me. This isn't your game. This is my game, no matter what you do to us."

Crowe was on her in three long strides, whipping a pistol down and across her face, drawing a sharp roar of pain from Savannah as the blow tilted her chair onto two legs, which then kicked out, slamming her sideways to the wooden chapel floor like a cheap Saturday pro wrestling trick.

She screamed a long string of profanity, some of it so guttural it was beyond recognition as anything other than unhinged hatred. He kicked her once in the stomach, which cut the string and turned her screams into the sound of a blacksmith's bellows, a telltale of a person who has the breath knocked clean out of them and can't get it back in. He bent down and whispered into her contorted face then straightened up and tipped her and the chair back into an upright position, like a stevedore would leverage a drum of motor oil.

Burch went slack-jawed then recovered quickly, shifting his face back into a stony set. He was sure Crowe was about to pump a bullet into his wife's brainpan. He was shocked when that didn't happen. To Savannah or him.

The moment passed. Now there would be a delay. Timeout for a word from our sponsor and host. Some verbal humiliation. An explanation. A nice, fat, juicy rationalization. Or the simple egomaniac's desire to hear himself talk to a helpless audience. To gloat. Or rev himself up once more for the kill.

Burch felt a worm of disgust curl up in his gut.

Be a pro, man. Get this evil shit over with. Shut us down, leave us dead and get gone.

Purely crazy thoughts on his part because any speech by Crowe bought them both a little more time. But the thought of being suckered by these two then having to listen to a little sermonette by Crowe before getting slammed into the land of the long goodbye screeched through his brain like a screaming parrot.

"I hope I have your undivided attention."

Jesus. Who wrote this fucker's script? And how did a guy who sounds like an assistant high school principal slick the greaseballs in New Orleans?

"This is where the bad guy tells the good guy how stupid he was, how he got played for a fool, how smart and evil will win out over slow but virtuous every time. And you know why that's such a cliché? Do you? Because it's true. Guys like you plod along, doggedly chasing your suspects and perpetrators. And the only ones you ever catch are the halt, the lame and the stupid. The ones who turn the corner and run smack into you while you're looking the other way. That didn't happen this time. You're here because I wanted you to be. Because you were helping her and, like her, have to pay the price for trying to beat me."

Burch said nothing, his face still stony, his eyes dead and staring straight at Crowe as the sermonette continued.

"I could have taken the easy way out. I could have scraped together some getaway money and written off what Savannah stole as the cost of doing business. But that would have been just a little too candyass for my tastes. Something that would have always bothered me, spoiling the taste of that first martini of the evening, ruining that perfect sunset at the beach. When I walk out of here and disappear, I want to leave you two as a calling card. For those dagos up in New Orleans and these greasers here. Nothing behind but two dead bodies and my smiling memory. Leave everybody grabbing for air. The greasers, the dagos, the feds. And all those fucks back in Houston. All their expectations, all those hard-ons and all that salivation about getting hold of me and making me dead and absolutely no payoff. Nothing. With their money in my pocket and an open file gathering dust in some cop shop up north."

Burch could hear Savannah's labored attempts to catch her breath and see the fear glittering in her eyes. He could feel the stone mask slip as he fought to keep contempt from showing on his face. It didn't work.

"Am I boring you?"

"To tears, son."

"What's the matter — the setting isn't picturesque enough for your tastes? I thought you and my lovely wife would appreciate my thoughtfulness, bringing you back to this isolated lover's hideaway. Have you lost your sense of romance — your appreciation of irony?"

"Look, shithead — people been tellin' me I'm dumb and slow all my damn life. They get in my face and brag about how quick and slick and smart they are. They usually right. But it usually don't matter because when the dust settles, I'm still standin' and they ain't."

"You're sitting now, hotshot. And you won't see the dust settle on this one."

"That just breaks my limp-dick heart, son. What you don't seem to notice is that I don't give much of a shit. You're gonna do what you're gonna do and my ass will be gone. I'm too tired and too old to care."

"Well ain't you just tryin' to piss on my parade. Man don't want to watch me do my touchdown dance. Man don't want to hear me gloat about how I slicked New Orleans and the feds and those coke whores up in Houston and these sorryass greaser motherfuckers in this nowhere village. No sir, man don't want to hear that."

"That is purely the worst black accent I've ever heard. An insult to every brother I know. I'd rather hear you preach some more. Better yet, I'd rather see you go about your business. C'mon man — be a pro. Get it done and get gone. Speeches are for amateurs. And suckers. You're playin' down to my level, now. And you know it."

"You're right. It's time."

Crowe pulled Cullen Mueller's Smith & Wesson from his waistband, cocked the hammer and pointed the barrel at the center of Burch's bald head. Burch steeled himself, hoping Crowe was good enough to make it a quick kill, hoping his would be a standup death.

Savannah screamed. Crowe, his concentration shattered, pointed the gun toward the chapel ceiling and eased the hammer down. Burch exhaled.

"Nnnnnooooooooooooo! I'm the one! I'm the one! Me! This is me and you have to know that! Goddam you Jason, this isn't about him! It's me! Look at me!"

"I'm sorry, wifey but that's not the way this is going to play out. You're going to have to sit there and watch your good friend and lover, Mr. Burch, die. Then I will deal with you. On my terms. Not yours."

Crowe cocked the revolver while it was still pointing vertical then slowly brought it back to bear on Burch's forehead. The barrel never got centered. Five shots boomed through the chapel — semi-automatic thunderclaps from God. Crowe's face exploded, then his chest, his body rushing toward the altar in a bloody sprawl of supplication, the reflexes in his fresh-killed hand squeezing off a round that shattered plaster just above the Madonna's head.

Burch grunted then blinked through the blood sprayed across his face. The bottom dropped out of his guts, then rebounded, forcing a gush of bile through his teeth and into his lap, dribbling down his face, his beard, his chest. Savannah screamed again but he blacked out.

Cold water in the face. A gasp for air. Sputters and blurred vision. Then the pocked face of a short, thin and middle-aged Mexican with a thick silvery pompadour, flanked by four younger men. The older man smiled at him.

"My name is Salazar. I am told your name is Burch."

Burch nodded.

"Ah, you understand me. Good. I thought your near-death experience might have left you in shock. But I can see it has only left you speechless. I am sorry we cut things so close but I had to hear for myself of Mr. Crowe's treachery. My son Cesar, had warned me about him but I had given Mr. Crowe my word. Still, a man has to keep an eye on his partners. Particularly his gringo partners."

Salazar motioned to one of the younger men.

"Cut Mr. Burch loose. Can you stand up? Help him to his feet."

Burch shrugged loose from the hands that reached to help him then stood on his own, wobbly but erect.

"*Bueno.* A man who refuses to let adversity make him less of a man. I like that."

Burch said nothing. Not out of tough guy but because no words came to his mind and mouth.

"You are wondering what happens next."

"No sir. I'm wondering how much longer I can keep standing."

Salazar laughed.

"Sit, Mr. Burch. Sit. I will do the talking. You have been chasing Mr. Crowe all over Texas, all the way to this little village. We have put him on a platter for you. You can take him back to Texas and prove to the authorities that you have run him to earth. You can tell as little or as much of how this happened as you please."

"What's in it for you?"

"A message. Notice to anyone who does business with me that I am a serious player and not a man to be trifled with. Notice that you gringos can't come down here and have us dancing like puppets on your string. You see, the story that will grow out of you taking Mr. Crowe back to Texas will become gigantic beyond the mere facts. It will become a bit of border legend, one that I will help spin, one that will build up my name."

"Maybe they'll write a song about this. Nothing like a little advertising."

Salazar chuckled.

"Yes. A *corrido* about me besting the clever gringo who thought he could outsmart everyone. Everyone but me. That's the perfect form of advertising for the border. Nothing like it at all."

"And the girl?"

"That is a bonus I give to you to deal with as you please. She would have killed you, you know. And in my mind, she is no different than our dead friend here. I would think you would regard her the same way, no?"

Salazar snapped his fingers. One of his gunhands racked the slide of a 9 mm Browning Hi-Power and handed it to Burch. Burch stood, hefted the slender black semi-automatic and looked at Savannah, red-eyed and sobbing in her chair.

He felt the ghosts of all the other people who had died because he was too slow and too dumb to keep them alive. He saw Krukovitch sitting at Louie's. He saw his dead ex-wife. His dead partner. And he burned to even the score and make them all go away with a loud blast of lead and spent brass.

The gun came up and Savannah's face filled the sights. She looked like a sick dog, shaking and whining, her curls slick with sweat. Or worse — a glassy-eyed mental patient with a shattered mind and a flamed-out soul, now that the object of her obsessive fury was dead.

The wreck centered in his sights held no power. The dead disappeared. The gun came down. He snicked on the safety and handed the Hi-Power back to Salazar's man.

"You keep her. Might help you settle your dead partner's account with some gentlemen from New Orleans. They can't have Crowe but they might settle for the next best thing — their money and his wife. Or not. I'll let you make that call and deal with her as you please."

"You're asking a bit much, my friend. She's far too troublesome for me to deal with. As for the money — that's a far more attractive bargaining chip to begin negotiations with New Orleans. But her — she is worth nothing to me alive."

"Then waste her. What's so tough about having one of your boys put a bullet in her instead of me? Not as entertaining for you but consider it my fee. Cheaper rate than you'd get on Madison Avenue."

"As you wish. Anything else?"

"Yeah — my *pistola*, the two horses I came in here with and a quiet place to slip across the river. Have the boys strap ol' handsome there across the pony that bites. And bury the guy who rode across the river with me. He wasn't a friend but he did watch my back."

"Give the man his gun. Consider the rest done."

Cesar stepped close and handed him the Colt. Burch racked the slide to put a round in the chamber then thumbed the safety. Cocked and locked. Condition One. Cesar gave him a sharp look.

"Don't be stupid, *pendejo*."

Burch met his eye, tucking the gun behind his back, wincing at the spike of pain in his shoulder. A growl at the younger man.

"I ain't a suicide, hoss. Your daddy is letting me walk out of here alive and I plan to do just that."

From the altar came the slow start of a woman's wail, shifting through the lower, then medium, then higher registers like an old hand-cranked air raid alarm. Laughter followed, high-pitched and shrill. Only one of the dead returned, his face rising in the mental mist. Krukovitch. A debt he had to pay.

Burch spun on his bootheels, ignoring the pain, the Colt rising in his left hand as he thumbed off the safety. Eight Flying Ashtrays boomed toward the altar, snuffing the laughter. Smoke curled from the Colt's locked-open breech.

Salazar and his men stared at him in the quick frozen silence. Two gunhands had their pistols leveled at Burch. The *patron* placed a hand on each gun, pushing them down as he spoke to Burch.

"My friend? Don't ever visit my little village again."

Burch nodded then turned and walked toward the open chapel door.

The sun was up. The mist was gone.

ABOUT THE AUTHOR

For more than 30 years, Jim Nesbitt was a roving correspondent for newspapers and wire services in Alabama, Florida, Texas, Georgia, North Carolina, South Carolina and Washington, D.C. He chased hurricanes, earthquakes, plane wrecks, presidential candidates, wildfires, rodeo cowboys, ranchers, miners, loggers, farmers, migrant field hands, doctors, neo-Nazis and nuns with an eye for the telling detail and an ear for the voice of the people who give life to a story. He is a lapsed horseman, pilot, hunter and saloon sport with a keen appreciation for old guns, vintage cars and trucks, good cigars, aged whiskey and a well-told story. He now lives in Athens, Alabama. This is his second novel.

Made in the USA
Lexington, KY
18 September 2018